the
RIGHT
swipe

Also by Alisha Rai

the RIGHT swipe

A NOVEL

ALISHA RAI

AVON

An Imprint of HarperCollinsPublishers

HarperCollins books may be purchased for educational, business, or sales promotional use. For information, please email the Special Markets Department at SPsales@harpercollins.com.

FIRST EDITION

Designed by Diahann Sturge

Library of Congress Cataloging-in-Publication Data has been applied for.

ISBN 978-0-06-287809-0

22 23 24 25 26 LBC 12 11 10 9 8

For anyone who has been made to feel weak and small.
You're stronger than you think, and more
important than you can imagine.
Thank you for being a part of this world.

Acknowledgments

A NEW SERIES can be an intimidating venture, and it's important to have the support of professional and personal superstars in your corner. Thanks to Erika Tsang and the team at Avon/HarperCollins, and to Corey, Jenice, Zee, Allie, and Lillie for reading early drafts of this book. A special thanks to Sarah Wendell, who is an invaluable source of kindness and inspiration.

All my love to Aly, my emotional support system, who lured me to the best coast and has made my transition such a joy (your glee in introducing me to people is secretly my favorite thing); to Kristin, my first (and finest) roommate and an eternal friend; to Jen, my most steadfast supporter and wine-tasting companion; and to my family, who are so proud of me but constantly ask when my books will be made into movies already. Call me, Hollywood, it would make my mama really happy.

Finally, I cannot thank *you* enough. Seriously. Every book feels like the hardest book I'll ever write, and the most satisfying part is when I reach the end and know that soon it'll be in the hands of readers who need it and love it and get it. To slightly paraphrase the great Jason Mendoza, you make the bass drop in my heart.

We're all in this together. Much love.*

---

* Unless you're a man who ghosted me at some point, in which case I am explicitly *not* thanking you and send you *no* love, I assume you're dead, it's the only explanation for your disappearance. Peace.

Chapter One

Rhiannon Hunter worshipped at the altar of no man.

Or woman, for that matter. She'd worked hard to carve out her own tiny empire where she was only accountable to herself and those she chose to be accountable to. It was a luxury and privilege she didn't take lightly.

So it was extra annoying when she had to cajole anyone for anything. Wearing heels, no less.

"Ma'am, you are not on the list."

Rhiannon flicked the button of her jacket open. Her modest cleavage in the crimson one-piece jumpsuit she was wearing had the bouncer's gaze slipping away from his iPad. She cocked her hip, the better to accent her legs, the dratted heels at least giving her a nice optical illusion of length. "I got an invite," she lied. "Can you please double-check? H-U-N-T-E-R." She spoke in what was her closest guess of what a sweet, soft tone might sound like.

The large, muscle-bound guy dragged his eyes back to his tablet and, with a sigh, scrolled through the list again. The light from the hotel's hallway reflected off his shaved head as he straightened. "Of course. Apologies, Ms. Hunter.

Here you are." He stood aside and opened the door to the ballroom.

She gave him a regal nod and sailed inside like she belonged in truth, pulling her phone out of her pocket to send a quick text. **I don't know how you finagled that, but I'm in.**

Her assistant, Lakshmi, responded immediately. **Didn't I tell you I'd handle it? And stop cursing your shoes. You only need to be in them for a little while.**

Rhiannon's lips curved. She could have worn her signature hoodie and Converse and not looked out of place during any other event this week—at a tech conference like CREATE, sweatshirts and sneakers mixed with silk and suits—but this particular party, an exclusive after-hours event, had specified a formal dress code.

She tucked her phone back into the roomy pocket of her jumpsuit and walked farther into the ballroom, snagging a glass of wine off a passing waiter's tray.

The place was packed. A band played onstage, but most people were circulating, their voices pitched over the music. Austin might be a music lover's city, but the majority of guests here tonight were conference attendees whose primary priority was to network and learn.

She surveyed the room with a critical eye. Formal wear was not her jam, and neither were stuffy hotel ballrooms, but Matchmaker had gone all out tonight. The company's signature M was emblazoned on everything from the heart-shaped ice sculpture to the dark blue napkins.

There were countless dating apps and sites now, but most North American serial singles knew only three mattered.

Swype, the original left and right swipe-based dating app built around Hot-or-Not bro culture; Crush, Rhiannon's pink and feminist response; and Matchmaker, that old-time behemoth website that had started back in the day when people wanted to spend days building their dating profile and had to scan their photos via a dedicated machine.

Rhiannon had studied Matchmaker in college classes, had picked the business and its strategies apart when she'd entered the dating industry. Despite a recent slowdown, the Kostas sisters were legends of the dot-com world, having outlasted most of their contemporaries through recessions and technological change.

Rhiannon's suspicion was most of that staying power had been fueled by the elder sister. Jennifer had died last year, reclusive and mysterious Annabelle had inherited everything, and the company now seemed to be in a holding pattern. Rhiannon was sure she wasn't the only shark circling Matchmaker since its visionary had passed away. Gruesome, but that was business.

Unfortunately, all of Rhiannon's standard and even more, um, stalky tactics to get to Annabelle had yielded zero fruit. Calls, letters, gourmet gift baskets, they'd all been returned or gone unanswered. In a moment of desperation, a few months ago she'd even traveled up the California coast to lie in wait near Annabelle's vacation home with a half-baked plan to, oops, bump into her on the beach.

Don't think about that trip.

Good idea, brain. Rhiannon took a sip of her wine and wrinkled her nose. She couldn't tell if it was the vintage or the memory of that weekend that left a bad taste in her mouth.

Anyway, through some last-minute miracle, she and Annabelle were scheduled to be on a stage together tomorrow for a live interview, their meeting inevitable, so crashing this party wasn't entirely necessary. But Rhiannon was too curious for her own good, and she wanted to get a sneak peek of the woman she'd been chasing. Plus, she wanted to see if there was a reason for her competitor to have poured out all this cash tonight for a fancy sponsored event.

Someone jostled Rhiannon. She stood still, not giving way, and glanced over her shoulder, resting bitch face firmly in place. She never knew what kind of reception she might get from guests at these kinds of industry gatherings. The chill and poorly concealed snickers from years ago had mostly died down, but there was always some fool who wanted to test her.

The pretty blonde gave her a dismissive look, then did a double take, her eyes widening. "Are you Rhiannon Hunter?" she asked, her voice pitched to be heard over the band.

Coming from L.A., where she was relatively invisible, it was weird to be in an environment where she was recognized. Rhiannon nodded, braced for anything.

"So cool." The woman stuck her hand out, gold charm bracelets jingling. "I downloaded Crush on my phone last week."

Rhiannon relaxed and accepted her hand. "Good luck with it." She meant that. Success stories were a dating app's lifeblood. Love was an industry fueled by hope. Whether that hope was misplaced or not was a different question.

She could practically hear her head of marketing hissing in her ear. *Maybe cool it on the cynicism when you're talking to a potential paying subscriber.*

"Thank you." The woman's nose wrinkled. "I'm not too optimistic. San Francisco is the worst city to be a heterosexual woman trying to date, I'm sure of it."

Rhiannon bit her cheek. It was a running gag at the office, that line. Almost every single felt like they lived in the worst city to date in. In reality, it was . . . everywhere. Everywhere and everything was terrible and on fire and if you did meet someone you clicked with, you could chalk it up to pure timing and luck.

Cool. It.

Rhiannon buried her personal weariness down deep and dug out a perky smile. Data was her friend, and she had a lot of it. "Actually, fun fact, by our internal numbers, San Francisco has a relatively higher ratio of heterosexual men to heterosexual women, so you might be in good shape."

The subscriber brightened. "Really? That's hopeful. Well, thanks. So far, I've definitely gotten less dick pics on Crush than I do on the other apps."

"That's not a bad legacy to have attached to my name, I guess," Rhiannon murmured, as the woman waved and walked away.

Rhiannon took another big gulp of her wine and surveyed the crowd again. The back of her neck itched, but it shouldn't. Lakshmi had vetted the guest list before hacking it for Rhiannon. No Swype employees were at this event, let alone its Chief Executive Asshole. Of course, that didn't mean everyone in this room liked her.

Her gaze lingered on a small woman not far from her, caught by her strange attire—all black and lace, with a weird hat and a veil that hid the upper half of her face, like she was some kind of old-timey widow—but then the band stopped playing. Rhiannon glanced away for a second, and when she looked back, the crowd had shifted, concealing the woman from view.

That nagging feeling of being watched disappeared, and Rhiannon was so grateful for that, she exchanged her empty wineglass for a full one. The applause died down and a tall man with salt-and-pepper hair stepped out onto the stage, took the mic, thanked the band, and smiled a Colgate smile at the audience. "Hello, all. Thank you for coming tonight. My name's William Daniels, I'm the CEO of Matchmaker." His smile widened when people clapped.

Rhiannon rocked back on her heels. She'd seen William around before, but his vaguely dismissive attitude had discouraged her from getting to Annabelle via her executive management.

A huge screen descended onto the stage and flashed a light blue, Matchmaker's big white M glowing.

"Over two decades ago, Matchmaker was created by a pair of sisters out of a small office in San Francisco." William paced the stage deliberately, a showman in his natural habitat. "Annabelle and Jennifer Kostas had a vision, to take their successful brick-and-mortar matchmaking business to the new frontier of the internet, to help more people find love than ever before. And they did. The small office in San Francisco may have turned into our current, much larger headquarters in Los Angeles, but we remain committed to you. We remain committed to our hundred-point matching system. We remain committed to helping you find the high of love, not the high of swipes."

It was an indirect dig at Crush and Swype, but Rhiannon didn't take it personally. She'd heard this spiel a million times, and William couldn't deliver it with Jennifer's charm. The kind-faced matronly woman had filmed commercials proclaiming the same a few years ago.

Rhiannon could afford to be magnanimous to the company she hoped to buy.

"We are so proud of our track record, with tens of thousands of successful matches."

Rhiannon clapped along with everyone else. Crush's headquarters were also wallpapered with engagement and wedding and birth announcements from the last three years. She treasured all of them. Not because she was a sentimental person, but because they represented dollar bills. Hope, man. Hell of a drug.

William's face turned grave. "This has been a year of change and reflection and regrouping for us after the death of our beloved founder and my predecessor CEO, Jennifer. I know many of you were hoping to see Annabelle here tonight, but unfortunately, she's not feeling well, and will not be able to address you."

Murmurs ran through the crowd. Rhiannon shared their

disappointment but she'd half expected this. Two appearances at one conference from a woman who had managed to stay out of the public eye for over twenty years had seemed like a lot.

There's still the interview tomorrow. You'll have your chance.

William spread his hands. "However, we're excited about what we have in the works. I won't take up your time tonight with talk about that—you're here to party, after all—but I hope you'll come to our open house tomorrow to find out more. Tonight, I'd like you to meet a friend of the company. As we say at Matchmaker, 'You never know who you'll find.'" William smirked and Rhiannon leaned closer, her competitive side engaged. That was totally the self-indulgent, smug face of a businessman who was about to reveal some new toy to the audience, and if Matchmaker had a toy, Rhiannon wanted it.

"Our slogan is appropriate, because to be honest, you really will never know who you'll find on Matchmaker. The love of your life, your next best friend. A doctor. A teacher. A scientist. A carpenter. And every now and again, a former football player. Please welcome our newest spokesman and Matchmaker client, two-time Super Bowl champion, son of a proud football dynasty, former linebacker for the Portland Brewers, Samson Lima!"

Rhiannon reared back, her heart thudding in time to the applause of the other people in the room.

Wait.

Waaaaait.

Lots of men are named Samson.

Lots of men who are built like linebackers are named Samson.

Lots of men who are built like linebackers and look exactly like the man whose face is on the screen now are named Samson.

Lots of men who are built like linebackers and look exactly like the man whose face is on the screen now, the face of the man who kissed you one night three months ago under a moonlit sky whose name was also Samson, are named Samson.

Oh, fuck. No. That was taking the train to Coincidence-Land a little too far.

Rhi scanned the smiling headshot on the giant screen, hoping to find some way to differentiate *this* Samson from the Samson she'd met on a beach more than a thousand miles away from here. The man who had kissed his way down her body, then filled her up with his body.

The man who had asked, no, begged, to see her again . . . and had *stood her the fuck up.*

Rhiannon didn't realize she had fisted her hands until her nails dug into her skin, and even the pain couldn't get her to relax, especially when the man, the *bastard*, walked onto the stage.

He'd worn faded jeans and a shirt when they'd met, his hair pulled back into a stubby ponytail. His scruff had scraped her inner thighs when he'd gone down on her, when he'd licked her up and down like she was a melting ice cream cone, when he'd whispered against her body that she tasted so delicious.

His massive body looked even bigger and stronger tonight in a tailored suit. His face was clean-shaven, nothing to hide his smile, his teeth flashing white against his brown skin. He'd cut his long hair short. But it was still him, even all cleaned up and respectable looking. Slick and shiny and so charming now, when he'd been rough and ready and sweetly hesitant with her that night.

Long ago, when Rhiannon had been a fresh Harvard dropout, a woman executive had patiently explained to her that no one took a woman who cried in the business world seriously. So Rhiannon had eradicated tears from her lexicon. Now she didn't even cry when she was alone.

Her nose twitched, and she beat back the prickle at the base of her throat, horrified at how close she was to leaking. Right here? Where anyone could see her? Not a fucking chance.

Theirs was a tale as old as, well, as old as a right swipe meaning you liked someone. They'd swiped, matched, met, fucked.

Leaving out the part where he snuck under your defenses and then ghosted you, I see.

She never thought she'd see him again, let alone here. Working for the company she wanted to buy? *Fate, you bitch.*

Inappropriate laughter tickled her throat, but she beat that back too. Her nails cut harder into her skin. She'd leave marks on herself, but that was fine. Anything to stay expressionless. Strong.

A man had stolen her ambition from her once before. She'd be damned if she forgot the vow she'd made to herself four years ago. *Never take your eyes off what really matters. Never again.*

Rhi relaxed her hands, one finger at a time. She could

leave now. The person she'd come to see wasn't here, so she could absolutely leave now.

Instead, she drifted closer to the stage, driven by the same impulse that might drive someone rubbernecking at a car wreck.

Never forget how terrible a person can be.

Samson finished shaking William's hand and smiled out at the audience. Despite her vow, Rhiannon's hardened heart squeezed. That smile had been devastating in a dark bar, sweet and tinged with sadness. Here, brilliant and charming and assisted by a lighting team? It was irresistible.

To other women. Not to her.

"Thanks, everyone, and thank you, William."

That voice. That deep, husky voice that had whispered all sorts of nonsense in her ear.

"I'm so honored to be a member of the Matchmaker family. People laugh when I say this, but it's hard for me to meet women."

Oh, this motherfucker. Rhi cracked her neck. *Maybe you shouldn't ghost the women you've met then.*

"But I'm thirty-six and I'm ready, past ready, to put some time and energy into my love life. So I decided to make the big leap." William handed him a tablet. Samson glanced behind him as the screen melted away to a Matchmaker profile, while the women in the audience hooted in delight. The main photo was a picture of Samson, casually leaning against a car.

"Now, I don't know much about dating sites."

Liar.

Samson swiped on the screen of the tablet. "But I was told I needed a photo of me with a baby, with a caption that says, 'Not my baby.'" The photo dissolved into one of him holding an adorable Asian baby. He smiled when people in the audience laughed and awwed. "That's my goddaughter, Miley. She's a cutie. Also, stereotypically conventional masculinity and a sense of adventure is important, right? So here I am posing on a safari." He swiped to a photo of him holding a stuffed tiger and lion. "These are also my goddaughter's. She's the real MVP, letting me borrow them."

This asshole, showing affection for an infant. Her ovaries were sighing, and she didn't even know if she wanted children.

He clicked to a photo of a younger Samson in a helmet and his green-and-black football uniform, face hard and intense. "I haven't played pro in almost a decade, but my friend said a work photo is appropriate."

That night they'd lain in bed together, he hadn't told her he was a former pro-football player. She could have found out but she'd consciously refused and unmatched him, releasing him to the wilds of dating other women.

There was a lot you didn't tell him too. Starting with your real name.

A good call, she'd told herself, the night he'd stood her up.

While he scrolled through the rest of his too-sexy pics and the rest of the audience hummed their appreciation, Rhiannon seethed. When Rhi had swiped right on him on Crush, he'd only had one photo, and it had been vague, his face in profile, his thick bare chest revealed, the line of hair on his muscular belly his main attraction.

She hadn't minded the photo, and since she owned the app—and the data people willingly forked over in their quest for love—she didn't fear for her safety in the same way other women might. Her own single pic was of her in a bikini, face also turned away. It wouldn't be the end of the world in terms of PR for someone to know who she was, but she didn't particularly want to advertise her identity.

On the rare occasions she was itching for a hookup, Rhiannon chose her conquests carefully, men who appeared to be far away from her world in both distance and work. Samson had looked big and eager for sex and they'd been almost 250 miles north of her home base in L.A. Just her type.

"And finally, a shirtless selfie," Samson said, grabbing her attention, and judging by the hoots from the audience, the attention of most of the women in the room.

The screen went blank, and he smiled. "Actually, you know what? You all can sign up to see that."

Rhi grit her teeth as people clapped and laughed. She'd had to rip and claw her way into the good graces of so many of the people in this room, overcome a reputation damaged by Swype's power-hungry, vindictive Chief Executive Asshole. A lot of people in her own industry still sneered at her, whispered about her, dismissed her, even though she'd worked around the clock to prove herself with a multimillion-dollar company that was poised on the verge of billion-hood.

This good-looking asshole walked right in, made some jokes, and Matchmaker was probably already getting new clients.

"All humor aside, though." Samson's face sobered. "This is serious." His profile took up the screen with blocks of text about who he was looking for.

Rhiannon's rage only allowed her to consume single words and short phrases out of the word salad he'd posted.

Sweet.

Kind.

Loyal.

Loves animals and children.

Looking for the real thing.

So funny, that he could type all these words for Matchmaker to describe the woman of his dreams. He hadn't even used all 250 characters that were allotted when he'd filled out his Crush profile.

Respectful and fully understand consent, not looking for anything serious, just a mutually satisfying physical relationship.

And now he'd just said, *This is serious*, with a straight face, and backed it up with a written thesis about his ideal woman.

Her eye twitched.

"If you're in the greater Los Angeles area and we match, we can go out. If you agree, parts of our date will be filmed for short online episodes and commercials. If you don't agree to the filming, we'll go get a steak anyway, my treat." He shrugged sheepishly. "This is a marketing campaign, yes. But it's also my heart. So sign up. Match me if you can.

Because as William said . . ." Samson's gaze drifted over the crowd. "You never know who you'll—"

His dark eyes landed on her and he stopped midsentence.

Rhiannon folded her arms over her chest, refusing to give him anything. She'd given him so much. Her body, her thoughts, her tentative trust even when she knew better.

Her hope for another night.

Even when she knew better.

Stone. Stone cold. That's what she was.

Someone in the audience cleared their throat, and Samson jerked. It might be the lights, but Rhiannon swore there was a trickle of sweat at his temple.

Let it not be the lights. Squirm, you bastard.

"Find." Samson's hand fell to his side, the tablet tapping his thigh. "You never know who you'll find."

Chapter Two

GETTING HIT was nothing new to Samson. He'd played football from ages six to twenty-six and had been hit so many times, he'd lost count. He'd gotten knocked out cold twice in his career, and each time his late mother had bolted from her seat to his side, sobbing in fear.

The concussions hadn't been fun, but it had been the countless subconcussive hits that had truly freaked Samson out. The ones that left him awake, but rattled everything inside his body, from the bones of his toes to his precious soft brain. Those hits had left him disoriented and confused, utterly discombobulated.

A person could still get up and play after a hit like that, their body on autopilot. Just like Samson could force himself to finish the speech he'd written and prepped in his hotel room last night without taking his gaze off the woman who was standing close enough to the stage that the light exposed her. "You never know who you'll find."

Like *her*. That face. The face of the one and only woman he'd ever met through his phone. The face he'd touched and kissed. The face that had haunted his dreams for months, so much so that he now thought about that night as That Night, in caps.

He'd wondered if he'd imagined how beautiful she was, or his memories had built her up to be more than she was, but no. Her long, lean body was all dressed up in a trendy siren-red number, a cropped jacket highlighting her nipped-in waist and curved hips, the vee of her neckline giving him a glimpse of shadowy cleavage. Her lips were painted red to match her outfit.

She'd worn lip balm That Night. Peppermint had never been an aphrodisiac but it was now.

Her hair was pinned up, one little almost-black curl escaping at her temple to rest against her cheek. That Night, her hair had been twisted out in tight curls, and the fading light outside the dive bar where they'd met had picked out dark and light brown, and every shade in between, copper and umber and russet.

They'd talked in that bar. Then they'd gone to her place. They'd done more than talk.

How was *she* here, at an industry conference in Texas? Yes, of course people could cross state lines. But what kind of coincidence would bring the woman he'd shared one perfect night with in a coastal California town to the hotel where he was being introduced as the spokesman for Aunt Belle's business?

Does it matter? You looked for her, and she's landed in your lap.

A rush of exultant satisfaction ran through him, the same satisfaction he used to feel when he ran a winning play.

I found her.

The applause distracted him. He only took his eyes off her for a second, but that was enough time. When he swiveled back to the spot she'd stood, his mystery woman had vanished.

Samson was so busy searching the audience, he barely noticed as William took the mic from him, wrapped up the presentation, and led him offstage. Matchmaker's CEO patted his shoulder. "Nice job. You okay, Lima? You look a little pale. Don't want you getting sick like your aunt."

The edge in the words told Samson the man had realized Annabelle Kostas wasn't exactly sick, and he snapped to attention, braced to defend her. Aunt Belle marched to her own drummer, and sometimes that drummer—or her horoscope—dictated her actions. "I'm fine." Narrator: He was not fine.

"Good." William directed him through the crowd. They smiled and nodded at some guests, and then paused at a pretty redhead dressed in a form-fitting blue dress. "Hello, Helena."

"William." The woman beamed at Samson, barely glancing at the CEO. "Mr. Lima, my name is Helena Knight. I host *Good Night Live.*"

"Of course, I'm familiar. Please call me Samson. Nice to meet you." It took every amount of discipline he had to keep his gaze fixed on hers. He was here for work, for family. He couldn't shirk those things, not even for That Night.

Helena was important. Television people were important. Not as important as social media influencers, according to the earnest Matchmaker PR guy who had briefed him, but given his internet-light life for the last decade, Samson barely understood what an "influencer" was.

"What an adorable campaign," Helena said, batting her eyes. She was flirting with him. He needed to flirt back. That was basically what this gig was all about, wasn't it? Getting paid to flirt with America.

"Thank you" was all he could cobble together.

William cleared his throat in warning, but Helena didn't seem to take offense to Samson's stilted reply. "I can't believe I'm meeting the Lima Charm."

Samson's smile tightened, but he relaxed it. *That nickname.* With his emergence into the public eye, he'd been prepared to hear it again, of course, but it was still a shock. The locals in the sleepy coastal town he'd grown up in and lived in for the past nine years had been so used to the Lima family, they hadn't called him anything but Sam or Samson or "the Lima boy."

Better this nickname than the other one, though.

"I'm a huge fan, and your father and uncle were my heroes." Helena waved her wineglass. "I'm sure you hear this all the time."

"I don't get tired of it. Thank you. They were my heroes as well." It was an automatic, harmless half lie. So many people had grown up watching his father and uncle on the field any given Sunday. Aleki and Iosefa "Joe" Lima were immortal legends in the minds of football fans of a certain age. No need to tarnish their memories with an explanation of his complicated feelings about his father.

"Will you be at the Matchmaker open house tomorrow?" Helena asked.

"I will, yes. As well as a panel discussion in the morning on modern dating." A topic on which he planned to stay mostly silent. He'd prepped for this gig, and could spout all sorts of information about Matchmaker, but theoretical knowledge was one thing. He'd been single and entirely celibate for almost five years before That Night. A modern Lothario, he was not.

"Well, I'm interviewing Annabelle in the afternoon, so hopefully I'll see you around. I'd love to talk to you more." Helena gave William a concerned look. "Annabelle will be well enough for the interview, won't she? I know this was a last-minute addition to her schedule."

"I'll make sure of it. Can you both excuse me for a second? I have to catch someone before they leave." William smiled at him and Helena and walked away.

Helena took a step closer and Samson knew what was coming after the second word. People had a very specific careful tone of voice they used when addressing the grieving. "I was so sorry to hear about your uncle. Please accept my condolences."

The shaft of pain was fresh. Uncle Joe had been diagnosed with Alzheimer's nine years ago, and Samson had moved in with him. The older man had been hit with another diagnosis, ALS, five years ago, and Samson had officially become his full-time caretaker.

He'd known that his uncle would one day die, that there was no cure for what he'd had. But the end had still stunned

Samson. "Thank you for your sympathy. I appreciate—"
A flash of black and red in the corner of his eye had him
swiveling his head, hope and desire brimming up inside
him, his resolve to focus on business vanishing.

The woman had her back to him as she walked briskly
toward a door with a neon Exit sign above it, but he knew it
was her.

"Can you excuse me?" he murmured to Helena, his body
already turning away.

"Of course. See you tomorrow."

As if she felt him stalking her, the woman glanced over
her shoulder when she got to the exit, and though the ballroom was crowded, he could see no one but her. He smiled
at her, so thrilled and relieved, but then he stopped dead in
his tracks. Her lovely face was no longer expressionless.

Oh, no. Here was an expression.

Fury.

She was mad. Wildly, incandescently mad.

Guilt rammed into him with all the force of a Mack truck.
Yeah, she was mad. She had every right to be, didn't she?

He'd only been on Crush for a day when they'd matched.
His well-meaning friends had pressured him to sign up,
and her sunlit bikini-clad body in her profile picture had
dissolved his wariness. She'd made it clear when she'd sat
down across from him in that bar what she wanted. *I'm in
town for a couple days. You're hot. We can have fun for a night.*

It had been more than fun. Sliding inside her had been
damned near a religious experience. He could still hear her
moans and sighs in his ear as he'd stripped her jeans and

sweatshirt and faded Metallica T-shirt off. And beyond the sex, he'd been intrigued. By her beauty, her secrets, her clear intelligence and subtle arrogance.

So he'd dared to ask for another night, got her to agree. He'd left her place that morning feeling a connection that he'd missed for so long, that bone-deep comfort that came from holding another human close.

And then he'd gone to his home, the house he'd shared with Joe. His uncle had started gasping for air around midday.

He'd forgotten all about their second date in his bed-side vigil, his world narrowed to his dying uncle. His grief and sense of loss had been so all-consuming, he'd only re-membered their date days later, after Uncle Joe had passed away.

When he'd fired up his app in a panic to message her, he'd discovered she'd already unmatched him.

Her lip curled up in a sneer, and he frowned. She should be mad at him, yes, but he could explain. He opened his mouth, her name falling from his lips, though he knew she was too far away to hear it. "Claire—"

She turned away and a large man stopped in front of him, blocking his view of her. "The Lima Charm, I can't believe—"

"Sorry, I'm trying to catch someone," Samson said hastily and swerved around the man, mentally cursing when he realized the door was slowly closing behind his girl.

No. He didn't want to lose her again. He moved faster,

shoving the door open and walking out. He looked one way, then the other, but the empty service hallway gave him no clues. He guessed and turned left, almost running down a bellhop who gave him an annoyed look. He apologized and started jogging, but when he came to a dead end, he cursed.

Damn it.

"Samson?"

Samson pivoted. If there had been more witnesses, he might have been ashamed of the yelp that fell from his lips at the sight of the small woman dressed all in black behind him.

Like, really, all in black, from the tips of her black satin heels to the small veil that covered her eyes. He bent his knees and peered under the veil, pressing a hand over his racing heart. "Aunt Belle?"

"Oh yes." She pushed up the veil, round blue eyes gazing up at him. "It's me."

Samson softened. His aunt had been eccentric for as long as he'd known her, which was as long as he could remember. She and Uncle Joe had started dating before he was born. She was the reason he existed; she had, in fact, matchmade his parents.

Aunt Belle was both intensely private and adored attention, depending on the size of the audience, her general mood, and the position of the stars. "Why are you dressed like . . ." *Like a ghost attending your rich ex-husband's wedding to his much younger wife?* "Like that?"

Aunt Belle petted her hat. "I wanted to watch the crowd's reaction to you, incognito. They loved you! How exciting."

Samson had no doubt people had noticed her more dressed like this than they otherwise would have, but he wasn't about to upset her by telling her that. "Ah, I see."

"I noticed you running out here. Is something wrong?"

"I was trying to find a woman. Did you see her? She left right before I did. About this tall." He placed his hand at his collarbone. "Black, beautiful, hair all pinned up, dressed in a red"—he gestured to the length of his body, unsure of what to call it—"one-piece thingy." He glanced around the deserted hallway again, like it would yield clues as to where Claire had gone.

Claire. If that was her real name. He'd googled Claire + Los Angeles after she'd unmatched him and discovered quickly what a fool's errand that was.

Annabelle shrugged. "I did not, sorry. Who was she?"

He puffed out his cheeks, trying to swallow his disappointment. "Someone I knew. Or thought I knew." He looked at his feet. "It's not important."

"Someone you knew . . ." Her eyebrows rose. "Biblically?"

His face turned red-hot. He'd forgotten that Aunt Belle's sweet, matronly facade hid a blunt tongue. "Aunt Belle."

"Ah," she clucked. "I know that tone. I said something an old lady shouldn't."

"You said something an *aunt* shouldn't."

"I never made an honest man out of Joe, so I'm not *technically* your aunt."

Not for lack of trying on Joe's part. But Annabelle had

been adamant about maintaining her independence, even to the point of keeping a separate residence. "Still my aunt."

She adjusted her silly hat. A tendril of bright red hair fell out of the black lace and touched her round cheek. "Always your aunt."

Samson's spirits rose, his natural response around Belle. *She's why you're here. You're not here to chase a ghost from your past.* He shoved his hands into his pockets, the silent hallway far too loud. "You know what? Let's get back to the party. I've barely had a chance to meet anyone."

"You did your part, Samson. If you want to go up to your room and rest, you can."

He wasn't even close to doing his part. He owed Aunt Belle, and not only because she'd been his emotional bulwark since Uncle Joe had passed. "Nah."

"One shouldn't do anything that doesn't serve them."

"You're paying me. Trust me, it serves me."

Annabelle pursed her rosebud lips. Joe had used to call her *cute*, an adjective she hadn't loved, but there was no other way to describe her. She was cute.

"You always were such a disciplined boy." Annabelle's smile was sly. "You must be really interested in this girl to let her lead you away from your job."

Uh-oh.

Annabelle wasn't entirely rational when it came to her business or love. He had no doubt Annabelle was genuinely hopeful something romantic would come of this, like he'd match with someone during the course of the campaign and fall madly in love with her.

A connection like that felt as far away as the moon to Samson. He'd sailed through life flirting with long-term relationships but never quite landing in one.

What would you have done if you'd caught your Cinderella then? After you profusely apologized?

He had no idea, like he hadn't known what had driven him to ask her out on a second date to begin with. He was all reaction when it came to her.

It was best he hadn't caught her, he supposed. "Nah. It may not have even been the woman I'm thinking of," he lied.

"Maybe you'll see her again. It's a small world, you know." Aunt Belle patted his arm.

The burst of pleasure at that thought was way out of proportion, but he embraced it.

"Tina gave you your agenda, right?" Aunt Belle fell into step beside him as they walked back the way they'd come.

"She did, yes." Samson wasn't sure he was going to be able to sleep tonight, which was a problem. He had a full day tomorrow. He'd told Matchmaker to utilize him as much as possible, which meant leveraging whatever infamy or fame he had attached to his name to promote Matchmaker. This was a big conference, covered by a good amount of media.

So big, he didn't understand why Aunt Belle had pushed herself to even attend, let alone commit to so many things. Perhaps because Jennifer had usually handled all this stuff? But Jennifer and Annabelle had taken care of two very different sides of Matchmaker's business.

"William said you have an interview tomorrow, right?

Do you think you'll be well enough for that?" He didn't judge her for not getting up on that stage, but he did worry she might have set herself up for more anxiety than she needed.

"Oh, I'm sure I will." Belle waved his concern away, a slight blush telling him she didn't want to talk about her anxieties. "Is there anything else you need?" She dropped her voice. "Has anyone been mean to you about your past?"

He patted her back and pasted on a smile he didn't feel. "No, Aunt Belle. Everyone's been really nice so far. I'm good."

Annabelle's nose wrinkled before she lowered her veil. "You return to the party if you truly want to, but I'm retiring for the night. I'll see you tomorrow. I'm so proud of you, darling. Thank you for all your help."

Warmth spread through his chest. He accepted a hug and kiss from Annabelle and watched her walk away before he turned to head back to the ballroom, a smile pasted on his face. No one would be able to guess how fake it was.

He was here for a reason. He had a purpose. And it had nothing to do with the beautiful, furious woman who had run from him. Again.

Chapter Three

HE'D *SMILED* at her.

That motherfucker.

Rhiannon fought the urge to curl her lip, for fear that the makeup artist might think it was directed at her. The poor girl didn't deserve snarling, especially when she was working so hard to disguise the dark under-eye circles that were a testament to how little Rhiannon had slept the night before, tossing and turning in her posh hotel's luxury bedding.

Lakshmi appeared at her elbow. Today, Rhiannon's tall and sturdy assistant was bright and cheerful in a yellow crop top and high-waisted black pants with rainbow suspenders. Her black hair was swept up to the side, revealing an undercut that was dyed purple and dotted with glitter in the shape of a star. Her brown skin glowed with good health and the effects of her daily ten-step skin care regimen.

They were in a different hotel from the one Rhiannon had been in last night, in a small room near the ballroom and the stage where Rhiannon and Annabelle would be interviewed live in front of a huge audience of CREATE conferencegoers. Tech people bustled right outside the door.

"Do you need another coffee?"

Since Lakshmi considered fetching drinks way below her pay grade, Rhiannon figured she must really look a mess. "No, I'm fine. Thanks."

Lakshmi waited for the makeup artist to finish and leave the room and then used two fingers to swivel Rhiannon's face toward her. She critically examined the makeup job, then reached for the blending sponge. Rhiannon waited patiently while Lakshmi redid her face with slightly darker foundation and powder. Lakshmi understood makeup and hair far better than most artists, especially when it came to brown and black skin, and Rhiannon trusted her implicitly to make her look her best. "How was the party?" Lakshmi asked.

"Fine."

"I heard Annabelle didn't speak."

"No, she was ill." Rhiannon studiously avoided thinking about who had come out on the stage. Or how he'd *smiled* at her, like he was thrilled to see her.

The sense of outrage wasn't bad, actually. It distracted from how much she was low-key disgusted with herself for bolting from the room.

Retreat isn't weakness.

Rhiannon curled her fingers around the arm of her makeup chair. She'd have to keep telling herself that.

Lakshmi dabbed powder over her nose. "It's no big loss if she doesn't show up today for the interview. With Helena killing it on her late-night talk show lately, it would be good for her to see you wrap an audience around your finger."

Rhiannon didn't pretend to play humble. When she was on, she was *on* and could easily wrap a crowd around her finger, even many of those people who might be poised to snub her on the basis of old rumors. "Yeah."

"Except, of course, Annabelle is your white whale. Meeting her here would be a lot easier than camping out near her beach house."

Rhiannon flinched, but she recovered as quickly as possible. Lakshmi was gently teasing her. She had no idea how little Rhiannon wanted to think of that weekend.

Katrina, Rhiannon's best friend and business partner, and Lakshmi had both been skeptical about her plan to rent a place a few houses down from Annabelle's beach home for a long weekend, but it had seemed like a great idea at the time. Despite Matchmaker's L.A. headquarters, Annabelle was reportedly rarely in the city, Cayucos the closest she came when she ventured off her Northern California estate.

Rhiannon had killed two days playing spy, and by the third, with Annabelle's house remaining dark and empty, she'd been climbing the walls in boredom. So she'd sat down with her own app, and, well, that night with Samson had been the result.

See me again.

He'd still been inside her when he'd whispered that in her ear. Dawn had been breaking, sending fingers of blue and pink over her rented bedroom walls. They'd wrecked all the bedding, the white ruffled duvet hanging off the bed, the pillows on the floor.

Normally she would have shuffled a man out after the first time they'd had sex or after she'd gotten off sufficiently, whichever came first. He'd lasted four times. Or had it been five? He'd merely had to kiss her or touch her, or look at her, and she'd dragged him back on top of her.

She blamed her dick-drunk brain for not shooting down his suggestion for another night immediately. Instead she'd skated her hands down his sweat-slick back. *I'm heading home to L.A. in a couple of days.*

Silly her, she'd held her breath, unsure of whether he'd say something that would mean she'd have to kick him out. Something long term, like *L.A.'s not so far*, even though a four-hour drive might as well be the moon as far as an Angeleno was concerned.

But he was smart and only replied, *Then we have a couple days.*

When he hadn't shown the next night, she'd felt—

She gave herself a hard mental shake. Nah. She was done with feelings. *Shove them down.*

She'd spent last night tossing and turning, marveling over the coincidence—horror?—of Annabelle's newest employee being her one-night stand, but it didn't matter at the end of the day. Whatever freak chain of events had led to him now working for the company she hoped to buy was irrelevant. She only had to avoid him for the next two days. This was a big conference, and he was her competitor's spokesman, not upper management. She'd be fine.

"Are we done?" Rhiannon asked.

Lakshmi finished painting her lips and stepped back. "Yeah."

Rhiannon checked her face in the mirror and nodded in satisfaction. "Thanks. I look good."

"As usual."

Whoa. "Thanks." Lakshmi must really be picking up on odd vibes from her if she was complimenting her this lavishly. Not that Lakshmi wasn't kind, but Rhiannon wasn't the type of woman who seemed like she needed complimenting.

Sweet. Kind. Loyal.

The funny thing was, Rhiannon could be sweet and kind, and she was loyal to death, if she loved a person. But no one would have ever described her as sweet, kind, and loyal. Because the world had decided long ago what a sweet, kind, and loyal woman looked like, and it wasn't her.

Rhiannon carefully picked a piece of lint off her black hoodie. When she'd found herself heartbroken and alone four years ago, she'd made a promise to create an alternate universe for herself. One in which she didn't spend hours and days and weeks and months losing time mourning people who treated her poorly. In the other universe, with her time reclaimed, she owned the world.

And today, with an interview in front of hundreds, livestreamed to God knew how many more, she'd take another step toward her lofty goals.

Samson? He was trash. A speed bump. A football player who said "nothing serious" a few months ago and now said he was "looking for the one" because he was getting paid? He could fuck right off. She wasn't going to let him live rent-free in her brain.

"Oh, I almost forgot." Lakshmi handed Rhiannon her phone from the table, interrupting her fierce musings. "Text your mom."

That was right. Rhiannon might own the world, but her mama owned her. "Thanks." Rhiannon opened her texts and scrolled to her mother's last message. She had two modes when it came to texts: reply immediately, or decide to reply later and completely forget, which was why she had Lakshmi to remind her.

Good luck with the interview! Lakshmi sent me the link. I'll be listening.

No pressure. Rhiannon typed her response. **Going on soon, thanks. ILU.**

Text bubbles. And then: **I know how much time you spend on your phone, you can type out I love you. I love you too.**

"Knock, knock!" Helena Knight billowed into the room. The former comedian/television personality/lifestyle magazine editor in chief and current evening talk-show host was taller than Rhiannon, her model-thin body clad in a stylish green cape dress. Rhiannon came to her feet.

Helena placed her hand on her bosom. "It's so nice to meet you, Rhiannon. I admire you greatly."

They exchanged air kisses, and Rhiannon gave her a genuine smile, something about her warm manner giving her a good vibe. "Likewise, Helena. This is my assistant, Lakshmi."

"Charmed. Oh my, I love your hair." Helena fingered her own red hair. "Do you think I could pull off that style?"

Lakshmi cocked her head and studied her critically. "Possible. You have a nicely shaped head."

Helena tittered, her hair tugging transforming into twirling. "Why, thank you. As do you."

Unnoticed, Rhiannon rolled her eyes. No matter the environment, men and women often gave Lakshmi second or third looks. Her assistant exuded some kind of magnetism that no one was really immune to. "Thank you so much for sending your questions in advance, Helena."

Helena dragged her gaze away from Lakshmi reluctantly. "Oh, not a problem. I may stray a bit or reword, based on how the interview goes, but those will be the main ones. And I'll stay away from the topics your team requested."

Rhiannon kept her expression placid, relieved. Like most people, Suzie, Crush's fearsome marketing leader, didn't have all the information on what had caused Rhiannon's career implosion at Swype, but the woman had diligently shoved that time period into a laundry list of other taboo interview topics. "Sounds good." Rhiannon pressed her hand over her belly, to quell the flutter of nerves there. No one would believe she got a bit of stage fright, but she did. "Are the questions from the audience going to be prescreened?"

"The moderator is requesting people write them down and turn them in, yes. She'll pick a few to read at the end." Lakshmi paused her fussing at the makeup table to assure her. "I've already threatened her if she picks a stinker."

"Now *that's* an assistant." Helena eyed Lakshmi with avarice, but Rhiannon wasn't concerned her assistant could be easily lured away. No one could afford Lakshmi. Rhiannon paid her better than some of her competitors paid their executives.

"She's the best," Rhiannon simply said.

"I'm so excited for this interview," Helena said. "I've been following your career for a while, and I love Crush's mission statement. It's about time that the conference highlights the women in this industry."

"I agree." Rhiannon couldn't have imagined four years ago that she'd be here, about to talk to Helena in front of a large audience at a major conference, joined by another woman entrepreneur. A lot changed in a few years. Global movements came and went, the tide shifted, people became marginally more accepting.

Not totally. Not where they should be, if everything was equalized. But margins were better than nothing, or so Rhiannon told herself.

Helena wrinkled her nose. "Now, I did come in here to break some bad news. Unfortunately, Annabelle Kostas won't be joining us. She's still feeling ill and had to step out at the last minute."

There went her chance to get to Annabelle. Lakshmi had called it. Rhiannon wondered if the woman was really sick or simply couldn't bear to face a crowd at all. Disappointed as she was, compassion moved through Rhiannon. She knew quite a bit about phobias. "I'm fine filling an hour on my own."

"I'd be fine with that, too, but she actually sent a proxy in her place. She assured me he knows everything about the company, has been around the business for years."

Rhiannon's heart lurched. "Oh?" It was William. It had to be William. Why would they send a flashy hot new spokes-man, when they could send the company's CEO, a longtime employee?

"He's a lovely man, I met him at the party last night. He's getting micced offstage. Come on, I'll introduce you." She waved and walked out.

Ask. Just to make sure it is who you think it is. "Did she send William?" Rhiannon asked, following behind her, leaving Lakshmi behind in the dressing room.

"My understanding is William already left to return to L.A., but we're in good hands."

Rhiannon's stomach roiled as they walked up behind a tall, dark-haired, muscular man standing not far from the stage. She fixed her gaze over his shoulder. The shoulder she'd dug her fingernails into.

It was fine. This wasn't the first time she'd sat across from a man she'd had sex with and had to pretend everything was fine. It had been years, but surely one didn't forget that skill.

So long as he kept his mouth shut and followed her lead, everything would be . . . fine.

At their approach, he glanced over his shoulder, and his eyes grew wide. Meanwhile, the knot in her stomach tight-ened. She could count on one hand the number of powerful men she knew who were capable of following a woman's lead. What were the odds he was one of them?

Sleeping with this guy was going to bite her in ways she never could have anticipated when she'd been sitting on that lounge chair in Cayucos, swiping away on her phone, cursing the rental house's slow Wi-Fi.

"Samson Lima," Helena said sweetly. "Please meet Rhiannon Hunter."

Chapter Four

R_{HIANNON}.

Samson rolled the name around his head, tasted it, examined it. It should have sounded wrong and foreign, given that he'd been thinking of her as Claire for months. Especially since *Claire* had been the name he'd groaned when he'd been inside her.

But Rhiannon suited her. Rhiannon was witchy and mysterious and secretive, and her shadowed eyes were all those things.

"Samson is the new spokesman for Matchmaker." Helena beamed at him. "Rhiannon is the founder and creator of Crush. It's the dating app for women, as they say."

"It's the dating app for everyone," Rhiannon corrected, and Samson didn't miss the steel beneath her pleasant reply.

He knew there'd be a rep here from Crush, but he hadn't had time to vet her identity. Aunt Belle had called him less than a half hour ago, weeping, and begged him to come here today and fill in for her. William was on a plane, she'd said, her voice wobbling. She simply couldn't get up in front of a big crowd and do this interview.

"Where are you?" he'd demanded. The sound of traffic had been loud on her end.

"Don't hate me."

"I could never hate you."

"I'm . . . I'm going to Australia."

He'd stopped and stared at the phone, then put it back to his ear. *Australia?* As far as he knew, his aunt didn't know a soul in Australia. "Aunt Belle . . ."

"Please. I thought I could do this, all of it. But I'm not Jennifer." Her voice grew faint. "I have to go. Please cover for me."

He'd grimaced. "Tell me what they're going to talk about so I'm prepared."

Spoiler: Aunt Belle hadn't mentioned that his coguest was the woman he'd been chasing through a hotel last night. Probably because his aunt hadn't known he was chasing her coguest. To be fair, neither had he.

Ah, jeez. Matchmaker's competitor. He'd slept with his aunt's competitor. In what world.

Samson held out his hand slowly, wondering what she'd do. There was no rage in her expression today, only deliberate calm.

She examined his hand for a second, and he wondered if she was thinking what he was thinking. About how she'd cried out when he'd made her come with his fingers, or how he'd cupped her breast in his palm.

She slid her hand in his. "Mr. Lima. A pleasure."

Her fingers were slender and long, the nails short and buffed. When she'd coasted them over his body, he'd thought they were a workingwoman's fingers, her palms calloused.

A tingle ran down his spine as they shook hands, brusque, personality-less, two strangers meeting each other for the first time. Today she was back to her jeans and black sweatshirt, though it was zipped up, so he couldn't tell if she had a vintage band tee on under it.

Her hair was loose again. Under the indoor lights, all the shades of black and brown that made up the curls were more muted.

"Call me Samson," he murmured.

She didn't tell him to call her Rhiannon, he noticed, but he could say it in his head. Replace the name he'd thought belonged to her.

She dipped her head and slipped her hand out from his.

He flexed the fingers she'd touched. He wanted to touch her again, but of course, he couldn't do that. It was apparent she didn't want anyone to know they'd met. Neither did he, really. His persona at Matchmaker didn't mesh with short hookups.

"You weren't at the party last night, were you, Rhiannon? Matchmaker's doing an adorable campaign," Helena prattled as she and Rhiannon got mics. "Basically chances to date Samson."

"Sounds like you're a prize bull." Rhiannon pushed her hair aside so the tech could access her collar.

"Hardly a prize."

Her eye twitched.

"I'm thrilled to meet you," he said gently, hoping she'd

get the hint. He wasn't about to reveal their past in a professional setting.

She dipped her head. Was that a flash of relief? "Very nice to meet you as well."

Helena gestured to the stage. "Shall we take our seats? There's a curtain, so we can chill up there while the crowd is still settling in."

That crowd sounded enormous to Samson's ears as they walked onto the stage, directed by staffers. Crowds didn't intimidate him, but then again, he'd never tried to do an interview for his aunt's struggling international business while sitting across from a woman he'd slept with and then flaked on in front of such a crowd.

He'd spent the whole night thinking about her, what he'd say if he ran into her again, how he'd apologize or grovel or say nothing. The scenarios he'd run through in his brain hadn't come close to this.

They settled into the white club chairs, Helena's seat in between theirs. When Helena was pulled away for a makeup fix, Samson saw his chance. "Rhiannon."

She ignored his whisper, examining her unpainted nails. "Rhiannon."

Nothing. He braced his palms on the arms of the chair and leaned forward, slightly annoyed at this childish game. "Claire."

Her eyes snapped to his. Ah, yeah. There was *an* emotion, but probably not a good one. "Don't." The single word was delivered between gritted teeth. "You don't know me. I don't know you."

A surreptitious glance told him Helena was still occupied. "That's fine. I won't say anything about us."

"Good, because there's no us."

Before he could answer, Helena dropped into the chair between them. "Now, I understand you two are competitors, so feel free to engage in some friendly banter, but I won't have any blood drawn here. Keep it clean."

"No blood." Rhiannon cracked open a water bottle from the side table. "Got it."

"No blood," he echoed.

"One minute," a stagehand hissed. An announcer's voice boomed out, quieting the crowd.

"Samson, I know you were briefed on the questions, but I also know this isn't your usual scene." Helena's smile was sympathetic. "If you get confused or overwhelmed, don't worry too much. I'm sure Rhiannon will be happy to jump in, and I'll moderate. Right, Rhiannon?"

Rhiannon capped the water bottle. If he was gauging her level of fury correctly, he was pretty sure she wouldn't toss the contents of it on him if he were on fire, but her mild expression didn't give that away. "Yeah, sure."

"I'll be fine." He didn't take offense to Helena's doubt. People were inclined to believe football players were stupid, and he hadn't been in the public eye for a long time. For all she knew, he wouldn't be able to handle himself.

Public appearances had never bothered him, though. One of his first memories was sitting on his father's shoulders after a Super Bowl win, the deafening roar of the crowd piercing through the giant headphones his parents had slapped over his ears. Being a famous man's son had taught him how to play to the public; being a pro athlete had taught him that his face and body were a tool. He hadn't minded doing endorsements. Until he'd retired, and they'd vanished.

"Here we go." Helena straightened up.

The curtain split open, and Samson was abruptly glad he had been able to step in for Annabelle. This big of a crowd, plus a recording? He didn't know if his aunt could have done this, if introducing him at the party had freaked her out. Even he felt a few nerves flutter alive.

Helena waved as the applause died down. "Gosh, thank you, Jason, for introducing me, and thank you all for coming! I'm so excited to be here at CREATE, and especially at this interview. I have so much respect for both of my guests today." She cocked her head. "Now, this panel is called Slow Dating vs. Swiping, and I think that's a bit of a mistitle, because I think real 'slow dating' would be, like, meeting someone at a café or a party and then seeing them once a week for four months and then deciding you want to be exclusive, and who the heck does that anymore, huh?" She placed her hand by her mouth and leaned forward, like she was imparting a secret. "If there's anyone here who's got a relationship that started like that in the last couple years, you're a freaking unicorn, FYI."

The smatter of laughter eased him. Helena was a good moderator, and this seemed like it would be a fairly softball interview. All he had to do was not focus on Rhiannon.

He might have been hit, he might be disoriented, but he could still play.

"But for our purposes, we'll use 'slow dating' to refer to a nonswipey dating app. And to that end, over here we have Matchmaker. Matchmaker was one of the first entries to online dating, almost a quarter century ago. While a number of those first sites have been lost to history, Matchmaker has remained strong, with almost eight million paid subscribers, and committed to its one-hundred-point matching system. Now, I know some of you were expecting to see Annabelle Kostas, cofounder of the site, but unfortunately, she had to bow out at the last minute. We have a very attractive stand-in, though. If you're a football fan like I am, some of you may know Samson Lima from his days as a Super Bowl–winning linebacker for the Portland Brewers or, before that, his college ball days at Notre Dame. He's taken a bit of a break from the spotlight, but now he's back. Hopefully, you all have heard about his gig over at Matchmaker, and how you, too, can score a date with this handsome bachelor. If you're just finding out right now, I'll ask you to hold signing up for the site until after the interview, please."

He smiled and waved as the crowd chuckled and clapped.

"And, over here, we have Rhiannon Hunter."

Samson raised an eyebrow as the audience erupted into cheers. There was no doubt who everyone was here to see.

Rhiannon took another drink of water while Helena indulgently waited for the noise to die down. "Rhiannon is the creator of Crush. Built on that familiar swiping platform, it's often called the more empowered response to app dating, where users have more control in curating who they see and how they communicate with their matches.

The customizability of the app seems to appeal to a lot of people. Crush currently has about twenty-six million subscribers."

Rhiannon crossed her legs. Her sneakers were a matte gold, a pop of color in her otherwise somber outfit. "It's closer to thirty million."

Helena chuckled. "Okay, thirty million."

Thirty million was a lot more than Matchmaker's eight million. Samson worried anew for Annabelle. Matchmaker had an app, but only due to Jennifer's insistence. Annabelle had fought her every step in migrating their platform or altering their time-consuming sign-up process.

Matchmaker was behind, and Jennifer had leaned into being the "old-fashioned" option, but Samson really hoped their lag didn't eventually tank the company. His aunt had had a rough year, what with losing Jennifer and Joe, and she didn't need any more loss.

Helena waited for the applause to die down, and then turned to Samson. "I think we can all agree that the internet has made dating so different now. Samson, why don't you explain what makes Matchmaker the place to be?"

Samson launched into his memorized talking points. "For anyone who's taken Matchmaker's questionnaire, you know how in-depth it gets, how long it takes. Now, some people may say that that's a negative, that time-intensive process, but I think anything that forces us to slow down and think about ourselves and what we're looking for is a good thing. Life is too fast paced. Your relationships shouldn't be."

Helena tucked a strand of hair behind her ear. "Do you

think apps are too fast paced for anyone to make a solid connection?"

"I wouldn't say that. Clearly people do make connections." He tried to tread carefully. He didn't want to attack Crush. This was a friendly panel, and the crowd was already here for Rhiannon.

Also, Rhiannon might murder him. "When you're on a phone and you're swiping, you're spending a second? A fraction of a second? On each person. That's not enough time to get to know them. That's more of a game than anything."

"Have you ever used a dating app, Samson?" Rhiannon interjected.

That felt like a trap. He answered honestly. "Only once, for a short period of time. I deleted it almost immediately."

"Is that how long you spent on each person?"

"No, but I think I'm an outlier." He'd scrutinized Rhiannon's—Claire's—single photo for a while and read her short profile ten times before swiping right. He had it memorized.

Looking for Mr. Right Now, not Mr. Right. Swipe right if you're down for a night of fun and you're not going to be a dick about protection or pleasure.

If he hadn't been staring at her, he would have missed the twitch at the corner of her mouth. "Well, even if some people view it as a game, and you can't deny that there are those who see any kind of dating as a game, this"—she made a swiping motion—"disrupted how we connect online. Fifty years ago, your potential mate was in a bar or a grocery store. Twenty years ago, your potential mate was on their computer. Today, this is where your potential mate is, on their phone, on their app, swiping for you. Maybe there are slower-paced ways to evaluate someone, but this is where you'll get the largest pool to choose from."

All that made sense, but he couldn't let her paint Matchmaker as a relic from decades ago. "It should be about quality, not quantity."

Rhiannon's teeth flashed, and she snapped the trap, looking out at the darkened audience. "How many quality people here are on or have been on Crush?"

The audience cheered. Mentally, Samson cracked his knuckles. Oh, she was wily. No blood, but she'd handily cemented the crowd's affection.

He would too.

Helena stepped in, perhaps sensing a need for moderation. "Crush does have a small quiz before you sign up. That's different from other apps."

"Yes. It's not a hundred points." The twist of Rhiannon's mouth made it clear what she thought about Matchmaker's system. "We ask simple questions, and most are optional: Do you have kids, want kids? Are you a smoker? How much do you drink? What's your political party? And then we have one required question: Are you looking for a platonic relationship, a romantic one, or a hookup?"

"Interesting that that's your required question."

"Our mission at Crush is to disrupt how you swipe. We're built on the principles of accountability, kindness, choice, and empowerment. We've found that this question encourages users to be honest about their intentions, and it helps curate who we match you with based on what answer you provide."

Samson thought back to when he'd signed up for Crush. He'd selected hookup and felt vaguely guilty doing it.

"You don't have to feel bad about what you pick." There was Rhiannon, reading his mind. "You can be honest."

"For heterosexual relationships, you also permit women to choose whether they prefer to initiate contact or not." Helena cupped her chin. "Why not default let the woman start the conversation? Isn't that the more empowered move?"

"There's no real one size fits all for empowerment. I will say, our data shows that women who choose to make initial contact do seem to receive less unsolicited dick pics, but that may be anecdotal." She grinned when the audience laughed. "We immediately block anyone who does that, of course. Zero tolerance on unrequested dick pics."

Helena turned to him. "Samson, what do you have to say to that?"

He opened his eyes wide. "I've . . . never sent a photo like that and don't understand why anyone would send one without explicit permission."

The audience laughed louder, and so did Helena. Rhiannon took another drink of water.

"Seriously, though, Matchmaker's app encourages accountability as well. In fact, if you came to our open house earlier today, you probably saw the launch of our new Face-Match system. It basically requires users to take a selfie to confirm that they are who they say they are." That feature had been a real hit at the open house, and it caused a ripple through the audience now.

Rhiannon raised a skeptical eyebrow. "Have you tried it? Because facial recognition is notoriously poor, especially when it comes to differentiating between the faces of people of color."

"There's no software. We have a team that personally reviews the photos and confirms the match. Matchmaker might be a huge company, but the Kostas sisters wanted everyone to feel like they're receiving the personal touch."

Helena consulted her notes. "Is it true that your parents met via Matchmaker?"

He blinked, but recovered quickly. Annabelle must have given that info to Helena's team. It wasn't a commonly known story, because the general public didn't know much about Annabelle, including that she'd been Big Joe's partner for close to forty years. That was a feat, given how cameras had followed Uncle Joe around at the height of his career. "Kind of, yes. They're both gone now, unfortunately."

"Right." Helena grimaced, and it appeared genuine. "I'm sorry. You don't have to talk about—"

"No, it's fine. It was a long time ago." If Annabelle had been willing to talk about this, he could too. "For those who don't know, my father was Aleki Lima." The rumble of excitement in the crowd gave him a minute to take a sip of water, swallow past the jumbled mix of pity and love and guilt that came with the thought of his father. "My mother's name was Lulu. She was born in Samoa and moved to San Francisco when she was in her early twenties. Lulu was looking for love. She came to Matchmaker's office to find it and took the original version of the questionnaire. Hard copy." He softened, thinking of his sweet, loving mother. "Annabelle and Jennifer set her up with bachelor after bachelor, and they all struck out."

"One of them was Aleki?"

"Oh, God, no. The Kostas sisters knew my dad pretty well, and they were sure that the only thing he might have in common with my mom was that his family was Samoan too. He had a reputation at the time. But according to the story I was told, my dad saw my mom leaving the Matchmaker offices one day. He fell in love at first sight. Family friend or not, Annabelle refused to introduce them until he took the test too. Once he did and she vetted him . . ." He shrugged. "They were married in six months, had me nine months after that."

Helena clapped her hands. "What a beautiful story. So this is a bit more personal for you than a standard spokesman gig, huh?"

"Oh yes. When I say Matchmaker works, I really mean it works." He hadn't told anyone outside his tight inner circle that story in a while, and he'd forgotten how sweet it was. No matter what had happened to his dad after, his parents had started their lives together in love. He took another sip of water and looked at Rhiannon. She didn't look as impressed with his origin story. "I'm guessing your parents didn't meet on Crush."

"Nah, they met at a grocery store," Rhiannon replied. "I'm sure we have users whose parents met on Matchmaker. Not as old as you, though."

Helena held up her hand to halt Rhiannon, chuckling. "Easy there, tiger. Why don't we talk about what features you both have in the works?"

They ran through some lighter, easier questions, designed to make the audience laugh. Forty-five minutes flew by quickly. Then Helena paused. "Before we get to questions from the audience, I want to just ask about one thing: the terminology. I've been married for five years, and I feel like the language of love has changed, hasn't it? There are so many new words, I can't keep up with them."

Samson was nodding before she finished speaking. For the last two years especially, he'd been so wrapped up in taking care of Uncle Joe, he hadn't been online much.

"Language changes when progress happens. I think the way we talk about behavior makes total sense. For example, benching someone is stringing them along in case your first pick doesn't work out. DTF is down to . . . mess around." Rhiannon's teeth flashed. "But really, maybe the most descriptive word we could possibly use is *ghosting*."

Chapter Five

An audible hiss ran through the crowd and Rhiannon smiled, despite the cold anger balled up in the pit of her stomach. If she didn't look too closely at Samson, she could forget that anger and the hurt.

Not hurt. Never again.

He didn't have the power to hurt her. She owned the world. She'd gotten through this interview, hadn't she? All by pretending Samson was someone other than the man who had stood her up. Who had *ghosted* her.

There were a couple times when she had been sucked in by his charm. Like when he'd gotten that knowing gleam in his eye when she'd made subtle references to how old Matchmaker was, or every time he'd articulately fielded Helena's questions, or when his face had gone all soft and sentimental, talking about his late parents.

Claire. Her fake name that she used on the app, murmured in that fucking voice.

So she'd remind herself of why, exactly, he was a bastard. If it jolted him and made him show remorse or chagrin, all the better.

"Ugh." Helena leaned into the audience reaction. "Ghosting is the worst."

"It's a terrible feeling. When you ghost someone, you're saying, I don't care enough about you as a human being to even tell you I don't want to see you again. How humiliating is that?" She tried to keep her smile intact, but she feared it was turning a little feral.

"No joke." Helena glanced offstage. "Okay, I am being signaled that we're running low on time, so let's take a couple questions from the audience."

Most of the questions were for Rhiannon, a tiny win that made her want to childishly stick her tongue out at the hunk of man sitting across from her. Some of the questions were silly and goofy, and Rhiannon answered them as such. There was a harmless one about the journey she'd taken to get to where she was, which Rhiannon significantly toned down, nothing that wasn't in her Wikipedia article: Harvard dropout, founder of a now-defunct social media startup she'd sold for a hefty sum at the age of twenty-six, an executive at a competitor app, and finally, starting Crush with a silent investor. She didn't name Katrina, who used a number of shell companies to keep herself out of the spotlight.

Those in the tech industry knew Rhiannon had departed Swype under a dark cloud, but even right after she'd left, the questions she'd fielded in public had been veiled and gossipy. No one had been bold enough to come right out and ask her directly, *Rhiannon, how do you feel about the fact that your former employer started a whisper campaign about how you were a gold digger and a whore?*

Not great, Chuck.

"Ah, interesting," Helena said as the next question came on the screen, but her lip curl told Rhiannon the woman found the question to be the opposite of interesting. Once Rhiannon read it, she liked Helena more. "The question is, 'Rumor has it Crush's staff is 80 percent female. Isn't it discriminatory to hire only women?'"

Rhiannon scanned the room, though the stage lights made it impossible for her to track down who in the audience had asked such an asinine question.

She said nothing for a beat. When she'd been embroiled in a messy employment relationship with Swype, the man in charge wearing her down, she'd dreamed of this power. The power to be silent while a man—though it could be a woman, patriarchy had no gender—waited for her answer, to force them to conform to her timetable.

It was petty and silly, but again . . . one could indulge in such things when one was in charge.

Finally, she spoke, directing her answer to the audience, not Helena.

"It's not a rumor, though the number's a little off." She didn't have to look offstage to know Lakshmi was probably plotting to strangle whoever had green-lit that question. "I am proud of how representative Crush is. An inclusive staff means an inclusive app, one that can be safe and welcoming and serve as many people as possible. Currently, approximately 72 percent of our workforce are women, both cis- and transgender, 18 percent are men, both cis- and transgender, and 10 percent are non-binary individuals. Let's look at the other companies of Crush's size. What's the makeup of their staff?" She didn't look at Samson, because she wasn't talking about Matchmaker. Matchmaker wasn't the enemy, and since she wanted to buy it, she wasn't about to rip it apart.

But she hoped everyone was thinking about Swype real hard. Her pettiness knew no bounds there.

Helena shifted. "I would imagine it's a majority of cis men," she murmured.

"I would say that too. So why do I constantly get asked this question? Why isn't every single one of these male CEOs asked why they're discriminating against anyone who's not a straight white cis man?"

A murmur of agreement went through the crowd. Someone started clapping.

Rhiannon placed her hands on the arms of her chair and leaned forward. "I see talent. Maybe you need to wonder why other companies aren't seeing the skills that I see in the people I hire. What's holding them back from being the best that they can be?" She was getting too passionate, too loud, so she leaned back and pasted a smile on her face. "I hope that answers your question."

Samson cleared his throat and raised his hand. Helena regarded him with amusement. "You can jump in, Samson. No need to raise your hand."

He shrugged. "I just want to say Rhiannon answered that really stupid question with grace and more eloquence than I ever would."

Rhiannon nearly smiled with the audience, but controlled it. Damn it.

But it was a nice thing for the bastard to say, especially when *she* couldn't come out and call that question stupid. Not without looking too angry or emotional.

"Okay, one more question." Helena tapped her fingers on the arm of her chair. "Oh, this is more of a personal question. I love it, I've always wanted to be an advice columnist. Are there any circumstances under which you'd give someone who ghosted you a second chance?"

"No," Rhiannon said flatly.

"Yes," Samson said, almost at the same time.

"Oooh, polar opposites."

No fucking surprise there.

Helena nearly rubbed her hands together. "Explain, Rhiannon first."

What a no-brainer. "My stance is, if a man ghosts you, he's literally ghosted you. Like, he's probably dead." The audience and Helena chuckled, but Samson only leaned back in his seat. "Please don't misunderstand me. I don't wish them dead. I assume they died. I'm kind enough to give them noble deaths, too, in my head." She rolled her wrist. "Saving a puffin from a fire, et cetera."

"Is there a word for people who come back into your life after a ghost?" Helena mused.

If there was one thing Rhi did know, it was the lingo. "The behavior is called submarining, but I prefer calling them zombies," she said dryly. "I don't know about you, but I'm not looking to let any kind of zombie back into my life."

"What about you, Samson? You said you would give someone a second chance."

Samson shifted. "I think, generally, you're right, Rhiannon. Too often people treat others as disposable. It's not right. But I think there are cases where you should, at the very least, hear someone out. What if someone doesn't intend to ghost the other person?" Samson asked, so quietly Rhiannon had to lean forward to hear him.

This time she did sneer. "Intend? Your intent is irrelevant, you either do it or you don't. If you—I mean, someone— makes a conscious decision to not call or stands you up, they've ghosted."

"What if the ghoster has a family emergency? Don't extenuating circumstances matter?"

Was he saying he'd had a family emergency that night? A flare of hope fluttered under her hurt and anger, but then she realized what it was and swiftly squelched it down.

Hope was the enemy of productivity, in her case, at least. "A family emergency of a sufficient degree may warrant a talk," she said, proud that there wasn't a single shake in her voice. "But trust in relationships is like fragile glass. How can you build on a cracked foundation? How can you be sure you're getting the truth? You have to protect your own heart. No one else will do it for you."

Samson's short lashes lowered, hiding his eyes. Helena jumped in, probably sensing their light interview was getting a little too deep. They wrapped up the Q&A and Rhi waited for the curtain to come down before she wrestled with her mic, yanking it off with more force than was necessary. The adrenaline that had fueled her through the interview was going to seep out of her soon, and she needed to get away before it did.

Shouldn't have brought up ghosting.

"That was fantastic," Helena enthused, as an assistant removed her mic and handed her a fresh bottle of water. "I'd love for both of you to be guests at some point on my show. Together, separately, anything."

God no, not together.

"Matchmaker would be all for that," Samson rumbled. She wondered if he was as drained as she was.

Don't wonder anything about him.

"That would be amazing." Rhiannon stood, Samson and Helena following her lead. "Why don't you have your people contact mine?"

"Will do." She and Helena exchanged air kisses and then it was time for Rhiannon to say goodbye to Samson. She held her hand out.

He took it, and that stupid little electrical shock ran up her arm. Why was it still there? It should be eradicated, that zing when he touched her. She snatched her hand back, and then felt mildly foolish.

Samson took a step toward her, but before he could open his mouth, Helena put her hand on his arm. "Samson, this is super unprofessional, but would you mind if I video called my dad? He's such a fan."

"That would be great." His words and smile looked forced to Rhiannon.

Why do you care?

That was right, she didn't. They were distracted, she was outta here.

She met Lakshmi offstage. The crew bustled around them to turn over the stage for the next event. "You killed it," Lakshmi enthused. "You three had such good chemistry."

They had had good chemistry, in spite of—or because of—the undercurrents of anger between her and Samson. Or at least, from her to Samson. She wasn't sure what he felt for her, because the man's public mask was as good as hers.

Whatever. She didn't care what he felt for her.

"Did Helena say anything about her show?"

"Yes." A belated thrill of excitement pierced Rhiannon's exhaustion as she relayed Helena's invitation. World domination was so close. "We'll get it set up." She glanced over her shoulder at the stage.

Samson was waving dutifully at Helena's phone while the other woman chattered away. As if he felt her gaze on him, he looked up and their eyes met. For the first time since the curtain went up, she saw his mask drop.

There was sorrow and guilt and apology there, and Rhiannon felt that stupid hope churning inside her.

A family emergency. Such vague words. They could mean anything from someone dying to a mild cold. And in the end, it didn't matter, because as she'd told the world . . . how could you believe someone who had already let you down once?

So she cut eye contact with the jerk and smiled at Lakshmi. "I gotta run."

"No problem. Go rest at the hotel." Lakshmi consulted her phone. "You don't have anything on the docket until tomorrow morning anyway."

And as much as Rhiannon hated running, that was exactly what she did. Because she knew she'd hate herself for running now much less than she'd hate herself for hoping later.

Chapter Six

CLASSICAL MUSIC swirled through the air, spilling out of the empty living room. Rhiannon peeked inside, then said, "Sienna, turn off the music." A small black device on the huge heavy desk turned red and the music cut off.

Katrina had a pretty set schedule, and usually that schedule included forgetting to turn the music off when she was done reading her newspaper to go make breakfast every morning.

Rhiannon sniffed the air. Whatever Katrina was cooking, it smelled good. She followed her nose, walking to the large, open-concept kitchen, the sun glinting off stainless steel appliances.

The sprawling Santa Barbara mansion belonged to her silent investor and best friend, Katrina King. As ambitious as Rhiannon was, she didn't require fancy houses to keep her happy. Big spaces meant more things to dust. As the kid of a housekeeper, she felt weird overseeing her own cleaning staff. Even if she had made sure her mother had a well-paid weekly maid service.

Dark lofts in transitioning neighborhoods had always

been more Rhiannon's style than something like this light and airy, mostly-constructed-of-windows hilltop home. In fact, she maintained her condo in L.A., close to Crush's offices, and crashed there for most of the week.

But weekends she spent here and had since about a year ago, when Katrina had far too casually asked if she'd be interested in living with her. Katrina rarely asked for anything, and Rhiannon had seen the sense in the setup. Rhiannon didn't have to worry as much about Katrina, and Katrina had some company in the house she didn't leave often.

Katrina was in front of the stove, bopping away to whatever music was coming through her giant noise-canceling headphones. She wore a camisole and short-shorts, the cotton barely containing her voluptuous body. Katrina had once confided that she loved wearing scanty clothing at home because every dimple and stretch mark and roll reminded her that she no longer had to please cameras and photographers and her agency . . . and her father.

Since she knew how much Katrina hated being surprised, Rhiannon clomped loudly into the kitchen and waved until Katrina caught sight of her in her peripheral vision. The younger woman jumped, then beamed and removed her headphones. "You're home early! I thought you were flying in tonight."

Rhiannon yawned and adjusted her silk scarf. She'd barely been alert enough last night to trade out her clothes and wrap her hair before she fell into bed. "I got in last night."

"I would have sent Gerald to get you from the airport had I known."

Katrina didn't offer to come get her herself, which neither surprised nor insulted Rhiannon. Katrina only left the sprawling mansion under very structured circumstances. "I took a car. Don't worry about it. What are you making? Do you have enough in there to share?"

"You know I always make enough for five. Go on and set the table." Katrina fussed at the stove while Rhiannon quickly set the small breakfast table with plates and spoons and forks and two glasses of fresh orange juice.

Katrina spooned creamy scrambled eggs and sliced avocados onto their plates. "Thanks." Rhiannon's stomach grumbled and she dug in as soon as Katrina sat down.

They ate quietly for a few minutes. Katrina could tell when Rhiannon was too hangry to be a good conversationalist.

Finally, Katrina broke the silence. "Why'd you come home before the conference ended?"

Because I was going crazy looking over my shoulder for Samson. One day of being skittish after the interview was enough.

Next time she tried to blow off some steam with a hookup—jeez, if she ever tried it again—she was going to find some nice boring accountant or truck driver. Someone clearly and explicitly far away from her industry. "Finished. I wasn't needed at the conference anymore."

Katrina pursed her lips, which called attention to the faint scar that ran down her cheek. Half Thai American and half white, Katrina had a unique and beautiful face, scars or not. "I thought you were going to stay for the weekend and sightsee. I haven't been to Austin in ages, but I remember how much fun it was."

"I don't need to sightsee, and we can order perfectly fine barbecue from that place downtown."

Katrina pointed her fork at her. "You haven't been on vacation since I've known you, Rhi. That's almost eleven years of nothing but work."

Rhiannon took a sip of her juice. Had it been eleven years already? She supposed so. She and Katrina had met at a party when Katrina was barely twenty-two and Rhiannon was twenty-six, fresh off the success of selling her first start-up. Rhiannon didn't make friends easily, but something about the other woman's vulnerability had yanked her right in.

"And before you say you took time off after you left Swype, know that year doesn't count."

"I went to New York twice this past year."

"Weddings also don't count as vacations. I want you to get away from your job and your phone and Wi-Fi and relax."

"No Wi-Fi? Um, that sounds like my personal hell." Rhiannon placed avocado on a slice of toast and took a bite, the crunchy buttery fat and carb combination making her hum.

Katrina dabbed the corners of her mouth. "Sonya agrees that you need a vacation. We talked yesterday."

Rhiannon groaned. That was what she got for not taking the time to spell out *I love you*. Her mother calling her friends.

"She said to tell her if you groaned when I told you she called." Katrina's eyes sparkled. "I love your mom."

"I know." Everyone loved Sonya.

"We had a lovely chat. Give her a ring when you can. She's annoyed you only text her lately, never call."

Rhiannon stabbed an avocado slice. "If I call, she's going to want to talk my ear off about the engagement party." Her little brother, Gabe, had announced his engagement, which meant Sonya was already preoccupied with a million wedding details, even though the couple had been engaged for a minute. Rhiannon had hoped she'd just be signing checks, but Sonya was determined to get her opinion on all sorts of things that Rhiannon had zero interest in. Like tablecloths. Why were there even options as to what you could put on your tables?

"You don't know that."

"Did she talk *your* ear off about the party and the wedding?"

Katrina looked away. "No comment."

Rhiannon snorted and continued to eat. "I'll call her. Later."

Rhiannon's father had died when she was young. Her single mother had been a housekeeper for one of the wealthiest families in the frigid midsized western New York town Rhiannon and Gabe had grown up in, and that meant they'd gotten some advantages other kids of housekeepers didn't, like fancy private schools.

Being able to go to those places didn't mean they'd fit in. Gabe had skated by a little less scarred, but she'd been acutely conscious of how . . . too much she was. Too much volume, too much melanin, too much ambition. Too much visibility.

Sonya had always tried to get Rhiannon to tone it down, ignore the haters, keep her head down. *The best revenge is success*, she'd preached, when Rhiannon had come home upset after someone was cruel to her. *You'll show them.*

And she had. Big picture wise, her mother had never tried to stifle Rhiannon's ambitions. Sonya had wept with pride when Rhiannon had gotten into every Ivy League school she'd applied to, then wept again when she'd dropped out of Harvard and headed to California to start her empire. Not with pride, the second time, but with worry that her daughter was throwing her future aside and going so far away. Rhiannon always felt a cocktail of guilt and love when it came to her mom, but that guilt trip had been epic.

Rhiannon hadn't spoken to her mom for almost a month after the debacle that was her exit from Swype four years ago. She'd been so ashamed, fearful of the I-told-you-so's. If success was the best revenge, what was failure?

Luckily, before Sonya could come out to California and investigate her daughter's radio silence, Katrina had swooped in with money and a plan to get Rhiannon's career back on track.

"So how did the conference go? Other than not getting a chance to get face time with Annabelle."

Rhiannon had tried to keep Katrina up-to-date on that front, at least. "Uh, great."

"Suzie said the activation went wonderfully, and we got some good press coverage."

The activation had been a walk-through interactive experience for guests, and it had been a hit. "Yup. Your shares are safe."

"You know I don't care about the shares. I care about a cat."

"Not this again. I'll think about it."

"One little kitten, that's all I'm talking about, roomie. You'll barely know it's here."

Rhiannon grinned at the long-running joke. They both knew she'd cave on the cat eventually, even if she wasn't an animal person.

A rush of love ran through Rhiannon, and she had to take a sip of juice to counter the lump in her throat. Katrina actually did care more about getting a cat than her shares.

When Rhiannon had been lost and alone, her reputation tarnished among those who might hire her, and her possibility for making it big almost nil, Katrina had pulled a last-minute Hail Mary.

Rhiannon had come to this house. Katrina had, silently, slid a blank check across the same table they were eating breakfast at. "I want to fund your next venture. I believe in you."

"Do you have any idea how much a start-up costs?" she'd asked Katrina.

Katrina's eyes had been kind. "Do you have any idea how much my husband left me? I have money. You have the brains. Make money for both of us."

At the time, Rhiannon had assumed Katrina's quiet but lush lifestyle was funded by her previous modeling career and truly hadn't had any idea how much money a famous Indian jeweler could leave his much younger wife. It turned out, a lot.

Katrina put her fork down, her plate cleaned. She was a fast eater. "I did happen to live-stream the audio of that interview you did. You were great, even handling that stupid question about your hiring practices. Was the football player as hot as he sounded?"

Rhiannon took a giant gulp of orange juice, draining the glass. She wished she'd thought to make mimosas. Not because she liked mimosas, but because then there would be a champagne bottle on the table. "Yeah, so. Funny story."

"Oh?"

"The football player was B.B."

"*What?*"

"Yup."

"Oh my God. Hashtag BeachBastard? How could you not text me immediately?"

"I was still . . . processing it." She'd processed it for the rest of the day after the interview and all of yesterday too. Processing it had given her such a stress headache, she'd moved her flight so she could leave after her very last commitment yesterday.

Rhiannon didn't keep many secrets from Katrina. She'd told her all about Samson when she'd returned from Cayucos, pissed and hurt. Katrina had been adequately outraged on her behalf. She'd initially referred to Samson as #BeachDick, but #BeachBastard had alliteration going for it.

"What on earth was hashtag BeachBastard doing *there*?"

"From what I gathered, Annabelle's a family friend."

Katrina bared her teeth. "He went from ghosting you to talking about how he's looking for love on Matchmaker? What garbage."

Rhi slammed her fist down on the table. "That's what I said! Total hot garbage."

"I should have asked you for his name when you came back from that trip, but I only wanted to call him a dick."

"Because he was a dick." Rhiannon rested her elbows on the table. "You know of him? Would you have recognized his name?" Katrina followed sports a little better than Rhiannon did.

"Yeah. I mean, he hasn't played in years, but he's more famous for his family than his career anyway. His dad and uncle were both Hall of Famers." She screwed her face up. "There was some drama when Samson retired, but I don't remember what, exactly."

"I don't care about his past." When it came to Samson, she knew quite enough, thank you.

"I can't imagine how awkward that interview must have been for you, and now I'm more impressed at how well you kept your shit together." Katrina gasped. "Ah God, all the double meanings now. Was he talking about you? How he didn't *intend to*—" Katrina paused and Rhiannon waited patiently for her to voice her outrage over how stupid it was to claim one wasn't intending to throw someone aside.

I didn't intend to ghost you was fast becoming the mealy-mouthed *I didn't intend to hurt you* of the dating world, and Rhiannon was sick of it.

"Wait a minute."

"What?"

"He said he had a personal emergency. That was why he ghosted you."

Rhiannon snorted. "A hypothetical."

A frown creased Katrina's otherwise smooth brow. She

often got skin care tips and products from Lakshmi. "Or real."

"If that's his excuse, it could mean anything. Or, yanno, he's lying."

"Oh yikes."

"What? Do you know something?"

"He may not have been lying. The timing would fit with . . ." Katrina hopped up from the table and retrieved her phone from the counter. She typed something in, scrolled for a minute or two, and then grimaced before sitting down again and placing the phone faceup on the table.

"What's this?" Rhiannon peered at the ESPN article.

"I remember hearing about Big Joe Lima's death a few months ago. That's his uncle, Rhi."

Rhiannon skimmed the article, each word increasing her sense of foreboding. *Long battle . . . ALS and Parkinson's . . . chronic illness . . . brain donated to the Concussion Research Alliance . . . survived by his nephew . . .*

The short bio ended with the date of death. Rhiannon compared it to her mental calendar. "His uncle died a few days after we were supposed to meet."

"That would probably be what he was talking about."

A sick feeling descended on Rhiannon, and she put her phone down. Underneath that sickness, there was another feeling, one she couldn't quite identify. "Probably."

Katrina's smile was pained. "Rhi."

"Don't say it." She could see it, the slight hopeful look in her friend's eyes, and she didn't want that hope to infect her.

"What do you think I'm going to say?"

Unlike Rhiannon, Katrina was a soft romantic, though she hadn't dated anyone in years. She couldn't go out to too many public places where she didn't fear a panic attack. "That he had a valid reason for not showing up that night."

"I don't know if I'd call it a valid reason, but it seems like extenuating circumstances."

Rhiannon pulled her sleeves down so she could stick her thumbs through the thumbholes. These were her favorite kinds of sweatshirts, the ones with the long sleeves so she could cover her palms. They hugged her best.

Katrina cocked her head. "Could he have reasonably gotten ahold of you to explain he'd had an emergency sometime between standing you up and the conference?"

She'd unmatched him on the app, she never gave anyone her real number. Plus, the fake name and all. "No," she said grudgingly, that sick feeling growing.

"Did he try to talk to you at the conference? I mean, when you weren't being recorded."

He'd *chased* her in that ballroom. "Kinda."

Katrina tapped her fingers on the counter. The silence stretched between them and Rhiannon finally made a frustrated noise. "Say what you want to say."

"I was only thinking . . . ninety-nine percent of the time, immediate block for ghosting, right? This might be the .01 percent time when a ghoster wasn't being a total cowardly dog."

Rhiannon folded her arms, then unfolded them. She thought of how tender Samson's hands had been on her skin. When he'd pushed inside her, he'd leaned down and whispered in her ear. *It's been so long since I've done this. Tell me if it's good for you.* "So? So what?"

"So he hurt you when he ghosted you. Doesn't it bring you some closure to know it wasn't about you at all?"

"He didn't hurt me," Rhiannon snapped, even though she knew the snap was unfair.

Katrina's eyes softened. "Of course."

"I am not easy to hurt. I am a stone cold bitch when it comes to men. No rose-colored glasses here."

Katrina toyed with her phone. "Rhiannon . . . you're not that much of a cynic. I think you're actually kind of a romantic."

Rhiannon gasped, like her best friend had stabbed her. "You shut your beautiful perfect mouth."

Katrina did not shut her delightful mouth. Oh no, she kept going. "You watch holiday movies every year. You try to hide it, but I see you crying."

"Find me the empty soul who doesn't get emotional over *While You Were Sleeping*."

Katrina rolled her eyes. "You send gifts to everyone who sends their success story in to Crush. Wedding and engagement and civil union and housewarming and baby gifts."

"I send *branded* gifts. I want that kid to be sucking on their Crush rattle from birth, damn it, so it knows from whence it came. That's business. It's almost automated."

Anyone else might be intimidated by her rising voice, but Katrina wasn't anyone else. She cleared her throat. "Is it business to send a personalized note of congratulations with the gift?"

"You're not allowed to talk to Lakshmi anymore."

"You were more upset than I've seen you over a guy when you came back from Cayucos. You may have had one night with him, but you liked him, and he betrayed you, extenuating circumstances or not. It's normal to have been hurt. It's normal to want to know what happened, and to be relieved when you find out it wasn't about you."

The sympathy in Katrina's demeanor should have warmed Rhiannon, but it made her want to claw her skin off. There was nobody in the world who knew as much about her life as Katrina did, and most days, that was fine. She needed one confidante who could be there for her 100 percent.

But being vulnerable wasn't easy for her. Her sense of vulnerability was compounded by the layer of shame she felt over bolting from the party. And again from the interview.

Weakness. Weakness on top of weakness. "I was fine. I'm fine now." Rhiannon picked up their plates and utensils and carried them to the sink. She rinsed them off and put them in the dishwasher.

"I know your rules when it comes to guys, and I know why you have those rules in place. Sometimes rules don't apply to every situation."

After a couple of moments of silence, Katrina blew out a breath. "Okay. I'll be in my office if you want to talk."

Rhiannon finished putting away the dishes and carefully washed her hands. A romantic? Hurt? Her? No.

So why did you run away from him?

Because she'd wanted to. She didn't have to explain herself to anyone! No one would blame her for running away from a zombie, five-time orgasm deliverer or not.

Rhiannon had about a million other things to do, but she found herself wandering down the hallway to Katrina's office. She hovered in the doorway. The light bounced off Katrina's shiny light brown hair when she lifted her head from the gold wire spread out over her desk. "Fine. I was hurt."

Katrina sat back in her chair. Her workroom was in another corner of the house, but she tinkered with metal and stones wherever inspiration struck her. "I know."

"You would have talked to him? Given him a chance to explain?" Rhiannon asked. Her throat felt rough, the words pulled out of her.

"Probably." Katrina tipped her head at the armchair opposite her.

Rhiannon came in and perched on the edge of it. "Why? You know the stats, as well as I do."

Katrina squinted at her. "Imagine I went out with a date one night. It was really good. We made plans for a second date. And then, before I could go on that date, I had a panic attack, one of my incapacitating ones, and I stood him up. For whatever reason, I couldn't immediately contact him, but I managed to track him down after a few months. Should he hear me out? Should he give me the benefit of the doubt?"

Rhiannon ran her tongue over her teeth. Katrina knew very well what Rhiannon would say to that, but then again, she was always on Katrina's side. "Okay. I see where you're going with this."

"Sometimes, good people make mistakes. It costs you nothing to hear someone out."

"No. It does cost you something." Because if you believed that person when you heard them out, and then they betrayed you, you ended up doubly hurt. Easier to give people one shot.

Katrina rose from her chair, walked around the desk, and sat in the seat next to Rhiannon's. "I misspoke. You're right, no one is entitled to your time and energy and forgiveness." She grasped Rhiannon's hands and pressed them tight, well aware of how much Rhiannon liked pressure against her skin. "You'd never believe someone blindly, and I'm not telling you to. But you can believe with evidence."

Rhiannon lifted one shoulder. "Okay. Fine. I do feel relieved I didn't totally misjudge him. And I feel . . . kinda bad for him. So what? What does any of this mean or change? Do I go see him now and let him explain himself?" As soon as she uttered the words, a terrifying sense of rightness settled over her.

"Would that make you feel better? If he wants to apologize, if there's an excuse he can give you that would lessen your hurt, you can let him. You don't need to take him back or date him—"

"I don't date anyway," Rhiannon reminded Katrina hastily.

"Right." But there was still a hopeful light in her friend's eyes that made Rhiannon nervous. "I'm just saying, do whatever will make you feel better. And if that's never talking to this dude again, fine, I will not say another word. I only want you to be happy and healthy."

Rhiannon swallowed. She momentarily shoved aside her defenses and let her vulnerability peek through. "I think I want to see him again, but not for an apology, necessarily."

"Then why?"

She whispered the words, like she was confessing a deep dark secret. "I ran away from him."

"What?"

Rhiannon exhaled. "I ran away from him. I freaked out when I saw him at the conference and I ran away. Twice."

"That's okay."

"No, it's not. That's his final sight of me, me running away. So maybe . . ." She sighed, working through it in her head. "I should see him. I can redeem myself."

"There's nothing to redeem."

Rhiannon shrugged. "My brain doesn't understand that. Okay. Fine. Closure, I guess?"

"I am a big fan of closure."

Decision made, Rhiannon raised her voice. "Sienna, call Lakshmi."

A pleasant woman's mildly robotic voice spilled from the speakers in the room. "Calling Lakshmi."

Lakshmi answered immediately. "Hey, boss."

"Hi. Katrina's here." Not everyone at Crush knew Katrina. Katrina had created a Fortress of Solitude up here, and she had her reasons for wanting to keep her identity as quiet as possible.

Katrina spoke. "Hello, Lakshmi."

"Hello, bosses."

"Can you get me info on Samson Lima?"

"Sure. He gave me his card after your interview. He wrote his personal cell on it."

Genuinely startled, Rhiannon exchanged a glance with Katrina. "You didn't tell me that." She and Lakshmi had been almost joined at the hip yesterday.

Lakshmi's voice turned dry. "You've told me, and I quote, *If a guy gives you his card to give to me, shred it.*"

Oh right. She had told Lakshmi that, but only because it was weird when people tried to pick her up or get at her through her assistant.

"I actually don't shred them, by the way. Or at least, I take a photo of them before I toss them. Want his cell?"

Rhiannon wrinkled her nose. Did she? Not really. She didn't like talking to people on the phone for non-awkward conversations. Awkward ones really should be in person. "Can you find out his social calendar? If he's going to any parties, events, engagements in L.A. anytime soon?"

"No problem. He's their face, his schedule will be easy enough to get. What are you gonna do, ask him to talk to Annabelle for you?"

Rhiannon opened her mouth, then closed it again.

Wait a minute.

Wait. A. Damn. Minute.

Had her brain turned to jelly? Why hadn't she thought of

that? All this agonizing over whether she should ever see Samson again, and she'd forgotten the number one practical reason to get back in front of him.

The night she'd slept with Samson, he'd said he'd grown up in Cayucos and moved back as an adult. Annabelle had a fucking beach house there. She'd introduced his parents! They were tighter than tight.

Lakshmi continued speaking when Rhiannon was silent. "Is tomorrow soon enough? I have to get the rest of our stuff squared away here in Austin."

"Take a few days," Katrina interjected and gave Rhiannon a warning look that shut her mouth. "Rhiannon needs to relax from her trip."

Rhiannon didn't know what relaxation was, but she couldn't admit that. It would prove Katrina and her mom right. "Yeah, what she said," she confirmed grudgingly.

"On it. Peace." Lakshmi hung up.

Katrina crossed her arms over her chest. "I don't like that look on your face one bit."

Rhiannon opened her eyes very wide, giving her best impression of what innocence might look like. "What? You wanted me to talk to him."

"Not to use him, Rhi," Katrina snapped. "Why are you so obsessed with buying Matchmaker anyway? I mean, I know buying your competitor and shutting them down is a time-honored technique to grab market share, but is it really necessary?"

"It's necessary."

"Explain."

Filled with restless energy, Rhiannon got up to pace the room. "What happens whenever there's progress? Backlash. It is progress that you can find someone to have a drink with from your phone. That's true. And it's also true that people long for what they thought they had before. I heard it at that conference, the rumblings getting louder. If we buy Matchmaker, we don't just buy their data and their infrastructure. We buy their name. Their respect. We modernize it a little, make it more mobile friendly, and then keep it as another option for our users. Crush for now. Matchmaker for forever."

"Damn." Katrina narrowed her eyes. "That's a slogan."

"It is." Rhiannon grinned, a little reckless. But most importantly, she felt strong again. Yes, finally. She had a good reason, a strong reason to see Samson again, one that had nothing to do with her feelings or their history.

Phew. A girl could only deal with her emotions so much.

"Matchmaker is our insurance against a backlash. We can stay on top, even if everyone decides to delete Crush tomorrow and try a method for love that doesn't include their phones. Sure, maybe they'll go to the bar or the grocery store. But more likely, they'll go back to their computers."

Katrina steepled her hands under her chin. "Does this have something to do with Peter?"

Ouch. Couldn't hide anything from her best friend. "This has to do with success." If that success was also about revenge, well. Rhiannon couldn't help that. "I'll talk to

Samson. Listen to him, talk to him, get my closure." Rhiannon shrugged. "And then, I'll ask him for a favor." When he was feeling bad.

Katrina looked straight-up worried now. "This feels manipulative. It's not the reason I thought you should see him."

"I'll only ask. Nothing more. It'll be a nice, direct, closure-heavy conversation. And then I'm done with him." What she didn't say, what she was thinking, was that yeah, Samson fucking owed her. If he was as nice as she'd originally thought he was, then he'd feel the same way.

And if it was manipulative to introduce a request when a person felt like they owed a person, well then, yes, she was being manipulative. Sue her.

"Well, you don't have to be done—"

There was that hope again, that malicious hope. Actively seeking out someone who had ghosted her was already borderline foolish, only acceptable because she had hard evidence to back up the excuse he'd inevitably give her. Getting back into bed with a zombie? That was inexcusable, given all that she knew about the dating world. Rhiannon slashed her hand across her throat. "Then I'm done."

Chapter Seven

"Samson?"

Samson shook his head and refocused on the young blonde sitting at his dining table. Tina was a sweet girl and had been his aunt Belle's admin since she'd graduated from college a few years ago. Her bubbly and cheerful personality was the last thing he needed right now. "Sorry. What's that?"

"No need to apologize!" She gestured at the open laptop screen in front of her. "I know you have company coming over soon, but I thought we could go through your next batch of matches while we have a minute."

He put down the knife he was using to slice salami and rinsed his hands. "Ah, sure. Are you certain you don't want a snack, though?"

Tina blew her bangs out of her face. Wearing her casual uniform of jeans and a loose T-shirt, with her legs curled under her on the padded dining table chair, her shoes kicked off under the table, she looked about eighteen. "You're so cute. No, thanks, I'm fine."

He wasn't cute. Samson just wanted to delay this as

much as possible. Also, he was his mother's son. He may be out of practice having people in his house, but he didn't know how to have someone over and not feed them.

Even if it wasn't really his home. The downtown L.A. apartment was filled with afternoon sunlight from the indulgently large windows that looked out over the city. He'd told Annabelle he could handle his own accommodations when he needed to be in L.A., but she'd insisted he stay in this corporate apartment owned by Matchmaker. It had a perfect view of the skyline and tasteful, impersonal furnishings, all leather and metal accents and modern shapes.

He sat down at the glass table, next to Tina. "Okay, let's get this over with."

Tina gave him a sympathetic look. "It's not so bad, is it?"

He'd been putting this off, but they had a small crew on standby to film the first date aka commercial/webisode. He was trying not to think about it too hard. "It is what it is." Samson shifted and did his best to shrink into his chair. Limas were born big, and he had always been supremely conscious of his size, especially when he was seated next to a much smaller woman. Tina didn't seem intimidated by him, but he knew sometimes women hid their fear well.

He'd been comfortable around Rhiannon. She wasn't that big, but her no-nonsense personality made her seem as large as him. At one point during that perfect, sweaty, lust-hazed night, she'd flipped him over onto his back with her strong legs and straddled him, using her palms against his to hold him down.

You have to protect your heart. No one will do it for you.

"I told you, I could pick someone for you."

He refocused, trying to tamp down his guilt spiral. In the week since the interview, Samson had managed to find breaks from thinking about Rhiannon, but she crept back in at the oddest of times.

You did all you could do. By the time he'd finished talking to Helena's dad and taking selfies with the crew and made his way offstage, Rhiannon had been gone. Someone had pointed out her assistant, and so he'd taken a chance and slipped the woman his card. Going by the arch look the intimidating woman had given him, Samson didn't hold out much hope on that front.

Still, he'd checked his phone eight hundred times in the past few days. At some point he'd have to accept Rhiannon wasn't going to get in touch with him. He'd left the conference the day after the interview, but even if he had stayed, he wouldn't have tried to find her. She'd made it clear she was furious with him. A next step, if there ever was one, would have to come from her. He wasn't about to stalk the woman.

In the meantime . . . "No, I'll vet my own dates." He ought to do something to justify the salary Matchmaker was paying him.

Reluctantly, Samson perused the faces of all the women smiling back at him from Tina's laptop. There were selfies and group shots and full-length photos. The group was diverse in body type and ethnicity. And not one of them looked like the woman who had occupied his mind for the last week.

He shifted, hating that he couldn't stop thinking about

her. Hating that he had a job to do, and he couldn't shelve her enough to do it. Hating that the job he was doing felt far too much like window-shopping for a woman. "This is a lot."

He meant everything, in general, but Tina misunderstood him. "No, this is about right. You usually get about ten matches at a time," Tina explained.

"Can I see their profiles?"

"Which ones?" Tina hovered the mouse over the first girl.

"Uh. All of them? Since I don't know anything about them?"

Tina blinked at him. "You don't want to knock any of them out on appearance alone?"

He looked at the women again and rubbed the back of his neck. He'd barely known what Rhiannon looked like before he'd met her on the basis of a sentence and a few messages, and they'd had an immediate connection. What if he got rid of someone based on her dimples or lack thereof and missed out on a good thing?

Uh, a good thing for the camera, that is. Not for him, personally. "They're all pretty in their own ways. I'd rather see what they have to say."

Tina beamed at him, though he wasn't sure what he'd said or done to get that response. They started going through the matches. A kindergarten teacher, a lawyer, a doctor, a receptionist. All perfectly normal women who didn't deserve to be used by him for a gimmicky photo op.

When Annabelle had come to him with this idea, he'd

proposed doing the whole thing with hired actresses, but she'd nixed that. He'd still been deep in his grief over Uncle Joe and hadn't protested too hard. He'd been happy to have some project forced upon him so the endless future hadn't seemed so endless.

He should have protested harder. Meeting real women hadn't felt so distasteful when it had been conceptual, but now that he was faced with a buffet of individuals, he couldn't get the sour taste out of his mouth.

"Can you filter based on profession?" he asked abruptly, when they were about halfway through.

"Sure," Tina said. "What are you looking for? Fellow athletes?"

"I haven't been an athlete in a long time." His main method of getting out of the house for the past five years in Cayucos had been twice daily runs on the beach, but that wasn't anywhere near his fitness regimen when he'd been a professional football player. "Filter it down to entertainment. Actresses, models, singers." This was L.A., and it wouldn't be hard to find at least one woman who was in the business. Being an actress didn't mean that his potential date's heart wouldn't be soft, but at the very least, she might get something out of a contrived hour that was more entertainment than a meeting of hearts. "Someone who will be good on camera and fine with this being a business thing."

Tina's gaze turned knowing. "Gotcha." She typed something, and all but two of the matches vanished. She leaned forward. "We got an actress and a model. Let me contact them and see if either of them are interested in our project, vet them a little to see which of them would be the most natural on film."

"Fantastic." He was so glad he wasn't actually emailing back and forth with them like he might if he really was looking for love on Matchmaker.

Tina gathered up the laptop and Samson shoved back his seat. "Have you heard from Annabelle?" His aunt had been pretty silent for the past week, though she'd sent him a quick text reply in response to his check-in.

"Yeah, a little, for some necessary business stuff. I keep her updated daily via email. She doesn't always respond. That's normal when she goes on the run like this. She gets overwhelmed, disappears for a while, but she always comes back." Tina wrinkled her nose. "I should have gone with you two to the conference. I told her the crowds might overwhelm her, but she was so dead set on trying to be Jennifer, she didn't listen."

Samson grimaced. He hadn't been very close to Jennifer, but the older sister had been protective of Annabelle and had kept her little sister out of the spotlight. "Yeah. Luckily, everything worked out for the best."

"Good thing you were there. You handled that interview with Crush like a champ. I hear Helena might even have you on her talk show? Good deal."

Oh, that was right. On her talk show with Rhiannon.

Hope at the thought of seeing Rhiannon again filled him. Pathetic.

The timer went off on the oven and he glanced at it. Tina waved him away. "You take care of that, I'll see myself out."

He was pulling mini pizzas out of the oven when he heard the door open and a deep male voice say, "Damn, I know we haven't seen Samson in a long time, but when did he turn into a small blond woman?"

Tina's reply was muffled, but the tartness of her response was clear from her tone. Samson grinned and dropped the pan on the counter and came out to the foyer.

Harris and Dean Miller both smiled when they saw Samson. For a second, none of them spoke, but then Dean erupted into a whoop and they closed in on him, engulfing him in a big hug.

His two closest friends were both settled in L.A. Getting together over the past few years had been a challenge, what with their lives taking them on different paths.

Harris slapped his back and stepped back. "Look at you. How long has it been, a couple years?"

"At least," Dean said. The two of them were cousins and were both tall, African American, and handsome, with some similarities in their eyes and the shapes of their face. Dean was way bigger, but he'd been a linebacker, like Samson. Harris was leaner, and still a quarterback. The three of them had played college ball together, but Samson and Dean had also been on the Brewers.

"What are you talking about? It's only been a month since I last saw Miley," Samson protested. He smiled at the gurgling baby in the carrier Dean held.

Dean picked up the bulging baby bag he'd dropped to

greet Samson. "That was an obligatory drive-by greeting of your goddaughter. Staying with us for a single night doesn't count."

Harris glanced curiously inside the apartment. "Couldn't believe that you'd come to the big city."

"I like it here. It's nice." He might have grown up in a sleepy beach town, technically, but they'd traveled a lot when his father had played ball, and then Samson's own professional career had taken him to Chicago and Portland. The big city life wasn't totally foreign to him.

He led the two men into the apartment. Dean placed the carrier on the dining table and unsnapped his daughter. "Want to hold her?" he asked.

Samson may have only seen the child once, but he knew the answer to that question had to be an eager yes or Dean would be mortally offended. "Can't wait."

Without ceremony, Dean deposited the baby into Samson's arms.

Samson jiggled the child, who felt too squishy and blob-like for his comfort. He had nothing against kids, but babies weren't his wheelhouse. "I'm holding her right, right?"

Harris had made a beeline for the food Samson had spread out on the island and already had crackers and meat headed toward his mouth. "Oh, yeah, hold the princess right or her daddy will kick your ass."

Dean shot his cousin a quelling look. "That's because you hold her like you're about to throw her. She's not a ball. Samson knows what's up." He gently adjusted Samson's hand on her butt. "Or at least, now he does. There."

Samson glanced down at the baby and couldn't help but smile. Her thick black hair stuck straight up, like she'd been shocked. Dean and his neuroscientist wife had adopted Miley from Korea, and the retired player's life had quickly devolved to answering only to the baby. She blew a bubble with her tiny rosebud mouth and returned Samson's stare with fascination. "How old is she now?"

"Almost eight months."

"Jesus." Samson shook his head. "Time flies."

"The days are long but the years are short." Dean hesitated, then moved Samson's other hand a tiny degree. Samson met Harris's gaze above Dean's head, and the other man rolled his eyes.

"How are you liking being a stay-at-home dad, Dean?" Samson asked.

"It's great." Dean beamed. "Miley's an angel. So smart too. She can roll over now and should be crawling in about a minute."

Samson made an appropriately impressed noise.

"Here, eat."

Dean accepted the plate full of food that Harris nudged him with. He folded a quesadilla into a square, ate it in two bites, and then flushed when the two of them stared at him. "Sorry. Since Miley arrived, I've been hoovering my food whenever I get a second."

"That sounds hectic." Samson allowed Dean to adjust his grip. Again. Miley kicked her legs against his stomach.

Harris swallowed his bite of food. "If you trusted anyone but you or Josie to take care of your baby, you could have a free hand. Damn, man, get a nanny. You guys got the cash."

"I'm not outsourcing my child," Dean said with some affront. He accepted the beer from Harris and took a sip in a more moderated manner than he had eaten. "Besides, I need this. You have no idea how lost I felt after I retired a couple years ago. Miley's given me a purpose again."

Samson knew exactly what Dean was referring to. It was weird to go from playing professional football, that intense life in a tightly knit group, to nothing, your days no longer regimented and controlled by an outside force. About a year after he'd retired, though, Uncle Joe had started showing signs of illness. After that, Samson had had his hands and his head full with his uncle's care. He hadn't had time to dwell on anything else.

"You'll understand when you go through it next year," Dean added.

Samson raised his eyebrows in surprise. Football had always been Harris's life. "You're retiring?"

"I'm almost thirty-eight." Harris braced his elbows on the counter and leaned back. "My knees aren't what they used to be. I'd rather go out on top than wait any longer."

"Dean's not wrong about how you'll feel after." Samson turned his head so Miley's little exploring fingers didn't go right into his mouth. His arm was falling asleep, but he was conscious of Dean's eagle eye on him. "Try to line up some work or projects or something."

"I've been talking to a couple of people. Charities, mostly. And there'll be endorsements."

"Though we could all be so lucky to get this spokesman gig of Samson's," Dean interjected. "Get paid to date hot girls and live in a swanky apartment."

"Seriously." Harris took a sip of his beer. "You go on any dates yet?"

Rhiannon popped into his head. Harris had been the one to gently badger him into downloading Crush all those months ago, but he'd never told his friends about That Night. It had felt too private, and he'd been ashamed of how it had ended.

More so now that he knew the word for what he'd done. *Ghosting.* Ugh.

But Harris wasn't asking about Rhiannon, he was asking about his time at Matchmaker. "Not yet. Soon."

"You nervous?"

"No. Why would I be nervous? I've been on dates." He winced when Miley's nails scratched his nose. Baby nails were surprisingly sharp.

Dean and Harris exchanged a glance. "Uh, do you want to come out with me some night to dip your foot in the shallow end first? The world has changed since the last time you were out there," Harris said.

"When it comes to how you find a date, maybe. Not the mechanics of actually talking to women, that hasn't changed. And I was always pretty good at that." He may never have had a long-term relationship or a grand love affair, but there were good, logical reasons for that. His focus had always been on something else: school, football, his dad, his uncle. He'd dated and had lovers, though he'd never reached Harris's borderline player status.

He'd be fine. Sit down with a woman for an hour or so, engage in some light banter that would play well for the camera? That, he could handle.

"Yeah, you weren't called the Lima Charm for—" Harris cut himself off. "Sorry, Samson."

Samson dipped his head in gratitude. He was resigned to hearing that nickname from strangers, but his friends knew exactly why it made him tense up. A little teasing and ribbing was normal, but he loved Dean and Harris because they weren't cruel in the name of joking around. "It's fine." He gently removed Miley's grasping hand from his hair, and the baby's face screwed up tight. Samson was shocked at the piercing wail that came out of her tiny mouth. "What did I do? Is she—"

"Hang on." Dean unzipped his jacket, revealing a baby carrier strapped to his front. "I got her. She's due for a nap. Miley's always on schedule." He took the baby from Samson and deposited her in the carrier, deftly maneuvering her kicking legs. His giant hand cradled her head and he moved away. Samson watched with bemusement while his buddy started doing walking lunges down the length of his big apartment.

"What are you doing?"

"It calms her down and puts her to sleep," Dean explained over his shoulder. Lunge. Step. Lunge. "We can go get dinner once she's out."

"Plus, the exercise maintains his figure. Gotta keep it tight for his hot wife," Harris explained mischievously.

Without breaking pace, Dean flipped his cousin off.

They watched him for a second, then Samson grabbed

a cracker and tossed it into his mouth. "He must be driving Josie insane." He dropped his voice so Dean wouldn't hear him.

"I think she's trying to convince him to adopt another kid so his attention will at least be split. There isn't a baby book, an opinion piece, or a parent forum that man hasn't read at this point." Harris shook his head. "I never thought I'd see the day Dean would be an expert on diapers and transracial adoption."

Samson huffed a laugh.

Harris sobered. "Hey. How are you holding up? I know it's been tough since Big Joe passed."

"I'm . . . I'm doing good. I think I was really in a fog for a while, but I feel better now." The gig had helped. It had given him a schedule. A purpose, as Dean might say.

"Yeah, you seemed pretty out of it at the funeral."

Samson barely remembered Joe's service. Harris and Dean had been the only contemporaries of his to attend. The rest of the mourners had been the few of Joe's friends that the man had stayed in touch with. And Annabelle, of course, her eyes still sunken from weathering Joe's illness and mourning her sister barely nine months prior. "Listen, I'm sorry if I've been distant since then. His death really hit me harder than I'd thought it would."

Samson had felt occasionally lonely when Joe had been sick, but with his uncle gone, he'd been totally alone. The last Lima, a short-lived dynasty over. Some charm.

"Nah, man. You did kinda disappear, but Dean and I got it. We knew you didn't mean anything by it."

His nose twitched. Here was the easy forgiveness he'd hoped Rhiannon would give him, but Dean and Harris knew him. They could afford to give him the benefit of the doubt in a way that Rhiannon could not. "Thanks."

The baby's crying rose in volume and intensity and Dean's lunges became longer, taking him into the bedroom. Harris shifted. "Did Joe . . . I mean. I know he talked about donating his, um . . ."

"His brain. Yeah. He donated it to the Concussion Research Alliance." Samson took a sip of water to wipe the taste of grief out of his mouth. Joe had been adamant about that donation. He'd wanted his brain to help with the research that was going on with chronic traumatic encephalopathy in football players. "Getting the results back takes time. Might be months longer." They could take as long as they wanted, as far as Samson was concerned.

Samson had had to fight his mother to get his dad's brain donated to science. Back then, CTE had only been diagnosed in a couple of deceased players. But Samson had had a hunch that his dad had the disease. He'd *wanted* his father to have the disease. He'd needed something. A diagnosis, an explanation for why the man had gone from a kind and loving father to a mood-spiraling, angry, unstable man.

The tests had taken a long time back then, when funding for CTE research had been nonexistent. Lulu had died before the diagnosis could come back. Aleki had had CTE, the buildup of tau proteins in his brain excessive and obvious even to a layman like Samson. Most likely linked to all the hard hits he'd taken over the years playing the game, the researchers had explained to Samson.

The National Football League had disagreed. Loudly.

Years after his death, in the big class-action lawsuit against the league brought by retired players, Aleki's brain and his seventeen years of pro football playing had been cited by more than one attorney as evidence of the link between football and CTE.

"Are you gonna try to get a piece of the settlement?"

Samson shook his head. "Joe wouldn't let me contribute any money toward his health care, so I'm okay, financially. I might have tried to navigate that mess for him, but he was lucky enough to have Annabelle. When his savings ran out, she took care of him." Everyone thought all football players were rich, but money went fast when illness kicked in.

Harris drained his beer. "Okay, good. 'Cause I was gonna say, you know that settlement fund is a clusterfuck, so you'd have to lawyer up hard."

"You know how it goes. Deny—"

"Until they die." Harris finished the dark rhyme one high profile former player had applied to the claims process. The NFL might have settled the class-action for a billion dollars to compensate retirees exhibiting symptoms of CTE, as well as late players' families who came with posthumous diagnosis in hand, but they were notoriously heavy-handed when it came to denials. "Hey, speaking of . . . You know, Trevor was asking me about you."

Samson's sneer was immediate. "I have nothing to say to Trevor."

"That's what I figured." Harris patted Samson's back gently. "It's okay, man."

Dean walked out of the bedroom, his baby's face smooshed against his chest. "Thank God, she's asleep," he said, sotto voce. "You want to order dinner now? Or we can go out. Heard there's a cool new vegan place on Melrose."

"You can't do those fucking lunges around a trendy restaurant if she starts hollering," Harris said bluntly.

Dean covered his sleeping daughter's ears with one hand. "What did I fucking tell you about swearing around her?"

Samson chuckled softly and slapped Harris's back. Christ, he'd missed this. His brothers. "Okay, come on. Dean, there's a family-friendly vegan place not too far from here. Let's go there."

Dean sniffed, his feathers still ruffled. "No swearing around the baby."

Harris sighed when Samson glanced at him. "Fine! Fine. No swearing around the nonverbal, sleeping baby. For fudge's sake."

Chapter Eight

Rhiannon resisted the urge to check her face in any reflection before she walked inside the huge historic hotel. There was no need. She hadn't bothered with makeup or her hair or changing out of her usual casual day hoodie.

She'd dressed up for this man once before, had slicked on some tinted Chapstick even, and he'd left her high and dry. Extenuating circumstances or not, she wasn't about to repeat the mistakes of her past.

Eye on the prize.

She walked inside the trendy place and glanced around with some interest. Matchmaker had chosen a good location to film their first spot in their Win a Date with Samson Lima contest or promotion or whatever it was. The ceilings were tall, the architecture was gorgeous, and Samson and his date would pop in a luxurious setting surrounded by expensive views.

How Lakshmi had gotten information on this, Rhiannon wasn't sure. She'd intended to casually stroll into a bar or a club that Samson was at some night, but Lakshmi had said the man didn't seem to be much of a party animal. So here she was. Crashing his date.

If this was solely about shedding her anger and finding inner peace or closure or whatever Katrina wanted to call it, she might have already left. But this was also about business, so she was all-in.

She bypassed the reservation desk and made her way through the chandelier-lit lobby to the hallway that connected to a restaurant. There was a discreet sign in the window that said the restaurant was closed, but Rhiannon ignored that and tested the handle. The door easily opened.

The film crew was small, only about five or six people, but even if the room hadn't been blocked off, she would have spotted Samson immediately. He towered over the other occupants, his broad shoulders big enough to block out the sun. He wore another suit, but no tie this time.

A shame. The sexy factor of a perfectly tied knot was undeniable, even to a casual dresser such as herself.

A small blond woman bopped her way, perky ponytail bouncing, a polite smile on her face. "I'm sorry, the restaurant is closed—"

"I'm not here for the restaurant," Rhiannon said gently. "I'm here for your star."

The woman raised an eyebrow. "I beg your pardon?" She blinked at Rhiannon, and recognition dawned in her eyes. "Hey, aren't you—?"

"Tina, it's fine." Samson appeared behind the sentry and placed his hand on her shoulder. "I asked her to come." His dark eyes were warm when they rested on Rhiannon's face, and she could almost believe he had asked her to crash his date. Or whatever it was called when a film crew was present.

Rhiannon tilted her head. "I was hoping I could have a minute to talk privately."

"Absolutely. Tina, how much time do we have?"

"Um." Tina looked back and forth between the two of them. "Your date is going to be here in a half hour. But you said you wanted more prep . . ."

"I'll wing it." Samson nodded at Rhiannon. "There's some space to talk outside. Let's go there."

She exhaled long and low as they walked away from Tina and the rest of the curious group. She'd expected Samson to be a number of things: shocked, panicked, annoyed. At the very least, she'd thought she might need to explain why she was here. She had a fast-talking spiel lined up and ready to go.

This had been relatively easy.

They exited to the patio, which looked out over a paradise of rolling hills and sprouting spring flowers. The view was designed to nourish and calm, but it had the opposite effect on her, ramping up the low-grade anxiety that had been humming under the surface since Lakshmi had told her where she could find the man.

Weird. She'd run from him and fought with him, but she supposed this was the first time since they'd been in her bed that they were alone with each other. She cast about for something to say. "Nice choice, filming here. Pasadena's picturesque."

Samson glanced at the surroundings and smiled. "Yes. Quieter than downtown for sure."

"Is that where you live?"

"Yeah. Not permanently, Matchmaker put me up. What about you? I know Crush is in L.A., but not sure where."

"Not far from there. Silver Lake." She hadn't wanted to be a Silicon Beach company, and the area had been more affordable when they'd established Crush.

"You live in that area too?"

"Part-time." If not for Katrina, she'd live and work in L.A. full-time, but she cared about her best friend more than the city. Santa Barbara had its own charms, and she could commute down easily after each weekend. "Why?"

"No reason. Making small talk."

She rolled her neck, trying to ease the tension there. "I'm not really here to make small talk."

His face grew grave. "I understand."

She gestured to a low stone bench, judging them far enough away from the restaurant and hotel that they wouldn't be disturbed.

He sat at one end of the bench. She took the other end, though it was a tight squeeze. Then again, he'd make anything a tight squeeze.

His body angled toward her. "How'd you know where to find me?"

"My assistant has some creepy powers."

Samson's smile was small. "Apparently."

She bit her lip, aware the clock was ticking. His hair was rumpled. She had a brief, untimely vision of it when it had been long, long enough to slip over his shoulders and brush her nipples and she looked away, focusing on a spot right over his shoulder.

Get this over with.

"Rhiannon—"

"I'm here for closure."

"Closure."

"Yeah. My best friend says I need it."

"Do you think you do?"

"I don't know."

"You're mad at me. I treated you really badly, and I am so sorry I hurt you."

She drew herself up, feathers ruffling. Bad enough, showing Katrina her vulnerabilities.

Don't get defensive. Don't run away, or you'll feel worse, as you discovered. This is what you're here for. The voice in her head sounded oddly like Katrina's, and it did calm her, but she still had to push back. "We knew it was going to be a temporary affair. It would have ended that second night anyway."

"Not like it did." Samson looked down at his hands. "The thing I said onstage, about the family emergency? That wasn't a hypothetical."

She wanted to cross her arms over her chest, but she knew what that would convey. She didn't interrupt him. Katrina may have connected the dots via Google, but that was a search engine, and she didn't trust that hope wasn't coloring their interpretation of what had happened.

There wasn't a more optimistic creature in the world

than a person who wanted to believe someone hadn't treated them like shit. Let him corroborate what they'd cobbled together.

"My uncle had degenerative neurological diseases—Alzheimer's, ALS. I was his caretaker. He was always on me to get out, take a night off, have some fun, and that's not always easy to do in a small town. I'd grown up around most of the locals, and the tourists weren't usually single people my age. I'd never been on an app before, but it seemed like the easiest way to see who was out there. Spending those hours with you was the first time I'd done something purely for myself in I don't know how long." His gaze on her was steady and sincere. "I swear, I did mean to see you again. But when I got home, Uncle Joe was having trouble breathing. I knew that it was inevitable, but his decline was rapid, and his death a few days later hit me hard."

Samson's recitation was matter-of-fact, but the underlying anguish and quiet sadness couldn't be faked. She didn't want to think anyone was cruel enough to try to fake it.

There are men who would fake it, her subconscious whispered. *Don't trust this.*

There was corroboration, though.

He could have let you know that day so you wouldn't have sat there waiting for him like an idiot.

Except she'd never given him her number. She rarely gave her number out to anyone, especially a one-night stand. A number was personal, and these sexual encounters were never personal.

As if he were reading her mind, he continued. "I could have—I should have—sent you a message through the app before we were supposed to meet. I didn't, and I apologize for that. I completely forgot until days later. By then you'd already unmatched me, and I didn't have a number to contact you otherwise." He didn't say it as accusation, but as fact. He shrugged. "I am sorry. I didn't intend—" He broke off. "I know you don't like hearing that, that you have no reason to give me the benefit of the doubt, but I truly didn't consciously stand you up."

She tried to marshal her chaotic thoughts. She hated feeling emotions. All these things inside her, anger, regret, sadness, relief, hope.

Stuff 'em down forever.

"I did try to find you afterward." His lips quirked, making her heart thud. "I went to the house you'd rented, talked to the owners. Googled you. Unfortunately, it's hard enough to find a Claire when her name is Claire. Much harder when her name is actually Rhiannon."

She finally spoke. "My middle name is Claire."

One snippet of personal information. It didn't mean anything.

He smiled, slowly, as if it did mean something. "It's a pretty name. I'm sorry, Rhiannon Claire Hunter. Truly."

She bit her lip. "I understand being out of it because a loved one dies. You had no obligation toward me, we'd only slept together once." She thought he was about to speak, so she lifted her hand. "That's the truth of what happened." Even if they had been silly about it, making plans for a second date. "So, um. Maybe you're not evil. Thanks for explaining. I am sorry to hear about your uncle. I don't follow sports, so I don't know anything about him, but it sounds like you loved him an awful lot."

His eyes flickered. "He was like a second father to me. I still can't believe he's gone."

Something tightly knotted within her unraveled and she frowned, confused at the feeling. What . . . what was that? Her anger at him dampening? Her anger at herself, for feeling fooled, unknotting? Was this what . . . closure felt like? This light buoyancy?

She didn't know. The last time she'd gotten burned by a man, it had been on a much more enormous scale than this, and she'd walked away in too many pieces to even risk getting near him again for anything as silly as closure. "I don't want to get together with you again," she added, for both their sakes. "But I . . . I believe that you had something tragic and unexpected happen to you, and it may have affected your state of mind and prevented you from seeing me again."

He nodded slowly. "Thank you for hearing me out."

They sat in silence for a while, listening to the birds chirping in the spring air. Rhiannon let the curve of her back touch the bench, though she didn't relax into it. Now what? What did one do when someone behaved badly and gave you a reasonable explanation for what motivated their bad behavior and apologized?

It was so much easier to write people off. Much harder to navigate the gray areas of interpersonal relationships.

A gentle brush came against her pinkie. She looked down to find his hand not far from hers. The giant Super Bowl ring decorating his finger winked up at her. "I didn't know you were a famous football player."

"I didn't know you were a famous entrepreneur." His big shoulders moved. "You could have found information about me, if you wanted to. You own the app. You have my data."

"I have everyone's data."

He eyed her. "How much data?"

She almost patted his hand but thought better of it. "Best you not know." Best no one knew. She wasn't evil. That data was safe in her hands. Ignorance was bliss. "And yeah, I could have easily found you, but I thought you were a dick." Even then, she'd wanted to track him down, but had resisted.

His smile was faint. He tilted his head up to the sun. "I hope you don't think I'm a dick now."

She didn't think he was. *So hard not to write people off.* "I don't want to think I slept with some bad boy football jock. My instincts about this sort of thing are usually good. I don't do assholes."

"You must have felt like you couldn't trust your instincts when I ghosted you. I'm sorry for that too."

She jerked one shoulder up, another knot in her belly dissolving. Her confidence in herself *had* been rattled. For other women, agreeing to a second date was probably nothing. For her, it had been a huge concession.

Instincts were all a person had in this world where anybody could be out to hurt you. Her gut was her only defense. She had to have confidence in it.

"You won't find any stories about that kind of bad be-havior from me. No string of pissed ex-lovers, no arrests, no complaints. You can google me, if you want." His head dipped. "You might find other stories, but not those."

"Then I won't google you."

"Should I google you?"

"No," she said flatly, though she wasn't sure why. She shouldn't care if he found some dude screaming about her on YouTube and repeating rumors from four years ago, but she did.

"Fine. A mutual no-googling pact." He shifted and pulled his phone out of his pocket. He grimaced. "It's Tina. They need to start getting me micced soon."

Ah, shit. Rhiannon straightened. All this time, and they hadn't even gotten to business yet. "Look, the apology is nice and all, but I didn't actually come here only for that. I want something else from you."

His dark eyes flashed up to hers, and there was some-thing so hot and knowing in them, she shivered.

She hadn't slept with the same guy twice in the last few years. She scratched, she left. There was an intimacy in sit-ting on the same bench with a man who had been inside her. All the little hairs on her arms stood up. *Stuff everything down.* "Not that," she said sharply.

His lashes lowered. "I don't know what you're talking about."

She rose to her feet, the better to ground herself. "Walk with me."

Without complaint, he followed suit, matching his wider strides to hers. "I want to buy Matchmaker," she said, as quietly as she could.

His steps faltered and he stopped. "I'm sorry, what?"

She clasped her hands behind her and faced him. This was better. Business was more comfortable than the nebulous world of feelings and emotions and interpersonal relationships. "I want to buy the company."

Samson scratched his chin. "I think you're confused. I don't own enough of Matchmaker for you to buy it."

Her eyes narrowed and she pounced on that new information. "But you own some of it?"

"A tiny percentage. Not enough for it to matter."

That was good to know. "You know Annabelle Kostas personally. She introduced your parents to each other. She owns a beach house in your hometown."

His mouth dropped open. "How do you . . . how do you know that?"

"You said it."

"I didn't say anything about her owning a house in Cayucos," he said sharply. "Were you in Cayucos for my *aunt*? She was your business there?"

"She's your *aunt*?"

He pinched the bridge of his nose. She thought he was angry, but then she realized he was laughing. "Oh Jesus. So you went there to get to her and we met? By pure chance of our fingers swiping?" He chuckled. "What are the odds?"

Rhiannon tried to redirect. She didn't want to think about

the moment she'd swiped right on him, not at all. "We need to get back to the aunt thing. If you're her nephew, why weren't you and your uncle living in her beach house?"

He sobered. "You knew which house was hers?"

"You're making me sound like a stalker."

"I'm just stating facts. If those make you sound like a stalker . . ." He shrugged.

She huffed out a breath. "Okay, yes. I did know which house was hers. I wanted to talk to her about buying her company. And yes, our night"—she gestured between them—"together was an accident. I definitely did not know you were her *nephew*."

"For someone who makes her living off cell phones, you're really weirdly committed to in-person meetings."

She bristled but caught the teasing glimmer dancing in his eyes. "Going to Cayucos was a desperate move. Annabelle hadn't responded to my phone calls or messages. I thought . . . there might be a reason for that."

"What reason?"

Ah, damn it. She didn't want to reveal that part of her past if he was untainted, and also because she had a standing rule not to speak of it with anyone. But then again, if Annabelle did listen to gossip about her unchallenged, she'd lose her last shot with Matchmaker.

Practicality won out over her pride, and she took a calculated risk, first glancing around to ensure no one was lurking behind a perfectly manicured bush or tree. They stood by a fountain, the closed doors of the restaurant within sight. "This is a small industry. I used to work for Swype. When

I left them, there were hard feelings. They spread rumors about me. Some people believed them." *They* was really *he* but Peter had been significantly assisted by others at Swype to shut her down and out. No need to let his bro friends and colleagues off the hook.

Samson swayed toward her, his concerned frown so real and authentic she wished she could believe that anyone cared that much about past Rhiannon. "What kind of rumors?"

"Not important." When he looked like he might press, she played on his empathy. "I don't like to think about it or talk about it. In any case, my name isn't totally blemish-free. So I wondered if Annabelle had heard those whispers, if that's why she wasn't responding to me and I . . . I took some more drastic measures than I otherwise would have."

He studied her for a long minute. She didn't mind his hesitation. Whether he did owe her or not, she was also asking him to trust her.

With his *aunt*. What pure luck, stumbling upon Annabelle's nephew.

"Annabelle isn't the type of person to believe rumors if she hasn't met someone yet. And she's not technically my aunt. She's more of a common-law aunt," he said, finally. "She and my uncle Joe were together for almost forty years."

"I didn't know she had a long-term partner." Lakshmi was good at ferreting out information, too, so it must have been super well-hidden.

"No reason you would have. Annabelle's always been private. To answer your question as to why we weren't staying in her home: my uncle and I lived in my childhood home."

He squinted at her. "What interest is Matchmaker to you? Aren't you outperforming us?"

Us. He might have only a small financial stake in Matchmaker, but he felt proprietary toward it. She filed that away in her little box of red flags, though she'd already decided to proceed as though Samson was a competitor. "I want to outperform everyone," she said mildly. Which wasn't a lie. She didn't have to tell him how badly she wanted to crush Swype, specifically. "Give me twenty minutes with her. Lunch, dinner, coffee, whatever she wants. Let her hear me out, and then if she's not interested, I'll vanish." Rhiannon snapped her fingers. "I only want a shot. That's all." *Stop.* She was coming perilously close to begging, and she wasn't about that.

He hesitated and looked out at the lush greenery. "I don't think Aunt Belle's in a rush to sell Matchmaker, but to be honest, we haven't exactly discussed it."

Rhiannon tugged her sweatshirt down over her hands so she could stick her thumbs into the holes. It hadn't occurred to her before, but what if he demanded something in return for this favor? Another date, or a kiss, or sex. She'd have to be ready for him to be awful. A dozen snappish retorts rose on her tongue.

"You know what? I don't see the harm of an introduction. Okay."

She opened her mouth and then closed it again. "I beg your pardon?"

"I'll ask her if she'll meet with you." He leveled a stern look her way. "But like I said, she's private, so anything

I've told you about her relationship with me or Joe isn't for public consumption. And if she does meet with you, you will treat her kindly and fairly. No hardball business tactics. Aunt Belle is a sweet woman and she's lost her sister and her partner in the same year. She might be an entrepreneur, but there's a reason she leaves the actual running of the company to others."

Don't get too excited. He could flake on you. "No hardball," she said quickly. "I know you may have heard differently, but I promise I play fair."

"The only things I've heard about you, Rhiannon, have been admiring."

She licked her dry lips. If she thought too hard about what Peter might still be saying about her, she might pull her sweatshirt hood up over her head and never come back out. She nodded. "Okay. Well. Thanks."

"It's the least of what I owe you."

Yes, good. That's how you want him to feel, like he owes you.

Now, though, the thought of him feeling indebted to her left a bad taste in her mouth. She knew grief. She'd been too young when she'd lost her father, but she had experienced loss.

The last of that knot eased up in her chest. "You don't owe me anything," she said gruffly. "Consider our past in the past. We're colleagues now."

His eyes darkened, and he took a step closer. She felt small and dainty with him so close. "Colleagues," he murmured.

"Competitors, actually, I guess."

"Mm."

"Samson?"

They both looked toward the restaurant, where Tina was standing in the door, her hands on her slim hips. "We're ready for you," she called out.

So his date was here. Cool.

"Good luck," Rhiannon said to him. She took a step back, then realized she didn't want to walk through the restaurant and see the woman.

Kind, loyal, sweet.

She had no designs on Samson, that part of their relationship was finito, explanation or not, but better to not know what his ideal woman looked like.

"Thanks," he murmured, though he didn't sound enthused.

She spotted a gate in the garden and gestured at it. The path should allow her to circumvent the building and get to the front drive. "I'll go. Let me know when you talk to Annabelle."

"Do you want to stay? This won't take long, and—"

"Nah, it's getting late, and, uh . . ." She had a vast repertoire of excuses on how to get out of a date, but her mind blanked. "My cat's sick."

"You have a cat?"

No. "Yes."

"I'm so sorry. What's wrong with it?"

She waved her hand. "It's nothing dire. I mean. She's fine. She's more my roommate's cat." She backed away as she spoke, patting her pockets for her valet ticket. Thank God, she never carried a purse. When you stashed everything in your pockets, you didn't have to hunt around for an extra device carrying all your essentials. Anything that could get you in and out of places faster was her jam.

Samson followed her, looking concerned. "Let me know if you need—"

"I don't. Anyway. Thanks again." She whirled away and tugged at the gate, confused when the artfully weathered wood only opened a crack. She yanked harder, but it barely jostled.

A warmth enveloped her, and she nearly groaned when he stepped up right behind her, his big, enormous body filling her with heat.

His hand came in front of her and gently pressed the gate shut. His forearm brushed her shoulder, and she waited, every muscle tensed. What would she do if he insisted she stay? If he dismissed the woman who had showed up for him? If he touched her now, after he'd been so sweet and apologetic, when they were alone, in a picturesque garden . . . ?

Nothing would happen. Because they were done. *Closure* meant *done.*

He undid the latch on the gate, and he took a step back, away from her. Her breath rushed out of her and she opened the door properly, feeling foolish.

"I'll call you after I speak with Aunt Belle," he said to her back. "It might be a few days. She's out of the country right now and she's slow to return calls."

She swallowed. Right. Yes. Annabelle. Business. "Okay. Thanks."

His voice was husky. "See you later, Rhiannon."

He'd whispered that in her ear when he'd slipped away from her bed, though she'd been Claire then. It was far easier to have impersonal sex with a person when they didn't know your real name. She hesitated, then glanced over her shoulder. "Call me Rhi."

He raised a thick eyebrow. All of him was thick, damn it. Or thicc. With two c's. All the c's. "Rhi? I like it. It's short, like Claire."

Peter had been the last man who had slept with her to use her full name, her real name. She'd been Claire to all her hookups. She didn't believe that a name gave someone power over you but . . .

Best not to risk it.

"Samson!"

Samson glanced over his shoulder, and Rhiannon took that chance to slip through the gate. She refused to look behind her, to see if he was watching her leave. It didn't matter.

Her phone buzzed as she got in her car, and she pulled it out to find a text from Katrina.

Are you okay? How did it go with #BeachBastard?

She gritted her teeth. She didn't think she could call him a bastard anymore now that she'd gotten confirmation over why he'd flaked. *A loved one died and I was overwhelmed with grief* was a way different excuse from *something came up.*

Rhi texted back. **It was fine. I got closure, I didn't fall into bed with him again. He's going to talk to Annabelle.** She hesitated. She finished typing, **By the way, why don't we go ahead and get that cat you've been wanting?**

Eeeeee. On all counts.

Rhiannon busied herself pulling up directions. She was grateful she wouldn't have to see Katrina tonight, that she was staying in her loft. She checked the time and groaned. Even if that meant she'd be sitting in traffic forever heading back to L.A.

There was no reason to be rattled over that momentary blip of panic and attraction. That had been as cool and calm a meeting as she could have imagined. Boom, they'd settled the question of why he'd ghosted her so she could, if not trust him completely, not carry this load of anger anymore. Boom, she'd gotten the promise of an intro to Annabelle that seemed somewhat legit.

Rhi.

How did he make her nickname sound sexy?

Boom.

She shivered and put her car into gear. Automatically, she glanced in the rearview mirror and paused when a shiny red Mazda pulled up behind her. A gorgeous girl with long red hair and a tight white dress clambered out of the car, dropping her keys into the valet's hands.

The sinking sensation in her chest intensified. His date? Was this what kind, sweet, and loyal looked like?

Well, that was fine. Totally and utterly fine.

If Rhiannon's tires squealed when she peeled out of the driveway, well . . . that must be what closure sounded like.

Chapter Nine

"Heyyyyyyy, Samson."

Samson groaned and lifted his head from his cupped palms. The fancy hotel restaurant was deserted except for him and Tina. "You don't have to use that tone."

"What tone?" The blonde slipped into the chair opposite him, where his "date" had sat twenty minutes ago.

"That *mustn't upset the talent* tone." Samson grimaced. "I know I stank."

Tina interlaced her fingers on the snowy tablecloth. There was a wine stain next to her thumb. "You didn't *stink*, exactly . . ." She stopped when he growled in disgust. "Okay. That was not you at your best."

Samson grimaced. That was a severe understatement. "Can we get that poor girl a consolation prize? Disneyland tickets?"

Tina cracked a smile. "She doesn't need Disneyland tickets. I told her we would reimburse her for dry-cleaning or replacing her dress."

Samson groaned again. The red wine he'd accidentally knocked over onto the woman's lap had left a glaring stain.

"I don't know what happened." He wasn't sure if he was talking to himself or Tina.

Tina patted his hand. "Listen, we all have off days. Sometimes there's no chemistry between two people, no matter what the match percentages say. Don't tell Belle I said that, though."

"She's going to be disappointed."

"We can work some editing magic, probably, and cobble together a few minutes, at least, of you two looking at each other like you were enjoying each other's company." She hesitated. "Or at least, not actively disliking and boring each other."

"You know, my friend Harris, he mentioned that I may be out of practice when it comes to dating. It's possible he got in my head? That's the only explanation." It was true, he hadn't dated for a long time. But he'd broken the seal with Rhi months ago. That Night hadn't felt so weird and awkward. When they hadn't been talking in that dark bar, they'd sat in comfortable silence, their knees pressing together.

Speaking of whom . . .

"Can you edit out the part where I called her by the wrong name?" he asked grimly.

Tina winced. "Yeah, that probably wasn't your smoothest move. In your defense, Rachel and Rhi do both, um, start with the same letter."

He scrubbed his hands over his face, then remembered that the makeup artist had blotted something on him to mystically create shadows where there were none. He used the towel to wipe the brown makeup off his palm.

"Also, you'd *just* seen her. Easy to misspeak." Then, more casually, she said, "I didn't realize you and Hunter were so close. I heard your interview when you were at CREATE, your rapport was good, but you, like, know each other otherwise?"

"Uh, yes. We're . . ." Friends? Exes? Neither of those terms really fit, and something made him viscerally cringe away from using the word *colleague* as lightly as Rhi had. "We know each other. From before. Somewhere else."

Curiosity brightened her eyes, but Tina only nodded. "Ah, gotcha. What did she want? How did she even know you were here?"

"I had some questions for her, at the conference," he lied. "She was kind enough to come by and talk to me in person. You know, since I'm new to the industry."

Tina raised a skeptical eyebrow. "I've never heard her called kind."

"What have you heard her called?" His tone may have been a bit sharp, but he hadn't been able to stop thinking about what she'd said.

Specifically, why did she fear Annabelle thinking poorly of her? What had her former employer said about her? And why?

He knew how rumors and backstabbing and blacklisting worked. This wasn't something he could google. And even if he could, he wouldn't want to. They'd made a pact.

"I stay pretty isolated from the industry, too, working with Belle on behind-the-scenes stuff for as long as I have. I don't know Rhiannon personally, but I've heard she's a shark." Tina perked up. "Actually, that's not quite right. I've also heard she's a fantastic and fair employer. Not always easy to find."

I play fair. "Fair is a good word for her." No wonder his behavior had so bothered her. It hadn't been fair.

He'd felt like a million pounds had lifted off him when she'd accepted his apology. Oh, she was still clearly and obviously wary of him, but at least she knew what had motivated his ghosting.

Closure.

Whatever had brought her to him, he'd take. He'd shoot Belle an email in Australia when he got home and hope that his aunt would respond somewhat soon. He didn't know what Belle would do with regard to Rhi wanting to buy Matchmaker, but it cost him nothing to put the message through. He owed it to his *colleague.*

She hadn't felt like his colleague when he'd stood behind her, when he'd brushed his arm against hers.

That spark of attraction had started a heat low in his belly, a heat he'd thought he'd banked when she'd run away from him. No wonder he'd been too distracted to properly talk to poor Rachel.

He still wanted Rhi.

"She's pretty too. Prettier in person. You two seemed comfortable with each other. We'll find you someone we can replicate that with." Tina came to her feet. "Too bad you can't date her."

"Yeah—" He stopped. Tina had already turned away and was walking to the door.

"If we can't edit you and Rachel, we'll trash tonight's footage. I'll see who the next girl is on the list," Tina said, over her shoulder.

Too bad you can't date her.

There were a few milliseconds before someone hit your body with the full force of theirs, when the world narrowed to nothing but the other person. He was there, in that tense, panting moment. "Things may not go any better with the next woman we find on Matchmaker."

She stopped and gave him a sympathetic look. "One bad date can make you feel that way, I know. We can expand past entertainment people. It might give you a wider net. You can also work on your acting skills before the next meetup." She rested her hip against the back of a chair. "What's the last great date you had? Pretend your next date is her."

The last great date he'd had.

He thought about sitting next to Rhi in that dive bar. That heart-pumping, soul-destroying connection.

The truth came upon him like a body blow.

Rhi may have gotten closure, but he hadn't. That connection was still there, the connection that had urged him to beg her for a second date, even though he'd known she was a tourist in his beach town.

I don't want to get together with you again.

That was what closure implied, huh? That she was done.

"That's it. Like that." Tina made a square with her fingers and peered through it. "Whatever feeling's making you look like that."

His brain churned. He wanted to help Belle vis-à-vis this campaign.

Rhi wanted to use him for his connection to his aunt.

He wanted to see Rhi again. Maybe as more than colleagues. No. Definitely as more than colleagues. It didn't have to be for forever, forever was terrifying. What fell between *colleague* and *happily ever after*?

Lovers. Temporary bedmates. Platonic friends. Lots of things. Why couldn't they all get what they wanted?

Why should he have to remember his last great connection? When they could re-create it, exactly. "Can you actually stay for a little bit? And get marketing and William on the phone. I have an idea."

Chapter Ten

"Y̶OUR MOTHER'S on the phone, and she said if you don't answer, she's going to start posting your most embarrassing baby photos on 'the Facebook,' one every hour until you pick up."

Rhi looked up from her laptop. She was curled in the window seat of her office. "Did you give her that idea?"

Lakshmi shrugged. She was wearing a rose gold crop top and overalls today. "I like your mom."

"Everyone does." Rhi rolled her eyes and held up her hand, catching the vintage pink phone headset Lakshmi threw into it. They had normal phones, but since Rhiannon used her desk as a catchall more than an actual workspace, this was how she did her business. This or her cell.

She put the earpiece on. "What's up, Ma?"

"Young lady, you are avoiding me."

Rhi cringed. She might be thirty-seven years old, but *young lady* always made her want to look for the closest cupboard to hide in. "I'm not." She was.

"Your brother responds to all my phone calls and texts immediately, you know."

Because Gabe is perfect.

That was unfair. Her little brother was far from perfect, but he was filled with an innate sweetness Rhi lacked. *Sweet, kind, and loyal.* Yeah, Gabe was sweet, kind, and loyal to a T.

Gabe understood both Sonya and Rhi. He kept in constant contact with their mother, happy to talk to her for an hour or more about nothing, and he kept his texts to Rhi short and to the point and with purpose. He truly was a code-switching saint, able to make his way through any situation.

"I'm sorry. I've been busy."

"I know." Sonya's voice softened. "I heard CREATE was a success. I listened to the livestream of your interview. Thank you for having Lakshmi send me the link."

Rhi wondered if she could give Lakshmi another raise. The woman just went ahead and did brilliant things like facilitate her relationship with her mother. "You're welcome."

"You did sound a little tired, though. Are you taking those vitamins I sent you?"

Rhi narrowed her eyes. She had been tired after a sleepless night fretting over Samson, yes, but how had her mother figured that out? Was she a wizard? "Of course I'm taking the vitamins," she lied.

Sonya clucked. "You're lying."

"I am not."

"I'm going to have Lakshmi put them in your coffee."

"Well, then, you'll double-dose me and I'll die," she snapped. "Is that what you want? To kill me via CoQ10?"

Sonya's voice was frigid. "Watch your tone, Rhiannon Claire."

Her mother invoking both names was worse than calling her a young lady. At what age, Rhiannon wondered, would she stop feeling the need to ram right up against her mother's limits? "Apologies," Rhiannon said.

"Hmph." Sonya thought for a second. "It's a little vacation you need. You could go to the beach."

Rhi looked out the window. Crush operated out of a small tucked-away two-story building, surrounded by other start-ups. Her office overlooked a green courtyard. "I live in California. I can go to the beach whenever I want."

"When was the last time you went to the beach, Rhiannon?"

She pulled her sleeves down to cover her hands. *When I met Samson.*

She felt a little bit like a sucker, for not hating him, for believing him so easily. But it was fine if she didn't hate him, so long as she didn't go and sleep with him again.

You don't give zombies second chances. "I went to the beach last month," she said. One of their employees had had a baby shower at a waterfront restaurant with a big patio.

"Sandy's baby shower doesn't count."

"Do you have cameras planted on me?"

"Don't need them," her mother said. "I know you."

Rhiannon imagined her mother in the kitchen of her comfortable Chicago home, a concerned frown creasing her still-smooth forehead, her hair in braids. Sonya had used to put similar braids in Rhiannon's hair when she was a kid.

Her mom had always made them too tight, pulling at her scalp, making her feel too restricted and hemmed in.

Rhiannon leaned her head back against the cushioned pink window seat. "I'll take a break soon," she said. She would. She'd go off somewhere and enjoy a nice day or two off.

Or a half day. A couple hours?

"I worry about you, Rhi."

Guilt crawled through her, that same vague sense of guilt she always felt around her mom. Objectively, there was no reason for that guilt. Her mother had never made her and Gabe feel bad about the fact that she'd worked so hard to support and raise them. Even if she had, Rhi had paid her back for that a million times over.

Still, that guilt remained, a guilt millions of dollars couldn't wash away, and she wasn't even sure she could ever pinpoint its exact cause.

Her mother liked the money, but Rhiannon bet she'd like having a daughter she understood better. "I'm fine. Is there a reason you called?"

"I wanted to make sure you'd booked your travel for Gabe and Eve's engagement party."

She made a face. Travel arrangements were not her strong suit. "It's so far away, don't worry."

"It's barely a month away. There are some excellent deals right now."

Travel was something Sonya liked to do with her trust fund. Rhi didn't begrudge her one mile, and urged her mom to travel first class to wherever in the world she wanted to go, but the older woman had become something of a budget flight hound. Every day she perused the airline deals. "Cool. I'll book it. Later."

"Rhiannon."

Rhi sighed. "I'll tell my assistant, Mom." Lakshmi would be bewildered at her planning something more than a week out, but she'd get it on her calendar properly.

"Tell her now, before fares go up."

"I will tell her as soon as I get off the phone, promise."

"And tell her to buy you a nice dress for the party. She has such good taste."

Rhiannon gritted her teeth. "I will definitely *not* do that." She looked down at her worn cotton sweatpants and old sweatshirt. When she was younger, her mother had always tried to stuff her in dresses and sparkly shirts.

Rhiannon's signature look wasn't an affectation. It was a necessity, a thing that made her feel comforted and secure. "I wasn't raised in a barn. I have acceptable clothes to wear."

"I love you, Rhiannon."

Another flood of guilt. "I love you, too, Ma." She paused. "I'm sorry I don't call you more."

"I would tell you to remember to call me every day but I know you won't do that. Call me at least once a week so I can stop talking to all your friends," Sonya instructed her. "And that way, you know I'm still alive. I'm not getting any younger, you know. I could break a hip and lie on the floor for days and you wouldn't even know."

"I would know," Rhiannon murmured. Her mom might

have a network of well-meaning spies in Lakshmi and Katrina, but Rhiannon quietly kept tabs on her mother's credit cards and bank accounts. If her paper trail ever varied or went silent for longer than a day, Rhiannon either checked up on her or had Gabe do it.

She and her mom were more alike than either of them wanted to admit. Wasn't that a scary thought?

"What was that?" Sonya asked.

"Uh, nothing. Yeah, I will call you. Sorry to make you worry, Ma." She hung up as Lakshmi appeared in her doorway. "If my mother tells you to dose me with vitamins, please don't."

Lakshmi cocked her head. "So does this mean I stop crushing vitamin D into your peanut butter sandwiches, or . . . ?" When Rhi narrowed her eyes, her assistant shook her head. "J/k. Hey, so, someone's here to see you."

"To see me?" They didn't have the kind of business where she got visitors. Any meetings were usually scheduled well in advance. She rose from the window seat.

Lakshmi glanced over her shoulder, then slipped inside, shutting the door behind her. "Samson Lima? The football guy?"

Her heart stopped for a second, then started again. In that second, she made an aborted motion to tidy her hair, but stopped herself. "Oh. Uh."

Lakshmi's gaze lingered on her hand. When her eyes met Rhiannon's again, there was a glimmer of understanding there.

One that Rhiannon did not want to see. "You know I asked him to get ahold of Annabelle for me," Rhiannon said sharply. "He must have received some news."

"Uh-huh." Lakshmi crossed the soft pink carpet to stand in front of her. She grasped Rhiannon's chin in her hand, tilted her face up, and eyed her critically. Then she reached into the purse she wore on her hip and pulled out two tubes.

"What are you doing? I don't need any makeup." Rhiannon didn't jerk her face out of Lakshmi's hand, even though it would have been easy enough to do so.

"You're absolutely right, you don't. You're pretty stunning no matter what. But you went to fix your hair when I told you who was here, which tells me you're not totally secure in how you look right this minute. Let me help you feel confident."

Rhiannon didn't protest anymore. In fact, she closed her eyes, letting Lakshmi put a coat of mascara on her lashes and quickly line and fill her lips in. Lakshmi took a step back and gave her a sweet smile. "Feel better?"

Rhiannon nodded. She didn't wear much makeup, but here was another layer. Lakshmi always knew what she needed. "Send him in."

When Lakshmi left, Rhiannon darted to her desk. She sat, opened the drawers, shoved the stacks of paper into them, and then arranged a notepad and a pen on the empty surface.

When the door opened again, Samson's huge form following Lakshmi in, Rhiannon leaned back in her leather chair, twining a pen between her fingers. She nodded at Lakshmi, dismissing her, then raised a cool eyebrow at Samson. "What a surprise," she said loudly as the door closed. Hopefully Lakshmi heard that.

He smiled, his eyes as warm as they'd been when she'd accosted him in that garden. So warm she dropped the pen. Damn it.

"I'm sorry to bother you at work." He sat down in the chair opposite her desk, adjusting his big body in the smaller pink chair. He glanced around her office curiously, and she tried not to bristle and guard her domain like a feral dog.

She was aware her office didn't look like what people expected from her. Crush's signature colors, sherbet pink and bright yellow, dominated. From the second a person walked into this building, Rhiannon had wanted them to feel like they were in a cheerful bowl of candy.

Her furniture was small and dainty, chosen more for aesthetics than sturdiness. It did mean that she curled up in her window seat to work more often than not, but that was fine. She had never really owned delicate furnishings. Working for other employers, she'd always had to be on guard against displaying her femininity for fear they would think she wasn't tough.

Here it didn't matter. No one could judge her for how she decorated her office because she answered to no one.

She shrugged. "I bothered you at work a few days ago."

He crossed one leg over the other. Gone was the suit he'd worn for his date; he was back in worn jeans and a long-sleeved ribbed shirt. The sunny yellow of his shirt made his skin pop a warmer brown. "So you did. That's actually why I'm here."

She sat up straighter. "You talked to your aunt."

"No, Aunt Belle hasn't returned my message yet. Hopefully soon."

She deflated a little. "Oh."

"But, in the meantime, I wanted to talk to you about another proposition." He glanced over his shoulder, and she followed his gaze. The panels on either side of her door were glass, and she rolled her eyes when she saw at least five of her employees, Lakshmi included, loitering at a desk within view of the both of them. "Do you mind if I . . . ?" He gestured at the glass.

She nodded and he walked to the door, closing the blinds with two snaps, making the small office more intimate. She settled deeper into her chair, pressing her palms over her belly to calm some of her butterflies.

He is not here to sex you up. Calm down. "What proposition?"

He nudged his chair closer to her desk, and sat again, handing her his phone. "I had my first date for the campaign after you left. Here's the raw footage."

Aw, shit. He was gonna make her watch him turn his sweet smile on that beautiful woman?

She sniffed, to make it supremely clear she did not give a fuck about anything he did or who he talked to, and hit play on the video. "She's gorgeous," she admitted in as flat a tone as possible. Just because she didn't dress up didn't mean she couldn't appreciate style. The woman exuded glamour, from the tips of her fiery hair to her high strappy sandals.

"Hmm," Samson agreed. "Keep watching."

Rhiannon refocused on the meeting, hitting the volume button up so she could properly hear their exchange. After a minute, her eyes went wide. After three minutes, she looked up at him. "Did you seriously ask her if she was wearing hair extensions?"

He rolled his lips in. "Keep watching," he repeated.

Rhiannon couldn't help but do just that, and her envy vanished as she watched the couple on the screen with all the horrified fascination of someone watching a train wreck. She winced when Samson choked on a french fry. He took a sip of water, which he then spit on the tablecloth when he was racked by a coughing fit.

She inhaled when Samson oh-so-casually asked his date if she liked to "Netflix and chill" with her *nephew* and his reaction when the far-too-patient woman explained what he was asking. "What did you think Netflix and chill meant?" Rhiannon demanded, pausing the video.

"Exactly what it says! Watch television and relax." He shook his head, bewildered. "I didn't know it was about sex. Why can't people say what they want to say?"

"Because we live in a puritanical society that can't use the S word out loud." Rhiannon shook her head. "You're not *that* old, how do you not know slang?"

He sniffed. "It doesn't have anything to do with age. I haven't been plugged in for a while. This is the internet's fault, going around changing words and meanings."

Rhiannon rubbed her hand over her mouth to hide her smile. But she had to bite her lip not to laugh when Samson's

big hand knocked the girl's large glass of wine over. Right
into her lap.

Samson cleared his throat. "Let's shut it down there.
That's enough for you to get the gist of what happened."

She turned the video off in the middle of Samson's frantic
attempts to dry the girl's dress, and put the phone on her
desk. Then she looked up at Samson, whose face was a deep
red under his brown skin.

Maybe it was because she'd been talking to her mother,
but all she could do was channel Sonya. "Oh, *honey*."

He groaned. "I know. It was bad."

"Not bad necessarily—no, you're right." Rhiannon
handed him his phone back. "You were a fucking hot mess."
She shouldn't feel good about that. It was mean to feel good
about it.

Ah, but she did. Not only because he definitely hadn't
been this graceless on their one and only date, but because
she wanted him to have some flaws. The man was too perfect and shiny otherwise.

"I'm aware." He leaned forward, bracing his elbows on
his knees. "That's why I'm here."

"I don't know how I can help you with your graceless-
ness."

"Aunt Belle's assistant, Tina, said something interesting.
About how you and I have much better chemistry than this
poor woman and I did."

Rhiannon narrowed her eyes, even as her heart skipped a
beat or two. "I don't follow."

Samson rose from his seat and walked around the desk.

She scooted back, to give him more room, because he required so much room. He perched on the desk and smiled down at her. "I have an idea for a better campaign. You and me."

"We date?" Her voice squeaked.

"Not exactly. The idea we came up with was airing this debacle"—he gestured to the phone—"online. I originally didn't want to do that, because I feel bad for Rachel, but I've talked to her since. She's an actress, and eager for publicity, and she said it was clear I was the fuckup, not her." His faint smile made it clear he didn't mind that description.

"She's not wrong. You will look bad, if that gets released to the public."

"I'll look foolish."

"Doesn't that upset you?" It would upset a lot of men she knew, to give the world the impression that they were anything but smooth as butter.

"Looking foolish? It wouldn't be the first time. And it's a pretty benign form of foolishness. After I got over my horror and embarrassment, even I found it funny."

People would eat it up with a spoon. There was something utterly charming about a handsome, attractive, otherwise together man fumbling when it came to women. "What's my role in all this?"

"All my matches are placed on hold. Instead, you and I go out to cool places around the city and chat about dating. We can say that you're teaching me, helping me get back into the game. No cameramen, no closed set, we shoot it on our phones."

"We're competitors."

"Like you said, we're colleagues. The public loves it when brands work together, according to our marketing team."

Not totally false, if the crossover was properly done. Rhiannon mulled that over. "And what do I and Crush get out of this?"

"You'll be viewed as an expert on love and dating."

"Meanwhile, Matchmaker will be cast as a clueless, old-fashioned ingenue in this setup," she pointed out.

"Matchmaker is old-fashioned. We lean in on that, people wanting love the old-fashioned way. And a lot of our base will identify with a guy who feels bewildered with the way digital dating has changed love. Your base will identify with a woman of the world. You and I know we have a good rapport. This works. For both of us. For Crush and Matchmaker."

She examined the idea all around, looking for more holes to poke into it. But other than the fact that it was something of a strange concept to craft a joint marketing campaign with your competitor—colleague, whatever—she couldn't find anything, on its face, to discredit it.

Except for the fact that she'd be with Samson. Again and again. Talking to him about love and dating and then walking away. Priming him to be the perfect date for some other woman.

But those were emotional reasons against doing this thing, and she wasn't ruled by her emotions. "You came up with this?"

His smile was sly. "Did I tell you my degree is in marketing?"

"You know you didn't. You haven't talked to Annabelle yet. She may not like this."

"She doesn't usually concern herself with this level of detail. William is happy with the idea, and our marketing people are ecstatic over it. She'll be fine."

"I have to talk to my team."

He nodded. "Why don't you do that today?"

"Is this time sensitive?"

"Anything meant for the internet is time sensitive, I've been told."

She mulled it over for a long moment. As if he knew she was wavering, he leaned closer and placed his hand on the back of her chair, boxing her in. Her breath caught as he brushed his other hand over hers, where it rested on the arm of her chair. "Come on. It'll be fun and benefit both of us. We do have good chemistry, Rhi," he murmured. "You can't deny that."

She licked her suddenly dry lips. *Rhi.* Not the first time he'd used her nickname, but it slid over her ears like silk in his deep, dark voice. His palm was so heavy, the calluses of his thumb rasping over her skin as he rubbed in the tiniest gesture. She wanted to flip her hand over and hold it. "We might."

"Might?"

His shoulders seemed to grow bigger. What was he, a peacock? If so, she was an animal too, because her heartbeat was responding to whatever mating dance body language he had going on. "I don't think there's any question about it." He straightened away from her, unboxing her body. For the first time since he'd walked into the room, his face grew grave and vulnerable. "Look. Let me address the elephant in the room. I clearly like you and am attracted to you, so if something were to develop between us, physically or whatever, it would be fine with me. I'm not going to badger you about it, though, or make you justify your choices if that choice is no. You have my number. You can come to me."

She tried to summon her voice, to explain the problem to him: she didn't fuck with the same man twice, especially one who had hurt her before. It was far too risky. She'd been decimated before, and by someone whom she'd thought was on her side. Samson was technically a competitor, and she needed to be careful.

Never again.

She couldn't force the words out, though.

When she sat silent, he lifted a shoulder. "Don't stress, Rhi. I have to go meet a friend right now." He named a downtown bar she was somewhat familiar with. "Someone recommended that place to me. I'll be there tonight, around eight. Since you like to track me down so much, if you make a decision, come there and let me know if you're ready to roll."

She rose to her feet when he did, the words that finally emerged from her mouth blessedly strong and assertive. "Or I'll call you."

His look was filled with kind humor, like he knew she'd come find him over calling him. "Whatever you'd like. I'll be there no matter what."

She pursed her lips, trying to figure out if there was some

double meaning behind his words. Was he trying to impress upon her that he was man of his word? Well, too bad. Nothing would help her learn to trust him again except his behavior.

She followed him to the door, and opened it for him. He nodded to her as he left. "I look forward to hearing from you, Rhi." The intimate use of her nickname made her toes curl. How could such polite words sound like a sexy veiled threat?

She watched him walk away, trying not to stare too hard at his butt, but what else was one supposed to look at when a hot man was walking away from you?

Aw, shit. The truth hit her like a tidal wave.

She was going to sleep with him again.

Yeah, yeah, she didn't sleep with the same dude twice, she didn't fuck with zombies. Her dating rules were going to go out the window with this guy. She could feel it. Gawd, maybe soon he'd send her a dick pic and she'd find it charming, thus cancelling every rule she'd ever made for herself.

She shuddered. *Let's not go that far.*

Fine. She might sleep with him again. But she'd do it on her terms. It would be within her control.

He disappeared from view as he descended the stairs that took him down to the exit, taking his bubble butt with him. That was when she realized a good dozen curious eyes were staring at her, the office chatter definitely at a lower volume than what it usually was. She frowned, and that was enough for everyone to get back to work. Or pretend to get back to work.

Everyone except Lakshmi, of course, who came clipping up to her in stilettos. "Were the layers a good idea?"

"Yeah," Rhiannon said. The lipstick hadn't been bullet-proof, so if she did see Samson tonight, she'd add a couple extra layers first. At the very least, she'd wear a pair of pants with buttons, and not these threadbare sweats. "Get Suzie and the rest of marketing into the conference room in five. We have an interesting opportunity in front of us."

Chapter Eleven

*S*HOULD HAVE *given her a more specific time frame.*

Samson sipped his second soda and tried not to stare at the entrance. He'd selected this place because it was dimly lit and intimate, a speakeasy tucked inside an unassuming restaurant. He'd chosen a booth in the corner. It was still early enough that not many people were drinking at the bar. He and Rhiannon could talk here.

If she showed up. He checked his watch again. She could easily vanish on him, he told himself, trying to manage his expectations.

Samson internally grimaced at the memory of her expression when he'd said he'd be interested in something personal developing between them again. That Night, when he'd asked to see her again, she hadn't looked that conflicted. Her agreement had been hesitant, but it had come. He truly hated that she'd taken a chance on him, on doing something she didn't normally do, and he'd let her down.

His mother had been a gentle soul, and she'd been the one he'd gone to for dating advice, from the time he was old enough to understand why he felt some kind of way about a girl. Especially once he hit his late teens and his father's personality had undergone a drastic reversal.

He remembered one epic lecture when he'd come home and told Lulu his ninth-grade crush had reacted in what he thought was an unreasonable way to something he'd said and started crying. First Lulu had dissected exactly all the way his words had been harmful, and then really lit into him.

Every time you hurt someone, you break off a little piece of them. Not only do they have to live with that broken piece, then the next person who comes along has to figure out a way to spackle that spot. Your behavior has ripple effects.

He owed Rhi for the piece he'd broken off her. This campaign might possibly make up for some of that. It would help her and Crush, which she seemed to love above all else.

Yes, he wanted her. But he'd meant what he'd said, and he wasn't going to pressure her for anything more than a business relationship. If *she* decided that she couldn't stand being around him without them both getting naked, well . . .

He snorted to himself. Fat chance of that happening, but it was a nice fantasy. His phone vibrated, and he pulled it out, frowning at the unfamiliar New York City area code on the screen. He had it set to Do Not Disturb for unknown callers, so it had gone straight to voice mail.

It wasn't particularly loud in the bar, but his hearing wasn't the best—another souvenir of his former profession—so he pressed one finger in one ear to hear the message. "Hey, Samson. This is Trevor. Trevor Sanders? I'm sorry to cold-call you like this, but I saw that you were back in the public eye and I was hoping to speak with you about this exciting new organization I'm starting. I'm going to be in L.A. soon and would love to sit down with you and talk. Or you can text me. Whatever works for you. Looking forward to hearing from you."

His phone creaked under his tight grip and he eased up. This fucking asshole. *Trevor. Trevor Sanders?*

Like he wouldn't know who Trevor was. Former star quarterback of the Brewers. Blond haired, handsome, that stupid Colgate smile. The most expensive caps money could buy.

He sent a group text to Dean and Harris. **Did one of you give my number to Trevor?**

The denials were instant.

Nope.

Nah, man.

He rubbed his finger over his lips. **Okay, thanks. He called me. I have nothing to say to him. Don't give him any info about me, and tell anyone else the same thing.**

The bubble popped up under Harris's name. **I didn't give him your number, but I have talked to him recently. He didn't give me all the details, but I guess he's setting up some kind of nonprofit to help retired players.**

Dean's reply came before Samson could finish his text. **Don't care what he's doing, he's a dick for what he's done. S, next time he calls, forward it to me.**

Harris answered. **Oh yeah. Not saying he's not a dick for the past.**

Warmth ran through Samson. He didn't need protection,

but it was nice to feel the brotherly camaraderie from men he'd known for forever.

Samson tapped back his reply. **I'll be fine. Let's meet up for lunch soon.**

"Is this seat taken?"

He jerked, his phone slipping away from him. "You're quite the butterfingers, aren't you?" Rhi remarked and bent over to scoop his phone up off the floor. "I guess I should be glad that wasn't wine."

He stood. "Literally no one's ever called me clumsy before."

She uttered an amused noise. Their fingers touched when she handed over his phone, and maybe it was his imagination, but he swore her gaze lingered on his hands.

Rhi slid into the booth, opposite him. She'd changed since he'd seen her earlier, into slacks and a snug blazer, with a Prince T-shirt on under it. Her thick hair was gathered up in a claw clip, but a few tendrils brushed her cheek. "You look nice," he said.

"I can clean up when I need to. I'm a board member for a domestic violence organization," she said crisply. "We have a meeting tonight, I'm going straight there after this."

"You look nice no matter what you wear." He tried to dismiss the pang of disappointment that he was a stopover before she went somewhere else. That was fine. He hadn't expected anything to come from tonight, except talk of their looming partnership.

Liar.

Okay. He hadn't *seriously* expected anything to come of

tonight. "Do you want a drink?" He slid the menu over to her. "According to reviews, they have good cocktails here—"

"I don't need a menu." Before he could signal the waitress, she raised her hand. "Vodka tonic with a splash of cranberry, please," she told the server.

Samson waited for the waitress to leave. "You know what you want."

"When it comes to drinks, yes." Rhi's face was unreadable. She clasped her hands on the table. Her nails were short and unpainted.

He straightened his shoulders, trying not to remember how those nails had pressed into his skin. And failing, terribly.

"Let's cut to the chase." Rhiannon cocked her head. "Crush is willing to get on board with this wacky idea of yours. My team actually loves it. They called it real Wholesome Content."

Odd phrasing, but okay. "Are you willing to get on board with it?"

"I am." Rhiannon's drink came, and she swirled the liquid with the straw, the pretty pink of the glass's contents matching her lips. There was something glittery in her lipstick, an added pop that might hypnotize him if he let it. "I have some . . . terms, let's call them, though."

"I assumed you would." There was no way Rhiannon wouldn't wrestle as much control for herself as she was able to.

She'd wrestled him in bed for the upper hand too. He didn't mind it. He'd had no idea this was his kink, but there was something supremely sexy about being with a woman who effortlessly displayed leadership.

"I like the scenario you proposed, us hanging out and talking about dating, basically an expanded version of the interview we did with Helena. We can keep it purposefully low budget, film it ourselves. We record on my phone. Crush gets first crack at editing, and then you can take over. We both have to agree to the final videos that are released."

He settled into his seat. "Interesting. Why your phone? What's your fear?"

"It's not a fear." She took a sip of her drink. "I want the footage in my control. If my image gets tarnished, my company's directly affected."

He trusted her not to tarnish his image but understood exactly why she might still be suspicious of him. "I'll have to talk to the team. But I think this should be fine."

"Second, we don't tell anyone that we've slept together. That includes our respective employees/employer, or the general public."

"That's absolutely fair," he agreed instantly. "I don't talk about my sex life with anyone."

Her shoulders relaxed a little, and he leaned forward, interested. "Can I ask you a personal question, though? Related to this?"

She examined him, then finally gave a short nod.

"You're in the public eye. You don't like bad publicity. I know I'm not the first man you've hooked up with off the app. Don't you ever worry that one of them will recognize you? What if they, I don't know. Go to a tabloid?"

"First of all, you make it sound like I have a long string of temporary lovers I've met through Crush. I won't give you the numbers, because I think that's crass, but it's not that high, it's a last resort when I'm feeling particularly itchy. Second, I don't do shit without thinking about how it'll affect my business, even the shit I do ostensibly only for me." She took a sip of her drink. "Like I said, I try to make sure the men I sleep with aren't assholes—I usually have good radar about that sort of thing—but I know there's a risk. If someone thinks they can get fifteen minutes of fame and goes to the press crowing about his lay, I am prepared for them." Her voice went up an octave, as if she were reading lines from a play. "Just because I don't want to have a relationship doesn't mean I don't have needs. You'd never shame a man for casual sex. Crush's business model is built on empowerment. I'm using my own app exactly as it was intended." She twisted her wrist. "And so on and so forth."

"Impressive. Very good answer."

"Business. You can have whatever you want so long as it doesn't cost you customers." Her smile was grim. "I learned that the hard way. Now. Where was I?"

He tipped his glass to her. "Your demands."

"Right. You still talk to Annabelle for me."

"Obviously."

"And one more demand, and this one is personal, and off the record."

"I heard you loud and clear, and I meant what I said in your office. You don't want this to get physical. I get it and respect it. I won't try to persuade you otherwise."

She half laughed. "Your butt persuaded me, Samson."

He opened his mouth, then closed it again. "I beg your pardon?"

"You have a great butt. I was never a butt person, but then you walked away from me." She pursed her lips. "Let's be real. I really like your ass, enough to bend another rule or two of mine. And you seem to like parts of me. So we might very well fall back into bed if we spend enough time together. I accept that."

"Wait, wait, wait." He held out his hands, palms out. "This is a one-eighty."

"I do those sometimes," she murmured. "It's not flip-flopping if you do it for a good reason."

"I don't mind flip-flopping when it comes to sex. You can flip-flop ten more times up to and during the sex act, and that's fine. I'm mostly confused how this flip-flop came about."

She placed her hand over his. It was cold, but he didn't mind that. She stretched across the table, and he reciprocated. Her eyes were so pretty, a deep, dark brown full of secrets. "Not to be crude. But it really was your butt," she said softly.

He bit the inside of his cheek to keep from laughing. He glanced over his shoulder. "It's that good? I don't even have to speak?"

"Let the cheeks speak." She sat back, slipping her hand out from his, but before she could he flipped his over and captured hers.

She glanced down, and then back up. "It doesn't mean

anything, though. I don't want anything more than that." She pinned him with a stern look. "Don't ask me for a real date, don't ask me for a future, don't ask me for anything beyond the time that we spend together. That's my last demand."

He'd let her go if she wanted him to, but she remained passive, letting him hold her. He wanted to hold her more. Exhilaration soared through him. He didn't care if it was his butt or his personality that had done it. She was willing to give him a second chance.

Kind of. No dating, no romance, no long-term stuff. He could deal with that. They were back in the same position they'd been in after That Night.

Except she'd been softer when he'd convinced her to give him a second date That Night. This coolness, this toughness, had been missing then. A stab of regret went through him. A broken piece to spackle.

So he'd take this time to spackle over some of the damage he'd done. Temporary or not, he could shower her with reliability and kindness. "I'm not looking for anything long term either," he said. He wasn't anti-love. He'd had some fairy-tale romances modeled for him. However, the thought of loving someone the way Lulu had loved Aleki or Annabelle had loved Joe—it filled him with anxiety, not anticipation. "I would like to be with you again, on your terms. So we have a deal?"

Her agreement came slowly, though he'd acquiesced to every request she'd made. "Yes. The contract will be for five meetups, in locations I choose, since I know the city better. Have they uploaded your debacle of a date yet?"

"Not yet."

"Okay, well, we can figure out the release schedule over the next couple of days. It should be fast, within a few days of each other. I'd say back to back, because people do like their binges, but keeping them waiting a little might not be a bad thing. Gives us time to shoot footage and edit and whatnot. Are you okay if this takes off? Goes viral?"

"Do you think it'll go viral?"

"Anything you put on the internet—a tweet, a picture, a video—has the capacity to go viral."

A hint of unease moved through him. The last time he'd been in the public eye had been ten years ago, and the internet then wasn't what it was today.

It was fine. He simply wouldn't read the comments. "A lot of attention would be good for Matchmaker. And Crush."

"Great. We can start on Wednesday. That gives us a couple days to get the contract ironed out. My legal team should have something over to Matchmaker by tomorrow morning."

"A contract?"

"Of course a contract." She squinted at him and drained the rest of her drink. "Oh honey, who does business without a contract?"

"The part about my ass won't be in it, will it?" he joked.

Her eyes grew heavy lidded. "Nah. Your ass is off the record."

His body tightened. For a second, he could forget they were in a dimly lit hipster bar in Los Angeles. Right now, they were back in Cayucos, in that dimly lit dive bar where they'd first met.

She pulled out her phone, opened the camera, and set it on the table, propped up against the menu holder, and hit record. "Might as well start now. Hey. I'm Rhiannon Hunter, owner of Crush, and this is Samson Lima, the hotshot former football player for the Portland—" She paused.

"Brewers," he supplied.

She wrinkled her nose. "I'm not much of a sports ball person. Let's agree to not talk about it too much."

Being with someone who didn't know anything at all about him, his family, and football was a godsend, not a bad thing. "We all have our strengths."

"Dating's not yours, though, right? That's why we're here."

Samson let his smile turn self-effacing. He was here to be made fun of a little. That was fine. "I used to be good at it. I think? But things have changed, and I could use some help. That's where you come in, I guess." Their knees brushed against each other. He let his leg slide between hers. Within view of the camera, they maintained a respectable distance.

The corner of her lips twitched, but that was her only reaction. "I like this. It's like pickup artistry, but instead of my teaching you how to manipulate women into bed, I'll be teaching you how to just . . . be cool."

"Bed isn't my first priority."

"What is your first priority?"

"Uh, I'd like to get through a date without spilling wine in a woman's lap."

"Or asking her if her hair is real?"

He winced. "It was so beautiful! I meant it as a compliment, I swear. Look, no need to rehash the whole thing for everyone."

Amusement danced in Rhi's eyes. "It's funny. Especially because you're this big, tough, handsome man."

"I'm a big tough guy who hasn't dated in a while," he said simply. "Help me, Obi-Wan. You're my only hope."

She snorted. "A nerd too."

For a second, he forgot they were recording. "Should I dial back the nerdiness?"

"Nah. I am a big fan of dialing exactly nothing back. Be yourself. Try to, like, lead with the most interesting parts of yourself. That's my only dating advice for anyone, ever. But we can discuss all this later." She turned the camera off. "I only wanted to see how you'd play on camera."

"Didn't trust me?"

"Checking to see if your mess of a date really was a fluke or a new stage fright you developed after the CREATE interview. We'll do proper intros later." She smiled. "I'm running late. Pay the bill and you can walk me to my car."

It was a humid night, the muggy air forcing a trickle of sweat to run down his neck. Or maybe she caused that physiological reaction, he wasn't sure.

She'd parked across the street in a parking garage. They rode down to the basement level in silence. He followed her to her car, a new silver Tesla nestled amid a sea of other electric cars.

His car was a six-year-old SUV sitting in his leased condo's parking garage. He had the savings to upgrade, but he hated spending a dime more than he had to on a vehicle that got him reliably from A to B. Then again, the bigger car, while good for getting Uncle Joe around, didn't really fit into this shiny city with cramped parking spots and high gas prices.

He opened the driver's-side door before she could. She glanced down. "You do like opening doors for me."

He didn't know what she was talking about at first, and then he recalled. Back on the beach, he'd had to almost lunge ahead of her to get to the bar door, her house door. She'd teased him then. *Oh, thank God, I don't know how I would have opened things without you here.* "It's manners. I open doors for everyone."

She braced her arm on the open door and tipped her head up to him. "You can kiss me, by the way. I'll allow it."

His smile was slow and real. This woman was tough and blunt and made no sense, but she was also super adorable.

He slid his arm around her waist. "Good. I've been dying to do that."

He didn't rush it, though, lowering his face to deliver a mere brush of a kiss. It wasn't their first kiss, but the distance they'd crossed to get to this moment made it feel like it was. Her head tilted, her lower lip dragging over his. "You smell good," she murmured.

"So do you." She smelled like peppermint again, but there was an underlying hint of chocolate mixed in with that. Like the sexiest cool-sweet peppermint patty he'd ever come across. Samson tugged her closer, squeezing the soft flesh above the waistband of her pants.

A feather light touch drifted up over the side of his face, up to his hair. Her fingers tunneled through the strands, playing over his scalp. He shivered and followed her cues, angling his head, deepening the kiss.

The first touch of her tongue against him was like dropping a lit match onto dry kindling, both of them turning needy and hungry. He stepped her back, so her car could give them a bracing surface. Her legs parted, and he settled between them. One of her legs slid up the side of his, and he grasped her limb under the knee. It was rude, and they were in a public place, albeit a deserted public place, but he anchored that leg against his hip, the better to keep her open and available to him.

His other hand slid up her side, under the hem of her shirt, and finally, finally, after months, he rediscovered the joy of her more intimate skin against his. He rubbed his thumb over the small of her back and she made a soft sound into his mouth. She made another noise when he found the clasp of her bra and plucked at it. One hook released. Then another. He slid his forefinger and thumb under the fabric and—

A car horn had them parting, the noise the equivalent of a bucket of cold water thrown over them. He stepped back and she huffed a small laugh. "That escalated quickly."

He winced and resisted the urge to adjust himself. That would be crass. More crass than making out in public? Possibly. "Tell me about it."

She blew out a breath, the tendrils against her cheeks vibrating. "I gotta go, or I'll be late for this meeting."

He almost missed her next words because she reached behind her to secure her bra clasp, arching her back.

"Keep an eye out for that contract."

The contract. Business. Right. He dragged his gaze away from her round breasts. "Will do."

She scowled at him. "Stop grinning. I could one-eighty on the sex again by the next time we meet."

"But you'd follow through on the business side," he pointed out. "Which means I'd see you, even if I didn't get to kiss you, and I like seeing you too."

She shook her head. "That Lima Charm thing isn't a joke, is it."

She was getting inside her car, so she missed his smile momentarily slipping. It was back in place by the time she rolled down her window. "I'll be in touch."

He tapped the corner of his mouth. "You may want to check your lipstick before you go to your meeting."

Instead of looking in the mirror, she smirked. "You may want to do the same. You got some sparkle on ya there."

He examined his finger, which did indeed have some pink glittery residue. His smile grew. "I'll see you soon, Rhiannon."

She peered up at him. "Rhi."

He'd call her whatever she wanted, and he couldn't deny that he liked the intimacy of a nickname. "See you soon, Rhi."

Chapter Twelve

It's okay to forgive him and trust him a little, but be careful.

Rhiannon ran her thumb over her phone screen in her pocket as the hotel's elevator took her up seventy floors to the rooftop bar, Katrina's text burning a hole in her pocket. Katrina was distracted by her new kitten, but she had taken the time to weigh in on this whole campaign when they'd video chatted on Monday, after Rhiannon had met with Samson.

While her best friend had been happy Rhiannon had gotten her closure, she'd been concerned about this new development, even without Rhiannon breathing a word about his butt. Or that kiss.

I don't want you hurt again, Katrina had fretted.

Rhiannon had reassured her she wouldn't make that mistake again anytime soon. Why, she'd barely obsessed over how good that kiss had been, pressed up against her car. Barely.

And it had been a stupendous kiss. She wanted more. She'd get more. All with her feelings in check.

Rhiannon stepped out of the elevator and zipped up her

hoodie. It was her favorite, the cerulean one that hugged all her curves tight. They might be filming this on her phone, but that didn't mean she couldn't look great.

The stern bouncer checked her ID and allowed her to pass through the hallway to the open rooftop. It was fairly quiet, given that it was a Wednesday. Suzie had made arrangements beforehand, and the hotel was accustomed to various parties using it for a backdrop. The establishment had set up a prominent sign that filming would be taking place and patrons might be on camera.

It took her about three seconds to find Samson's huge frame leaning against a railing. It was good that he had his head turned in profile, looking out at the twinkling city lights. That gave her a chance to at least try to suppress the little jump of excitement in her belly before he saw her.

She crossed over to him, passing the cabanas and Ping-Pong tables. This rooftop bar she'd chosen was a cool combo of sophisticated and kitsch. Most importantly, though, it had one of the most stunning views of downtown L.A.

Samson spotted her when she was about four feet away, and his beaming grin almost made her stumble. He was so clearly happy to see her. That had been the first thing she'd liked about him, that night in Cayucos. In a world that played it cool and cynical, his obvious interest had been a breath of fresh air.

Be careful.

"Hey," he said, and waved the waitress down. He'd dressed casually in jeans and a light sweater, the knit clinging to his biceps.

Rhiannon rested her elbow on the railing and looked out over the city, the distance all the way down dizzying. Fondness for her adopted hometown lifted her mood. Weeknight or not, the never-ending traffic was bustling. "Hi. Did you have any trouble finding the place?"

"Nah, I walked."

She lifted an eyebrow. "Walked?"

A dimple popped into his cheek. "Yes, I walked. It was barely a mile, it would have taken me longer to hitch a ride."

"Weird."

"No one in this city likes to walk. I miss it."

"No one in this city likes to walk because you could get hit by a car. But I'm glad you were able to make it in one piece."

"Here you go," the server interrupted them and handed Rhiannon a drink before walking away with a full tray for other customers.

Rhiannon lifted the glass of pink liquid. "You ordered for me?" No one had ordered for her in a very long time, save for Lakshmi.

"Wasn't hard to guess what you'd like. You always get the same thing." He frowned. "Was I wrong? Do you want something else?" He was already raising his hand, and she shook her head.

"No, I do always get the same thing."

"I didn't expect that. Wouldn't have pegged you as a creature of habit."

"I'm not, but I am efficient. I was told a long time ago that staring at a menu and dithering over what you want to order is a sign of weakness." When she'd first started out, her mentor had told her to pick a signature drink and be done with it, so as not to waste a chance to talk about business. Back then, it had been a gin and tonic, clear and boring.

When she'd started Crush, she'd felt free to order the splash of cranberry juice, tinting the drink pink.

"A sign of weakness?" He stared at her, baffled. "What an odd thing to consider a sign of weakness."

Lord, if he only knew. Sometimes she felt like her whole life was navigating what was weak and what was strong and always ending up confused and unsure. She nodded at his drink, what looked like a Coke, the same thing he'd ordered the first time they met. "You don't drink alcohol." He wasn't the only one who was observant.

"I don't. I never really have." He looked out over the cityscape and gestured at the video being projected on the building across the street. "That's cool."

A change of subject, which was fine. Alcohol consumption could be a testy subject. "They usually pick a single artist and broadcast their greatest hits. Must be MJ tonight." They watched the zombies dancing for a minute. "'Thriller' is my favorite."

"Mine too." The touch of wind blew a strand of his hair over his forehead. It had grown out since the conference. She wondered if he would cut it short again or let it go long, like when she'd seen him in Cayucos. She'd liked those wavy locks.

She shifted and placed her drink on the table nearby. "You ever think about how the music video wouldn't make sense if it was shot today?" She continued when he shot her a questioning look. "I mean, technology could take care of this whole problem. Car breaks down? I have a battery starter in my glove box, it's the size of a tablet. If that doesn't work? A cell phone would call AAA and help. You wouldn't have to leave your car to walk down some spooky path with a werewolf."

"Eh. I don't know about that."

"What do you mean, you don't know about that? A cell phone solves like 99.9 percent of the problems that created conflict in media prior to 1998."

"Hear me out. You didn't charge that car starter. You're out of cell service, or, as is usually the case with me, your phone battery's run out." He spread his hands out in front of him. "Boom. Zombie dance. Technology's only good if it's functional."

"Okay, but the setup still might not work." Rhiannon gestured to the terrified young woman on the screen. "That poor girl's on a date, possibly a first date? Today's day and age, she's got pepper spray or a Taser on her. I'm on a first date, and a guy's car breaks down, and he magically 'doesn't have' cell service?" She used air quotes. "I'm going to have one hand in my pocket or purse, on my weapon and my keys, 'cause something's fishy there. A woman with a hair bow that jaunty, she's a fighter."

He mulled that over. "You think pepper spray would work on zombies and ghouls?"

"Open membranes are open membranes, son." She

couldn't hide her smile at his laugh. He had a beautiful laugh, all deep and hearty.

She sobered. It would sound good on camera, which is what they were here for. Rhiannon pulled out her phone and a tripod, setting it up on the table so it would capture some of the scenery. She adjusted it so the music video wasn't in view. The last thing she wanted was for legal to bitch about how they couldn't air the thing because of licensing.

"You have a little phone tripod?" He peered at her setup. "How clever."

"I didn't invent it, but it is clever." She hit record and took a step back. She glanced up at him and then pressed his shoulder, angling his body so they were both visible.

"You know what you're doing," he rumbled.

She dropped her hand away from his shoulder, that nice, solid shoulder. Because business first. Pleasure later. "Sometimes." She fixed a smile on her face for the camera and gave a brief intro, including where they were standing. The bar manager had been kind enough to allow them to do this for free, in exchange for a mention, so she dropped the bar's name a couple of times.

A few people glanced their way, but this was L.A., and there were more exciting things in the world than two possibly vaguely familiar-looking people talking to a cell phone set up a foot away from them. They'd be left alone.

She looked up at Samson. "Samson, I'm not even sure where to start with you. How long have you been out of the dating game? Years, right?"

"Five years." There was a shadow of a smile on his face, and she knew they were both thinking of their one night together.

Which they couldn't. Not now. "Phew. Too long. We gotta get you up to speed. Where to even start with you."

He grimaced. "I'm afraid I was so awkward I may have come across as a jerk on my last date."

"I think you were more nervous than anything. Got in your head a little too much about it?"

His cheeks slightly reddened, and it was so cute, she hoped the camera would pick up the color. "Yeah."

"Everyone's got nerves or awkwardness on their first date. That's okay, you can usually recover from those things. Just don't be a jerk. In fact, let's start with talking about some general dating no-nos for people. Number one: don't be an asshole."

"This seems totally doable." He patted his pockets. "Should I take notes?"

"Commit my words of wisdom to memory." She held up a finger. "Okay, second rule, related, but more specific. No dick pics without invitation." Their target audience was adults, they could be adult.

He choked on his soda. "Yes. I'm on your side, 100 percent." He looked down his body. "It's not even that pretty. No one wants that in their texts."

She ran her tongue over her teeth. His penis was, actually, delightful, and she had firsthand knowledge of that, but she wasn't about to say that on camera. There were limits. "The prettiness of a dick might be subjective."

"Breasts. Breasts are universally pretty." He shook his head, and she was certain his bewildered expression was genuine and not an act. "Penises are floppy and boring and messy looking. God give me the confidence of a man who thinks the sight of his dick will lure all the ladies to the yard."

This time she allowed herself to laugh and leaned back against the railing, relaxing. She could almost forget the camera was there, which was odd for someone who almost always had their professional mask on when a camera was rolling.

She'd grown up in the age of YouTube. You never knew when you were being recorded, so when you knew you were being recorded, you acted right. "Let's just say, there might be times when you want your partner to send you a picture of their private bits, because you find it arousing."

He looked doubtful. "Okay . . ."

"But then it's not unsolicited. A solicited dick pic is great. Go with God. Send your penises all over town."

"Send your penis all over town if asked." He tapped his temple. "Got it."

"I guess all of this could be shelved under the general advice of don't be a fuckboy," she mused. "Unless you're being upfront and honest about being a fuckboy, and that's what your partner wants too."

He squinted. "What's a fuckboy?"

"What's . . . a . . . fuckboy." She tapped her lip. "You don't know?"

"No. Is it someone who just wants sex?"

"Oh no. You can just want sex and still not be a fuckboy. You can want a relationship and be a fuckboy. Fuckboys are on Matchmaker, on Crush, on every platform." *Though they probably heavily congregate on Swype given the Chief Executive Asshole's top-down culture of boys will be boys.* "But you know, I don't know if I've ever had to give a succinct explanation of what a fuckboy is, and I'm pretty sure the phrase has hugely evolved since it first came into general modern usage."

Two women passing by cast them amused glances, clearly having heard their conversation. They were both in their early twenties, wore short skirts and tall boots, and were gorgeous enough to be models.

Rhiannon made an abrupt decision and waved at them. "Excuse me." She gestured at the phone facing her and Samson. "We're filming for a thing."

The closest girl, blonde and poured into a red dress, looked unimpressed. "Who isn't filming in this city?"

"I know, right? Listen, we're trying to come up with some dating don'ts. Can you give us a description of the worst person you've dated or could imagine dating?"

"I'll stay off camera," her companion said. She was Black, had a smoothly shaved head, and wore a white leather mini and a crop top. "But that's an easy one. Someone who sleeps with you once, doesn't call you the next day, and then hits you up with a 'got any pics?' like, two months later."

"If you do text them, they leave you on read for, like, days," her friend chimed in.

"Oh yeah, he totally has his read receipts on, even though there's no reason for such a thing in this decade." The woman shook her head. "He also bails on plans with you, but gets pissed off if you have a genuine reason why you can't see him at the spur of the moment."

"They regularly use the phrase 'bros before hoes.'"

"He posts a million mirror selfies of himself but makes fun of women who do the same thing."

"He sends dick pics, and they're never framed well."

"You can text him something hilarious and witty that you spent a lot of time thinking up, and he'll respond four hours later with *haha*."

"He's shallow."

"Egotistical."

"And he always comes crawling back."

The girl in white clapped. "Al-ways."

Her friend scowled. "Says all the right things."

"Mmm-hmm."

"You give him a second chance. And then blam. The whole thing starts again. Ghost or most, rinse and repeat." The women sneered.

"Well." Rhiannon cleared her throat. "Uh, thank you, ladies. That was extremely . . . thorough."

The pair waved and left, and Rhiannon looked at Samson. His eyes were wide. "My God," he whispered. "That's so much."

She snorted a laugh. "So don't be that guy. Unless a woman wants you to be that guy, in which case, be up front about how you're that guy and have fun."

He nodded but seemed preoccupied. "What did that young woman mean when she said ghost or most?"

"Ah, mosting. That's a newer one. You know how ghost-ing is when a person disappears, no contact on a person? Mosting is when a person disappears, no contact, and does it after making the other person feel . . . special, in a very short period of time. Sweeps them off their feet. There's no good reason to do either, but at least you can recover from a so-so date when someone disappears. Harder to get over a person who takes you on a magic carpet ride and then vanishes."

His skin grew lighter, and she realized why when he made a rough noise. "Rhi."

Just that, only her name, and she realized he thought she was talking about him. Them.

Maybe she was, she didn't know. But she didn't want to do it on camera. She gave a tiny shake of her head. "Let's switch gears and talk about how you communicate with your matches," she said brightly, eager to get them off a topic that was so close to home for them both.

Samson rolled his shoulders. For a second, she thought he might object, but he followed her lead. "Again, no dick pics."

"Right, yes. No being a jerk either. Try to find something in their profile to talk to them about, whether that profile is short, like on Crush, or long, on Matchmaker."

"One thing I like about Matchmaker is that you only get a small number of matches, based on the personality test, and you can really focus on—"

"My God." A visibly drunk man stumbled up to them. He grabbed Samson's arm and leaned in really close. "Are you—are you Samson Lima?"

Rhiannon didn't like the look of this. She turned the camera off, stuck her mini tripod and her phone in her pocket, and balanced on the balls of her feet. She hadn't brought her pepper spray with her. A mistake.

Samson disentangled the man's grip from his arm and took a step to the side. "I am."

"Ugh. Fucking hate the Brewers."

"I'm sorry to hear that." Samson subtly positioned himself so he was between her and the guy.

Rhi stood on her tiptoes to look over Samson's shoulder. "Excuse me, sir, but we are in the middle of something here." She gasped when Samson gently reached behind himself and placed a hand on her arm, pushing her farther behind him. What the hell?

Was he . . . protecting her?

"Used to love them, but they all got fucked up after you turned traitor. Haven't won a Super Bowl since."

"You'll want to walk away now, sir."

The man's face contorted and he curled his lip at Samson. "Lima Curse."

Samson went entirely rigid. "Say that again."

Whoops. What was that? She'd never heard *that* rough whisper from her smiling, sweet colleague. Worried now, Rhiannon made eye contact with the huge bouncer by the elevators and jerked her head. The man immediately started jogging over.

"Curse," the drunk fool hissed, and Samson took a step toward him.

Rhiannon tugged at Samson's arm. She'd always assumed

if she was ever in a bar brawl, she'd be the one starting it, not playing the role of an anxious girlfriend. "Come on," she said as she scanned the rooftop. Her gaze lit on the egg-shaped cabanas on the other side of the roof.

The bouncer arrived and took a firm hold of the drunk.

When the guy started walking, Samson allowed Rhiannon to lead him away, too, but he balked when she got inside the pod. The hard plastic had openings on either side, and a cutout on top, to look at the stars. It was large and could probably fit like five or six people. It was also weird. "What is that thing?"

"It's a cabana." She gestured at the pool not far away from them, the water lit blue and green.

"That is not a cabana."

"They call them cabanas."

He tentatively touched the mattress she was sitting on. "Is that a waterbed?"

She settled on to the surface, letting it jostle her. These things usually had a waiting line for them on weekends, but they were empty on this weekday night. "Yup. Come on in."

Gingerly, he got inside, the mattress waving with the weight of his body. He ran his hand over the cotton surface of the covering of the mattress. "They wash these, right?"

"I'm guessing very much so." She tried to sit so her back was against the plastic wall, but the mattress made being upright difficult. "Don't think about it too hard."

"Got it." He adjusted himself, but no matter what he did, she was going to be attached to him. The waterbed wouldn't allow them to sit on opposite ends, and she rolled right next to him.

She hadn't planned on wrapping herself up in him. Her instincts had only urged her to get them far away from the source of his agitation.

It had been so long since she'd cared after the emotional well-being of a romantic partner like this, and she didn't quite know how to feel about it, but that was something she could dwell on later. Finally, she gave in to water and gravity and rested her hand on his belly, her head on his chest. He froze for a second, and then his arm went around her shoulders and he pressed her against him. The mattress stopped waving, and they sat there quiet for a few minutes. The lights from the stars and buildings around them bathed them in a blue glow.

It wasn't silent. The noise from the bar and the pool filtered through, but in this odd egg-cabana, they were alone. It was nice. Peaceful.

He let out a deep exhale, the air coming from his toes. "You want to know what that was all about, don't you?"

"I mean, I may not understand. Anger over sports isn't really in my wheelhouse. I reserve my anger for other things. As you've seen."

"People can get real emotional over sports. And me."

"I've heard you called the Lima Charm before. Why did that guy call you a curse?"

His hand rubbed up and down her arm. "When I was a kid, my dad and uncle played for the same team for a while. I would go to some of the games. The games I went to, they won. My dad started calling me his lucky charm. As I went up through college, the name morphed. I had a way with the media, with the public, with women. It turned into the Lima Charm, among my teammates, and then the media heard, and you know how it goes." His body tensed, then relaxed. Like he was forcing it to relax. "It became the Curse when I retired. Or rather, how I retired."

"How did you retire?"

"I walked at halftime in the middle of a game."

"What?" She lifted her head. "You can do that?"

"I did." That big, calloused hand ran up her back to her neck and he massaged her there.

At the first touch, she wanted to melt into him and forget talking, but she couldn't do that, not without satisfying her curiosity about one more thing. "Why did you do it?"

His chest rose and fell. "My friend got knocked out with a hard hit. Like out cold. He came to, and they wanted to put him back in the game. He was clearly concussed. Could barely recognize any of us, was seeing double, and they wanted to put him back in the game so he could get a concussion on top of a concussion. I told them, if they tried it, I'd walk. Then they tried it." He grimaced. "So I had to walk."

"You walked for your friend." *Do not let that melt your cold dead heart.*

But as much as she might wish otherwise, her heart was neither cold nor dead, so there it went. Melting into a puddle.

"We were closer than friends. We were teammates. We played college ball together. He was my brother."

"I can't believe they wanted him to play with a concussion."

"I can." He lifted a shoulder. "I knew better, because of—well, anyway, the week before, they'd distributed a pamphlet in our locker room about how concussions wouldn't lead to permanent problems if each injury was properly managed." He smiled bitterly. "But they didn't even want to manage my friend properly." He resettled his weight, the waterbed shifting with him. "Anyway. A lot of my teammates and the fans were angry with me. Someone coined the Lima Curse, and I guess there are still people who remember that ten years later."

She ran her palm over his smooth jaw. He was leaving things out, but she wasn't going to badger him. "I'm sorry."

He grunted. "I can't believe I spewed all this out. I don't usually like to talk about myself like this."

"It's the waterbed," she said solemnly. "The waterbed of truth."

He chuckled. "Makes sense." He played with her fingers and sobered. Without another word, he leaned down and pressed his lips against hers.

It might be that he was embarrassed by the vulnerability he'd revealed and was simply deflecting any further questioning, but that was fine with her. She kissed him back, eager. Damn it. She did like him.

Which was fine. You could like temporary bed partners. *Keep telling yourself that. Emphasize the temporary.*

Their lips parted, both of them panting. "Do you remember, back on the beach, when I went down on you?" he murmured. "That first time, right after we got inside the house?"

"Yeah," she exhaled.

His hand slid over her ass. "I can't stop thinking about it. Since I saw you again, it's all I've thought about."

"Is that right?"

"Mm-hmm. Camera's off, yeah? Now we can get personal?" There was that blasted dimple again. "As per the terms of our contract?"

"Mine is, but I can't guarantee other people's are." She shifted. "These cabanas are dry humping pods, I'm sure."

He looked around them with disgust. "Okay, as unique as this experience is, I'm ready to leave."

"Why don't you walk me to my car?"

His body wound tighter as he followed Rhiannon to the garage where she'd parked. Some other time, he might worry about her wandering around these deserted garages by herself instead of parking at a street meter or surface lot, but not today.

He should have been anxious that he'd opened up to her as much as he had—only a select few knew such personal things about him—but the emotions that had driven him to tell her about his past had morphed into something else, something dark and heavy.

Though, to be fair, he'd been consumed with varying degrees of lust since he'd watched her walk across the rooftop, her bright blue hoodie unzipped enough to give him a peek of shadowy cleavage. When had sweatshirts become an aphrodisiac? The same time peppermint had become one, he supposed. More specifically, when he'd met Rhi.

She got into the back seat of her car, shoving the driver's seat up and making space for him. He got inside and reached for her immediately. There wasn't much room, but that was okay. He didn't need much room to please her.

And he wanted to please her. He wanted to play her body like a concert violinist. He wanted her to remember tomorrow what his tongue and hands felt like, so he could do this a million times more.

He came up for air from her lips and immediately pressed kisses to her cheeks, and down her throat. His fingers went to the waistband of her pants. She wore stretchy leggings today, thank God. Jeans were stiff and inflexible and difficult to wrestle off in the confines of a back seat. He knew, because his jeans were currently strangling his dick.

"I want to lick you until you come," he heard himself say, and the guttural, deep tone of his voice startled him. He sucked the pulse at the base of her neck. "Will you let me?"

Her yes was almost soundless, but he heard it. That thready, breathless verbalization of consent was sexier than anything on this planet. Even sweatshirts and peppermint.

She raised her hips for him, and he pulled the stretchy pants down to her ankles and then completely off, taking her panties with them. The blood rushed away from his brain.

Her legs gleamed. He ran his hands up her muscular calves and to her round thighs, and then shifted both of them. He placed one of her feet on the seat and the other on the floorboard and crouched between them on the seat.

Samson reversed his decision to get a new car. He needed

his SUV for situations like this. This electric car was not built luxuriously enough for such shenanigans.

Not that he was going to let some tight quarters get in the way of Heaven. He kissed his way up her thighs to the spot between. He wanted to bury his face between her legs but he controlled his greed.

The car was dim, the only light a distant fluorescent bulb in the parking garage, but it cast an oddly romantic glow over her body. She was all these perfect shades of brown here, her black hair trimmed. He used two fingers to open her up and studied the pink revealed. He hadn't gotten to thoroughly indulge his senses when they'd been together the last time. He probably wouldn't get to tonight. He didn't want to fuck her here, in such cramped quarters.

Next time. There has to be a next time.

Basically the exact words he'd thought to himself the first time he'd gone down on her That Night. He rubbed his cheek on her soft inner thigh. This passion and excitement was raw and uncomplicated and utterly untouched by all the other stuff that clouded their relationship. It was like they were new to each other.

"I should tell you, I don't usually come from oral sex," she said, and her matter-of-fact words jerked him out of his contemplation of her pretty pussy.

He rubbed two fingers up and down her sex. Her flesh glistened. "You came for me plenty the night we were together."

"Not while you were . . ." Was her face red? Was Ms. World Weary blushing? "I didn't come while you were going down on me."

He thought back to that night, the X-rated memories making him harder. That was true. He'd either been fucking her or playing her with his fingers. "You liked it, though?" His mouth was watering, but he'd go no further if she didn't want him to.

"I loved it. I just can't come easily from it, and most men don't want to stay down there forever."

The stab of jealousy that ran through him was annoying, so he ignored it. "I'm not most men," he murmured and licked her swollen clit.

He used his hands to grip her legs and settled in to feast, taking more space for his head and shoulders when she arched. She was silent, but he could tell by the way her thighs trembled and the way she gripped his hair that she enjoyed it.

Samson had no idea how much time had passed, but when he heard her moans, he opened his eyes and left her for a breath of air. Her skin was flushed, turning her face and neck a dark burgundy rose. The lines on her forehead were deep. "You need to come," he said, his breath coming as fast as hers. He scraped his chin over her clit, delighting in how she jumped.

"I told you, I can't . . ."

He pressed two fingers deep inside her. He chuckled at the noise she made, though his erection made humor almost impossible. "That Night, you made that noise when I slid inside you. Does this fill you up like my cock did?"

"I think you're a little bigger," she purred.

He swallowed, the ego stroke going right to his dick. He

pressed a third finger inside her and she gasped, her legs widening. "Perfect."

He thrust inside her, using his thumb to stimulate her clit. "You can't come from my tongue, I get that. But you came just fine when I fucked you with my fingers, didn't you?"

She didn't respond, so he stopped, lowered his head, and sucked her clit. She cried out.

He came back up. "Didn't you?"

"Y-yes."

"Yeah." His hungry gaze locked on his fingers moving in and out of her body, the sounds of sex filling the car. How would he let her go? Like, ever, but especially tonight?

Rhi tensed and he followed the cues of her body, not letting up until she came with a shudder and a sigh, her fingers relaxing over his arm.

Though his body was clamoring at him, he rested his head against her thigh, exhilarated accomplishment making him smug and happy.

He petted her calf. "Rhi," he murmured and gave her clit a gentle kiss. "Rhiannon."

A new tension invaded her limbs. He could feel the instant she transformed from postcoital lethargic to anxious. She sat straight up. "Rhi?" he repeated. "You okay?"

Her hair had escaped its ponytail. She nodded so hard the curls vibrated. "Yes. I—I have to go." She grabbed her leggings and pulled them on.

"Go?" He frowned. She didn't sound okay. She sounded freaked out. "Did I do—"

"You didn't do anything." She lifted her hips and pulled

the pants on over her hips, tugging her shirt and sweatshirt down over the waistband. Then she pulled the sleeves of her sweatshirt down to cover her hands. "You were great. Thanks for, um, everything. I'll— I'll see you."

She clambered out of the back seat, and he followed, blinking at the harsh glare of the parking garage, no longer diffused through the windows. He straightened and touched her arm. "Rhiannon."

"Don't call me that." Her snap was loud and stern. She opened the driver's-side door with jerky motions.

"I won't." He kept his tone as gentle and nonthreatening as he could make it. "Rhi. I'm sorry."

Her shoulders froze, her face in profile. Her words spilled from her lips too fast, like something was forcing them out involuntarily. "My ex was the last person to call me Rhiannon in bed. Things didn't end well. Guys I hook up with, they use Claire, if they call me anything at all. I didn't know how much I'd hate it, but I can't handle you calling me my full name. Especially when we're intimate."

His first instinct was to find this mystery ex-boyfriend and punch him in the face, but that wasn't helpful right now. He raked his hand through his hair. "I'll call you whatever you want, even if that's Claire or some other name you haven't told me yet. Say no more. I didn't know it was such a big deal, but I hear you. I'll be more careful." He dared to rest his hand on her back. Her muscles slowly unclenched.

She faced him, and he was floored at the sheen of tears in her eyes. Rhi put a lot of stock in appearing tough and strong. She was probably kicking herself for even having this outburst. She wouldn't like him seeing her cry.

He pulled her in for a tight hug so she could have the illusion of privacy. She rested her face against his shoulder and breathed deeply while he rubbed her back. "I'm sorry. This was an overreaction."

"No. If it's important to you, it's not an overreaction. It's okay, Rhi."

At the repetition of her nickname, she relaxed. She pulled away and he gently freed a curl from where it was stuck to her damp lips. He squeezed her shoulders. "Why don't you go on home. Get some rest?"

Her smile was wobbly, but there. "I will. Thanks for, um. Everything."

"Thank you."

Her tone went businesslike and brisk. "I'll call you about our next meeting."

He matched her tone with a faint sense of amusement, given where his lips had been a few minutes ago. "Sounds good." He waved and waited until she'd reversed out of the spot and drove down the ramp before he walked away.

His body was still clamoring for more, but he also felt an odd sense of peace that not even the memory of that drunk calling him a Curse could shake.

This was the best business decision he'd ever made. What an interesting, demanding, adorable puzzle of a woman.

Chapter Thirteen

I'm so glad you're here this weekend. Feels like it's been forever since we've gotten to catch up."

Rhiannon smiled at Katrina, who was sprawled next to her in a lounge chair on the Santa Barbara mansion's porch. It wasn't that hot out, but Katrina wore the skimpiest of white sundresses and looked like a voluptuous goddess, her golden flesh spilling out and over the fabric.

"I'm glad I came up for the weekend too." It was only Thursday, but she could work remotely tomorrow. She'd been feeling guilty over how little she'd seen of Katrina over the past couple of weeks.

She'd been busy, not only with the business, but with Samson as well. They'd shot four of their five videos so far.

Samson's initial terrible first date with Rachel had gone about midlevel viral, like Rhiannon had thought it would, but in the best possible way. People who had no idea who he was were invested in the bumbling hot former pro athlete, and people who knew of him were awash in nostalgia. As for Rachel, she was doing fine. Samson had mentioned to

Rhiannon that the aspiring actress was delighted with the free publicity.

They'd already released two of their videos and they'd had good metrics on their social media and a bump in app downloads. As Samson had predicted, they'd both played well to their respective customer bases: a dating ingenue taken under the wing of a cynical romance expert. In fact, the internet was responding so well to Rhiannon's brand of snark, she'd felt free to get a little spicier on camera. Suzie and marketing had been surprisingly chill.

Except for when she'd said she'd rather gouge her eyes out than be in a relationship with someone. Suzie had edited that part out of the second video and glared at her while she told her to, of course, *cool it.*

"Have you heard from Annabelle yet?"

"Samson's been in contact, but she doesn't want to talk business until she's stateside, which should be any day now." Rhiannon had eyed him suspiciously when he'd told her that, because it sounded like a delaying tactic, but he'd thrown up his hands, pulled out his phone, and played a voice mail from Annabelle that was, almost verbatim, what he'd said.

She'd apologized, but oddly enough, he hadn't seemed terribly put out by her general distrust. It was kind of nice, not to have to explain herself constantly.

"How was the beach yesterday?" Katrina asked.

Rhiannon adjusted her laptop screen. This was another reason she'd been staying in her L.A. apartment lately. Katrina saw too much. "Great. Samson is a natural in front of the camera."

"He sure is. So are you. You have good chemistry."

The words were delivered without inflection, but Rhiannon could hear the question in them. She kept her gaze glued to her computer.

What could she say? That after every filming, they sat around and talked about the most mundane stuff on the face of the planet? That she was learning more about him than she had any man in recent history? That "walk me to my car" had become a code for heading to whatever remote spot she'd parked her car and fooling around? "We haven't had sex yet."

"I didn't ask if you had." Katrina paused. "Oral sex is sex, FYI." When Rhiannon cast her a startled glance, Katrina laughed. "Well, that tells me everything I need to know. Be—"

"Be careful. I know. I am."

"I love you."

"I love you too." Rhiannon sighed. "He's a good guy. And I never thought I'd say that about someone who ghosted me."

"You know, in certain special cases, it's okay to give someone the benefit of the doubt." Katrina tapped her finger on her chin. "Someone wise in this house advised exactly that, no?"

The benefit of the doubt? More like a recipe for being let down. Or at least, that was what she'd always assumed.

Still assumed, that is. "Spoken like a romantic."

Katrina snorted. "Hardly. Romance hasn't come knocking on my door lately." A meow came from the concrete.

Katrina leaned over the side of the chair and picked up the kitten she'd adopted about three minutes after Rhiannon had given her that panicked go-ahead.

Rhiannon and the kitten eyed each other in respectful tolerance. She was glad she had agreed to this new roommate. Katrina needed more companionship.

"I went to that pho place yesterday."

Rhiannon stopped pretending to work. "You didn't tell me that."

Katrina rubbed her face on Zeus's head and smiled. It was a small, secret, vulnerable smile. "I couldn't believe it."

Rhiannon whooped and placed her laptop on the table, curling up to look at Katrina more head-on. "What are we up to now? Seven?"

"Yes." Katarina's chest rose and fell and she looked off into the distance. Her round, makeup-less face was soft and sweet. Back in the day, when she'd spent lots of time outdoors and at beaches and concerts, her skin had been burnished a golden tan at all times, but now her coloring was dependent on the time of year and whether she felt like sitting in the sun. "Seven establishments I've managed to comfortably patronize."

"That's amazing."

"I never thought I'd see the day when I would celebrate being able to walk into a handful of places that aren't my own home."

Rhiannon didn't care for the hint of disgust in her friend's tone. "Hey, don't think about what you may have done in the past. Think about how hard you worked to get here."

Katrina gazed at the sprawling view laid out before them, the city of Santa Barbara spread like a necklace, the view of the Pacific obscured by fog. Other mansions dotted the hill, but this one was especially secluded, the backyard lush with greenery and flowers. When Katrina wasn't creating high-end wearable art, she was gardening. "I am pretty happy with myself."

"You should be. I'm happy with you."

"I was telling my therapist . . . if I can frequent at least ten places, maybe then I'll try dating again."

Rhiannon's first instinct was to tackle Katrina right then, wrap her up in cotton, and keep her safe. "Um."

Her best friend's smile was rueful. "I know. I'm a romantic and you're a cynic, and you're scared for me to even try." Her smile faded. "I'm lonely."

"I'll come up more," Rhiannon said immediately. "Or I'll live here full-time and commute every day. Or—"

"No." Katrina held up her hand. "I love you, but it's not that kind of loneliness. I miss being held. I miss sleeping with someone at night. God, I miss spooning."

Rhiannon rolled off the deck chair and nudged Katrina over. Her friend laughed as she complied and Rhiannon squeezed next to her. "I'm too big for us both to fit on here," she protested.

"You're not big. We fit fine." Rhiannon pulled her closer. Zeus clambered over them to rest over their chests.

"As much as I appreciate and value all cuddling, this isn't exactly what I miss either," Katrina said with a chuckle. But she hugged Rhiannon back, and they sat together for a few minutes in silence.

Rhiannon closed her eyes, enjoying this. Nobody spoke enough about how much bodies could be starved for platonic affection. She knew she gave off strong Do Not Touch vibes, but she needed occasional hugs too.

Rhiannon's nose wrinkled as Zeus dug her tiny claws into her skin. "If you want to start dating again, that's fine. However, you're rich and you've been out of the game for a while, so please understand I'm going to vet any dude you happen to meet." She shuddered. "And we're only handing out benefits like doubt for rare special cases, like you said. Not everyone gets that."

Katrina lifted a shoulder. "It'll be a while. I still have to be able to regularly go to three more places without drugging myself."

Ten was an arbitrary number, but Rhiannon knew from experience that Katrina didn't like anyone questioning her goals. "Whenever."

The ringing coming from the small black cylinder on the table beside them startled Rhiannon. "Sienna, patch the call through," she said out loud.

There was a brief pause, and then Lakshmi's voice filled the air. "Hey, boss."

"Hey. Katrina's here."

"Hi, Lakshmi."

Lakshmi's voice warmed. "Katrina. Okay, first of all,

Rhiannon, I got your travel for your brother's engagement party booked."

Sonya would be delighted that this chore was done. "Can you—"

"Already emailed your mom."

"Thank God."

"Second, I have some great news. Helena's people called, they want you and Samson to do a little segment on her new show. They said, and I quote, 'Helena is *charmed* by your little videos.'"

A little stab of irritation hit her that she'd have to share screen time with someone else. Cooperating with a competitor was all well and good, but she didn't want her's and Samson's names linked forever.

Unless you buy Matchmaker.

She liked the idea of working indefinitely with Samson a little too much. "Any way for it to be just me?" Rhiannon absentmindedly stroked Zeus's fur and rested her head on Katrina's shoulder.

"They want both of you."

Fine. "Book it."

"I'll try to do it around the time of the engagement party so you won't have to go to the East Coast twice."

"Perfect." She hated jet lag and lost time.

Lakshmi blew out a breath. "Now, to the bad news."

She sat up at those dire words, and so did Katrina. The kitten bounced into Katrina's lap. "What's the bad news?"

"Swype's Chief Executive Asshole has reportedly been cozying up to William Daniels."

Her heart jumped and she tried to wrestle it back down. "Cozying up how?"

"They were seen playing golf. Having dinner together."

Rhiannon didn't doubt Lakshmi's sources, they'd never been wrong before. There were a million perfectly good reasons why Swype's CEO and Matchmaker's CEO might be buddying it up together.

And one scary reason why they might, as well.

When Rhiannon didn't speak, Katrina jumped in. "Thanks for the information, Lakshmi." She made their goodbyes, which Rhiannon barely heard. Her mind was going a mile a minute, thinking of everything she needed to do to circumvent this possible sabotage.

She jumped when Katrina placed her hand on her shoulder. "Rhiannon, they could be having dinner, no ulterior motive. They're in the same social circle."

She and William were in the same circle, but he'd never play golf with her. Or take her out to dinner.

Because of Peter, probably. She clenched her fists tight. "That fucker."

"Hard agree, he is a fucker. But you need to take a deep breath."

Instead, Rhiannon launched off the chair to pace. "He's trying to buy Matchmaker from under me."

"You don't know that."

"I do. He saw the videos. He's annoyed about how fucking wholesome and cute it is and he's pissed he's not a part of it." She got to the end of the patio and whirled around. "Do you know what he's like when he feels left out of something? Did I tell you about the time I went to a friend's birthday party and didn't think to invite him? He didn't talk to me for a week. He broke the vase my brother made for me, the one I kept in my office." Peter had said it was an accident, and at the time, she'd believed him. She gripped her elbows. "He knows I want Matchmaker. He's gonna try to get it."

She jerked to a stop when Katrina stepped in front of her and put her hands on her shoulders. "Stop. Take a deep breath."

"This isn't a fucking panic attack," Rhiannon snapped, and then flinched at her own thoughtlessness. "Oh my God, I'm so sorry. I—"

"Stop," Katrina repeated again, slower this time. She pressed her hand on Rhiannon's collarbone. "Take a deep breath."

Rhiannon complied, more out of regret than an actual belief it would help. Sure enough, her heart continued to pound. Sweat had popped out at her hairline. "Katrina, he can't win. He can't—"

"Name three things you see."

She almost whimpered. This was stupid, and a waste of time.

But she'd already minimized Katrina's issues once, and she owed it to her to listen. "Your eyes."

"What color are they?"

"Brown. Medium brown."

"Name two more things you see."

"The orange marigolds you planted in the window boxes."

"One more."

She blinked, the better to clear her vision, which had narrowed and blurred. "The city. A sliver of the ocean."

"Now name two things you can hear."

"The birds calling to each other. The wind chimes on the tree over there."

"Name one thing you can smell."

She inhaled and exhaled deeply. "The roses."

"Good. Good girl. Can you think a little clearer now?"

Rhiannon blinked back the tears in her eyes. She could think clearer, but that meant the panic and anger had receded and she could taste loss and defeat. She didn't know if that was better or worse. "He can't win."

"Even if Peter does buy Matchmaker, Rhi, that doesn't mean he's won. You're a better businessperson than him. You'll trump him, one way or another."

Rhiannon worked her jaw. No, Katrina didn't understand. She couldn't let Peter win at anything, or even think he'd won at anything.

The best revenge is success.

If she couldn't get success? Then what? What did she have?

"I have to . . . I have to do something." She walked to the table and picked up her phone, sending a quick text.

"What are you doing?"

"I can't cozy up to William." Especially now that it was confirmed that Peter and he were chums. There was no way William hadn't been given an earful about how evil she was. "But he's not the majority shareholder of the company anyway. I have to get ahold of Annabelle." She grabbed her laptop. "I'm going to go down to the office."

"To the office, or to see Samson?" Katrina asked astutely.

Hopefully the latter, but Samson needed to text her back to confirm that. In the meantime, she'd start driving down to L.A. She grunted.

"Rhi, be—"

"Careful. I know. I will be, I promise. I . . . I can't let Peter have this. If anyone buys Matchmaker, it has to be me."

Katrina was quiet for a second and then nodded. "Okay. Go. Let me know what you need from me."

This. This acceptance calmed her down more than breathing exercises ever could. "I will." She reached out and squeezed Katrina's shoulder. "I'll keep you updated."

If there was anything to update. Worry and fear had her walking at a fast clip, and she kept glancing at her silent phone. She'd been so preoccupied with this little project with Samson and their canoodling, she couldn't believe she'd taken her eye off the prize, the prize she'd already gone to great lengths to attempt to secure. She couldn't lose this.

Not to *him*.

Chapter Fourteen

SAMSON'S PHONE vibrated in his pocket, and he almost reached for it, a Pavlovian response he had to consciously beat back. He'd never been tied to his cell as much as he had for the past couple weeks. The hit of dopamine to his brain every time it was Rhi on the other end of the line had become addictive.

This time, though, his hands were full, so he did his best to ignore it, even when it buzzed a second time. He'd check it after lunch.

Samson kept a gentle hold of Miley's fists while she stood and balanced on his thighs, her tiny feet encased in trendy white sneakers that matched her dad's. She beamed at him, her fat cheeks creasing, and took a wobbly step.

". . . anyway, that's why sometimes it's that greenish-brown color." Dean looked at Samson expectantly.

Oh, thank God. His friend was done. "I never knew there was so much variation in baby poops," Samson managed to say. Miley babbled, as if to agree, and plopped down like her legs had gone suddenly boneless. Samson grasped her around her waist and secured her. A few visits with his goddaughter, and he was feeling ten times more at ease with her size. Infants were like a ball of cheeks and rolls held together with drool, but they were surprisingly sturdy.

Dean paused with his water glass halfway to his mouth. "Oh no. I did it again, didn't I? I overdadded."

Yes. "Not at all."

"You're being too nice to me. Harris would have stopped me the second I started talking about diapers."

"No, I don't—" Samson rethought that. "Yeah, he would have. To be fair, I probably should have."

They'd met up at a popular Irish pub that was owned by a well-known retired basketball player. It had been a trek to get here, but Samson was glad they'd come. It was busy, and they were relatively anonymous.

More people than usual had started recognizing him since the Matchmaker/Crush collaboration had hit the digital airwaves. He'd stayed off the internet and out of the comments. He didn't want to really know what people were reminiscing about him or what the campaign had stirred up.

The Lima Curse.

He'd known, going into this gig, people would talk about his retirement. So long as he wasn't slapped in the face with it, he was fine. If he could go the rest of his life without hearing about the Curse, he'd be better.

"Do you want me to take Miley back?" Dean wiped his hands on his napkin.

Samson wrapped his arms around the child protectively.

So long as she was happy, holding a baby was rather soothing. Like having a therapy animal. "No. Finish your burger."

The new dad took another bite, but Samson noticed that he kept an anxious eye on his daughter. "Have you asked Harris why he ribs you so much about Miley?"

"He says I'm going overboard." And then, surprising Samson, Dean continued, "I think he's right."

"Do you?"

Dean took another bite of his grilled portabella burger. His friend wasn't eating at a breakneck pace today, Samson was happy to notice. "I'm working with Josie to dial it back. Miley's my world, but I don't want our marriage to get lost in being parents. Josie's mom's gonna come stay in our guesthouse for a while. Give me a break." Dean's face brightened. "So when my best friend's in town, I can actually see him without toting a diaper bag along."

Samson smiled, and nodded, relieved. "All that sounds good. Bonus: you'll get Harris off your back for a while."

"Godsend. Can you imagine growing up with that ass—" Dean stopped, gestured, and waited until Samson cupped his palms over the oblivious baby's ears. "Asshole," he whispered.

Samson smoothed Miley's fuzzy hair. "I don't have to imagine it. I basically grew up with both of you."

"So you did." A half-reminiscing, half-regretful smile played over Dean's face. "I honestly don't know how you did it, man, retiring so early. After I retired, I felt . . . I don't know if I can describe it."

Samson could describe it. "Aimless and trapped?"

Dean snapped his fingers. "Yes! Exactly that. I didn't know you could feel both those things at once."

Joe had been the one to guide Samson out of his immediate post-retirement funk. *Son, I know what it's like to go from being a part of a pack to being alone.* His uncle had coaxed him out of the house, gone on runs with him, had helped ease him from that regimented life to solitary retirement. "Neither did I, until it happened."

Dean nodded, thoughtful. "Yeah. At least I was somewhat prepared. You got shoved into retirement."

Samson hated the tinge of guilt in Dean's voice. "I'm fine with my decisions. And yeah, it was tough for a time, but I had you and Harris and most importantly, I had Uncle Joe. Not long after, he got sick." Samson shrugged. "I didn't have much time to worry about anything else then."

Dean's gaze was sympathetic. "Big Joe was kind of like your Miley, huh?"

Samson almost jerked back, but then he remembered the baby in his arms. "What do you mean?"

"He gave you a purpose. Distracted you from your own feelings." Dean's expression turned contemplative.

"My uncle wasn't a distraction." His words were sharper than he intended, but he'd be damned if anyone considered his uncle anything but a whole human in his own right, sickness or no.

"I'm sorry, I didn't mean it like that. I meant, you had someone other than yourself and your feelings to think about. It's not a bad thing. People like you and I, we function better when we can focus on a team objective over a solo one." Dean leaned over and pulled out a round blue plastic snack container from his daughter's diaper bag. At the sight of it, Miley bounced in Samson's lap. "Do you want some cereal, angel?" Dean crooned, and opened the container, setting it next to Samson's empty plate. "Check out that pincer grip, will you? She's so advanced. Gonna be a surgeon, this one."

Samson pretended to admire whatever a pincer grip was, but his brain was occupied. When Uncle Joe had gotten sick, he'd sat Samson down on the deck of his home. *Your aunt badgered me into going to the doctor, and it's not good.*

Almost a decade later, he could vividly recall the bolt of fear that had run through him at the news, the trauma of his father's decline far too fresh. It had been Joe who had consoled Samson. Joe who had suggested Samson come live with him and take care of him. At the time, Samson hadn't questioned it, they were each other's closest living relatives, it made sense.

But now, he wondered if it was because Uncle Joe, even in the midst of his own fear and uncertainty, had known what Samson needed even if he didn't.

A lump of quiet grief rose up in his throat. "You're right." He moved his fork out of the baby's range. "I didn't feel so aimless so long as it was me and Uncle Joe against the illness. When he passed away, I guess it was like I was lost all over again."

"I'm glad you got the Matchmaker gig."

"Me too." He could help Annabelle. Be a part of another team.

Dean's voice was gentle and compassionate. "What are you going to do when it's over?"

When he stopped seeing Rhi. When he had no one to help and nothing to show up for. "I don't want to talk about this."

Dean immediately backed off. "I gotcha. Sorry, man."

"Don't be sorry."

Their waitress popped up, and Samson was so relieved at the interruption, his smile might have been larger than it would have otherwise been.

"Gentlemen, how's everything going?"

"Everything's great, thanks," Dean said, but the waitress didn't look at him.

She beamed at Samson. "You're that guy from those Crush ads, aren't you?"

"The Matchmaker ads," he corrected her.

She waved her hand. "Yeah. Your videos are so cute."

Samson picked a piece of cereal off Miley's shirt and placed it on his empty plate. "Thanks."

The waitress's blue eyes slid over him and she placed her hand on the table. "Let me know if you need anything else."

He glanced at Dean, who was waggling his eyebrows like mad while he slowly ate a french fry. "Will do."

When she left, Dean stretched over and snatched the napkin she'd left behind before Samson could hide it. "I remember those days," he said, with nostalgia. "The days women flung their numbers at me, before a baby ruined my figure."

With Miley in his lap, Samson couldn't retrieve the napkin from Dean. "Your figure's fine and if any woman had even looked at you after Josie locked you down, they would have lost at least an eye."

"No joke." Dean grinned, clearly delighted with his wife. He waved the napkin. "Is this happening often?"

"More often than I thought it would."

"You can't go around being a halfway decent guy and holding a criminally cute baby and *not* expect women to throw their numbers slash panties at you." Dean lowered his voice. "My sister tells me stories of the guys out there, man. The bar is, like, set at a negative level for decency."

"I'm learning that. No reason for us to go negative, though."

Dean tossed the number to him. "No lies detected. Have fun with that."

Samson tucked the napkin into his pocket. He'd do with it what he'd done with all the other napkins he'd received over the last couple weeks. He'd toss it, once he was out of her sight.

There was only one woman's number he was interested in right now.

"Well, well, well. Look who it is."

They both froze at the familiar voice. Samson slowly looked up at the man standing next to their table, where the waitress had just been. What the fuck.

"Trevor," Dean said, and his grim tone echoed Samson's lack of desire to see this asshole.

Trevor Sanders smiled at both of them. Tall and still fit in spite of his retirement a few years ago, the Brewers' former quarterback had the kind of blond good looks the media loved.

Samson was definitely not in love with him. "How did you find us here?" He'd dodged two more calls from Trevor, had considered blocking the number, but figured it was better to know what the snake was up to.

What the fuck was up with this trend of people somehow knowing where he was and showing up? It was one thing when Rhi did it, she wasn't his longtime nemesis. Was this an L.A. thing?

Trevor's toothy grin disappeared. "Dean posted a photo. It was tagged."

Samson scowled at his friend. "Dean has clearly forgotten that he could have stalkers out there, and he will no longer be telling the world where he is."

"My social's private," Dean protested. "But not private enough, I guess."

"Look, guys, I get it." Trevor pulled a chair over and sat down without asking them, which was a very Trevor thing to do. He paused to smile at Miley. "Cute baby, Dean. I love all the photos you post of her."

Dean pulled a wet wipe out from somewhere. He carefully cleaned his hands, sanitized them with a squirt bottle, and grudgingly nodded. He wouldn't turn down a compliment to his baby. "Thanks. And thanks for the baby present. We really love that stroller."

"I'm glad. It was my girlfriend's—well, ex-girlfriend's—favorite stroller for our kid."

Samson passed Miley to her dad and immediately wished he had her back. Therapy baby indeed. "I have nothing to say to you, Trevor."

Trevor's sigh was long and low. "Listen. I know you hate me, Samson. I even get why. But please, can I have like ten minutes of your time?"

Samson gritted his teeth.

Dean placed Miley carefully in her carrier. "Harris said you were starting an organization. That true?"

"It is," Trevor responded.

Dean buckled his daughter in, then pinned Trevor with a stern look. "You going to ask Samson to help?"

What was Dean talking about?

"I am."

Dean pursed his lips. "He doesn't owe you—"

"It's okay, Dean." Samson didn't want Dean in the middle of this feud. He could handle Trevor. "You need to get home, right?"

Dean glanced back and forth between them. Miley was due for a nap soon, but Samson knew his friend wouldn't leave if he thought Samson needed him. "I guess . . ."

"Go on. Trevor and I will have a quick chat, and then we don't ever have to talk again." He kept his tone pleasant, though his stomach was coiled into a knot.

Trevor was smart, confronting him in a public place like this. Samson wouldn't, couldn't, make a scene. Too many people knew who they both were.

The last thing he wanted was another wave of headlines pitting him and Trevor against each other.

"He's loyal to you, all right," Trevor said, after Dean gathered up his baby and left, with another warning glare for Trevor.

"That's what friends and teammates are. Loyal."

Trevor flinched, probably because he'd said almost that sentence, verbatim, to a journalist the day Samson had walked mid-game, but he stayed seated. "Like I said, you have every right to hate me. But this isn't about me. It's about something bigger than both of us."

"You always were dramatic."

Trevor was silent for a beat. "I don't know how much Harris has told you, but I'm starting a nonprofit. For retired players who are showing signs of CTE but can't access the NFL settlement, either because they were denied, or because their symptoms don't fit in the covered class." When Samson stared at him blankly, Trevor continued. "The settlement only covers a narrow window of neurological, degenerative diseases like ALS or Parkinson's. There are players out there with anger, depression, suicidal ideation. They have to cobble together their own emotional and financial resources. I want to create a central place they can go to for assistance."

"You have got to be kidding me."

"What?"

"*You're* going to be the face of a CTE organization?"

"No, actually. I was hoping you would be."

Samson's laugh was short. "Are you serious?"

"We're serious. I'm serious."

"There are a lot of players, current and former, who are more famous than me," he said flatly.

"Your career aside, you're a Lima." Trevor spread his hands out. "The son and nephew of two beloved players. Your father's case made that settlement possible. The irony is, he wouldn't even be eligible for compensation from it if he was still alive. Both because he retired before the cut-off, and because he didn't have the right diagnosis. Your uncle—"

"My uncle's results are not back yet," Samson snapped. With every word Trevor was saying the throbbing at the base of his skull grew. He didn't want to think about where his uncle's brain was, or who was poring over it, or when the results would come. Bad enough when it had been his father, though he'd prayed for an explanation then.

He knew exactly what had caused his uncle's decline, he didn't need the confirmation.

Trevor dipped his head, acknowledging what he must have realized was a sensitive subject. "You quit the game," he continued, in an even softer tone. "At the height of your career, loudly and publicly, because you disagreed with how head injuries were being managed. You were one of the first to take a stand for yourself and other players. In the history of activism for this condition, you are an icon."

Samson linked his hands together under the tablecloth. Another person might say they were shaking, but he was a big, strong man. Big strong men's hands didn't shake.

He'd played football for four years after his dad died. Four years of being gaslit by his employers about how the scientists who had studied his father's brain matter didn't know what they were talking about, and that Aleki had been a special, unusual case.

On the day Samson had retired, when he'd knelt next to Dean, he hadn't been thinking about activism. He'd been thinking about his dad. And how, if people had stopped Aleki from going out in the field with concussions, maybe he wouldn't have suffered as much as he had in his final years.

"You're forgetting part of that story," Samson said, his voice hoarse. "When I left the field, you declared me a coward and a traitor." A *curse.*

"I did." Trevor's shoulders hunched forward. "I absolutely did. I'm so sorry. It was a different—"

"I don't want your excuses. I'm out here to help out a family friend, that's all. It has nothing to do with CTE or the NFL or football."

Trevor's brow furrowed. "Man, haven't you been looking at how the sports world is covering this? Whether you want to or not, your whole past, your father, your uncle, it's all getting rehashed. I'm not the only one calling you an icon."

Samson's shoulders tightened, like there was a target painted on his back. "I stopped caring what that world thought of me a long time ago." He dropped a wad of cash on the table, not looking to sort out how much was there, just eager to get gone. The waitress could have a big tip.

"Samson . . . I retired because I started having depressive episodes."

Samson froze. Trevor's voice lowered. "It was bad. I couldn't play, I couldn't get out of bed. After I quit, it got worse. I had other mood changes. Paranoia, anger. I'd pick fights with my girlfriend, stupid fights, sometimes over the same damn thing again and again. She finally left me one day when I accused her of stealing my phone. I couldn't stop yelling at her." Trevor's jaw worked. "She took our son. I only get to see him in supervised settings now. I actually don't mind that. I'd never hurt him, but I don't know."

"I'm sorry." An inadequate bouquet of words, but they were all he had.

Trevor swallowed, his Adam's apple bobbing. "I have help. There are guys out there who are way worse off than I am. I want to help them. I've assembled a good team. Please, will you meet with the whole group? Then decide."

Slowly, Samson shook his head. Ice had seeped through his veins, leaving him cold. He couldn't think about Trevor's organization or his problems. He couldn't think about Trevor's son. "I don't want to work for you. When this gig with Matchmaker is over, I'm going to—" He stopped. He was going to . . . what?

"You could save lives, Samson."

Samson wanted to laugh at that, but not because it was funny. He hadn't been able to save his own father, or a man he considered a father. What good could he do for anyone else? "Goodbye. Good luck."

He was sweating by the time he got outside, and he ripped off his light jacket, though there was a nip in the air. He pulled out his phone to call for a ride, and that was when he saw the text from Rhi.

Can I come see you?

He didn't know what she wanted—they didn't have anything scheduled today—but it didn't matter. Could she come see him? What a ridiculous question. The answer would always be yes, but especially right now.

He typed out his reply. **I'll be at my place in an hour.** He gave the address and hit send. Her response was immediate. **See you then.**

He knew he needed to sort out the complex tangle of emotions in his brain, but not now. Not yet.

For now, he wanted Rhi.

Chapter Fifteen

Rhiannon's frenzied panic had cooled a little on the drive from Santa Barbara to L.A., especially after Samson had finally—finally!—texted her back, but not enough for her to cancel seeing him. The edge of fear and anger was still there when she pulled up in front of Samson's high-rise condo.

She avoided looking at herself in the mirrors in the elevator on the way up. She didn't want to think about what she looked like. Probably a mess, since she'd intended to lounge the day and weekend away and not see anyone but Katrina.

Her knuckles barely hit Samson's door before he opened it. Angels didn't sing, but a halo of light surrounded him.

Or he's backlit by the sun, calm down.

He opened the door all the way, and his biceps looked so big and strong and sweet. She wanted to bite them and lay her head against them. "Hey. Good to see you. Come on in."

She stepped inside and glanced around. Curiosity pierced through her other emotions, though it was misplaced. There was nothing personal in this open-concept corporate-furnished condo. It was all black leather and metal.

"Do you want me to take your sweatshirt?"

She rubbed her hands over her arms, letting the worn material hug her closer. "No."

He didn't insist, only gestured at the living room. "Have a seat. Wine?"

"No, I'm fine."

"Water?"

She hadn't realized it until now, but her throat was parched. "Yes. Please."

He went to the kitchen and opened the fridge door, grabbing a bottle of water. Restless, she walked to the couch, but didn't sit down. There were three framed photos on the side table, the only personal effects in the entire room, as far as she could tell. That curiosity reared its head again, and she welcomed the diversion from her darker emotions.

One photo was of Samson crouched next to a wheelchair with who she assumed was his uncle Joe, with the ocean in the background. The older man looked tired and fragile, but happy. His smile was identical to Samson's, down to the tiny dimple.

She didn't want to prick his grief by asking about his late uncle. She ran her finger over the photo of Samson and a handsome young couple. Samson held a baby in his arms. The same baby from his Matchmaker profile, the one that had made everyone in the ballroom at CREATE sigh. "This is your goddaughter, right?"

"Yes. My best friend, Dean, and his wife, Josie. Their daughter, Miley." He walked out from around the granite island and handed her a glass of water. She drank it in a few gulps and handed it back to him. "Thirsty, huh?"

Rage took a lot out of a person. Rhiannon ignored him and touched the last frame. A young Samson, maybe at twelve or thirteen, smiled out at her from a football field.

She could see where he got his size and looks from now. A couple stood behind him, both beaming. The big man's hand was on Samson's shoulder, his pride evident. The woman was almost as tall as her husband, statuesque and gorgeous, her hip-length hair in a braid, love radiating off her. Sweet and loyal and kind. This was the type of woman who inspired that kind of description.

"Those are my parents," he said, and there was an odd tone in his voice. Banked grief and something else.

"I'm sorry. They look lovely."

"It's been a while. My dad died right after I was drafted to the Brewers. My mom lasted a couple months after him."

He'd lost them almost at once? She inched closer to him. "That's tragic. I didn't realize your mother died so quick after him."

"They said it was a heart attack. She was a lawyer, worked a lot. She'd been under a heavy stress load for years." He grimaced. "But I really think it was losing my dad that did it."

"My dad died when I was young. I was too small to really know him, but I had my mom." She might drive Rhiannon crazy, but she loved Sonya.

"What's your mom like?"

"Guilt trippy, but she loves and supports me in her way. She lives in Chicago, but travels a lot."

"Do you wish she lived closer?"

Rhiannon grimaced. "I should. But no. We're both a little too power hungry to live in the same house."

"You both like to be head of the household?"

"Basically."

"One brother, right?"

Rhiannon nodded. "Younger, yes."

"I always wished I had siblings."

"I don't know how I would have dealt with being an only child."

"My parents made sure I was never too lonely."

"You look like them. Your father, especially."

"I know." He picked up the photo and looked down at it. That was when she noted the air of preoccupied sadness clinging to him. Had it been there since she'd walked in? Or was it in response to this conversation?

She stuffed her feelings down for a minute and moved close enough to study the picture with him. "Had you just won some important game?" she asked.

He nodded, still staring at the photo. His finger traced his mother's face. "Yeah. My dad was really proud I was following in the family footsteps. This was before the Switch."

"The Switch?"

He blinked at her, and shook his head. "Sorry. That was what my mom called it. A nice euphemism." His laugh was hard and unexpected.

She hesitated. This was veering fast into personal territory, and she wasn't sure how personal she should get with this man, when they'd already blurred so many lines, but . . . "A euphemism for what?"

His lips flattened into a tight line, and she wondered if he would answer her, but he finally did. "Right before I started college, my dad started having issues."

"What kind of issues?"

"He'd get angry. Depressed. At first, it wasn't too bad. My mom and I chalked it up to him not having enough to do. She tried to get him involved in activities, hobbies. Ballroom dancing with her, golf. Whatever might get him out of the house. Every month, it was like he got worse, the episodes getting longer. We took him to different doctors, neurologists, psychiatrists."

Ah. She didn't watch sports, but she heard what was going on in the news. "CTE."

"Yeah. He played pro for seventeen years. He'd had God knows how many concussions, let alone subconcussive hits." Samson shoved his hands in the back pockets of his jeans. "The episodes escalated. He stopped coming to my college games. Barely paid attention when I was drafted. He holed up in the house, drank, gambled, raged. My mom made excuses. I don't think he ever laid hands on her, but I was always scared for her. Not that I expected her to leave him. I couldn't leave him, no matter how angry my face made him, toward the end." He cast her a quiet, anguished look, and Rhiannon's heart clenched.

Samson's affable charm was such a huge part of his personality it was startling to see something else in its place. She placed her palm on his back, wishing she could absorb some of his pain for him.

It's dangerous to care this much.

Nah. She'd be concerned about what kind of a person she was, if she could coolly turn the subject to business right now. Bluster over how strong and tough she was aside, she'd never been someone who walked away from another's pain.

Especially someone she kind of, well, liked.

"Do you know what it's like, to love someone who hurts you? Because you know they can't help how they act?"

Her fingers spasmed. "I know how it feels to love someone who turns out to be someone other than who you think they are. It's not quite the same, though."

The corners of his lips turned down. "Not quite."

"I'm guessing it was difficult to get him help?"

"We tried. The league denied us more disability. Said their doctors had found no definitive link between playing football and long-term neurological issues." His smile was bitter. "We had independent research proving otherwise. In the end, he died as we were filing an appeal."

It took a second to connect the dots and the timeline. "He passed away . . . while you were playing pro? And you knew that his behavior was linked to concussive injuries?" That must have been a conflict for Samson.

"You're wondering why I didn't quit immediately?"

"No, not at all."

"You should. I wondered." He lifted a shoulder. "Even after I got the diagnosis, I tried to convince myself I was wrong, that my dad was a unique case. Deep down, I knew

I was fooling myself. I only needed something to push me into realizing it."

Realization dawned. "Your friend. The one you walked for."

"Dean." He put the frame down and gestured at the other photo, the one of him and his goddaughter. "When the reporters asked why I was retiring, I said I feared players' head injuries weren't being managed properly. The press went nuts, especially since my dad's death was so fresh. There were already rumblings of the class action coming." His words were halting. "I know the league was my employer, not my friend. But they spend all this time—the coaches, the media, my teammates—they tell you you're part of a family. And it was like my family turned on me. My coach said I walked 'cause I couldn't handle the pressure. Our quarterback said I was a traitor, that I'd left the team when they really needed me. I went from the Charm to the Curse." He snapped his fingers. "Like that."

"I'm sorry." She wondered if anyone had seen much of this brooding, dark side of Samson Lima. Words didn't feel like enough, so she wrapped her arms around his waist. "That must have been painful."

He held stiff for a minute, then relaxed, putting his arms around her, engulfing her in his body heat. "I loved the game. I loved my family more."

She lifted her chin so she could look up at him. She opened her mouth to say something. What, she wasn't sure. Something smart and clever and kind. But the next thing she knew, his lips were on hers.

His hands slid over her back, to her butt, and rested there for a second. She pressed tighter against him, taking the kiss deeper. The energy shift between them was seamless, from comforting and pained to needy and lustful. The adrenaline that had fueled her flight to his place returned in a vengeance, channeled into lust. He pulled away to speak. "I'm sorry, I don't know what I was thinking."

"We don't have to think." Better to think later. Putting her brain on a small time-out was necessary right now.

Let the anger and fear transform into mutual greed.

"I like that plan," he muttered.

Her clothes were easy to remove. She only had to slide her yoga pants down her legs and yank off her hoodie and shirt. One of the plus sides of athleisure.

When she was naked, he surveyed her. She hadn't worn a bra today, and her nipples peaked when he ran his gaze over them. His big hands reached up to cup her breasts and they both shuddered.

He was far too overdressed. She attacked the button on his jeans, struggling with the stiff denim. He tried to help, but his hands were more in the way than anything else. "You do your shirt," she ordered, trying to concentrate.

She had to stop when his T-shirt cleared his head. Their hurried interludes in her car hadn't given her enough time to appreciate his body. Not at all. His chest was so wide, the perfect size to curl up on and take a nap or pet or bite or lick . . .

Bottom line, she could do a lot to that chest.

"Bedroom," he said, in a guttural tone, distracting her

from her plans to world tour his upper torso, and she placed her hand in his, happy to comply. Their foreplay had lasted weeks now. She wanted his body driving inside hers.

They could forget, like they'd forgotten for that night in Cayucos. Forget about who she was and who he was and all of the baggage that made up Rhiannon Hunter and Samson Lima.

He tugged her into the bedroom. The sun was setting outside, but the blinds were pulled in this room, making it dark and cool, the only light spilling in from the living room. She shoved the comforter down and got in the bed while he undressed.

She might actually break her final rule and solicit pics of this dick. Pretty indeed.

Rhiannon tried not to lick her lips for fear it might come across as too lascivious, but her mouth watered when he walked over to the nightstand. He pulled a fresh box of condoms out of the drawer and ripped it open.

He donned the condom, pushing the latex over his curved, thick cock and turned to her. She'd hoped to lick him, play with him, take him in her mouth, but he moved over her so quickly, his body sliding over hers.

"Can this time be quick?" he asked, his voice rough.

This time. This time implied more times, and she squelched the surge of happiness that came with that possibility.

None of that dangerous hope nonsense. Not now, not ever. But she didn't want to explain that to him now, when he was so close, his body heat alone making her ache. He bent his head when she didn't respond immediately and licked her nipple.

She gasped. "Yes. Quick. Do it."

He pushed her leg aside and sank inside her. She groaned and arched, forcing him to speed up to a faster pace. His fingers clenched over her thigh and he moved harder, deeper, shafting her in long, fast strokes.

Delicious.

She slid her hands down over his back, slick with sweat, and grasped his pumping buttocks. He pressed his mouth against her neck and kissed her, his tongue working over her sensitive skin. "Fuck," he moaned.

Rhiannon wound her leg over his hips. "Harder."

He took her request, his body slamming into hers. The coil of passion inside her belly went tighter, but that sliver of a peak remained out of reach.

Until he put some space between them and his fingers went searching between her legs. He rubbed a slow seductive circle around her clit, his delicate fingers at odds with the furious pace of his cock. Again. And again. She broke, the climax washing over her.

He groaned, his body tensed for a long moment as he came. His arms caught his body weight before he could collapse on her.

Fool. Didn't he know?

Of course not, how could he. She pressed down on his shoulders. "Rest on me. I like it."

His breath panted against her neck. "I'm too heavy."

"No such thing." She tugged at him, and he finally complied, relaxing on top of her, shoving her into the expensive mattress.

Ah yes. She felt completely covered and hugged and smushed. She loved it. Like one giant sweatshirt covering her whole body, only this one was made of muscle, not fleece.

She didn't realize she'd made the comment out loud, until he turned his head, a puzzled smile on his soft face. "I'm a hoodie?"

"It's the same feeling, like I'm being hugged," she tried to explain, though she wasn't sure how. She felt loopy and punch-drunk, like a balloon that had had half the air leached out of it. "Never mind. I'm tired."

"Me too." He pressed a kiss against her neck. "Stay here and keep warm." He rolled off her and she admired his back and that stupendous butt as he moved away.

Seriously, that butt could launch a thousand ships.

She lay there for a second or two as he did whatever he needed to do in the bathroom, but relaxing wasn't her style, even if she was in a postcoital glow. She sat up. This room was as impersonal as the rest of the apartment, but there were more signs of Samson here. He was neat, she was happy to note, his open closet showing her his clothes hung up and organized by style and color.

The only mess were his jeans on the floor. She rose from the bed and picked them up, tossing them and his boxers on the armchair. A slip of paper fell out of one of the pockets.

She didn't mean to look at it when she picked it up, but

the phone number, smiley face, and words scrawled on the napkin were impossible to miss. *Janet. Call me.*

Oh.

She held the napkin for a second while the faucet turned on in the bathroom. She didn't know what this feeling was. Disappointment. Jealousy, perhaps. Sadness.

Okay, she knew what the emotions were. This was a cliché, wasn't it? The lover finding another woman's number in her man's pocket.

Only she wasn't his lover, and he wasn't her man. These emotions didn't belong to her.

The reason they were seeing each other was, ostensibly, to prep him to date other women. She was the one who had told him ten million times this was temporary. She had no right to be jealous of Janet, whoever she was. Even if Samson had deemed the woman worthy enough to keep her number.

Rhiannon's fingers tightened over the napkin. Was Janet sweet and loyal and kind?

The faucet shut off in the bathroom and it galvanized her into action. She shoved the napkin back into his jeans and went to the living room. She had her T-shirt and panties and pants on by the time he came to the door. He'd donned his boxers and was scratching his beautiful, perfect, smooth chest. His expression of sleepy satisfaction faded as he took in her fully-dressed appearance. "Are you leaving?"

"I'm sorry, I have to go into the office. Dating emergency," she half joked and put her hoodie on, making sure to zip it all the way up.

He crossed his arms over his chest. "Not a sick cat this time?"

"I do have a cat, for your information. That wasn't a lie." Well, it had been at the time, but she'd made it true.

A frown appeared on his forehead, one she didn't like. His sadness had vanished while they'd had sex. She may not like that he was collecting other women's phone numbers, but that wasn't his issue to deal with. It was hers. She took a step forward. "I really have to go. I'm sorry."

"Don't be sorry." Still, he puffed out his cheeks.

His visible disappointment was so cute, she had to come closer and slip her arms around his waist and press a kiss on his chest. "I'll see you soon. Thanks for everything. This was really great."

He returned her hug. "Thank *you*. Uh, was this why you came over here, or did you need something else?"

Ack. How had she forgotten? She almost slapped her forehead. The man had some kind of magical power over her, addling her brain. "Right. Are you going to talk to Annabelle soon?"

"I told you, she should be home any day now."

She thought for a second, grateful the sex had cleared her head. She couldn't tip Samson and Annabelle off to other buyers if Peter really didn't have any intention of going after Matchmaker. The last thing she wanted to do was bid against herself. "I really need to speak to her, is all. It would be good if we could get together soon. I would love to do a deal that helps both of us out."

If Samson thought it was weird that she'd raced over

here to impress upon him how badly she wanted to speak to his aunt, he didn't say so. "The second she's stateside, I will tell her you want to talk to her. Promise."

His promise shouldn't carry so much weight for her, but it did. She allowed him to walk her to the door. His bare chest and thick thighs called to her, but she tried to ignore them, because she couldn't go curl up in his bed and cuddle.

Janet. Think of Janet.

He bent down to kiss her and she almost swayed into another hot, wet kiss. It was only the knowledge that it would lead to other hot, wet things, all with the undoubtedly lovely Janet's number sitting firmly in his pocket, that gave her the strength to pull away and walk.

She'd reaffirmed Samson would talk to Annabelle without tipping her hand, and gotten sex in the bargain. What more could she ask for?

Rhiannon closed her eyes and rested her head against the mirrored wall of the elevator, trying not to think about the delicious ache in her sex and inner thighs. Probably best to avoid answering that question.

Chapter Sixteen

SAMSON HAD never been much of a coffee drinker, but sleeping had come hard after his uncle's death, and he'd learned to appreciate the glory of caffeine. He'd set up the fancy coffee maker's timer in his loaner apartment the first night.

As was his new habit, he padded out of his bedroom, grabbed his full mug, and took his first sip in front of the giant windows overlooking the downtown skyline, the freeway traffic in the distance already bumper to bumper though it wasn't quite six. He liked this view. Matchmaker had furnished him with a nice little spot, even if it was one he'd never have thought to choose on his own.

The house he'd grown up in Cayucos had been a homey environment with bright splashes of color and comfy furnishings. When he'd become independent, he'd barely paid attention to where he lived, figuring he could have a real home at some shadowy point down the road. And, then, of course, he'd been with Uncle Joe.

Samson frowned out over the buildings. Where would his next place be? He'd sold his own condo years ago and had no interest in returning to Portland anyway. His childhood home in Cayucos was sitting vacant, but it held so many memories. Leaving there after Uncle Joe's death had been both heart wrenching and a relief.

Trapped and aimless.

He shifted. He still had time to think about his next move after this gig was over. He didn't have to come up with it right now.

His day was packed with various Matchmaker-related engagements, including a photo shoot. He needed to get showered and dressed, but he took another sip of coffee, wishing he could inject the caffeine directly into his veins. He'd stayed up all night thinking about Rhiannon and the sex. And the aftermath.

He'd been looking forward to smushing her all night when he'd sauntered out of the bathroom, his body all loose and relaxed, and instead, he'd found her almost out the door. He didn't know what had made her dart out like that. Or really, what had made her come to him in the first place. Surely she hadn't really run over to make sure he did what he'd already said he'd do and contact Belle, right?

He should have pressed her before she left, but he'd been too thrown by the sex. And his own internal upheaval.

He never talked about his parents. The only people in the world he'd confided in had been Uncle Joe, Aunt Belle, and Dean and Harris. Though he knew Rhi wouldn't tell anyone, he was shaken by how easily the details of his life had spilled out of his lips.

At first, he'd stayed silent because his father wouldn't have wanted too much about his final years made public. Everyone knew about the depression, yes, and some of Aleki's erratic behavior. The anger, though, he and his mother had kept under wraps, had shielded the world from. Flying into uncontrollable rages was the thing his father would have found most horrifying about his personality change. Aleki had been gentle. He'd never so much as raised his voice before the Switch.

Samson's hand shook as he took another sip of coffee. He was a fucking thirty-six-year-old man, bigger than average, and the mere memory of his father's rage made him shake like a boy. How did a person reconcile the man they'd loved with a man who was controlled by a brain that had been fundamentally altered by hit after hit? How did you reconcile adoration and fear? Fear for his dad, his mom, himself.

How do you think Trevor's son's feeling?

He had to put his mug down, lest he spill it. He may have initially hidden his history for his father's sake, but it was also simply too difficult for him to think about, let alone share with another human.

He'd go shower, and get dressed, and try to forget all these feelings Trevor and Rhi had stirred up. He couldn't handle them, not right now.

His phone rang, and he welcomed the interruption to his trip down memory lane. He grabbed it, relief coursing through him when he saw who was calling. "Aunt Belle."

"Hello, Samson."

He frowned. Aunt Belle sounded like a timid, hesitant

version of herself. "Hey there. I was talking about you with someone yesterday. Are you stateside again?"

"I am. I got in last night."

"Are you up north?" Belle's main estate was a lovely home near San Francisco, surrounded by tall redwoods.

"Yes." She paused, then spoke in a rush. "If you're mad at me, can you get it all out?"

"Mad at you?" Samson sat down on his couch. "Why on earth would I be mad at you?"

"Because I left everyone in the lurch." His aunt's tone grew thick. "I called William first, and he told me . . . well, it doesn't matter what he told me."

Samson's frown deepened. It wasn't William's place to chide his boss. Jennifer may have been the former CEO, but Annabelle controlled the company now. "You didn't leave me in the lurch."

"Well. I suppose I should have thought before I got overwhelmed and ran away, especially when the company isn't having its best year. I was in fairly constant contact with Tina, but not as much as I should have been. Not as much as Jennifer would have been."

"I think everything ran fine even with you gone for a few weeks," Samson said soothingly. "I didn't notice any hiccups."

"I saw you changed the campaign. That was smart, after that mess of a date."

The amusement in Aunt Belle's voice was a relief. "I guess match percentages can't promise perfect dates."

"They can't, but I will defend my test. I accessed your

account and you didn't have the highest match percentage with sweet Rachel."

Samson shook his head. Joe had once privately told him Belle had made him take the damn test, in hard copy, before agreeing to go on a first date with him. What their match percentage had been, Samson didn't know. As far as Samson was concerned, the infamous test was nothing more than a personality questionnaire.

"I found another girl in your matches who would work so much better. I asked Tina to set up a date with her for you this week."

Samson leaned forward and placed his arms on his knees. "Uh, I still have one more filming session with Rhi." They hadn't talked about when that meeting would be scheduled yet. "And my schedule is pretty tight this week. Podcasts, some other interviews, a photo shoot. It's not all in the city, so I'm going to have to travel."

"You can do the last session with Rhiannon later, and we can make some room in your schedule for another date. I don't want you to miss this woman. So pretty and such a high percentage match, dear."

Samson could tell she wasn't going to budge on this. What did it hurt, to go film a fake date with another woman? Rhi wouldn't care.

You wished she cared.

He grimaced. "Sure. Did you watch the videos with Rhi?"

"I did. And I know you and the company didn't need my blessing, but Tina and I talked about the change in the campaign, and I was on board." There was a defensive lilt to those words.

William must have really made her feel guilty for going off the grid for a while. "Teaming up with Crush wasn't so much a change as it was a detour. The campaign that you came up with will go on after." He emphasized the fact that she had come up with the idea to put him on the site. Aunt Belle wasn't a bad businesswoman. She was just different.

Aunt Belle's voice warmed. "I like the idea of working with our competitor for mutual gain. The world has become far too cutthroat. Not to mention, that Rhiannon girl is lovely."

"Rhi's great." He thought about what Rhi had confessed about her fear. "Have you heard anything about her?"

"Oh, no. Tina says she's a good person, and that's all I need to know."

Phew. "You know, she's actually the reason I left you a message. She wants to meet you."

"Oh. Why?"

"She wants to talk to you about buying Matchmaker." When the silence stretched, he rushed to fill it. "Of course, it's talk. It doesn't mean you have to sell."

Her voice was very small. "William said he has at least three buyers interested in the business as well. He recommended I consider selling if I wasn't interested in running the company like it deserves."

Fresh annoyance struck Samson. "Well, William has no say in that. It's your company."

"He's not wrong, though. I understand Jennifer was far more hands-on than I ever could be. No doubt William misses her. Of course the sharks have been circling since she passed."

Samson hated hearing his aunt so sad. "You've had a hard year, losing Jennifer and then Joe. You don't have to decide this right away."

"Oh, trust me, my instinct would be to procrastinate on this forever. But people's jobs are on the line, if the company continues to do poorly. An ad campaign is nice, and William says we've seen a boost in sign-ups and traffic since we started this—especially since you released those videos with Rhiannon—but that's a temporary fix. Jennifer wouldn't have dillydallied if she'd ever considered selling. She would have ripped the Band-Aid off immediately. Or at least, met with the buyers to see what they might offer. I could talk to them."

"I don't think that would hurt. You don't have to commit to anything."

"I don't, do I?" She paused. "Are you free next weekend?"

"Yes. You want to meet them that soon?"

"Like I said, Jennifer didn't dillydally."

"You don't have to be Jennifer, Aunt Belle."

"I want to do right by the employees. I'd like you there if I meet with a potential buyer. You do have some stake in this, after all."

A very small stake. Against Uncle Joe's wishes, Aunt Belle had transferred her partner 5 percent of the company. Samson had inherited that when his uncle died.

Should he disclose his and Rhi's personal relationship? Only he didn't know what way that might sway Annabelle, and he didn't want Rhi to not get a fair shake. He'd simply recuse himself from advising her on Rhi's offer. "Okay."

"I have to think about how I'll do this, what I feel most comfortable with. You know I don't much like conventional meetings and lunches and so on with people."

"I know." Before his dad had gotten sick, it hadn't been uncommon for Aunt Belle to ring their doorbell at midnight for an impromptu tea, or come and stay for a couple of weeks because she was craving domestic life.

Like business, Annabelle socialized according to her mood. Or horoscope. He had no idea how she'd handle meeting with potential buyers. "Tell me what you need from me. I'll be there, wherever there is."

"Don't say anything to Rhiannon for now. I have to consider what I'm doing."

He didn't love that. If Rhi really had come over last night just to make sure he spoke with Annabelle, this was clearly a big deal for her.

He wondered why she hadn't gone to William now, actually, if the other buyers had felt free to do so. Had she felt that the CEO would have heard shit talk about her? "I won't say anything, but it's already Friday, so if you want to do something next weekend . . ."

"Yes, of course. I'll speak with Tina right now. Goodbye, dear, and don't forget that we'll have to schedule a date for you during the week too."

He hung up and grabbed his now cold coffee. It tasted

like ashes in his mouth, and he knew that wasn't because it was cold.

He didn't want to go on another date with another woman from Matchmaker. He wanted to see Rhi. In bed, in her car, on a rooftop. She was his Green Eggs and Ham, he'd take her anywhere.

He really did need to get up and shower now, but instead, he killed some time scrolling through the news headlines. Finally, his fingers tapped their way over to what he really wanted to do and opened his messages with Rhi.

He wouldn't tell her Annabelle was going to meet with her. But he could calm some of her anxiety. Also, he'd slept with her yesterday, and temporary or casual or whatever, he didn't feel comfortable not texting her today.

Spoke with Annabelle, and she's thinking about it. No promises or guarantees yet. Don't worry, she's only heard good things about you.

He stared at that. There. That was practical and business-like and he didn't have to say anything more. Nothing that would betray Annabelle. Nothing that was too personal, nothing about the mind-blowing sex they'd had, nothing about how his sheets still smelled like her, and nothing about how he'd pressed his pillow against his nose last night to capture the scent of her body.

That would all be too much.

He hit send and put the phone down. Then he snatched it back up when it dinged immediately.

Thank you.

He swept his thumb over the words. Also stilted and formal. Colleagues. Not lovers.

He scowled. Scratched his belly. Finally, he typed, unable to help himself.

Yesterday was amazing. Let me know when you want to meet up again.

There. She could take that however she wanted. *Meet up* could mean sex, or it could mean their final, contractually obligated videotaped thing.

Business or pleasure. Her choice.

Of course, when his phone remained silent—at least when it came to texts from her—for the rest of the weekend, he realized he'd played himself.

Because she could easily choose neither.

Chapter Seventeen

Rhiannon stayed in L.A. for the weekend rather than traveling back up to Katrina's home. Partially because she wanted to bury herself in work and partially because she was still feeling low-key ashamed for her meltdown in front of her best friend, though she knew Katrina would never judge her.

She didn't want to dissect her feelings about Matchmaker or Samson or Peter. She wanted to *work*.

An impossible task. She tried hiding her phone so she wouldn't check every two minutes for updates from Samson. When she did cave and grab it, she found herself staring at Samson's last text to her like an infatuated teenager.

Yesterday was amazing. Let me know when you want to meet up again.

What the fuck did that *mean*? Meet for what? Did the fact that he'd used a period convey something extra serious? Serious as in business serious or serious as in personal serious? Why was there no flirty emoji? Had he texted the mysterious Janet? Had he used a period and a flirty emoji in his text to her?

Gah.

Monday morning brought with it a host of issues to deal with, and given that they were on the West Coast, Rhiannon started her day playing catch-up with New York. There was a reason Peter had moved Swype to Manhattan and it wasn't only because, as Katrina had hypothesized, his soul was too dark for the California sunlight.

So, yeah, she had a ton of shit to do, and she ought to be obsessing over whether Peter was slithering in to take over Matchmaker while she waited around for Annabelle. But here she was analyzing Samson's lack of flirty emojis to death.

A knock came on her office door and she dropped the phone on her desk in a clatter. Hopefully, she didn't look as guilty as she felt. "Yes?"

Lakshmi stuck her head in. "Um, can you come out here for a second? Something was delivered for you."

Rhiannon didn't like that odd, suppressed glee in her friend's voice. She warily got to her feet. "Is it April Fool's?"

"No. Come out here."

Rhiannon followed Lakshmi out of her office. The problem with open layout was that everyone could see everything. About twenty or so of her employees were gathered around, with the others craning their necks from their desks.

The attraction was a giant cake sitting in the middle of the floor. Actually, giant was probably an understatement. At least five feet tall, six layers, it was made of Styrofoam, decorated in purple and pink and white, with fat flowers on top.

The small, youngish blonde standing next to it was familiar, but as unexpected as the cake. She stepped forward. "Ms. Hunter."

Rhiannon slowly accepted her hand. "Tina, right?"

"Yes." Her smile was rueful. "I am so sorry for this disruption. I told Annabelle you wouldn't love it, but I couldn't talk her out of the idea. I figured I would come with, to minimize any trauma."

"I'm fine with some disruptions but . . . wait, did you say trauma?" Rhiannon looked around but her employees were no help. Though at least half of them had their phones out and up. "What is this?"

Tina bit her lower lip. "It's an invitation."

Rhiannon took a step closer to the cake. She leaned forward to read what was on top. "An invitation to—"

She staggered back when the cake exploded. "Surprise," shouted the well-built man in tight leather pants who now stood in place of the cake. He tossed something in Rhiannon's direction, and she recoiled at the puff of glitter.

"What the fuck?" she yelped.

The man cleared his throat and unfurled a piece of paper. "Hear ye, hear ye. Rhiannon Hunter, you have been invited to the home of Annabelle Kostas to take part in a corporate extravaganza. You have a week to prepare your presentation and pitch for you know what. Please me, and perhaps you shall be pleased. Signed, Annabelle Kostas." The man rolled up the paper and presented it, with a smaller cake, an edible replica of the giant fake cake. "You can eat this one," he said with a wink.

When no one moved, Lakshmi accepted the offerings. "Um, thank you."

"God, I'm so sorry." Tina wrung her hands.

"I'm not eating a cake that was closed up with a sweaty man for God knows how long," Rhi heard someone murmur as the guy clambered out of his cake and started wheeling it away.

"Fuck, it's cake. I'll eat it," another employee said.

Lakshmi looked around. "Lin, would you like to take this, um, man cake to the break room. And everyone get back to work."

There was good-natured grumbling as the crowd dispersed, one of the employees snagging the cake from Lakshmi. Rhi turned slowly to Tina and enunciated each word. "I have glitter in my hair."

Tina grimaced. "Uh, yes. Would you like me to . . ."

"Help me remove the *herpes of crafts* from my *hair*?" Rhiannon nodded. Glitter tumbled to the carpet.

Lakshmi handed her the note and brushed at Rhiannon's curls. "At least it's your favorite color," she remarked.

True. Unfortunately, she wore a black sweatshirt today, which meant the pink glitter was showing up really well. "I don't like any color glitter."

"Again, I am so sorry," Tina said. She timidly dusted at Rhiannon's shoulder. "Annabelle is . . . eccentric."

Rhiannon glanced around to make sure no one was listening. She trusted all her employees, but no need to get anyone's hopes up if nothing would come of this. "What that stripper was saying . . ."

"Not a stripper," Tina said hastily. "I nixed that idea."

"What is Kostas's deal?" Lakshmi wondered out loud. "Is she nuts?"

Tina drew herself up to her full height, and haughty arrogance replaced her contrition. "My employer is not *nuts*. She's a woman who has a whimsical, fun sense of humor. She's not stuffy."

Lakshmi straightened, too, and glowered down at the smaller woman. "You know, there's a pretty broad spectrum between stuffy and a stuffed cake."

Tina's nose twitched, as if she agreed with Lakshmi, but her stubborn chin didn't waver. Which was good. Rhiannon respected that, and she bet Lakshmi did too. Lakshmi might argue with her in private, but she'd defend her until the death to a third party.

Rhiannon cleared her throat to bring them back on track. "This party next weekend. The pitch and presentation. Is that for what I think it's for?"

"It's an introductory meeting, yes." Tina nodded at the piece of paper Rhiannon held. "Those are the details. Dinner on Friday evening, pitches on Saturday. It'll take place at Annabelle's beach house in Cayucos. Driving is probably the best way of getting there."

"I'm familiar with the place," Rhiannon murmured, because she couldn't admit she'd stalked the shit out of Annabelle already.

"Great."

"Will there be multiple interested parties?"

Tina nodded. "Four at the moment."

Fuck. She could guess for sure who at least one of those four were. "Can you tell me their names?"

"I'm afraid not."

Rhiannon backed off. No need to badger Annabelle's assistant. "Were they all sent glitter-grams, though?"

Amusement danced in the blonde's eyes, and Rhiannon wondered if she hadn't taken some enjoyment in this unconventional invitation, despite her profuse apologies. "No. They were sent couriers with invitations. The glitter-gram, as you call it, is a token of Annabelle's affection for the recent partnership our companies have enjoyed."

Rhiannon nodded. More glitter rained down. "Lucky me."

Tina's tone turned businesslike. "Can I relay your acceptance for the weekend?"

"Yes. Of course. I'll be there Friday evening."

"Wonderful."

Tina turned to leave and Lakshmi launched into motion. "Let me see you out. We've talked on the phone, but I don't think we've been formally introduced."

Tina nodded, but didn't look entirely ready to forgive Lakshmi for her jab at her employer. "I know who you are. The Lakshmi with no last name."

"Correct." Lakshmi smoothed her loose tie. She wore a slim fit pinstriped three piece suit today. "À la Beyoncé."

Rhiannon left her assistant to handle Tina and escaped to her office. She closed the blinds, placed her hands over her mouth to muffle the noise, and squealed.

Yessssss.

She grabbed up her phone, no longer capable of thinking

about things like periods and a lack of emojis. Samson's low, husky voice came on the line, and Rhiannon's brain went a little soft. "Rhi. Hi. I'm so glad you called."

"I am covered in pink glitter," Rhi blurted out.

There was a beat of silence. "I am not."

She suppressed her laugh.

His voice deepened. "Is this slang for something? Does glitter mean something other than glitter?"

"No, actual glitter. Your aunt. Your aunt is the reason I'm covered in pink glitter."

A longer pause. "Uh."

Rhi quickly brought him up to speed.

"Ahhh," Samson drawled. "Aunt Belle does love sending ridiculous invitations. It was singing telegrams for her sixtieth birthday, I believe. To my locker room."

"I bet your teammates got a kick out of that."

"You have no idea. I'm glad Tina was there to clarify, at least."

"Did you have an idea she was planning this?"

"She asked if I was free next weekend, but other than that, no. If I'd known what she was planning, I might have given you a heads-up. Or at least talked her down from the glitter."

Samson would be there. She suppressed the thrill of excitement. Business. This was business. "Do you know who the other guests will be?" Even if Tina couldn't tell her, maybe Samson would.

Manipulative.

Yeah, this was veering into conflict-of-interest territory.

Samson's first loyalty was to his aunt and the company he had a stake in, and she didn't want to force him to inadvertently betray the woman. She almost retracted her question, but he spoke first.

"I don't, I'm sorry. She said there were three others who were interested in buying the company, but I don't know the details."

The others, one of whom may be Peter. She opened her mouth, and the toxic bitter words were there in the back of her throat. Words like *evil* and *harassment*. But she bit them back.

The best revenge is success. Even if Peter was there, she'd kick his ass. She didn't need Samson's assistance.

She picked at some glitter on her hoodie. "Cool. Anyway, I'm busy, so I'll go. Gotta work on my pitch. I wanted to thank you for talking to Annabelle."

"My pleasure."

She shivered, hating how beautifully he said that word. *Pleasure.* She wondered if he'd invite her over again, for more sex. She didn't have any time between now and Friday, but she wanted him to invite her anyway.

"I'll see you next weekend then. I don't think I'm going to get a glitter-gram with my invite. I guess that's a good thing."

She grinned. "It's a very good thing."

"Put together a great pitch, Rhi."

She bared her teeth. "It'll be the best pitch."

She could tell he was smiling. "I don't doubt it. We should drive up together."

Like Rhiannon would ever be able to get into a vehicle with him and not think about sex, after all that "walking her to her car." Please. "I don't know when I'm leaving yet."

"Ah. Right. Text me if you have any questions about your pitch. Or we could meet up—"

There was the invite she'd craved but couldn't take. She shook her head, though he couldn't see. "I'll be swamped trying to juggle everything and get this pitch done."

"Got it."

Was it her imagination, or did he sound as disappointed as she felt? Her hand clenched over the phone. "Guess we'll move filming our last video to after the weekend."

"Yes. Good."

She swallowed, but her mouth was dry. "Goodbye."

"See you soon, Rhi."

She hung up and looked around her pretty pink office, filled with dainty white furniture. If she acquired Matchmaker, she'd have to move to a bigger office to accommodate her larger staff.

When, not if.

She cracked her neck. Eye on the prize. And the prize was world domination. She had no room in that world for a man.

She texted Katrina a photo of the invitation and a bunch of exclamation points. Her silent partner might not fully understand Rhiannon's obsession, but she'd freak out with her.

The door opened, Lakshmi walked in, and closed it behind her. The two of them looked at each other for a minute, then squealed in unison, neither of them bothering to muffle the noise.

"This is amazing," Lakshmi said, quieter, when they'd gotten that out of their systems.

"Amazing." Rhiannon walked around her desk. "Do I still have glitter on me?"

"Tons, but it's mostly out of your hair." Lakshmi squinted. "Well, like 70 percent out."

"This woman's making me work."

"No shit." Lakshmi's grin was gleeful. "But we're getting that company."

Rhiannon allowed herself another bubble of glee. *This was her chance.* "Clear my weekend and this week. We're going to put together the mother of all proposals."

"Will do." Lakshmi casually indicated the closed door. "I'm gonna marry that girl, by the way."

Rhiannon's eyebrows shot up. "Uh, what?" People got smitten with Lakshmi, not the other way around. "Tina?"

"Mmm. Don't worry about it. I'm in no rush." Lakshmi plopped into a chair. "I won't let that stop me from prioritizing this takeover. Shall I fire up the PowerPoint?"

Rhiannon's phone buzzed. Samson.

One tip I can give you: Aunt Belle hates computer presentations. You'll want to talk.

She touched the phone. This was good, valuable inside information.

The distrustful monster in her brain woke up. *Or he's sabotaging you.*

To what end? She hesitated. "We'll make a decision on the PowerPoint later."

"Got it." Lakshmi started tapping away on her phone.

"Get Suzie in here. Accounting too. This'll take all of us."

Lakshmi stood. "So, like, this eccentric billionaire is inviting a bunch of people to her home to pitch her on taking over her company."

"Yes." Rhiannon nodded. "I got the allusion too."

"She's Willa-Wonkaing you." Lakshmi shook her head, admiration stamped on her face. "Imagine being this rich, having the ability to make other rich people dance to your tune. That's the dream."

"Indeed." Rhiannon pushed her phone aside and opened her computer, fresh resolve flooding her. "In the meantime, let's Charlie Bucket the fuck out of this whole situation."

Chapter Eighteen

Tuesday 10:52 a.m.

    RH: Did you send me something

                                      SL: I did

    RH: A junk food basket? Isn't this for college students studying for finals?

          SL: I thought Cheetos might give you the energy you need to power through this week.

    RH: Those are radioactive. Just because I dress like a teenage boy doesn't mean I eat like one.

          SL: Nothing about you screams teenage boy

Tuesday 11:37 a.m.

    RH: You didn't have to go to the full-on Vegan/Paleo option, you know.

SL: Do you like it more?

RH: . . . yeah. I'm eating the carrot sticks right
now. Thanks, I don't have time for lunch.

SL: 😊 I thought about sending another
glitter-gram to lift your spirits but . . .

RH: I would never forgive you. I never realized how
anti-glitter I was until I had it literally all over my
carpet. A stripper might have actually been better.

SL: You might have still had glitter everywhere,
even if Aunt Belle had sent a stripper.

Tuesday 4:25 p.m.
RH: Are you sure no powerpoint

SL: Positive. 100%. William might like a ppt but
he's not the one making the decision.

RH: William's gonna be there?

SL: Yeah, most likely.
Is that a problem?

RH: No.
What kind of presentation should I do?

SL: How do you feel about interpretive dance?

RH: I can't tell if you're kidding or not.

SL: Kinda kidding.

Aunt Belle responds best to feelings and people, not computers and numbers.

RH: She built this business during the dot-com boom. She doesn't like technology?

SL: Not that kind. Talk to her. Tell her why you want her business and what you'll do with it.

RH: No numbers?

SL: Some numbers. Mostly you.

Tuesday 8:20 p.m.

SL: You still making the powerpoint?

RH: I'll keep it in my back pocket.

SL: I wouldn't lie to you.

RH: I didn't say you would. I like to be prepared for anything.

Wednesday 12:40 p.m.

RH: Thanks for the pizzas. My office is delighted.

SL: How'd you know I sent them?

RH: No one else would.

Wednesday 9 p.m.

SL: Want to get a drink?

RH: Still working.

SL: I miss your face.

RH: Well, you'll see me in two days.

SL: You're not even going to send me
a photo of yourself?

RH: You asking me for nudes? I'm in the office.

SL: Photos of your face. Here's mine.

RH: Boo, you gotta work your angles better.
Selfies from above, not below.

SL: You'll have to teach me how to selfie too I guess

About those nudes . . .

RH: I thought you said you wanted my face.

SL: I'll take anything.

Wednesday 9:22 p.m.

SL: why did you send me a pic of a brown shoe

RH: They're nudes.

SL: Unbelievable.

RH: 😂

Thursday 12:25 p.m.

RH: Mexican today, I see.

SL: I thought your employees might like a taco truck.

RH: Tomorrow I expect you to show up
and cook for everyone, FYI.

SL: I'm not that fancy a cook, but I can make a mean
chili. Unfortunately, I have to work tomorrow.

RH: This is kind of extravagant. Do you have money to throw around like this?

SL: Uh, yeah. Don't worry. I have savings.

You and your staff need to eat.

Consider it a courtesy from a colleague.

What do you want tomorrow? What's your favorite food?

Thursday 3:27 p.m.
RH: Thai.

SL: Got it.

Thursday 11 p.m.
RH: I'm so tired.

SL: You want me to come over?

RH: No. You'll make me more tired.

SL: We could cuddle. Watch tv.

RH: Netflix and chill huh

SL: I will never live that down!!! I
continue to mean it literally.

RH: I'm good, thanks.

SL: I learned how to take a selfie. Look!

📷

RH: Oh. Uh. Normally I am a hater of shirtless mirror
selfies, since you do have a perfectly good front-
facing camera, but this one is nice. Ctrl save.

SL: How about this one?

📷

RH: You lower those sweatpants any more,
we're going to be in dick pic territory.

SL: I'd never.

RH: You could. I would not mind. Yours is pretty.

SL: Pretty??? No.

Really?

RH: Really. I'd delete it after, promise.

SL: 📷

RH: That, my friend. Is a beautiful dick pic. Nicely lit, just a hint of flesh at the base of the shaft, outlined in your sweats. Your hand is positioned artfully, holding the dick. 14/10 for solicited dick pics. Actually, you have a beautiful hand. I could do with some hand pics too.

SL: 😌

RH: It pains me to delete this photo.

SL: Please delete it. I did.

RH: Haha, okay. Now make sure you delete it from the cloud.

SL: The cloud? Oh fuck.

RH: I'll help you with that when I see you tomorrow.

SL: The cloud or the . . . subject of the pic?

RH: Both if you're lucky.

Friday 11:30 a.m.
RH: Thai food AND massages?!

SL: You have a road trip ahead of you. I imagine you're exhausted. You need to be in top shape.

RH: Thank you.

See you soon.

                                        SL: 🙂

Chapter Nineteen

SAMSON FINISHED pumping his gas and waved to the owner of the station, visible through the little window of the building. He knew the guy well, as well as he knew the Mexican American family who owned the tiny unassuming deli annexed to the left of the building. They made the best fish tacos and ceviche he'd had in his life.

He got into his car and buckled his seat belt. It was freeing, being back in his hometown after a while away. He didn't have to keep a constant smile on his face now or be on guard against anyone calling him the Curse. He wasn't a dynasty in Cayucos.

As comfortable as it was, he'd had trouble sleeping last night, after he drove up to the little town. The sound of the waves should have been soothing, but it was almost too familiar. His apartment in L.A. didn't belong to him, but he missed the traffic and noise and bright lights like it was home.

He missed Rhiannon. Like she was home.

That dopamine hit sparked his brain awake when his phone pinged from where it was mounted on his dashboard. He smiled when he checked the text.

On my way and stuck behind a car accident. You should send more pics.

He rubbed his finger over his lip, trying and failing not to smile.

Samson had wondered if he should tell Rhi about the fake Matchmaker date he'd had a couple nights ago. The girl had been lovely and charming, and they'd spent a nice ninety minutes together.

Since all he'd wanted to do for those ninety minutes was check his phone to see if Rhi had texted, he'd ultimately decided against it. That had been business. This was personal. No need to mix the two.

He took a picture of his hand and sent it to Rhi.

The phone rang before she could reply. He frowned at the unfamiliar Boston-based number. "Hello?"

"Samson, this is Barry Kamau from Concussion Research Alliance."

"Dr. Kamau. How are you?" Dr. Kamau was their contact at CRA. He had, in fact, been the one to diagnose CTE in Aleki all those years ago.

Dr. Kamau's gruff voice gentled. "I wanted to call you personally with our findings, son."

Samson placed his wrist on the steering wheel, his lungs growing tight. "You told me it could take up to six months."

"Yes, but we're working on streamlining our process. Is this a good time?"

No. "Yes."

The doctor cleared his throat. "We found an excessive buildup of tau proteins in—"

Samson didn't need to hear any more. He'd already been through this once. He tipped his head back and closed his eyes, waiting until the other man was finished speaking. "Are you going to issue a press release?" was his first question. His uncle had given them permission to publicize the research.

"We are, but it'll be a week or two at least. If you need more time, I can delay. We are more than willing to work with you, in case you'd like to release a statement first."

His first instinct was to decline, but then he thought of Aunt Belle. "Let me speak to my uncle's partner."

"Of course. Please feel free to text or call me over the weekend. I am so sorry for your loss. I know how traumatic this can be."

Samson didn't know how long he sat there, but he stirred when the owner of the gas station came out of the building, his creased brown face concerned. Probably wondering why Samson was loitering at the pump for so long.

He pulled away and drove through the small downtown, past the cookie company storefront and the café and the pizza place Uncle Joe had liked best. With his windows open, the crash of the ocean on sand overpowered the muted sounds of traffic. It was windy today, and still too cold for tourists.

He pulled into his aunt's driveway. Her mansion stood tall and imposing, blocking the view of the beach from the street. Directly to the left, not too far down, was the house Rhi had rented That Night. Around the curve was his childhood home.

Aunt Belle's place was giant, a compound compared to

the relatively cozy three-bedroom home he'd grown up in. Aunt Belle and his parents had bought their lots around the same time, back when beachfront property in this area hadn't cost the equivalent of a small country, but they'd built very different homes.

He nodded to Aunt Belle's housekeeper as he made his way through the house, though the older woman barely glanced at him. Aunt Belle's staff had been thrown into a tizzy in preparation for their impending houseguests. It had been so long since Annabelle had entertained.

Samson hesitated with his hand raised to knock on Aunt Belle's office door. He didn't want to be the bearer of this particular news, especially now, right before she engaged with an important potential business deal.

Before he could decide, the door opened, and he and Tina both reared back. "Oh, hey."

"Hey."

She gave him a distracted smile and spoke over her shoulder as she scooted around him. "I'll get this handled, Belle. The first guests will be arriving soon, you may wish to get ready."

He stepped inside the cluttered office. This room was Aunt Belle's favorite, smaller than one might expect from a woman as wealthy as his aunt, and crammed full of books and papers and pens. Annabelle loved pens.

He closed the door behind him and inhaled the familiar woodsy scent of the room. His aunt looked up from the computer, eyebrows raised above her reading glasses. "Oh Samson. I'm a little busy."

"I'm sure you are." He braced his hands on the back of a chair. "Can you spare me a minute?"

"For you, of course." She clasped her hands in front of her on the cluttered desk. "What's on your mind?"

"I was out, getting gas, and I got a phone call." He resettled his weight, doing his best to look her in the eyes. The words were easy enough to draft in his brain, but when he opened his mouth, nothing came out. *The call was from CRA. They got the results on Uncle Joe back. Do you want to write a statement?*

She studied him as the silence stretched, then sighed. "Oh dear. You found out, didn't you?"

Oh. That sounded like she already knew. "Yes. I did. Did he . . . did he call you first?"

"Well, it was a few weeks ago."

He frowned. A few weeks ago?

"I only had your best interests at heart, sweetheart. That boy is genuinely trying to make up for his mistakes."

Oh, okay. They were clearly talking about different things. He opened his mouth to correct her, but she continued. "I think, given your background and family name, you would be a perfect fit for his new organization."

Realization dawned, and he mentally shelved his uncle's diagnosis. "Aunt Belle, are you saying you gave *Trevor* my number?"

Her hands fluttered. The bells on the sleeves of her turquoise caftan jingled. "Oh. You didn't know. What were you talking about? I mean, never mind, look at the time. I have so much to do."

"Aunt Belle! You know what he did to me."

She paused mid-jingle. "I know. I also know what he's doing. Samson, the job he's offering you is right up your alley."

He gestured to the office, to encompass her own business. "I have a job. Remember?"

"Yes. I gave it to you. But it'll end, and then what will you do?"

What *would* he do?

Her tone softened when he went silent. "Trevor's job offer makes sense for you, Samson. You are good with the public, good at being in the spotlight. You're sympathetic. You could make real change."

None of that was wrong, but his stomach cramped at the thought of working with Trevor ever again, especially on this topic. Especially with Dr. Kamau's words ringing in his ear. "Last time I breathed a word about my concerns about head injuries, I got shunned." Even though his father had died from it, even though he'd already started to fear for his uncle.

That day he'd walked, he'd known what he was throwing away. Had he wanted to go to another team, he'd have been completely blacklisted. Some family.

"Times have changed, my love. People change. Look at Trevor! Why, look at the comments on any of the videos you and Rhiannon release."

"No, thanks." If there was one internet rule he knew well, it was *don't read the comments.* He set his jaw. "Don't meddle like this again, Aunt Belle."

She sighed. "Fine, fine. But you should think about it."
She wagged her finger at him. "It would be good for you and
good for the world."

"Aunt Belle—"

She fiddled with the ring on her pinky finger. She might
have turned down Joe's marriage proposal, but she still
wore the big diamond ring he'd given her. "I'm so lucky to
have you, you know."

Damn it. Like that, his anger deflated. "I'm lucky to have
you too."

Her computer gave an alert and she glanced at it, brow
furrowing. "That's William. He's being so difficult about
this weekend."

"Difficult how?"

"Saying that having potential buyers come to my home
is excessive and over-the-top. That it's not what Jennifer
would have done." The lines around her mouth deepened.
"Tina told me not to tell him about the glitter-gram I sent
Rhiannon, she said he'd be even more scornful."

"You know, you are his boss. You don't have to put up
with this." The reminder was gentle, though his annoyance
was not.

Aunt Belle waved that away. "It's fine, really. What did
you want to talk about, if not Trevor?"

Samson ran his tongue over his teeth, her diamond ring
winking up at him. He didn't want to tell her, not now. She
had enough on her plate. Let her have the weekend. "Nothing." He forced a smile, and it took all of his energy. "Don't

work too hard. And don't listen to William. I'm sure anything you've planned will be great."

"Why don't you go have a drink and relax on the porch for a while? I had the chef put some delicious virgin cocktails on the menu for tonight."

The last thing he felt like doing was sipping a nonalcoholic margarita in the sunshine, but he nodded and left. At some point, he'd have to have a more serious talk with Aunt Belle about giving his personal information out to his nemesis, but not when both their emotions were running high.

He turned sideways in the hallway so a maid could scurry past him. His shoulder brushed a framed painting. It was an amateur seascape, the initials A.L. in the corner.

He studied it for a moment. His dad had painted this, in one of the classes his mom had dragged him to, back when she'd been convinced his depressive episodes had simply been a matter of too much free time.

Samson remembered when Aleki had gifted the painting to Joe over dinner at their house. *What the hell am I supposed to do with this crap?* Joe had barked. The brothers had always been growling at each other, though their tight bond had been more than obvious to anyone who spent any time with them.

Aunt Belle had taken it from him and exclaimed like it was a piece of fine art, and to her, it may very well have been. *Hush, Joe. It's the view from our house, can't you tell? I'll cherish it forever, Aleki, thank you.*

Samson scrubbed his hand over his face. The majority of the people around that dinner table were gone now, him and Belle the only ones left.

His phone vibrated in his pocket and he pulled it out. Rhi. Her text popped up under the photo of his hand.

LOL. Dork.

A ray of sunshine threatened to pierce through his fog of grief and loneliness, and his brain beat it back, even though a part of him was aware he needed it right now.

What is wrong with you? You knew this diagnosis was coming.

He shook his head, but he couldn't dislodge the darkness, the vast emptiness that waited for him if he took a step toward it. He tucked the phone away without answering, and wished he could tuck his emotions away as easily.

The guests would be arriving soon, including Rhi, but he was in no shape to mingle with strangers now. He'd work out, go for a run on the beach.

Perhaps then, he could outpace his feelings.

Chapter Twenty

"ARE YOU texting Samson?"

Rhiannon glanced around guiltily, but Lakshmi was in her ear, not in the chauffeured town car whisking her to Annabelle's home. She switched from her messages back to the video call with Lakshmi. "No." Not a lie. She hadn't been texting Samson. She'd been ogling the photo he'd sent of his hand. Silly, yes, but still so fucking sexy.

"That is one goofy grin you're sporting there."

She consciously wiped her face clean of any kind of grin. "Fuck off."

Lakshmi chuckled. "Can you thank him for the food and massages, if you do happen to text him?"

No one had been more grateful for the extravagant gesture of week-long lunches than her. She'd basically been sleeping at the office for the past week. Eating had been the furthest thing from her mind. She rolled her neck. The massage therapists he'd sent today had been nice too. "You don't know where the food came from."

"Girl, please."

Her staff had grown curious after she'd shook off their

thanks for the free lunch the first day, except for Lakshmi, who had cast her knowing looks. They'd started calling their mysterious benefactor Santa. How had Samson known that the way to her heart was to also take care of her too-dedicated employees?

Wait, not her heart. The way to her . . . sincere admiration. Yeah, that was right. She admired him.

Him and his sexy almost-dick pic. She, who could have given a keynote speech on how much she hated dick pics, had stared at the outline of his penis in his sweatpants for longer than she cared to admit. Guess it mattered who the dick was attached to.

Damn it. She liked him more today than the last time she'd seen him, when they'd had sex. How was that possible?

For all you knew, he was chatting up sweet, kind, loyal Janet when he wasn't sending you food.

So? He had the right to do that.

Lakshmi sobered. "By the way, I've had all my feelers out for the past week. I still can't get any intel on if that bastard will be there."

For a second, Rhi thought Lakshmi was talking about Samson, but then she realized Lakshmi didn't know about the now discarded hashtag BeachBastard. Peter. That was the once and always bastard king. "Oh, he'll be there. Peter won't miss a chance to fuck me over."

Lakshmi uttered a disgusted noise. "I don't understand how you stayed with him for as long as you did."

Rhiannon faltered. She might be oversensitive right now,

but it was painful to hear that. "He was very, very good." Peter had been a master manipulator. She'd been like a frog in a pot of water, the temperature on the stove nudged up and up and up by tiny degrees.

It was easy to see danger when someone flung knives at you. Harder when they quietly, subtly poked you full of holes.

"No doubt. I didn't mean to imply you should have known or anything," Lakshmi reassured her. "Anyway, we don't know if he'll be there. It's a worst-case scenario."

"No, he'll be there. I'm sure of it." She forced a smile to her lips. "And we'll beat him." Yes. Those were the right words to say. Strong, tough words. *I'm scared to be face-to-face with my ex for the first time since he ran me out of his company* were not strong, tough words.

"Damn straight we will." Lakshmi tossed her head. The shaved sides of her head were new. A rush of affection filled Rhiannon when she realized the pink and yellow of her hair was a perfect match for Crush's colors.

She clutched that close to her. She had people in her corner. Lakshmi and Katrina, via her phone.

Samson. Right there in the house.

She wouldn't be facing Peter alone.

The driver turned off the small local highway to navigate the town's internal roads, and soon Annabelle's house came into view. It was a magnificently large mansion with huge windows, nestled in a row of luxury homes. She knew at least one of those houses well, a few doors down. It had been the place she'd rented, where she and Samson had had their night together.

She said her goodbyes with Lakshmi as the driver pulled into the circular driveway. An older man in a suit walked out of the house and up to her vehicle as if he'd been watching for her.

"Welcome," he said as he opened her door and offered his hand. His voice was low and deep, his cheeks hollowed. "Ms. Hunter?"

"Correct."

"My name is Logan. I oversee the house here. I will take your bags to your room. Lisa is at the door, she will escort you to the drawing room where the guests are gathering."

"Am I late?"

"Not at all." He pronounced it At-Tall. "The itinerary does not have anything on the schedule for the next hour."

A smiling woman in a Mrs. Potts aproned outfit met her at the door. "Hello, I'm Lisa," she said warmly. "Would you like me to take your jacket, Ms. Hunter?"

"Call me Rhiannon, and no." She adjusted the blazer at her wrists in a nervous flick. She'd tried to anticipate what would please and impress Annabelle and had ended up going with a simple black pantsuit. She'd subbed the button-down shirt Lakshmi had picked out for her with a snug white T-shirt. It wasn't as comfortable as her normal wear, but it would do, especially paired with plain black flats.

The hell she'd wear high heels all day in an unfamiliar environment. Charlie Bucket hadn't won the factory by teetering around on heels.

The housekeeper gestured to the left. "If you need to freshen up, I can show you to your room first."

"I'm fine, thank you."

She followed Lisa through the winding hallways of the mansion. The walls were crammed with decor, frames touching other frames. Rhiannon's art education was lacking, but she recognized more than one expensive artist. Those artists were side-by-side with amateur art, mass-produced prints, and even children's crayon-scribbled drawings. It was as if the owner of the home had slapped up anything that caught her fancy.

It should have been overwhelming, but the eclectic collection combined with the bleached wood floors, expensive worn rugs, and the hint of sea salt in the air was oddly homey.

"Here we go." Lisa's cheery smile widened and she gestured to a set of open French doors.

Rhiannon murmured her thanks, which the housekeeper took as her dismissal. Multiple voices spilled out of the drawing room. Tina, she recognized, and two men.

Neither of them were familiar to her. *Don't get too relaxed.* It was early yet, she had to be braced for Peter's presence.

Rhiannon tugged at her blazer and straightened her shoulders, then walked in. She surveyed the three individuals, unable to halt the relief that Peter wasn't one of them.

Or the disappointment that Samson was missing as well.

Tina spotted her first and split off from the group. "Hello, Rhiannon."

"Hello."

"I see you got all the glitter out of your hair."

Rhiannon fluffed her hair and smiled at the teasing. She liked Tina. "It was a trial, but yes."

"Let me introduce you to some of the other guests."

Tina led her across the large room to the small group and gestured to a slender, dark-haired young man in his twenties. "This is Rhiannon Hunter, the creator of Crush. Rhiannon, this is—"

"Martin O'Donnell." Rhiannon nodded at the man.

He grinned, revealing expensive caps. "Have we met?"

"No, but I know of you." O'Donnell was a vulture, had picked up a couple of smaller regional dating apps recently. If he bought Matchmaker, it would be so he could strip it down, siphon its assets.

On the other end of the spectrum was Chris Hwang, the Asian man in his fifties standing next to Martin. "I know we've met." The lines around Chris's eyes crinkled, and he inclined his head. British-based, he headed up a powerful conglomerate of apps and sites across Europe. He'd been one of the only people who had reached out to Rhiannon when she'd left Swype, had even offered her a job on his marketing team. She would have seriously considered it, if it hadn't meant a move to London. She'd been too raw at the time to consider hopping across the pond solely for a job offer from a powerful man, even if that man was as well-respected as Chris. "How are you doing, Rhiannon?"

"Well. Quite well."

"Rhiannon . . ." Martin tapped his finger over his lip. "Did you used to work at Swype?"

"A long time ago."

Speculation entered the younger man's gaze, and Rhiannon knew he must have heard some talk about her. "Uh-huh."

"Wasn't *that* long ago."

She stiffened at the too-familiar voice behind her. Goddamn it.

She counted to three, with Mississippis in between. He deserved to wait for her time and attention. If there was no one in the room, she'd make him wait longer.

She'd make him wait forever.

She turned, her movements slower than usual, aware that he'd hate having to conform to her time table. The man behind her was tall and lanky. He'd been a swimmer in college, and he'd maintained both his physique and his boyish good looks well into his thirties. His brown hair was sun-kissed, his normally pale skin tanned, which meant he'd probably been on his yacht lately.

She'd been there when Peter had bought his yacht. She'd been so excited for him. They'd had sex on that stupid boat.

This was happening. She'd known it was coming. She was prepared.

She was Charlie fucking Bucket, and she'd kill this.

He didn't look at all surprised to see her, and she immediately did her best to match his expression. Blasé. Uncaring.

Like this man hadn't slowly isolated her until she feared she had nothing but him. Like he hadn't harassed her and made her professional life miserable when she finally managed to break things off. Like he hadn't started a whisper campaign to smear her name to make sure no one would believe her if she did come forward.

Like he hadn't forced her out of a company she'd loved, one she'd helped build from the ground up without so much as an iota of credit for her contributions.

A snarl started deep in her throat, but she reined it in. She arched her eyebrow at Peter, and inclined her head slightly. "Peter. Good to see you again."

"You as well." He clapped her on the shoulder and she barely refrained from flinching. Especially when he kept his hand there for a moment too long before he turned to Martin and Chris. "Gentlemen, it's a pleasure."

She sidled away, her gaze drawn to the large shadow in the doorway.

Samson.

Her relief at seeing him would have worried her, if Peter didn't worry her more. She smiled as he walked toward them.

It took her a second to realize his return grin was missing. Actually, everything was missing. The light in his face, the eagerness in his step, the little lines crinkling around his eyes.

Her smile faltered. What was wrong?

"Who's this?" Peter's booming voice dragged her attention back to him. Which was what he'd meant to do, she realized, when she beheld his frown as he looked back and forth between the two of them.

He didn't like that she'd smiled at Samson. She didn't give a fuck what Peter liked, but there were other ways to establish her dominance that didn't involve Samson.

Before Tina could introduce Samson, Rhiannon took up

the cause. "This is Samson Lima," she said smoothly, speaking to the other men. "He's the new face of Matchmaker. He and I have been working on a little project together."

Samson shook hands with everyone. "Hello."

"I've seen the campaign," Chris enthused. He winked at Rhiannon. "Wholesome. Very much what the internet needs right now. It's that kind of thinking that would have made you a great CMO for my company, Rhiannon."

"It was Samson's idea, and I personally think I make a better CEO of my own company." Her words were firm, but kind. Chief marketing officer at Chris's megaconglomerate would have been a big step up from Swype, but her step was bigger.

Chris laughed, not taking offense, and her liking for him grew. "Absolutely right."

Martin eyed Samson with the kind of hero worship children usually reserved for their sports heroes. "I'm sorry to hear about your uncle," Martin said. "I'm a big fan of your family."

Samson's lips curled up at the corners, but his eyes remained dull and blank. "Thank you. Everyone's here, right, Tina? I think we can go in to dinner."

"Yes, everyone's here."

Samson placed his hand on Rhiannon's elbow. It was a light, platonic touch, but a frizzle of excitement went through her when she thought of the photograph he'd sent her a few hours ago, of that very hand.

The photograph he'd sent her yesterday, of the same hand holding something else.

"You okay?" she murmured, when everyone else went ahead of them.

"Sure. How are you?"

"Fine," she responded automatically, though that wasn't true. A formal response to a formal inquiry. Rhiannon studied him, worried about his uncharacteristically subdued greeting and affect. It was like someone had sucked every ounce of charm out of Samson, leaving only an automaton. She'd never seen him look so expressionless, especially when greeting new people. Had he gotten some bad news or—

She glanced away, her stomach tightening when she met Peter's gaze. He swiveled his head around, but she inched away from Samson.

What was wrong with her? She didn't have time to dwell on why Samson's smile was missing, or analyze his mood. She was here to work, damn it.

Eye on the prize, and that prize included no man.

Chapter Twenty-One

FROM THE time Samson was ten until Aleki had started to decline, Samson had gone on barefoot runs with his father and uncle on the beach. At first he'd lagged far behind his elders, but as he'd grown, he'd easily caught up with the two star athletes. They'd jogged for miles, until sand covered their bodies, until they could taste it in their mouths. In the colder months, the three of them would return home with their faces tight and immovable.

He hadn't run far enough when Tina had texted him Chris had arrived, but his face was still frozen. Which was a little worrisome, because he had to be on, but it was also a blessing, because his stew of feelings were ice-cold too.

Samson glanced across the dining table. Rhi didn't know it, but that numbness was a blessing for her too. Had he been in his right mind it would have been difficult not to grab her up in a hug when he'd spotted her, especially when she looked so tidy and businesslike.

She would have murdered him. She was here to work, after all, and he intuitively knew she'd carve him up with a rusty spoon if he let on that they knew each other intimately in front of her competitors.

The French doors to the dining room opened, and Annabelle appeared. She'd elaborately curled her red hair and giant black glasses perched on her nose. She changed caftans from when he'd seen her last, opting for a flowing red one, and matched it to the red paint on her lips. His aunt posed in the doorway, one hand on her hip. "Hello, everyone! Welcome to my home. I am Annabelle Kostas."

Samson had seen this entrance many times. He dutifully rose to his feet and the others followed.

Annabelle swept into the room and grinned at all of them, clearly delighted with herself. She may not enjoy being the focus of large crowds, but Annabelle did like attention when it came in the form of small gatherings like this. Once upon a time, she and Joe had often hosted weekend soirees for their closest friends. "Please, everyone! Have a seat, have a seat. No need to make such a fuss over me. Rhiannon, Martin, Chris, Peter. Lovely to meet all of you."

The ice on his soul melted, at least in one corner. He'd considered ignoring Tina's text earlier and running forever, but that would have been an impossible option. Today wasn't about him. He was here for Aunt Belle. He had a job to do too.

The butler held Annabelle's chair out for her, and they all took their seats. "Did everyone have good travels?" she asked, in a deceptively sweet tone that didn't give away the fact that the games had begun. She flicked her hand, and servers appeared with silver domed trays of food.

This was elaborate. The last time he'd come over to Aunt Belle's, they'd grilled hamburgers and ate corn on the cob on her porch.

Martin leaned back for the server to place his plate in front of him and remove the dome with a flourish. "It was fine, thank you."

"Coach always gets a little crowded on these transatlantic flights," Chris said smoothly.

Annabelle smiled at the distinguished older man approvingly. She might be lavish at times, but she generally appreciated frugality in the rich. Chris had done his homework.

"And you, Rhiannon?" Annabelle picked up her fork and knife.

"The drive was fine."

Samson cut into the chicken he didn't want. Annabelle didn't believe in a salad course. An entrée and dessert were the only two meals a person needed to survive, she'd once told him.

"Oh, my, I have been remiss. Does everyone know everyone else?" Annabelle surveyed the table like a queen with her subjects. "Why don't we go around and introduce ourselves? Let's do . . ."

Samson eyed his aunt. Whenever she'd come over, she'd done exactly this. Gone around the table and had them all answer a question she posed. It had driven his father crazy. Aleki had always just wanted to eat, had barely been able to wait long enough for grace.

But he'd indulged Annabelle, because as he'd explained to Samson, *the woman allowed me to meet your mother. If she wants us to talk about our favorite memory or whatever before we carve the turkey, then that's what we'll do, damn it.*

Before the Switch. Of course.

Don't think about the Switch, don't think about your father or your uncle or CTE or the future. You're here. Focus on the here.

"Name and a bit about yourself and one of your greatest fears. Here, I'll do me. I'm Annabelle—hopefully you all already know that since you're here to put in a bid for my company. My greatest fear is . . . dogs." She shivered. "I was bitten by a large dog as a child."

When the guests appeared varying degrees of perplexed, Samson roused himself. "I'm Samson, I'm a close friend of Annabelle's, as well as Matchmaker's current spokesman and a minority shareholder. And, uh, my greatest fear is . . ." He stalled. He wasn't about to tell this room of strangers and Rhi his actual fear. "Clowns. Hate 'em."

Martin introduced himself and skipped talking about his fears entirely, and Chris chose something as generic as Samson's.

Rhi commanded his attention. Her voice started out thready and rocky, but it strengthened as she spoke. "I'm Rhiannon Hunter. I created Crush. And my greatest fear is . . ." She hesitated. "Not having options, I suppose."

It was a good answer and sounded sincere. Annabelle smiled approvingly and turned to the only man left. "And you, sir?"

"I'm Peter Roberts. I created Swype, the first swipe-based app—"

"In America," Chris quietly interjected, and Samson

wondered how often he had to step in with that correction. He'd read up on Chris. The man had many companies under his belt, and his apps were number one in multiple Asian and European markets.

Peter flashed a brilliant smile. He was a good-looking man with a face some people might call trustworthy, but Samson wasn't impressed.

This was Rhi's former boss, the head of the company that had spread rumors about her. He'd be watching the man.

"Yes, I was going to say that. The first swipe-based app in America. I suppose one of my greatest fears is the dark." His brow wrinkled. "I'd rather not talk about why, but I can't stand to be in dark rooms now."

Samson ate a bite of his chicken and considered Peter. That sounded sincere, but there was something odd about the too-innocent look in Peter's eyes, the earnestness in his face, like it was a mask constructed by someone who understood those concepts but had never actually practiced them. Samson might be a little biased in Rhi's favor, but he didn't think this man was on the up-and-up.

"Of course you don't have to discuss that, Peter." Annabelle dabbed the corner of her lips. "It's an honor to have such distinguished guests here. The best and brightest in the industry."

"You would top that list, Annabelle." Chris beamed at Annabelle. Samson added him to the list of people to watch. Samson would not have the guy try to influence Belle with flirtation.

His aunt tittered. "Why, thank you."

"You're not going to, like, use our fears against us or something, are you?" Martin looked around. "Is this one of those sick horror movies where the doors all lock and the windows shutter now?"

"My, no." Annabelle daintily ate a bite of mashed potatoes. "I don't have the energy for that. I've found you can really get to the heart of a person when you catch them off guard with an unexpected question."

"What did you learn about me? I didn't answer your question."

"It told me you're a nonconformist, who perhaps cannot stand having a probing question aimed at you." Annabelle cocked her head. "Am I wrong?"

Martin shrugged.

They occupied themselves with food and small talk for a little bit. Samson noted Rhi was still on the quiet side, though she conversed fine with Chris next to her and Annabelle when spoken to. Samson grimly ate and went through the motions of talking football with Martin, conscious of his aunt's eagle eyes. He didn't want Annabelle to notice his mood had deteriorated since he'd come to her office and wonder why.

The waiters took away the remnants of their dinner entrées and placed lemon syllabub in front of them.

Ah. He almost pressed his hand over his heart for a second to dull the ache that threatened to pierce through the fog. Joe had loved lemon anything.

His aunt took a single bite of the syllabub and closed

her eyes. The lines between her eyebrows deepened. He wished he was close enough to reach over and touch her hand.

But he wasn't, and they weren't alone, so instead he cleared his throat. Aunt Belle put her spoon down and straightened her shoulders. "Why don't you all check under your seats? I've left a present for you there."

"Under our seats?" Martin repeated.

Samson didn't entirely blame him for his confusion. Rhi might be the only one here with a more intimate idea of Aunt Belle's theatrics, and having them grope under their chairs like they were on a daytime talk show and about to win a car was pretty much peak theatrics. Samson reached under his seat.

He straightened with an envelope in hand and opened it, the others doing the same. When he reached inside for the cardstock, a bunch of glitter fell into his hands and lap.

"Oh, look," Rhi said with no inflection. "More glitter."

If Samson could feel anything, it would have been amusement.

Annabelle cleared her throat. "This is an itinerary for tonight and tomorrow."

"Eight p.m. until question mark, exam. Saturday, ten to four, feats of strength. Five, rose garden ceremony. Exam? What is this exam?" Chris asked.

"When you go back to your room, you'll find tablets so you can complete your Matchmaker questionnaire."

Chris crossed his arms over his chest, then uncrossed

them to pick glitter off his well-tailored suit jacket. "Are we here to find love interests or to submit a bid for your business, Annabelle?"

"The quiz is nothing more than a personality test," Belle explained. "I want to know who you are, in your heart of hearts."

Martin scowled at Annabelle. "What the hell are feats of strength?"

Annabelle smiled thinly at him. "Please don't swear," said his aunt, who could swear like a sailor. "To answer your question, you will all be pitching me and my CEO, William, when he arrives tomorrow. When you aren't doing your individual presentations, you may make use of the property as you see fit. I have boogie boards if you'd like to see how cold the water is, an exercise room, a well-stocked library, and multiple places to stretch out and relax. Feats of strength implies physical strength, but I am quite aware there are all kinds of strength. I wanted to accommodate everyone, even those who may have issues with activity."

"I have no issues with it," Peter said, his smirk annoying. "I'm very fit."

Samson stirred. "As am I. But I also tweaked my back last week, so I'll probably be taking a rest tomorrow, if anyone wants to join me on a lounge chair on the deck out back." His gaze flitted over Rhi's bowed head.

Aunt Belle beamed approvingly at him. "Yes, son, listen to your body. Anyway, before you leave tomorrow, you'll know whether I wish to pursue a business relationship with you."

"Is that the . . . rose garden ceremony?" Rhi asked.

"Yes. Correct." Aunt Belle's curls bobbled when she nodded. "It's a lovely environment and will make bad news easier to digest."

Rhi tucked the card back into the envelope and brushed the glitter on the table into a neat pile. "This is quite an experience."

"This is bullshit," Martin said flatly and came to his feet. He tossed his napkin on top of his uneaten syllabub. "I don't need to play games to scoop up a slowly dying company. I'll snag Matchmaker for pennies when it goes under. The rest of you can't possibly want to put up with this either, right?"

No one else moved, and Martin rolled his eyes. "Fine. Whatever. See you all at the next conference, suckers." He stomped more than walked out, and Samson half rose from his seat. He didn't quite trust the man-child to not tip over a vase or something on his way out the door in his annoyance, but Annabelle waved him back down.

Probably for the best. He wasn't the type to needlessly fight, but in his current void of an emotional state, he wasn't fully in control of how he might respond to a spoiled rich guy.

"Well," his aunt said with a secret smile. "That makes my decision easier, eh?"

Peter tossed his longish hair. "Martin has always been impatient. Good things come to those who wait."

"Oh, certainly." Belle steepled her fingers under her chin. "So now, I suppose . . . there were three. May the games begin."

Chapter Twenty-Two

ONE OF *my greatest fears is the dark.*

What a fucking lying sack of shit. She should have blown up his yacht when she had the fucking chance.

Forget Peter. You can't murder him. It's an isolated house party, you'll be the first one they arrest.

She took a deep breath, then let it out. *The best revenge is success. The best revenge is success.*

She curled her legs up under her in the armchair and struggled to focus on the last few questions of this stupid questionnaire. In the beginning, she'd tried to answer the questions as she thought Annabelle might want her to but had quickly realized that a lot of the hundred points in the hundred-point questionnaire were the same questions masterfully reworded, making it difficult to game the system.

She clicked the last button with a satisfied sigh and tossed the tablet onto the side table. The room she'd been given, while not lavish, was decorated expensively, in soothing ocean blues and greens. The walls here, too, were groaning with the weight of multiple frames, but these were all photographs of the ocean.

Rhiannon switched one screen for another and pulled out her phone. There were texts from Katrina and Lakshmi, but none from Samson.

That was fine. Absolutely fine. Totally fine.

She scrolled up through her texts, to confirm that he'd sent her that kissy face and the silly photo of his hand earlier today. There could be a good reason for his coolness and distance since she'd arrived. Perhaps he was self-conscious, here in his aunt's house. She wanted to keep their relationship, temporary or not, low-key too.

He could have texted her, though.

Running hot and cold is a red flag.

Catch and release was the name of that game. Lure someone in, then as they were getting comfortable, toss them aside because the thrill was gone.

He played you once. This is why you don't trust a ghoster.

No, no. She wasn't going to torture herself like this, with her brain running through every possible scenario of bad dating behavior. She'd shoot him a message and ask him if everything was okay.

Even if she had been the last one to message, leaving her committing the cardinal sin of the double text.

Before she could type anything, though, a knock came on the door. She launched out of the chair. It was a sign of how much she hoped it was Samson on the other side that she didn't first check to see who was knocking—to her regret.

She opened the door and took a step back in surprise. A tactical error. That was all it took for Peter to muscle his way into her room, closing the door behind him so fast she didn't have a chance to stop him.

Fucker.

Show no weakness. She lifted her chin. "What do you want?"

He spread his hands out. She'd once thought those hands were sensitive, the fingers long and slender, like a pianist, but they were a predator's hands. "We haven't had any time together, alone, in so long. I thought we could talk."

"Have your assistant call mine."

"Very funny." He leaned back against her own door and perused her. She was abruptly very aware that she'd taken her blazer off. Her T-shirt didn't cover her arms, and she couldn't even cross them and hug herself in front of him. That wasn't a power move.

He met her gaze. "Look at us, both competing for the same company. Isn't that funny?"

"I wouldn't say funny, but you always had a terrible sense of humor."

"Did you finish up the absurd test?"

"I did."

Peter snorted. "Imagine, this company making any money when people's attention spans have shrunk to .06 seconds."

"Imagine. Imagine being the sucker who buys it."

His thin lips curled up. She glanced around the room, instinctively seeking escape. She'd left the windows open. She could jump, if she had to. Second story, but sand below.

He'd never been violent with her. But then again, she hadn't thought he would systematically try to ruin her career and life's work all those years ago either, and here they were.

How did you stay with him for so long?

Because he hadn't shown her this side immediately. She hadn't gone on her first date and looked for exits. She hadn't woken up from their first overnight together fearful for her safety. A frog in slowly boiling water. "Spit out whatever you want to say, Peter."

"Have a seat."

"No."

His face darkened. "You—"

Her phone chimed, and she pulled it out of her pocket.

"You're talking to me, put your damn phone away."

"It's for work," she lied. Peter might be wholly lacking in empathy, but he would understand work.

It was, actually, a text from her mother, with something silly about the engagement party. She ignored it and, listening to her instincts, clicked on Samson's name.

Please come to my room. Right now. If I don't answer, open the door, no matter what you hear or don't hear.

It didn't matter if Samson barging in would confirm Peter's assumptions about the two of them. She didn't want to be alone with her ex. She tucked the phone away and hoped Samson would get the text soon and that his recent coolness wouldn't extend to ignoring her now.

"You want to work on our presentations together?" Peter's smile was smarmy.

She snorted.

"Please, Rhiannon. It's been years. Can't we put this unpleasantness behind us and be colleagues? I'm sorry for the way you felt you were treated when you left Swype."

The way she *felt* she'd been treated, and not the way he'd treated her. Ugh, this asshole. "Peter. Get out of my room. Go away."

Once when they'd been dating, he'd told her that men thought in black and white, that they were literal creatures, and she'd taken issue with the flip-side assumption of that statement: that women were emotional, wishy-washy, shades-of-gray ambiguous creatures. Funny enough, he didn't seem to have enough self-awareness to understand his argument was full of holes pierced by his own behavior. He'd never been able to take simple, direct orders. Not from her, at least.

He ignored her literal *go away* now too, though his mask slipped. "Bet you wouldn't tell Samson to go away. You seem chummy."

Aw shit. "We've been working together."

"You're closer than colleagues."

"You're hallucinating."

"Am I? I think you're sleeping with him. If so, it's unfair you have an inside track on this bid."

"It's not an in. Samson doesn't have enough ownership in this company to make any kind of difference. I need to prepare my presentation for tomorrow. Now please leave."

The smile dropped, and so did any illusion that he wasn't an asshole. "If you think fucking that idiot football player is going to get you anything but a lousy lay, you're as stupid as I always thought you were."

"Lousy lay? If that's not the pot calling the kettle black."

His cheeks flushed red. "I could show him the pictures."

She went rigid. "You know what happens when you go down that route."

A knock came on the door. It startled Peter enough that he stepped away. Before either of them could speak, the door opened and Samson stuck his head in the opening.

She'd never been happier to see someone.

Confusion crossed Samson's face as he took in Peter's presence. "Excuse me. I didn't realize something was—" Then his gaze fell on Rhiannon's face, and he stopped and shoved the door wider, stepping over the threshold. "Is everything okay in here?"

"Everything's fine," Peter snapped.

"Peter was just leaving," she said, with as much calm as she could muster.

"I was not."

"I want you to leave," she insisted, dropping all pretense.

"But you want him here? I see what's going on." That familiar cold fury was in Peter's voice, the fury she'd always shrank away from toward the end of their relationship. "Fuck you, you bitch—" He strangled on the last word because Samson strangled him.

It took a blink. That was all. The same fraction of a second it might take someone to swipe right or left on a photo.

Samson pinned her ex against the wall with his arm across Peter's throat. "If I hit you," Samson said, in a calm, quiet tone, the same chilling tone he'd used when the drunk on the rooftop had called him the Curse, "I could kill you. Do you see how that's possible?"

Peter gave a short nod, his range of motion limited by Samson's grip.

"I don't care what your relationship with Rhiannon was, but if you ever speak to her like that again, if you ever ignore her request to leave her alone, I will find you. One hit is all it would take. Understand?"

"Yes," Peter choked out.

Samson waited a beat, then stepped back, releasing him. "Leave," he said, and Peter bolted like his feet were on fire.

Samson closed the door and looked at Rhiannon. "You okay?"

She should say yes. She should nod and grab her sweatshirt and put it on. Layers on layers. No vulnerabilities.

But instead, she sank to the side of the bed and dropped her head into her shaking hands. The bed depressed next to her, and a big hand rubbed up and down her back in a soothing motion.

This wasn't so much a reaction to Peter scaring her, though that was part of it. No, this was about Samson.

He'd come, right when she'd asked him to. She hadn't really even doubted that he'd come, not if he got her text. When had she decided to trust him like that? When was the last time she'd dared to trust a man like that?

Hope, her enemy. It had crept in and taken root.

The remnants of fear and anxiety twisted her up inside. He scooted closer and she pressed herself against him, pathetically grateful for his warmth. "*I'm* scared of the dark."

"What?"

Her words spilled over each other. "It's me. Not Peter.

My little brother went missing one day during a game of hide-and-seek. I went looking for him and got locked in a shed. They didn't find me for almost nine hours." Her mom's employer had taken an ax to the door, because no one had had a key to the old shed. She could still recall the smell of her mother's sweat when they'd gotten her out. "I'm not claustrophobic, but I can't stand the dark."

He seemed to know exactly what she needed and when, because he shifted and drew her into his lap. He squeezed her so hard, she made a noise. He loosened his grip immediately, but she rested her hand on his arm. "No, you know I like being held like that. Can you do it again?"

He squinted at her, but obliged. "You'll have to tell me if I hurt you."

"Tighter," she said instead, and murmured happily when he complied. Her own little head-to-toe compression force.

"You two had a personal relationship? You and Peter?"

She was held so snug, it was like she was in her own world of comfort, a world where she could confess anything. "Peter and I dated when I was at Swype. He had pursued me for years, and it was flattering. He was a great boyfriend at first. Then he stopped being a great boyfriend. He started to make me feel . . . small. I hated it. It took me a couple months, but I ended things."

"And you left Swype?"

"I didn't want to, but I had to. Because I stopped sleeping with him." She hadn't realized her hands had tightened into fists until her nails cut into her skin. "He couldn't fire me because of my contract. So he set out to tell everyone I was a gold-digging whore who was terrible at my job. People in the company, people out of it. He harassed me daily until I cried every day on my way to and from work. He told me he'd stop if I came back to him. How could I go back to him after that?"

"Why didn't you sue him?"

"He told me he'd destroy me if I did. When we were together, we sexted. He had sent me some sexy photos. I'd reciprocated. Nudes. A video. We were dating, it was fine." Her voice faltered. "If his nudes got out, he'd be high-fived. If mine got out, I mean, now, yes. I could spin them, it wouldn't hurt my business. But they'd still be out there. Everyone would see me." Naked. She shuddered and burrowed deeper into his embrace.

His exhale was long and low. "When we were filming, you said you wanted our footage in your control. Makes sense now, after what he did."

She nodded. "Quitting felt like I was admitting to everything he was saying about me, but I didn't know what else to do. He gave me a settlement for a fraction of what I was owed, and I left." Her smile was bitter. "He kept those photos quiet, but the damage was done. Everyone believed him or, at least, was wary of me. Getting a job at the same or higher position seemed impossible. If it hadn't been for Katrina putting up the money for Crush, I don't know what I would have done."

He kissed her neck. "I'm sorry that happened to you and I'm glad you had your friend. I'm going to punch Peter tomorrow. Don't worry, I won't really kill him."

Her laugh was choked. He sounded suspiciously like

Katrina. "Please don't. No one can know about this, Samson. I mean it. Especially not Annabelle."

He rubbed his hand up and down her back. "I can't let Annabelle do business with a predator, Rhi."

"He's not a predator, not to anyone else." She leaned back, more anxiety piling on. Why had she said anything? How could she have abandoned her usual tight-lipped stance on this subject? "He has a vendetta against me, personally, that's all. Please don't tell Annabelle. I can't have him saying I won by snitching on him. I have to beat him fairly. I—"

"Okay, okay." Samson pressed his finger over her lips. "I won't tell Annabelle."

She moved her head away so she could speak. "Promise?"

"Totally promise."

He sounded sincere. Rhiannon sagged against him and rested her head against his shoulder. "I should have checked to see who it was before I opened the door." Hadn't she had the rules of how to be wary drummed into her from the time she was a young girl?

"Don't blame yourself. He shouldn't have come to your room."

"I don't want to sleep here. Not under the same roof as him. I can't."

He brushed a kiss over her head. Either she'd imagined his disinterest earlier in the day, or it was simply gone now, because his response was filled with warmth. "You don't have to. Grab your sweatshirt and put on your shoes and take anything else you'll need for the night."

Chapter Twenty-Three

SAMSON WANTED to run along the beach again, but this time, it wasn't grief and loneliness guiding him.

It was barely banked rage.

You can't hit Peter.

He'd wanted to, even before he'd learned of the full extent of Peter's villainy. The second he'd seen the fear in Rhi's eyes and put together a rough understanding of why she'd sent him that cryptic text, he'd been ready to smash something.

Samson's fists clenched.

His threat had only been a mild exaggeration. He may not be in the shape he'd been in during his pro-athlete days, but he could put enough power behind his blow to lay a man out cold.

Samson consciously shortened his stride when he noticed Rhi was trotting to keep up with him. He'd told her to grab her shoes, but she'd yanked them off the second they'd hit the soft sand.

It was silent this time of night, the townspeople snug in

the glowing warmth of their houses. The full moon cast a silvery curtain over everything, turning the ocean and the large rock formation in the distance into a magical landscape.

Rhi tilted her head toward the ocean. The moonlight caressed her cheeks and forehead, a natural highlight for her luminous dark brown skin. The vibrating tension that had shaken her body in her room had eased as soon as they'd hit the beach and started walking.

She wasn't herself, though. Normally, her dynamic personality gave her the illusion of being so much bigger. Tonight, with her shoulders hunched and her heart-shaped face pinched, he was conscious of how physically small and fragile she actually was compared to him. Compared to Peter.

He breathed in deep, the familiar salty air and the cool sand between his toes calming him down a little as well. He couldn't go back to the numbness that had protected him earlier, not while Rhi needed him, but red-hot fury wasn't productive either. "Can I hold your hand?"

The look she shot him was startled, but after a beat, she held out her hand, and he took it. "You're a hand holder?" Even her voice was smaller than usual.

"I don't know," he admitted. "I guess so. Is that a problem?" He'd never been with a woman long enough to determine if he was a hand holder.

Her cold fingers clenched around his. "No."

Another slice of his mad slipped away. He'd concentrate

on making sure she had a safe place to sleep tonight, the night before her big pitch.

Ah jeez. No wonder she'd asked who else was pitching. "Did you know Peter would be here?"

She sighed, the sound carrying on the breeze. "I had a hunch. That night I rushed to your apartment, I had heard a rumor he was cozying up to William."

His mother had liked to say, if you waited long enough, everything made sense. "Ah." He didn't like keeping his aunt in the dark on this, and there was no way he'd let Belle do business with Peter, despite what Rhi had said about her being the only target of his cruel behavior. But he'd figure that out tomorrow. He didn't want to upset Rhi any more tonight.

"Where are we going anyway?"

He nodded at the weathered blue home as it came into view. "My place." He'd been relieved That Night, when she'd proposed going to her rental. He wouldn't have felt comfortable bringing someone into the home he shared with his uncle. When his uncle was alive, that is. Now it was nothing but an empty house.

They walked up the steep stairs leading to the back porch from the beach. The spare key was under a green frog-shaped planter, as it had been his entire life.

He slipped inside the back door and entered the security code. He should change it at some point, he supposed. It was his mother's birthday still. "Come on in."

He flipped on the lights in the living room and the kitchen while she placed her small bag on the couch. The place wasn't musty at all, so he suspected that Aunt Belle had directed someone to come over regularly and air it out. "This is, uh, it."

"It's nice. Not what I expected. I thought you would have grown up in a huge house like Belle's."

Samson looked around, trying to see the home through Rhi's eyes. Though sitting on prime real estate, the place was relatively cozy, one giant room split into a kitchen, dining area, and living room. The furniture was large and of good quality, to accommodate his large-framed family, but decidedly dated. Except for his and his uncle's bedrooms, no one had redecorated in here since his mom had passed. "My parents were pretty frugal."

"A beautiful place to grow up."

He softened. Sometimes he avoided thinking about his parents entirely, because his father's behavior after the Switch had been so painful, but he should probably work on that. They'd had so many good times together. His childhood here had been idyllic. "It was." He rested his hands on the back of the floral couch. "The place was closed up for a long time. Since my uncle died, and before, too, since my mom died."

At her questioning look, he continued. "When I started taking care of Uncle Joe, we lived in the big house. A little over a year ago, it started to get challenging. He kept getting lost, not remembering where anything was, not recognizing Aunt Belle when she visited. He was calmer here." He nodded at the mantel of the fireplace and the display case next to it. It held photos and memorabilia from his uncle and father's football-playing days. Samson had moved the elder Lima's Super Bowl rings to his safe deposit box, but they'd carefully been enshrined in the case when Uncle Joe had been alive. "He liked to sit up here and look at all of that. He could remember."

Rhi drifted over to the display case and peered inside. "This is really cool."

"I suppose I should donate it or something now." That was something else he'd put off, along with thinking too much about the endless future. There was a reason this place had been preserved so well. Packing it up and deciding what to do with it had always been too painful of a chore.

"Or keep it. For future Limas."

Samson blinked. He hadn't considered having a family or children for a long time. "I have to think about it. Some of it might be better off in a place where fans could see and enjoy it."

"You must miss him an awful lot."

"My uncle? Yeah. I do miss him." The words that had been so hard to say to his aunt spilled from his lips. "I got a call today, confirming his CTE diagnosis."

She faced him. "I'm sorry."

He nodded. "I knew it was coming."

"Still hurts, I'm sure."

Again, it was remarkably easy to make his confession. "More than I thought it would. Like I lost him all over again."

She walked toward him, skirting the flowered couch. "Is that why you've been so distant today?"

He scrubbed his face. "Was I?" Samson didn't need to ask, though. He'd chased down and welcomed the numbness. "I'm sorry. I guess I have a tendency to shut down when I'm upset." He grimaced, thinking of the fog he'd been in after his uncle's death. "I'll work on it."

The corner of her lips kicked up. She didn't tell him that he didn't need to work on anything for her, because what they had was temporary, and for that he was grateful. Instead, she wrapped her arms around his waist and hugged him tight. "I don't know exactly what happens in situations like this, but I presume his diagnosis will be released to the public?"

"Yes. My uncle wanted that. It's good," he added, to convince himself. "It'll increase the pressure to make the game safer." Two brothers, long NFL careers, both passing away over fifteen years apart due to the same degenerative brain disease? Headline writers would have a field day.

Her hand moved over his back, and it was then that he realized how tense he'd become. He was glad she was calmer than she'd been in her bedroom, but he didn't much like that she was now the one soothing him.

"You're good with publicity."

He should put an end to this line of conversation, show her to a bed, but he couldn't. "Not this kind." His throat grew tight. "I was the one who pushed for my father to be diagnosed after he died. I wanted a reason, some scientific proof that explained why he'd changed. I didn't need a diagnosis for my uncle, I knew what was wrong with him.

I guess it's not just grief that upset me today, but apprehension about what will happen now. The inevitable public reaction."

She peered up at him. "I understand that, but can I say, as someone who has had to weather a good deal of negative gossip myself and who is fully aware of the current conversation around you, I am pretty sure any attention you get from this will be positive and supportive."

He tried to scoff. "How are you fully aware? Did you google me despite our no-googling pact?"

"Nah. But occasionally someone will show me the comments. I have football fans who work for me. I'm an outsider, but even I can see that your retirement was a flashpoint for CTE activism."

Samson's face flushed. "I didn't set out to be an activist."

"No, but it seems like you are one anyway." She hesitated. "Guys like that drunk on the rooftop, he's going to be the odd man out. Like, do I think your former employers are going to be happy? No. They're in the business of men smashing their bodies against each other, not health care. But the majority of public opinion will be firmly and loudly on your side, I bet. You made your industry better for the young men who came after you, and the older men who came before you, and you did it just by living your life. You'll be a sympathetic face for the disease, whether you like it or not. I don't think that's a bad thing."

He thought about Trevor. "I was recently asked to represent a CTE nonprofit. I turned it down," he admitted.

"Why'd you turn it down?"

"My team's old quarterback runs it. He was the one who started calling me the Curse." Samson's jaw tightened.

"Ah, he's done a one-eighty. I'm familiar with those." She shook her head. "I am like the queen of dead-to-me so I don't feel comfortable telling you whether you should forgive him or if it's worth hearing him out. But it sounds more like you hate the guy and not the idea of working for this place."

He pulled her close and squeezed her tight, because he didn't know what else to say. He hadn't brought her here to comfort him, but that was exactly what she'd done.

He didn't know how she'd take it if he told her how sweet and kind she was. Would she think he was getting too attached and cut him off?

Because he was. He was getting frighteningly attached. "Let me show you to my room. You need to sleep."

SAMSON'S LARGE BEDROOM was the only place in the house, as far as Rhi could tell, that looked like it had been touched in the last decade. Here was some of the personality that was missing from his slick L.A. apartment and in the rest of this home. She crossed her arms over her chest and chafed them, though she wasn't cold, and glanced around with curiosity. The walls were painted a soft gray, the king-sized bed covered in a fluffy white duvet. The end tables were clear, the closet doors open, revealing a few shirts, still in dry cleaning bags. A painting above the bed depicted an open-air hut with a thatched roof nestled on golden sand.

"I've had that since I visited Samoa as a kid. It's a beach near where my mom grew up."

"It's lovely."

He pulled back the comforter. "Do you want me to sleep in here or would you like to sleep alone?"

His question was matter-of-fact, leaving the decision up to her. "Yes. I want you." Rhiannon would brush her teeth and wrap her hair later. They wouldn't be sleeping yet. There was too much restless energy jostling around inside her, both from her confrontation with Peter and from the surge of empathy for Samson.

It had been a busy night.

Samson pulled her close once they were in bed. She didn't know how long they cuddled. Or when they started kissing.

He stripped out of his clothes first, and the sight of all that tan, smooth flesh made her mouth water. He was such a nice specimen of a man, all his slabs of muscle layered on top of each other, his belly wide and thick.

He pressed her back against the bed and brushed his lips over her cheek, her lips. Her hands fluttered, then came to rest on his hot, naked shoulders. Samson slid his hands around her waist and untucked her shirt, skimming his palms up her sides.

His touch was tender and sweet, and part of her, the part that was still terrified by the evidence of how much she'd grown to trust him, hated how much she loved it. So she ran her fingers through his hair and tugged his head up until he could clearly see her. "Right now, I need you to fuck me hard." She deliberately used the crude word. He drew back, and she wondered if she'd hurt or offended him, but he nodded.

As soon she had his consent, she kissed him again, and it was rougher this time, dirty, their tongues rubbing against each other, their bodies doing the same. His hands grew surer.

Their fingers fought with one another as they tried to get her clothes off. Her shirt went first, and then her bra. Samson stripped her pants and panties off in one smooth move.

He sat back and stared at her. "How are you so perfect," he marveled. A shiver of pleasure ran from her head to her toes.

Rhiannon scrambled onto her knees. His cock was thick and heavy and she cupped it in both hands. "Can I take you in my mouth?"

"You never have to ask."

"It's more fun to ask." She stroked his shaft down and back up again. A shot of heady power ran through her. "That way you know what's coming." She bent forward, letting her hair tickle his thighs. "You can anticipate it." She licked the tip, delighting in his groan of pleasure. "And I know you want it."

"I want it. I definitely want it."

She'd given him a taste, and he was reacting like she'd given him a feast. The sweet man.

She took more of him in her mouth, sucking him deep. Normally, blow jobs weren't something that turned her on. Rhiannon liked to be good at everything, so if she wasn't an expert, she didn't see the point in putting forth her whole effort. But Samson didn't seem to care that she wasn't some blow-job queen.

He didn't need to resort to hair tugging for her to understand his urgency. It was there in the contracted muscles of his stomach and the sounds he uttered, a sexy symphony of sighs and groans.

Rhiannon was so into it, she was startled when he drew away. "You said you want it hard?"

She nodded.

"Get on your hands and knees."

A thrill of need and desire shook her. Her movements were less than graceful as she got into the position he'd demanded, but his groan when her ass faced him told her he didn't care much about grace.

She heard the rip of a condom wrapper and then the bed depressed behind her. Her fingers curled into the bedspread when he parted her folds. "Are you wet?"

"Yes—Jesus." Her fingers clenched tighter as his tongue swiped over her pussy.

Teasing laughter filled his words. "Just making sure."

The man was sweet, but that sweetness hid a streak of filth. Pure filth.

She moaned when he thrust inside her, and he raised her ass higher as he set a steady and rough pace. He laid his palm flat on her back, pressing her upper body down so he could fuck her even harder. "Tell me if it's too much," he gritted out.

"It's not enough," she managed.

"Oh no?"

Uh-oh. That was definitely a *challenge-accepted* if she'd ever heard it.

He snaked his hand under her body and pulled her upright, so there wasn't any space between their bodies, and gave her short, fast thrusts. She cried out. "Yes, perfect. More."

His thick arm tightened around her breasts, his heavy breaths tickling her ear. "Look." He nudged her with his forehead. "Look at us in the mirror."

She turned her head and almost came right there and then. The full-length mirror on the wall gave her a perfect view of the two of them in profile, his much bigger body tight against hers, penetrating her. No one had ever called her a woman of small stature, but right now she looked tiny, caught up in his grip. Helpless.

He pressed his forehead to her shoulder, his pained expression reflecting back at her in the mirror. Or he was the helpless one.

Or they were both helpless.

He kept one arm around her breasts to plaster her to his front. With two fingers he opened her up to rub his thumb against her clit. A kiss glanced off her ear. "You close?"

"Yes."

Samson guided her back down to the bed. She pressed her cheek to the pillow so she could keep watching in the mirror, gasping when he held his hand gently but firmly against her neck to keep her pinned down while he hoisted her hips higher. The biological function of sex became a cinematic masterpiece, each muscle contraction in the side of his ass and his thighs hypnotic and amazing.

The orgasm hit her hard and fast out of nowhere and she

shuddered. His thrusts grew harder, rougher. She was still shivering when he groaned loudly and pushed deep inside her a final time.

Rhiannon couldn't budge, not even when he moved off her and collapsed onto his back. All she could do was lay there in a ball of wasted energy and limp muscles as he got off the bed and dealt with the condom.

It was only when he returned to the bed that she lifted a finger, and it was mostly to sleepily let him arrange her so he could big-spoon her. His hand coasted up her arm. He had calluses that teased the hair on her flesh. "Your skin is so soft, Rhi."

Rhi. He didn't slip up anymore. He'd respected her demand immediately, even when he hadn't known the story behind how Peter had tarnished the thought of a lover using her full name.

He was a good guy. The fragile bloom of hope dug its way out of the frozen ground of her heart, and she almost whimpered.

He stroked her back, settling her. There were things they needed to talk about, logistics for the morning to plan out. As if he could read her mind, he kissed her ear. "Go to sleep. I'll wake you up early, and we can sneak you back into your room at Aunt Belle's house before breakfast."

"I asked for breakfast in my room." She'd wanted to psych herself up before her pitch. The best way to do that was to be alone.

"Before anyone else wakes up, then."

"Thank you." Rhiannon meant the thank-you to apply to

everything. Coming to her rescue, bringing her to his home, sharing why he'd been so distant. Fear and worry trembled awake under her contentment, but his arm flexed and she fell right back into the warmth of his grip.

It's okay. Tonight, she'd let him hold her and protect her. And then tomorrow, she would win. All by herself.

Chapter Twenty-Four

RHIANNON WASN'T going to win Matchmaker.

She could see it in the slightly bored look in Annabelle's eyes, in every doodle William made on his notepad. She had scrapped the PowerPoint, but she still had to give Annabelle her numbers and projections, didn't she? Speaking from the heart sounded cute, but it couldn't tell the woman cold hard facts about the terms of her deal.

Rhiannon crossed her legs. They were doing their pitches in the library. Unlike the rest of the house, which was light and airy and open, the library was darker, with navy walls and heavy furnishings. She'd been in more masculine, stuffy enclaves than this, but that didn't mean she liked them.

Rhiannon sat in a wing chair facing the big windows, open to the lovely garden on the side of the home. Annabelle and William sat opposite her, behind a desk. Annabelle's chair was larger than William's, almost thronelike, so the man appeared smaller than his boss.

Rhiannon wondered how he felt about that. It was a power move, one Rhi might copy one day. But then again, odds were low that she'd ever hire someone like William.

"As far as employee retention goes—" Rhiannon broke off midsentence when William covered his mouth to hide his yawn. She couldn't blame him, she was boring herself, and this was her presentation.

She rethought her entire presentation and decided to go with her gut.

This is another performance, another show. Imagine you're up on that CREATE stage again, and kill it.

Only this time, the stakes were so high. She had to be successful. "Annabelle, may I go off script? Why don't you ask me what you'd like to know about me? Get to know me better."

The older woman straightened. "I love going off script." She picked up a piece of paper in front of her and ripped it in two, tossing the scraps in the air. "Scripts are for fools."

Ah, jeez. Rhiannon wondered what important section of her proposal the woman had just destroyed. She forced herself not to dwell on that and refocused when Annabelle spoke. "Tell me about yourself. From the beginning."

An open-ended question Rhiannon often asked her prospective employees. "I was born and raised in western New York. My mother was a housekeeper, my father was a groundskeeper. He died when I was young."

"Do you have any siblings?"

She softened. "Yes. A brother. Gabe. He's perfect."

Annabelle grinned. "I loved my sister dearly, but I never would have called her perfect."

"Gabe's perfect," Rhiannon insisted. "He's kind and sweet and everyone likes him. He's getting married later this year."

"You're close to your family."

She thought about how her mother badgered her to call and winced. "Yes. Though my mother might say I don't call her enough."

"I used to go weeks without contacting my loved ones when I got busy or distracted. Luckily, the people I loved, I chose wisely. When I did reach out, they were right there." Annabelle squinted. "I regret that now, a little. Seems like I can't remember some of the things that made me busy, but I remember most conversations I had with my family and friends."

Rhi shifted. That didn't sound like it needed a response, so she settled for a noncommittal "Hmm."

Annabelle consulted the tablet in front of her. "You have an impressive educational background."

"My parents were employed by a wealthy family. They sent my brother and me to an expensive private school." She left out how she'd been tormented at that school, how she'd thrown herself into every activity so she could prove she was better at everything than everyone, no matter how much money her family had or didn't have. Sure, she'd had friends, those who had had her back. In that sea of rich, privileged snobs, her skin color and working class background had still made her a prime target for the assholes.

"How kind of them."

"Very kind," she echoed.

"And then you went to Harvard?"

"I'm a Yale man myself," William interjected.

"I got into Yale as well." She'd picked Harvard because

she'd had a photo of her father visiting the campus. She'd liked to imagine, when she walked across the grounds, that she was retracing steps her dad had once taken. A silly, sentimental reason to choose a school. "I didn't graduate, though. I dropped out and moved to California." For a while, she'd thought she'd found a home, with Swype and with Peter. With a man whose intellect seemed to match hers, who seemed so dedicated and consumed with her.

But that had turned dark so quickly and quietly, she hadn't even realized she was lost again until she was.

"I never graduated from college either," Annabelle confessed. "There was no matchmaker major, and I knew what I was destined for."

Rhiannon jumped on that. "We have a lot in common, the two of us. I wish I had known you when I was starting out. I could have used your mentorship."

Annabelle's face softened. "I don't know how much help I would have been. Matchmaker was created almost by accident, and it wouldn't be what it is today without Jennifer. And the executives she hired." She tipped her head at William, who looked smug and mollified at being credited with the growth of the company. "As far as I can tell, you did everything on your own."

"I did. Though the seed money for Crush came from a friend. Now my silent partner." Annabelle and Katrina could meet if the deal progressed further.

Samson and Katrina should meet too.

She mentally shook herself to get rid of that far too enticing idea. As it was, it had taken all her concentration not to think about Samson since he'd snuck her back into Annabelle's home this morning after a blissfully deep night of sleep.

Rhiannon crossed her legs. She'd dressed in her usual casual wear today, unable to stand the thought of not being comfortable. William had definitely given a judgy sniff at her choice of jeans and T-shirt, but he wasn't the first man to sneer at her.

"Why did you start your company, Rhiannon?"

There were easy, pat responses she could offer. Annabelle, with her unexpectedly perceptive gaze, might see through those. "I grew up in a town where everyone knew your business, or if they didn't, they made it up. Everyone's life was set on a certain path. People were shocked when I got into every college I applied to. They were more shocked when I made my first million."

Annabelle rested her chin in her hands. Today she wore a loose canary yellow top and jeans, her feet clad in UGGs, and she looked more like a college student than a veteran of the industry. "You wouldn't be the first person in the dot-com—I'm sorry, app—industry to start your own company to prove people wrong."

"No, I started it to prove myself right," Rhi corrected. "To prove what I already knew—that I'm right to be proud of my brain and confidence."

Annabelle's smile was approving. "Do you feel like you've proven yourself right yet?"

She hesitated. "I don't know." She'd set so many goalposts in her head. If she could make a million, if she could make a billion, if she could beat Peter . . . had she proven herself yet? If not now, then when?

William shifted. "This is all fascinating, but I think you skipped something in your oral résumé. You worked for Swype, yes?"

She braced herself, made sure her face was wiped clean of expression. "I did. Yes."

"In what capacity?"

He already knew this, but she indulged him. "I was VP of marketing." She'd had her hand in every aspect of that company, but she wasn't allowed to say that or anything else which would imply she'd had a primary role in creating the app, according to the terms of her exit settlement.

"And you had a relationship with your employer?"

Well. This was brazen, but she'd roll with it.

Annabelle shifted, her frown disapproving. "William, how is this relevant?"

"I'm fine answering." She wasn't, but it would appear shadier if she didn't answer. "Peter and I dated for about a year. It was well known throughout the company. We broke up. I left Swype and started Crush. These things happen." She almost choked on that last meaningless nothing sentence, but managed to get it out.

These sorts of things were bound to happen. Bound to be forced to make nice with a man who had tormented her and almost run her out of her own industry and faced no repercussions for it.

That was life.

Annabelle smiled with approval. "I like your calm attitude. Be like the Europeans about past lovers, that's what I always say."

Did Europeans often want to murder their exes? If so, then Rhiannon was very European. "Sure."

"It's interesting you built an app so similar to Swype's."

She narrowed her eyes at William. Now this, she'd fight him on. "Swype didn't invent swiping right and left. I did not lift one proprietary bit of technology from them." She resisted the urge to say she knew that because she'd helped build Swype. "Swype has had years to test us in court and they've refrained because they know they'd lose. Not sure where you have standing to litigate for them, though."

Annabelle tapped her fingers on the desk. "William, why are you being so confrontational?"

William scowled at his boss. "I am not. I merely want to clarify Ms. Hunter's history."

Nah. He believed the lies Peter had spread about her years ago. Hell, Peter was probably still spreading lies about her, about how she'd slept with him to get ahead.

It was easier for William to believe those lies. They probably confirmed what he'd already thought: that there was no way a woman like her could get as far as she had without cutting corners.

She could address the lies right here and now. Tell them she had been in the right all those years ago and it had been Peter who had been the liar and cheat. She opened her mouth, then closed it.

Damn it, no. She ought to be able to win this company

on her own merits, and not out of sympathy. "I'm happy to answer any questions about my past," she said simply.

William grunted. "I think we're at the end of our time here. Do you have any more questions, Annabelle?"

Annabelle thought for a moment. "Tell me, Rhiannon, why do you want Matchmaker?"

A million corporate-speak answers rose to Rhiannon's tongue, but she went with her gut again. "I want my company to be the best in the business. I want to be so big, no one can ever threaten my livelihood again."

Annabelle dipped her head. "You don't like failure."

"Does anyone?"

Annabelle smiled. "I suppose not."

"I've tasted failure. I like success more." Rhi shifted. "I have worked hard to get where I am, Annabelle. I will not purchase your company and fail."

"And the employees?" William interjected. "You pride yourself on a high percentage of women employees. What will you do with all our men?"

Castrate and murder them. She almost rolled her eyes at that stupid question and bit back her snarky reply. "We pride ourselves on hiring the best. If your people are the best, they'll be retained. I've outlined our full plan for employees in the proposal, as well as timelines for any layoffs we might have to make. I'm not in the business of destroying lives. My people will tell you, I am a good employer."

"You're quite the self-made woman, Rhiannon," Annabelle said. "And I do like your emphasis on ethics and fairness. Unusual to see in a company in this day and age. Tell me, if you could do anything other than what you do right now, what would it be?"

Rhiannon blinked, caught off guard by the question. "I wouldn't do anything else," she said, honestly. "If I couldn't do this, I'd be lost."

"Interesting." Annabelle pursed her lips, and Rhiannon wasn't sure if she'd passed that odd test or not. The dismissal was apparent, though.

Rhiannon rose to her feet and dipped her head to both of them. "Thank you for your time."

She was almost out the door when William called her name. She glanced over her shoulder.

William cocked his head. "I understand you're in a personal relationship with Annabelle's close family friend. Please understand Mr. Lima has no say in our decision-making process."

Rhiannon's face went hot, then cold as she stared at William's smug face. He looked like a well-groomed cat that had eaten a particularly delicious treat.

Annabelle slowly faced her CEO. "Uncalled for, William. Putting current business aside, Rhiannon and Crush are friends of ours, or we wouldn't have partnered with them recently. Also, please understand that *you* have no say in my decision either."

Ugh, if only she wasn't so mortified so she could properly appreciate Annabelle's burn.

Annabelle smiled at her, and there was a hint of steel in it. "Apologies, Rhiannon. Enjoy the rest of your afternoon.

Please gather in the rose garden at five. I'll be announcing any definite no's then."

Rhiannon's face was cold, matching her emotions. It had been a long time since someone had accused her of essentially fucking her way to the top.

She exited the room and stood there for a second, attempting to process. She could go out to the deck or the beach and find Samson. He'd told her where he'd be when he'd left her with a kiss this morning. That was what her gut wanted her to do.

No. Not right now. Given the thinly veiled accusation William had spouted, she had to keep some distance. No need to add fuel to the fire. She wouldn't, couldn't be accused of sleeping with the man to get ahead.

This house was too big and expensive, she decided as she went upstairs. Easy to feel that too-familiar loneliness, like she didn't belong, in here. If only she could go back to Samson's cozy beach house with its old-fashioned floral patterned sofa.

Text him.

No. She'd hole up in her room. At the very least, she could comfort herself with how annoyed Peter must be to have to sit around all day waiting for Annabelle's decision.

When she was in her room, the churning loneliness still hanging over her like a dark cloud, she pulled out her phone and typed **I love you.**

Then she copy-pasted it to her mother, brother, and Katrina.

Before she could put her phone in her pocket, her phone chimed three times:

I love you too, but didn't we just talk about how you'd call me more? It's been almost a week, Rhiannon. I could be dead. In fact, maybe I am. My ghost will haunt your phone, daughter.

Hey Sis, love you. 😚 Anything up? I'm sorry if Mom's bugging you about the engagement party, I'll tell her to cool it.

I love you most! How's the weekend going? Call me whenever.

Rhiannon swallowed the lump in her throat and tugged the sleeves of her hoodie down.

The people I loved, I chose wisely. When I did reach out, they were right there.

Her sweatshirt hugged her, and Samson would hug her better, but to be honest . . . she tucked her phone away. These texts had accomplished kind of the same feeling.

Chapter Twenty-Five

SAMSON FOUND Annabelle in her office. "You wanted to see me, Aunt Belle?"

Annabelle half turned from the window. The dying sun lit up her red hair. "I did."

Samson took a seat as she paced the floor. He folded his hands in his lap, though his mind was screaming in impatience.

It was twenty to five. In no time at all, Annabelle would decidedly eliminate one or more of the contenders for her business in her beloved rose garden.

According to the staff, Rhi had asked not to be disturbed all afternoon, so he'd refrained from knocking on her door or texting her. He had seen Peter, for exactly one minute, in the hallway, before the other man had caught sight of him and scurried away. It had taken every ounce of self-control in Samson not to chase him and smash the rat's teeth in.

He wanted Rhi to win, but he was aware he might be too biased at this point to function as a proper adviser. One thing was certain, though, Peter couldn't buy his aunt's life's work. The man didn't deserve it. He didn't deserve winning anything, but especially not at Rhiannon's expense.

The only issue now was how to make sure Peter got cut without breaking his promise to Rhi.

"Chris is out of the running," Aunt Belle blurted out.

"Oh?" Odd. The older man had seemed legit.

"He said he only came to see me again." A light flush colored her cheeks. "We may have had a slight fling once upon a time."

Samson coughed. "I'm sorry. What?"

"Before I met Joe. Our match percentages weren't that high, so I ended things." His aunt's brow was furrowed deep. "But his test from yesterday shows a higher match. Perhaps we've both changed."

Or the test wasn't that big of an indicator of relationship success, though he wouldn't tell Aunt Belle that. "Are you going out with him?"

"I don't know. It would be a date. Or I suppose that's what dinner at a nice Italian place is? That's what he proposed."

"Which place?"

"Oh, I don't know Rome that well."

He raised his eyebrows. "Yeah, that's a date. How do you feel about it?"

"He's very handsome. And his accent is rather sexy, isn't it?"

"I suppose so."

"Oh dear." She twisted her fingers together. "I don't know much about dating anymore. I haven't . . . not since Joe."

He softened. "I didn't know much about dating these

days either. I think it's more work to really be able to communicate above all the other noise out there, but otherwise, I don't think it ever really changes."

"Joe's only been gone a few months." Annabelle poked her finger into a hole of her knit shawl. "Dating someone before his diagnosis is even confirmed? No. People will say it's too soon."

"Since when do you care what people say?" He took a deep breath, and this time the words came easy, possibly because he'd already broken the seal with Rhi. "I didn't want to mess you up this weekend, but the doctor called and confirmed the CTE yesterday."

Her lip quivered, but she bit it. "Well." She straightened her shawl. "That's amazing. Good. He'd be so happy. We talked about this."

"You did?" His uncle had only briefly informed him about the donation plans he'd made.

"You didn't? Of course you didn't. He probably thought it would bring up too many painful memories about your father." She drifted to where he sat and touched his shoulder. "Joe had the most generous heart hidden under all that bluster. The second he got sick, he said to me, *Belle, if the tests come back positive, you make the biggest stink the world has ever seen. Don't let them sweep it under the rug like they tried to do with Aleki.*" Her eyes grew misty. "He didn't want anyone else to go through what his brother and nephew did."

He had to blink hard a couple times. *You made your industry better for the young men who came after you, and the older men who came before you.* He didn't know if Rhi's words applied to him, but he wanted them to apply to his uncle. "I guess we'll have to make a stink."

She squeezed his shoulder, as if she sensed his lingering apprehension. "I'll have Tina work on our joint statement. You will not be alone in this."

"Right."

"This is good. Closure."

"Closure," Samson repeated. He shifted, and his shoulders did feel lighter, like he'd shed a weight. "Back to your question, I'd be concerned if Chris was flirting with you to get to the company, but if he's no longer in the running, and you want to, you should go out with him. If Rome is too far, we have Italian restaurants here."

Annabelle mulled that over. "Yes, I was concerned he might have ulterior motives so I told him if I did date him, he would have to withdraw his offer for the business."

"What did he say to that?"

His aunt blushed. "He said he didn't come here for that anyway. I dismissed William during Chris's presentation time slot and we simply chatted."

Samson smiled. "Joe would have wanted you to be happy, more than anything."

"I think so too." Annabelle sat down at her desk, adjusting her shawl. She folded her hands on the table. "Back to business. That leaves Rhiannon and Peter."

No, not Peter.

Samson waited. No need for him to say anything if Annabelle had already decided against Peter.

"I like Rhiannon," she finally said. "For some bizarre reason, William has the most terrible impression of her. He's a good executive, but not a good judge of character when it comes to women. He's been married and divorced four times, you know, and I warned him each time that he wasn't suited to any of those lovely ladies."

"I like her too."

"I know you do." She paused. "You have a close relationship, don't you?"

He remained silent and she smiled. "No need to answer. I know you do. Would you like me to tell you your match percentages?"

"Nope."

"Very well." Annabelle played with her pen. "On paper, Peter is the better choice. He's offered more money than Rhiannon."

"Counter Rhiannon."

Annabelle steepled her hands in front of her face. "Why would I counter Rhiannon when I could just take Peter's money?"

"Because you don't want to do business with that man." He braced himself, ready to launch into an argument that didn't betray Rhiannon, but to his surprise, his aunt nodded.

"I agree. Something about how Rhiannon parted from Swype left a bad taste in my mouth. I dug harder and found some rumblings about Peter from a couple of women. One of those women got back to me today. Her story was . . ." She shook her head, distaste written across her face. "I directed her to a lawyer. I'm unimpressed with Peter."

Samson tugged at his earlobe. Did Rhiannon know there were others Peter had treated poorly? Based on what she'd said, he didn't think so. "What did you say to the woman? What were her allegations?"

Annabelle waved him away. "That's private."

"Okay."

"If there's anything you want to add, though . . ."

Samson bit the inside of his cheek. As much as he wanted to spill out Rhi's story, he couldn't do that without talking to her first. "I believe them. Whoever you talked to. Whatever they alleged. I believe them. Listen to them."

"You don't even know what they said. Or if anyone corroborated their account."

He thought of Rhi's face last night. Of Peter's barely leashed aggression.

Of what might have happened if she hadn't sent him that text. When a person felt free to cross one boundary, they often felt comfortable crossing multiple boundaries. "I don't need to know what they said. I believe them."

Aunt Belle studied him for a long moment and pursed her lips. "Well. I suppose my decision is fairly easy then."

THE ROSE GARDEN was on the west side of the house, the garden Rhiannon had seen from the library. Rhiannon imagined Annabelle had been peeved not to do this bit of theater when the roses were in full bloom, though they were still pretty lovely, the sweet fragrance teasing her nose the second she stepped outside.

Peter stood in the clearing. Rhiannon didn't turn around and leave, or trip over her own feet, or back down.

She squared her shoulders and walked into the rose garden, hands down and relaxed at her sides. Now that she was clear-headed following a restful night of sleep, she understood it didn't matter if she fidgeted or stuffed her hands in her pockets, Peter wouldn't see it as a weakness. Peter had never been able to pick up on the nonverbal cues of when she was discomfited. Or the verbal cues, for that matter.

Samson could tell after a couple weeks. He also held her properly. Peter had never cuddled her like that.

Think about Samson later. Business now.

"Peter."

He raised an eyebrow at her cool tone. As usual, he was buttoned up and down in a suit, though he'd left his tie off, probably as a nod to the weekend and casual atmosphere. "Rhiannon. How did you sleep last night?"

This fucker. "Like a log, thank you." She beamed at him, the better to irritate him.

He picked a piece of lint off his sleeve. "And Samson? I saw him briefly today, in gym shorts no less. What exactly is that meathead's job when he's not filming dumb ads?"

"Talk a little louder. I'm sure Annabelle would love to hear you calling her close family friend a meathead."

Peter bared his teeth. "Ready to lose?"

"Nope." Her smile was thin, and she hoped she looked every bit as confident as she didn't feel. "Won't happen."

"I guess we'll see." He checked his watch, his annoyed frown lifting her spirits a little. For all that she rolled her eyes at this drama, it was satisfying Peter hated it more.

"I'm here!" Annabelle swept into the garden. The older woman had changed out of her casual clothes. She wore a glittery pink evening gown that clung to her curvy figure. Her hair was caught in a sparkly headband, and her earrings were flamingos.

Annabelle beamed at them and motioned them closer so they stood in a triangle. "Update: Chris has opted to withdraw from bidding on Matchmaker."

"And then there were two," Peter murmured, and he gave Rhiannon a smug smile.

How strange. Chris wasn't the type to drop out of any race. Rhiannon wondered what had happened. She couldn't tell if Peter had known about Chris, but he clearly didn't think it affected his chances either way.

Annabelle took a deep breath and Rhiannon prepared herself to wait. If the older woman stood true to form, she was going to drag this out until kingdom come. Were there cameras? Was she going to pin roses on their lapels?

Annabelle looked Peter dead in the eye. "Peter. I've opted to decline your offer." She switched her gaze to Rhiannon before either of them could react. "Rhiannon, come to my office." And with that, she swept out the way she'd come.

It took a second for Rhi's feet to move. Holy shit. Had she . . . won? Was that what had happened?

"What just happened?" Peter wheezed.

So she wasn't the only one in shock. "I think . . ." Rhiannon said slowly. "I think you got rejected." An unholy glee took over her shock. "I know you don't handle that well, but hopefully you can refrain from melting down like you did when I rejected you."

Rhi started walking away, to follow Annabelle, but Peter blocked her path. She cocked an eyebrow. "Move. I have a deal to close."

An angry red flush suffused Peter's face. How had she ever thought this man was attractive? Or good for her?

Because you didn't know better.

When you were in a stew of toxicity, sometimes you reached for the least bitter piece of meat. She wasn't going to beat herself up for how good he'd been at tricking her.

"If you think this somehow makes you better than me, you're mistaken," Peter hissed.

It was probably unwise to taunt a man who looked as angry as Peter did, but . . . eh. Fuck it. "I don't *think* I'm better than you," Rhiannon explained. "I *know* I'm better than you. And pretty soon the whole world will know it, too, won't they?" She dropped her gaze to Peter's fists. "Do you want to hit me?" Exhilaration made her brave, or maybe reckless. She took a step closer to him, on the path she'd follow to speak with Annabelle and claim her crown. "Go on. How will you explain a black eye? That I was asking for it?"

Slowly, he unclenched his fingers.

Tough talk aside, the knot of apprehension in her chest eased. She nodded. "Now move."

They waited in a tense standoff for a few seconds, but Peter finally budged. She could feel his gaze on her back, drilling a hole, but with each step she took, pride and accomplishment took the place of her fear and nervousness.

She found Annabelle in her office, seated at her desk, scribbling something. The older woman looked up when Rhiannon entered and gestured for her to close the door.

Her beautiful Willy Wonka.

Rhiannon's butt had barely hit the chair when Annabelle shoved a folded piece of paper across the desk. "That's my counteroffer," she said crisply.

This was a little unexpected, but not wholly so. Rhiannon had anticipated some negotiation. So long as she wasn't the one angrily grabbing her bags and exiting the mansion right now like Peter undoubtedly was, she was fine with some friendly wrestling over dollars and cents.

Rhiannon opened the paper and choked at the number written there. "This is a much higher counter."

Annabelle folded her hands on the desk. "It's what Peter offered."

That son of a bitch. He'd been willing to *overpay* for this company, just to make sure Rhiannon got shut out? Because that's what this amount was. A vast overpayment.

She folded the paper. "I'll have to check with my partner." This was much higher than what she and Katrina had agreed their final number would be.

"I'll give you a week." Annabelle's smile wasn't so friendly now. She might not be her older sister, but there was a businesswoman underneath all those eccentricities. A shark of a businesswoman. "There's also some terms in Peter's proposal that I liked that weren't in yours. I'll send you a list tomorrow, but those would also be included in the counter."

Annabelle's tone was stern and dismissive, something Rhi never heard before from her. "We can consider some additional terms, but again, I have to speak to my partner."

"Perfectly acceptable." Annabelle stood. "Well, that's that, I suppose. Congratulations, Rhiannon. I look forward to hopefully doing business with you."

Rhiannon rose to exit the office, but a tiny itch between her shoulder blades stopped her from leaving. "Was there any part of my proposal that you liked more than Peter's?"

"Oh yes." Annabelle peered at her over her glasses. "I liked the words you spoke from your heart."

"But the actual proposal?"

"Well, Peter offered more money. And 100 percent employee retention."

Rhiannon wasn't sure she could guarantee employee retention, especially if everyone at Matchmaker was as snotty to her as William was. She definitely couldn't imagine retaining and working with William. "That is an extravagant promise," she said cautiously.

"Oh, I know. I wasn't expecting it."

"If you don't mind me asking then . . . why didn't you take Peter's offer? If it was so good it could hardly be true?"

"Personality and heart matter in all aspects of life, business included."

A suspicion bloomed. "I didn't think you disliked Peter."

"Appearances can be deceiving." Annabelle's smile was fake. "Are we done? I'm sure you have to get on the road."

Rhiannon hesitated. Her stomach was a mess of knots. "Annabelle . . . this isn't because of what William said about me being involved with Samson, is it? Because I would hate to think that influenced your decision making."

Annabelle reared back. "Of course not. I don't make business decisions based on who my nephew likes."

That sounded genuine. "Okay."

Annabelle shrugged. "I didn't care for some of the things I heard about Peter's past, that's all."

Instead of easing it, the sinking sensation in Rhiannon's stomach intensified. *Why are you looking a gift horse in the mouth? She's willing to bargain with you, not Peter.* Still, she persisted. "Do those things in his past have to do with me?"

Rhiannon knew she was on the right track when Annabelle looked away. "Of course not."

Bingo. Rhiannon swallowed the lump in her throat. It tasted like bitterness and defeat. "Thank you for your counter. But I have to regretfully decline."

She made it to the door before Annabelle found her voice. "You're refusing the company? Why?"

Rhiannon shook her head, unable to fully explain. How could she tell Annabelle that the sale would feel forever tainted and handed to her out of pity and default? How could she verbalize this complex ball of emotions? "I don't believe I need a reason. Thank you for your time and your consideration." She left the room before Annabelle could speak further.

She was thankfully already packed. Instead of summoning the housekeeper or butler, she grabbed her bag herself from her room. She hadn't cried in forever, but as she jogged back downstairs, her sinuses grew dangerously clogged. All she could pray was that she didn't run into Annabelle or Samson.

The strap of her duffel caught on the door handle of the library as she passed it, and she tugged it free. She froze, gaze on the floor, when Samson called her name from down the hall.

The anger she'd expected, but not the hurt. She deliberately ignored him and continued walking to the front door.

"Rhi? What happened? Rhi!"

God, her name on his lips. It hurt to hear it. It made her angry to hurt when she heard it. Peter had tainted her full name, and now Samson had tainted her nickname? Would she have any name left?

"Rhi!" He grabbed her arm and she shoved him away so violently she dropped her bag.

"Don't touch me," she said coldly and got madder at the hurt in his face. *He* had no right to be hurt. She was the one who had dared to hope and had that hope smashed to smithereens.

He held up his hands. "Okay, okay," he soothed. "I won't touch you. What's wrong? Did Annabelle refuse your offer?"

Ugh, like he could take care of things, if Annabelle had refused her. He couldn't take care of anything for her. "No, she refused Peter. She countered me."

He appeared mystified. "But that's great news?"

"She refused Peter," she repeated, enunciating each world carefully, in case the fool didn't get it. "Because you told her what I told you about me and Peter, didn't you? After I said not to say anything?"

"No. I didn't. She—"

"She said she learned something about Peter she didn't like, and I could tell the thing she learned was about me. How did she know anything about me and Peter? You were the only other one here who knew." Her voice was getting dangerously loud. Too loud, too much, too emotional.

He held out his hand in that beseeching universal gesture for *calm down, little lady.* She almost swatted him away. "I didn't—"

"What? You didn't *intend* to tell her anything?"

"Let me explain. Belle was leaning toward Peter. He had the stronger bid. I—"

"I wanted this company on my own merits. Buying Matchmaker would have proved . . ." Something. She wasn't sure what. "I didn't want to cheat."

"You didn't cheat. I didn't tell her, but for God's sakes, Rhi, even if I had, what he did to you, it's the truth. Telling someone the truth is not cheating. Him getting away with hurting you? Him getting rewarded in spite of it? That's cheating."

The blood roaring in her ears made it impossible to process what he was saying. "I can't believe I trusted you."

His face turned gray. He took a step closer. "You were right to trust me."

"No. I wasn't. You forgot about me once before. You disregarded my feelings here entirely. Even after—" She broke off, because what did they have together? The start of something maybe, but not even that now. "It was my decision to tell someone about this. Not yours. Mine."

"Let's talk. We can go to my house."

"No." Rhi shook her head so hard her hair whipped her in her face, her vehemence fueled by how badly she wanted to do exactly what he said. "I have to go. I . . . I have to go. Goodbye, Samson."

He didn't try to stop her from leaving, and for that she was grateful. She might have stayed and heard him out if he'd uttered one more plea, and she couldn't do that right now.

Did you learn your lesson now? This is why you don't hear people out. This is why you don't give second chances.

She pulled her hood up so it covered her hair, but she was naked. Exposed. Someone, a colleague who wasn't Katrina or her assistant, knew the truth of what Peter had done to her. It might only be a snippet of the truth, only the tip of the harassment iceberg, but it was enough that her fight-or-flight reflex had been well and truly triggered. She needed to be alone.

Thank God her scheduled ride was already in the driveway. Rhi got into the luxury sedan without waiting for the driver to open her door. She acknowledged his greeting and placed her duffel next to her. As they pulled away from the big house, she didn't look behind her to see if Samson had come out on the steps to watch her leave. She did, however, yank out her phone and delete him from her contacts. Her thumb hovered over blocking him, but she couldn't go that far. Deletion you could do on a whim. Blocking was the ultimate goodbye.

She kept her gaze on her lap, head bowed, so the driver wouldn't see her tears if he looked behind him. She pulled her sleeves down and hugged herself tighter. In a few hours, she'd be home and Katrina would hug her for real.

She just had to hold on. She was good at that.

Chapter Twenty-Six

SAMSON ROLLED to his back, his head cushioned by Rhi's lap. She smiled down at him, the sunlight reflecting off her glowing skin, and ran her fingers through his hair. He hummed with pleasure at the massage.

"Samson?" Someone shook his shoulder, hard, and rudely jerked him out of his perfect dream.

He recoiled when he opened his eyes to find his aunt's face mere inches from his own. "Aunt Belle? Why are you here?"

She dangled his childhood home's spare key in front of him. "Dear, we have to talk about you leaving that key under the planter. The world isn't as safe as it used to be, you know."

He glanced around in confusion. "Why are you in my bedroom, though?"

Aunt Belle perched on the side of his bed. She wore overalls splattered with paint, with a ribbed tank top underneath. A pink strip of cloth was wrapped around her head, a jaunty bow tied on top. "It's the middle of the day. I came over to see if you needed help."

He scrubbed his hand over his face. Samson had told

his aunt he was packing up his parent's home. It was slow-going. "I must have been tired."

"You've been tired a lot this past week."

He sat up and tucked the blanket around himself better, though he was dressed in shorts and a T-shirt. "How's everything going with William?"

"Fine." Aunt Belle waved the topic aside. She'd grown more confident in dealing with her CEO since the house party. So confident, William had announced his intention to step down. Aunt Belle didn't seem fazed by that decision, so Samson wasn't either.

"Did you want to talk about the campaign then?" They'd aired his last Matchmaker date with the young woman Aunt Belle had picked out for him. After edits, the meetup had looked even better.

"Oh, I think we should press pause on the campaign. You had a miserable date, you had lessons, you had a great date. That narrative arc is simple, and complete."

He still had one contracted shoot with Rhi, but he supposed that was over. "Cool." Cool, cool, cool, cool. His job was done. Now he had endless days ahead of him.

Belle interrupted his melodramatic thoughts. "What's going on, Samson? They told me you pulled out of the interview with Helena. That was a nice opportunity for exposure."

He rested against his headboard. "I know. I'm sorry. I couldn't do it."

He hadn't been able to stand the thought of sitting across from Rhi, separated by Helena and miles of distrust. He'd done it once before with her angry at him and that had been bad enough. He couldn't do it now, with her livid at him, thinking he'd betrayed her.

And he couldn't do it when he also felt a little angry with her. For turning on him, on them, so easily.

"That's fine. We do only the things we're capable of doing." Aunt Belle's tone was very gentle. "You've been so depressed lately, Samson. It hurts me to see it. I thought it might help you, coming over here, but I don't think it has."

"I haven't really gotten far." He'd only sorted his uncle's records this week. He knew he had to make a decision about the place soon, but piling a heavy task on top of his current glum existence wasn't an exciting prospect. It would wait, right? He could give himself a pass on this.

He'd only finalized his statement about Uncle Joe and sent it to CRA yesterday. Thinking of Rhi was painful, but she'd eased a lot of his apprehension about what might come after the statement was released, at least.

"This is about Rhiannon, isn't it?"

He clasped his hands on top of the comforter and considered saying no. What was the point? Annabelle would see right through it. "Yes."

"What happened with her?"

The words spilled out of him, like he'd been waiting for a confidante. "She thought I told you something I didn't."

"About her and Peter?"

He couldn't nod to confirm it, even though Rhi was already gone.

Aunt Belle pursed her lips. "I didn't need you to tell me anything. I told you, I found other women who Peter hurt. The one who called me back, she'd worked at Swype around the same time as Rhiannon. She said there were rumors swirling that he was treating Rhiannon poorly."

Samson wondered if Rhi knew there had been people at Swype who'd known Peter was the bad guy in their feud. Probably not. "Well, I knew about it and she made me promise not to tell you. I guess when she turned down your offer she came up with this scenario where I spilled the beans and refused to even give me the chance to set the record straight. Straight-up assumed I had betrayed her."

"Her questionnaire did indicate a lot of trust issues," Aunt Belle admitted.

"She has those in spades." He cracked his knuckles in agitation. Samson understood when he'd exacerbated those issues, when he'd stood her up. He hadn't *done* anything this time, though, damn it.

"Do you know what your test results indicate?"

"What?"

"Patience," Aunt Belle said.

Samson looked down at his comforter. "I don't feel patient. I'm mad at her for believing the worst about me. It was unfair. I'd never hurt her like that." *Not true.* He had ghosted her, after all.

Okay, he hadn't hurt her since they'd gotten back together, though, had he?

"Your anger is valid. Keep in mind, though, her response may seem unfair and irrational to you, but based on the very little I know, Peter traumatized her. This may all make sense within the framework of her experience."

He exhaled, the air coming from the soles of his feet. Her words made sense, and his anger was already wavering. "I understand that. Anyway, it doesn't really matter how I feel, at the end of the day. She doesn't want anything to do with me." There was the real issue. Bleh. He hated how plaintive his words and tone were.

"Have you tried contacting her?"

"I talked to her when she left the house." When she'd run. Like a bat out of hell.

"I meant after."

"No. Of course not."

"Why not?"

"Because I'm not going to shove myself at her when she doesn't want me. How does that make me any better than Peter?"

Aunt Belle snorted. "There's a very real difference between Peter harassing her for not sleeping with him and you texting her a nice, sweet explanation to try to open the channels of communication again."

He shook his head. "I don't know."

Aunt Belle considered him for a long moment. "Do you know what I've observed about you, Samson?"

"I'm scared to ask."

"You love so deeply. You take care of everyone." She cocked her head. "But you haven't cultivated a long-term relationship with anyone since, say, college or your early twenties. Why not?"

"That's not true."

"Isn't it? You have your friends, but those are relationships you forged a long time ago, under very specific conditions."

Was she right? He tried to come up with the name of one person who could prove her wrong, but couldn't. "Rhi and me, our thing was meant to be temporary. Casual. That was what she wanted."

"Was it what you wanted?"

"It's all I can have."

"Why? Why can't you have a long-term, romantic relationship with someone? Do you prefer to sample the buffet, so to speak?"

His face burned. "No." He'd never been a player. Hell, he'd been celibate for almost half a decade before he'd hooked up with Rhi.

"Then why?"

He squirmed, but he couldn't get away from Aunt Belle's probing gaze. "Because I don't want to."

"Interesting. Why?"

"Because."

"Because why?" she persisted.

"Because they'll leave me!" The words fell between them with the weight of a thousand broken hearts.

"Ahhhh." Aunt Belle drew out the word. "There it is. You don't expect love to last, do you? Everyone leaves you, eventually. And you've come to accept that they'll all leave you, so you let them go before they get too close. Or, in this case, because she's already close, you're letting her go when you could fight for her."

He laughed, but it sounded desperate. "That's some psychoanalysis."

His aunt lifted a shoulder. "I haven't gotten this far with this many marriages under my belt without having a keen knowledge of human nature, darling. I am right."

Was she?

Samson thought about how he'd tried to find Rhiannon back when he'd stood her up at the beach house, when she'd been Claire. Had he tried hard enough? Had he exhausted every resource? He'd craved Rhiannon enough to chase her down and talk to her and sleep with her, but hadn't he freaked out a little with every vulnerability he'd revealed?

Annabelle swung her leg off the side of the bed. "Do you remember, last summer, when you took Joe to the brewery on the water?"

"Yeah." Annabelle had sat at a nearby table, hungrily staring at Joe. A year or so ago, Joe's Alzheimer's had progressed to the point where he couldn't readily recognize Annabelle. If she spent much time around him, he'd grow agitated. When she was in town, Samson had gone out of his way to get Joe in her vicinity, where she could at least see him.

"When you went to grab menus, I walked up to the table. I knew I couldn't stand there long, or he'd start to wrack his brain over who I was and get upset with himself. So I asked if I could borrow the ketchup. Do you know what he said to me? He said, 'Has anyone ever told you how beautiful you are?'" Her eyes sparkled with tears. "In that moment, I was nothing but grateful. Grateful to have another moment with him, even if he didn't remember all the other moments we'd had together."

"Don't cry." He grabbed a tissue from the box on his nightstand and offered it to her. She dabbed at the corners of her eyes.

"I'm grateful for these tears. I'm grateful I was vulnerable enough to love him. I'd do it all over again, even knowing I would lose him eventually. Your mother would have said the same about Aleki. You would say the same about all of them, wouldn't you? Aren't you grateful to have had as much time as you did with them?"

He pressed his lips together. "Yes." Even with his complicated feelings about his father, he was grateful.

"Being vulnerable is a risk. Love—romantic, platonic, familial, it doesn't matter what kind of love—is a risk." She closed her eyes tight, tears leaking out. "Because you're right. They can leave. They can die or be hurt or simply walk away." Her eyes opened. "But a moment of that love, child, is worth it. If you have a second, a minute, a month, a year, a decade with that person? You count yourself lucky. You can use that love and the lessons it taught you to plant more seeds for love. You can live off that love for a lifetime. Are we clear?"

His chest hurt. He unclenched his fist, laying his palm flat on his leg. "Yes ma'am. We're clear."

"Call Rhiannon. She's perfect for you. I knew it from the second you chased her out of the hotel—" She bit her lip, cutting herself off, but it was too late.

Samson slowly straightened. "What?"

"Nothing."

"Were you going to say, when I chased her out of the hotel ballroom?" At CREATE? When he'd spotted her standing in front of the stage?

"No. Of course not."

His aunt was such a shitty liar. "You said you didn't know who I was chasing, Aunt Belle."

She winced. "I heard her say her name when I was spying in the ballroom, before you took the mic. When you described her, I realized who you were talking about."

His eyes narrowed, a thought occurring to him. "Did you fake your fear the next day? To throw me and her together at the interview with Helena?"

"I have many real phobias." She fiddled with her earring. "Perhaps I didn't try to fight that fear too hard, though."

"Aunt Belle!"

"I was trying to help you! And I didn't think you'd go work with her or anything. That was all you. I wasn't in the country, remember? I put you two face-to-face once. You took it from there."

"Did that push include inviting her here? The whole house party? So you could meet her?"

"Um . . . I mean, I did want to seriously meet everyone interested in the company . . ."

"Oh my God." He dropped his head in his hands. If you waited long enough, everything made sense. "The test. The Matchmaker quiz. I thought that was weird. You made everyone take it, so you could check on the match between the two of us."

"Okay, that part is true."

"Aunt. Belle."

"What?" His aunt's eyes went wide. "I wanted to make sure she was right for you, Samson! Sue me for loving you."

He pinched the bridge of his nose. "I can't believe this."

"Do you want to know your match percentage with her?"

"No!"

They sat in silence for a moment, until Samson cracked. "Is it over ninety?" He shook his head when Belle nodded and moved her thumb upward. "No, I don't want to know."

"Suit yourself. But rest assured, dear. You should call her. It's a *good* match." She slapped her thigh. "Should we think about what to have for dinner? I—" She frowned when her phone rang, and she dug it out of the pack slung around her hips. She plucked her reading glasses from where they were hooked in the front of her overalls and peered at the screen. When she gasped, Samson reached across the bed to touch her arm. "What's wrong?"

Worry was written all over her face. "The woman I talked to, the one who told me Peter harassed her. She went to the press."

Chapter Twenty-Seven

Rhiannon sat in Helena's green room and watched the news broadcast on television. The breaking-news banner, combined with Peter's name, had prompted her to turn the volume up. She listened in increasing disbelief, then accessed the article in the national newspaper that the broadcaster had referenced and read it on her phone.

There it was, in black and white. Three women and one man, accusing the CEO of Swype of sexual harassment and misconduct. Two women had permitted their names to be used.

Some of the accusations were similar to what Rhiannon had experienced, some were far worse than she could have ever imagined. Peter, demanding sexual favors for continued employment. Locking his office door to ensure the victims had no way out, physically. Threatening to blacklist them if they didn't comply.

Her eyes went back to a quote in the middle of the long report. *I should have known better, because I was there when he bullied his former girlfriend out of the business. Everyone saw it. We all felt so bad for her. She was an executive, with some power.*

Why did I think he'd treat me any differently? I was nobody compared to her.

Rhiannon covered her mouth with her hand and scrolled back down to the end. *Why come forward now?* The reporter had asked one of the victims. *I would have never said anything, but I guess Swype was looking to buy another company, and the owner of that company called me. It brought up all these old memories, and I couldn't bear to live with them anymore in silence.*

She looked up when the door to the green room opened and Helena Knight walked in, somber. They'd greeted each other an hour ago, when Rhiannon had arrived at the Manhattan studio. Helena had delivered the news that Samson had canceled at the last minute. Rhiannon had been relieved.

She didn't feel relieved now.

"Darling, did you see the news?"

"I did."

"Would you like to get your publicist on the phone?" Helena asked gently. "Because you know I'll have to ask you about it. You worked for Peter."

Rhiannon shook her head. Her phone was vibrating in her pocket, probably Suzie or Lakshmi, but she couldn't deal with that now. She didn't need them for this. "I understand. No need for anyone else. Let's talk."

HELENA PUT RHIANNON at ease first and gave her a chance to discuss Crush and build a rapport with the audience. Then she turned to the topic on everyone's mind. "Today a story broke accusing the CEO of Swype, Peter Roberts, of multiple counts of sexual harassment and in one case, at least, assault." Helena gestured to Rhiannon. "Everyone who knows Crush knows Swype. You two are the largest players in the app-dating business. You also used to work for Swype. Do you have any comment on the story?"

Rhiannon opened her mouth. The silence stretched, and out of the corner of her eye, she noticed the producer taking a step forward.

Her gaze fell on the first row, the people watching her intently. All in their twenties and thirties.

Oddly enough, a snippet of what she'd said to Samson as they stood in his home, surrounded by his memories, came to mind. *You made your industry better for the young men who came after you, and the older men who came before you.*

Helena cleared her throat and Rhi snapped out of it. Live television. No time to fuck around.

It was my decision to tell someone about this.

Never again.

She clasped her hands in front of her on the table. "I saw the story. I believe those who came forward."

"Across the board, no hesitation?"

"No hesitation. In general, I believe survivors. And when I say that, I don't mean to say I blindly believe them or that I blindly believe the alleged perpetrator guilty. But the societal impulse is to disbelieve survivors, and we don't really do that when it comes to any other misconduct. When someone claims they've been mugged, we don't treat them with skepticism. We believe them. We investigate, but we believe them."

Helena nodded. "And in this particular situation?"

"In this particular situation . . ." Rhi licked her lips and reached for her most coldly dispassionate tone. She might be speaking from the heart here, but she needed to sound like she was doing nothing more than reciting facts and figures. "I believe the survivors because I have personal experience. I was involved in a relationship with Peter. It wasn't a secret. I ended things. Peter decided Swype wasn't big enough for the both of us and harassed me out. He spread rumors. He made my life there so miserable, I begged to leave." Her hands curled into fists. "I hated begging most of all. He knew that."

Helena took a sip of water, and Rhiannon could practically see her brain racing. They hadn't gone into this much detail in the green room, but Helena was a good journalist. The cameras were rolling, and a juicy follow-up to a sensational story had landed in her lap. "This isn't common knowledge."

"One of the survivors in the newspaper article, she mentioned having been employed when Peter harassed an executive. That was probably me. Most likely me. I didn't think anyone noticed, at the time. The rumors he spread about me are still prevalent. I still meet people in the industry today, who, despite my accomplishments, believe that I'm dumb and lazy and a gold digger." She thought about William. An executive of a well-respected company who had viewed her with contempt. "My reputation was solid gold before I dated that man. And then after I left . . . I was radioactive."

"Did you take money to leave the company?"

"I need to talk to my lawyer about what I can and can't

say about my separation agreement." She smiled faintly. "I would have been far better off financially staying at Swype than I was leaving it, if that's what you're asking. I received no financial benefit from quitting."

Helena crossed and uncrossed her legs. "Why didn't you sue him when he started harassing you? You also held a position of some power."

Rhi's defensiveness kicked in, but then she caught the encouraging, empathetic look on Helena's face. The woman was giving her the chance to get the jump on those who would rip her story, and her, apart limb from limb.

The magnitude of what she was doing, unplanned, unrehearsed, with no warning to anyone, not even the people of her own company, made her want to throw up.

Too late. You couldn't stuff a cat back into a bag. Well, you could, but there would be blood.

Anyway, she wasn't a company or a brand at the end of the day. She was a person.

The last thing she wanted to do was bring up the pictures Peter had held over her head to get her to quit. There had been other reasons to quietly leave. "When you're a minority, in any industry, you feel so visible, and like the only way to get ahead is to be tougher than everyone else. You don't cry. You don't show weakness. You can't be a victim." Even now, she flinched away from the word. *Victim.* It was wild how, at the end of the day, even language was an elaborate ruse to keep hurt people compliant. "Victim" implied weakness; if she claimed to be hurt, she was a victim; ergo, if she was a victim, she was weak.

Bullshit.

She hadn't *done* anything wrong, she'd merely taken a chance on loving someone. She hadn't harmed; she'd had harm done to her. That didn't make her weak. Peter's behavior reflected only upon himself.

Helena gave her a second to compose herself, and then prompted her. "Why speak up now?"

Rhiannon looked at the rapt young people in the front row again. "I assumed no one would believe me then. Times have changed."

"It's only been a few years. You think our society has evolved so much since you left Swype?" Helena lifted a skeptical brow.

"We didn't have movements then, or hashtags." Rhiannon tugged at the cuffs of her hoodie. The blue one, her best one. The one she'd worn on that rooftop with Samson, when they'd been silly and cuddled in a waterbed cabana, and he'd kissed her against her car. "Even then, I wouldn't have said anything, probably, if I'd continued to believe I was the only one. As far as I'm concerned, there's no benefit to me coming clean right now, like this, except it might help someone else." She looked directly into the camera, the red light hurting her retinas, but she didn't flinch away. "I read that article today, and I feel so awful, for anyone Peter hurt after me and before me. Thank you, to the people who put up their hands first, who made me feel safe enough to tell my story. I hope, if anyone else is out there, what I'm doing right now helps you."

Helena's lips thinned. "I hope so too. I think it's clear how much workplace harassment has been swept under the rug for years."

"I was lucky. I happened to have a friend who stepped forward and believed in me and gave me the capital to start Crush. If I hadn't had her, my career would have been, if not over, at least severely set back. How many people can say that? How many brilliant minds have been suppressed because a toxic workplace ended their careers?"

Helena glanced at her producer, then back to Rhi. "Is there anything else you'd like our audience to know?"

Rhi twined her fingers together and summoned all her public speaking skills. Whenever she ended an interview, she did it with the knowledge that the sound bite she gave would be used again and again. She needed to close this out with something simple, but powerful. "I built Crush on the platform that the world needs more accountability. Peter should be held accountable for what he did. He shouldn't be allowed to ever do that to anyone again. No one should. Every industry needs to be cleaned up, so we can all get back to work. Let's start here."

The crowd broke into applause as the taping wrapped, but the noise was filtered through a thick layer of Vaseline. Her brain was fuzzy, like she'd been enveloped in a fog.

She accepted Helena's fierce hug and nodded when the other woman whispered in her ear. "I'm sorry. I believe you, and thank you. Please let me know what you need from me. I can put you in touch with a *Times* reporter or . . ."

Reporter. News. This interview was originally supposed to have been a fluff piece in a millennial- and Gen Z–friendly format. When she walked out the door, her life would change.

Or it already had, she realized, as she caught side-eye from the crew backstage.

She deliberately didn't pull her phone out of her purse. The show had arranged for a limo to take her to the airport, and she stared out the window at the garish neon lights, bright and colorful. She shivered at the blasting A/C in the car and turned it down. All she wanted was to be home on the left coast. Curled up in front of the firepit in Katrina's backyard or gazing out at the downtown skyline from her loft.

Unfortunately, she was scheduled to fly from here to western New York for her brother's engagement party. Her departure time was still a few hours off, but she could settle into the airline club at JFK and hide as best she could.

The lounge had small private offices, and one was blessedly empty. She closed the door and pulled out her laptop to start an email. She should call Lakshmi or her lawyer . . . but she didn't know what to say to them. *Hi, I know I set off a not-so-small public relations bomb.*

Instead, she dug through her archives. She didn't send the email, but attached every document she could find with meticulous attention to detail.

After she had that ready, she dug out her phone. She ignored all the calls and messages filling her notifications, and video-called Lakshmi.

"How mad is Suzie?" she asked, when Lakshmi answered.

Her assistant had kept Crush's colors in her hair and added a rose gold septum ring.

"Not mad." Lakshmi's tone was incredibly gentle. "You want to see? We're at my place for a watch party."

Rhiannon almost groaned. She'd forgotten that Lakshmi had arranged a watch party for the staff. "Fine. Yes."

Lakshmi flipped the camera and walked her out of her kitchen. "Guys, Rhiannon is on the phone."

Rhiannon nearly dropped the phone when the roar of approval came out of the speaker. The frame was filled with her people, smiling, misty-eyed, crying, but so . . . on her side.

She'd thought she felt like she belonged in L.A. because she was anonymous there, but no. She belonged because these people were her family too. Family she paid, but family.

Her cheeks were wet, and she almost covered the camera to block anyone from seeing her cry, but she was too tired.

Suzie came into view and took the phone from Lakshmi. The permanent frown on her head of marketing's face was etched deeper, her short platinum hair standing straight up, like she'd run her hands through it. "Bitch," she said, and her smoker's voice was rougher than usual. "Don't you ever go do something like that without me physically by your side to run interference. It's my job to protect you. But you did an amazing job without me, come back soon so I can lecture you in person." She handed the phone back to Lakshmi.

Rhiannon sank deeper into the plush seat. Lakshmi walked away from the crew, her tone turning brisk. "Peter's lawyers have already called legal. They're threatening to sue for defamation and theft of trade secrets."

Rhiannon hit send on the email she'd prepared. "Tell them to go ahead. Show them a couple of the attachments I sent you."

"What are they?"

"Every email Peter sent me telling me I'd never work in this industry again if I didn't get back together with him. Calling me a bitch and a whore." Rhi paused. "I'm still debating releasing them no matter what. But if Swype wants to go the lawsuit route, all those words are definitely getting released to the public. Tell them I saved my text history and voice mails too. Those are even better."

Lakshmi's grin was wide. "With pleasure. Chelsea's gonna be so excited."

"Any lawyer of mine should be. She ought to know that there might be some compromising photos of me in Peter's hands. He didn't use them, because he knew I had all this, but he might go nuclear now."

"Girl, my nudes could wallpaper my house. We'll take care of you."

Rhiannon's shoulders relaxed. "Thank you."

Lakshmi brought the phone closer to her face. "You know we all believe in you, right? My living room is full of heart eyes right now."

Rhiannon licked her lips and tasted salt. "I see that. Thank you. Can you let Katrina know I'm okay?"

"Of course. She was actually watching virtually in the

living room through my computer, though, so she saw you. Are you sure you want to go to your brother's right now? You could come home."

She yearned to go back to California. But no. She couldn't flake on Gabe's engagement party, not when her family had undoubtedly seen this piece. "How many times has my mom called you?"

"Not important."

"Yeah, I have to go to my brother's." Funny how she couldn't bring herself to call the town she'd grown up in *home*. Her family, though, that was a home. "Only for the party. Get me out of there by late tomorrow evening."

"Hang on." The screen went blank, Lakshmi was silent for a moment, and then she was back and spit out some gate info. "Go there. Private jet. I'll charter another one to be waiting for you tomorrow. You want me to intercept your calls and texts for now?"

"Yes. Actually . . ." she hesitated. She'd never said the following words before, in her life. "I'm going to turn my phone off for the next twenty-four hours. If there are any emergencies . . ."

"There won't be. We can handle it. I'll call Sonya and tell her when to pick you up from the airport. Turn your phone off and keep it off."

"I will. Hey. Was that Tina I saw in your living room?"

Lakshmi gave a sheepish shrug. "What can I say? Don't worry, we're only friends for now."

Rhiannon smiled, even as a wave of sadness went through

her. *Samson*. God. She'd avoided thinking about him since she'd left Annabelle's house. Had he seen the show? Had he texted or called her?

Would he, after she'd accused him of something he hadn't done? *I guess Swype was looking to buy another company, and the owner of that company called me.*

It was highly probable Annabelle hadn't found out about Peter from Samson, but from her own due diligence. Meanwhile, she'd flipped out on Samson.

"Rhiannon? You have to get to your gate."

"Right. Goodbye." She hung up and looked down at her phone. It only stayed silent for a second before it buzzed with another text.

She almost braved her in-box, to see what, if anything, Samson had sent, but she simply couldn't do it. She pressed the button on the side and powered it off.

She tugged her sleeves down and grabbed her bags. Since she still felt exposed, she pulled up the hood of her sweatshirt and kept her gaze down as she made her way through the airport.

Her phone, a useless piece of glass and metal now, was blessedly, finally, silent.

Chapter Twenty-Eight

Her little brother had always been a soft soul, but from the second he'd picked her up from the airport Gabe was extra gentle with her. Rhiannon knew he must have seen the show, or at least the clip of her interview, but he danced around discussing it, instead chatting inanely about the engagement party.

She'd rather talk about the show. She'd rather talk about literally anything else.

"Anyway then the cloths were more an off-white than an eggshell, so I said—"

"If you explain the difference between various shades of not-white to me now, I will tuck and roll out of this moving car," she said, without opening her eyes.

He clicked his tongue. "Fair enough, fair enough."

She rolled her head to look at him. He was her adopted brother, so they didn't look alike—Gabe was white passing, big and strong and bearded, like a lumberjack. He was also tattooed all over, a side effect of his profession as a tattoo artist.

He was marrying an heiress, so he had cleaned up a bit

for the engagement party tomorrow. His beard was neatly trimmed, his hair a little shorter than shoulder length. But he was still her little brother. "You saw the show."

Gabe kept his gaze determinedly on the road. "Let's wait to get home to discuss it."

They rode the rest of the way in silence, though Rhiannon looked around in surprise when he pulled up in front of a tidy little house. "We're not staying at the Chandlers'?" Gabe's fiancée, Eve, lived in her family mansion, and Gabe had moved in there a while ago, leaving his own home vacant.

"No. I thought it would be more comfortable for us to stay here."

And they'd have privacy. Always thinking of people's feelings and whatnot, her brother. She got out of the car and followed him to the door.

They'd barely cleared the threshold of the living room before Rhiannon was swallowed up in a giant hug. She wrapped her arms around her mother and hugged her back, burying her face in her neck and inhaling the scent of apples.

She started to cry when her brother also put his arms around them. She was embraced from every side, and the sensation was so beautiful, she couldn't contain herself. They weren't delicate, tiny tears, because nothing about her was delicate or tiny, but deep and racking sobs.

Her mother let her carry on for a few minutes before pulling back and wiping at Rhiannon's cheeks. She was also weeping, Rhiannon noted, through her own haze of tears. "There, there," Sonya whispered. "You're with family now. No one's going to hurt you or point a camera at you here."

This was true. No one would come here to Rockville to shove a mic in her face. "I'm thirsty."

Gabe ushered her to the couch. "I'll make some tea. Sit down."

Sonya perched on the coffee table in front of Rhiannon and seized her hands, chafing them between her own. Rhiannon wasn't cold, but it felt so good to be touched and held in any way, she didn't complain. "I'm glad he's calmed down," Sonya whispered. She tipped her head at the wall.

Rhiannon raised her eyebrows at the fist-sized hole in the drywall. "Gabe did that?"

"He got so angry when we watched the interview. I've never seen him like that. Don't say anything."

Sweet, peaceful Gabe?

Rhiannon took in her brother's scratched-up knuckles when he came back to the living room. Yeah. He'd punched the wall. For her?

Gabe handed a glass of whiskey to their mother and gave her a mug. Rhiannon dunked the tea bag into the mug and took a deep breath. "I'm sorry."

"What are you sorry for?" Sonya demanded. "I knew that Peter was bad news. From the moment I met him, I knew he wasn't any good. Something weaselly in his face."

Rhiannon had thought Sonya loved Peter. He was wealthy and traditional and had also criticized Rhiannon's taste in clothes. "I'm sorry for the inevitable blowback this is going to cause for you guys."

Gabe rested his mug on his knee. "If there's any blowback, it's going to be on you, Rhi. We're way more worried about you."

"Why didn't you go public with this when it happened?" Sonya demanded.

She'd known her mom would want to know that. "For the same reason I said on the show. Because I didn't see any positive upside to it. Sure, some people may have believed me, but most would have taken his word over mine. I thought I could give it less fuel if I stayed quiet."

"No. You should have defended yourself right then."

The last thing she wanted or could deal with was for her mother to lecture her on her past choices. She scrubbed her face.

Gabe slung his arm over her shoulders. "She did what she thought was best."

"I focused on beating him instead." Rhiannon's smile was wobbly. "It's like you used to say, Mom, success is the best revenge."

Sonya's brow furrowed. "When did I say that?"

"In school. Don't you remember? When kids were mean to me."

"In school? That was ages ago."

"I remember it like it was yesterday." That horrible period of being too much.

Sonya squinted. "Oh. I vaguely recall."

"Uh, I've basically used that one piece of advice to cope

for the last few years. It was the only thing that kept me going sometimes." And her mother only vaguely remembered it?

"Well, if it's helped, that's great, but I wouldn't advise you to use every snippet I said to you as a child in your adult life. Half the time, I was throwing stuff at the wall in the hopes it would keep you balanced and well-grounded in that school full of toxic assholes."

"What?"

"I hate to admit this, but I don't know everything." Sonya drained her glass of whiskey in one shot and made a face. "Do you have any idea what it's like, to be the mother of a prodigy? To know your child is brilliant and destined for greatness but will still have to work four times as hard as people with a fraction of her intelligence? I was furious when your classmates were rough on you, but I figured my job was to keep you calm and focused and not let you lose this opportunity. I couldn't let you be angry, or at the very least, I couldn't let you show that anger. Because then you would be that angry Black girl, and everyone would dismiss your intelligence or worse, suppress everything that makes you you. So I—" She stopped, and inhaled sharply. "I guess I suppressed you. My God. I'm so sorry. This is all my fault."

Guilt and love coursed through her when her mother started weeping, and she rose from her seat to put her arm around Sonya. "No, Mom. It's not—"

"Mom."

The steel in Gabe's voice had them both looking up. "This

isn't about you. Don't make Rhi comfort you tonight. We need to be here for her."

Sonya sniffed and surprised Rhiannon by nodding. "You are absolutely right." She cupped Rhiannon's face. "My dear, let me make it clear. Success is the best revenge? No. Sometimes, revenge is the best revenge."

Gabe took a sip of his tea. "What you did wasn't revenge, though, Rhi. It was justice. Justice is the best justice."

"Exactly that," Sonya said. "Even if it took four years, I'm glad you finally came forward."

Rhi stirred. Physical and emotional exhaustion had taken root, and she didn't want to think about Peter anymore. Especially when that thinking included the very real possibility that everything she'd done tonight was for naught and Peter would emerge from this unblemished. "Can we stop talking about this for a while? I'm beat."

"Of course." Sonya made a face. "Did Gabe tell you about our napkin crisis today?"

RHIANNON SLEPT WELL in Gabe's guest room, her mom snuggled in the bed with her, quietly snoring. When she awoke in the morning and puttered into the kitchen, she was welcomed by a scene from her past: Sonya making smiley face pancakes while Gabe cut fruit.

Rhiannon found solace in their familiar banter and the rhythm of her small family, especially when she realized they were going out of their way not to talk about Peter. As kind as they were, the walls of the small home pressed down on her. She excused herself after breakfast, and went outside to enjoy the weak spring sun and the rustle of trees.

Gabe wandered out a few minutes later and got to work chopping wood. His house wasn't too isolated, but there was some land behind it. This was a normal pastime for him.

Rhiannon glanced up at a particularly loud crack and eyed her brother's form. She'd grown up chopping wood too. He was using more force than necessary. She marked her place in the art history book she'd snagged off Gabe's bookshelf. "Did you put a hole in your living room wall, yesterday? Watching the show?"

Gabe paused and swiped his arm over his forehead. If he was discomfited by the abrupt question interrupting their companionable silence, he didn't show it. "I did."

"Why?"

"'Cause I was mad." With a grunt, Gabe set up another log and brought the ax down.

"Why?"

"What do you mean why?"

"Why were you so mad?"

He cast her an incredulous look. "Some dick hurt you, I didn't even know, you think I won't be mad?"

"You're not a violent person."

He raised an eyebrow. He was a big guy, her brother, yet those huge fingers could manage the most delicate fine-line tattoos. "Anyone's violent with the right provocation. I choose not to be violent, that's different."

She fiddled with the edge of her blanket. "Are you mad Peter hurt me, or mad you didn't know?"

Gabe put the ax down carefully and walked over to her. "Both."

She scooted over, making room for him on her blanket. "That doesn't make sense."

He gathered her hands in his and paused for a moment, like he was organizing his thoughts. "I'm your brother. I'm supposed to protect you."

"You're younger than me."

"Right, which mattered when we were both young. In school, I couldn't stand up for you because I wasn't big enough. I barely saw you after you went away to college. But this? I find out some guy hurt you so bad, it almost destroyed your career? The career that's your life? How do you think I'm supposed to feel?"

"I don't need anyone to protect me."

He frowned. "I love you, Rhi. Of course I'm going to protect you. It's not failure to accept protection sometimes."

She thought of how she'd called Samson to her room to scare Peter away. Could she have done it herself? Maybe. Had it been nice to have a shield? Yes.

Gabe squeezed her hand. "I know you've always considered yourself the provider of our little family. I never thought of the toll it must take on you. *My sister, she's one tough bitch.* That's what I'd tell my friends."

"I'm a bit concerned you called me a bitch to your friends."

Gabe chuckled. "Only in a good way. You're an alpha. But alphas need to rest. And they need to recoup. And they need to cry and be vulnerable and take a break from taking care of everyone."

Her throat grew tight. "I always thought I couldn't show any weakness. Like my career depended on me being strong."

"You're strong no matter what. You're strong for speaking up about Peter, you'd be the same degree of strong if you'd stayed silent." He tapped her shoulders, and she consciously lowered them. "It's not a weakness to take care of yourself. Asking for and taking what you need to function should never be considered a weakness."

"I don't think I know how to ask for what I need."

"Think of it this way. You delegate a million and one things at work, right? Lakshmi makes your plane reservations. Suzie runs interference on marketing stuff. All of your employees take something off your plate, either because they're better at it or because it's stuff you don't want to do."

"Yes."

"So delegate in your personal life."

"Delegating. That I understand." She licked her dry lips. "Trust is harder to figure out."

"Mmm." He looked off into the distance, and a soft smile played on his lips. She knew that smile. He was thinking about his fiancée. "Trust is the only reason the world ever functions as it should. Sometimes it works out and sometimes it doesn't, and I know that uncertainty is scary, but that's the only way you figure out who your closest people are."

They sat in silence and listened to the birds chirping. There were no traffic noises here, no concrete. Out of habit, she patted her pocket. No phone.

She inhaled and released a deep breath and finally allowed herself the freedom to think about the man she'd been forcing herself to avoid obsessing over since yesterday. Hell, since she'd left him, standing in a home that belonged to neither of them. "There's a guy."

"Samson Lima." Gabe smiled at her surprised expression. "I watch the videos. Not a huge football fan, but I know of him. He seemed cool and you were clearly into him."

"Clearly?" She'd thought she'd done a good job of maintaining a friendly distance between them on camera.

"Clearly to anyone who knows you like I do."

That was a relief. "He . . . it's a long story." She ran through what had happened at Annabelle's home.

Gabe wrinkled his nose. "Gave him the old Rhi-Rhi deadto-me treatment, huh? How do you feel about that decision?"

"Not good. I mean, I was miserable about it before, but now I'm pretty sure he didn't actually tell Annabelle about me and Peter. I jumped the gun and assumed the worst. Probably because I was already low-key freaked out about how close we'd gotten." The first time she'd cut him out, he'd at least done the thing she'd accused him of doing, extenuating circumstances or not.

Her stomach churned. The way she'd treated him at Annabelle's hadn't been fair.

Gabe shrugged and bent his leg, resting his arm on his knee. "So tell him you're sorry."

"He probably wouldn't take my call. I'd never take anyone back if they treated me like that." She twisted her fingers together. Why would he want someone as difficult and downright annoying as her? She'd watched the video Matchmaker had released last week, of Samson with a pretty young woman.

He hadn't told her he'd gone on another date, though it must have been filmed before they'd met up at Annabelle's home, during that week when he'd been wooing her by sending her food. Sweet, kind, loyal. The girl had been a kindergarten teacher, for crying out loud, and their rapport had been excellent, both of them smiling, nice people. She couldn't compete with that.

"Even if there were extenuating circumstances for their behavior? I mean, your trust issues didn't happen in a bubble, Rhi. You have a traumatic history. It's not like you were being a dick for no reason."

A little sliver of hope peeked through her gloom. The truth was, she had given someone a second chance, fairly recently: Samson. He was so much nicer than she was. Surely he'd take her call, at least? "You think there's hope?"

"Only one way to find out. Text him. Call him. Hell, your phone is off. He may have already contacted you."

"I'm scared."

"Trust is scary. I learned that, for sure, with Eve. But when it's right, Rhi? When the stars align, and you have a partner you can be vulnerable with? There's no such thing as weakness or strength or power battles. There's just a person who loves you. And it's amazing." He shrugged. "You could use a ride from the airport when you get back, I'm sure. Perfect excuse to call him."

She fiddled with the corner of her book. This was so

much to think about, when she was already overloaded, but her brother made sense.

More importantly, she wanted him to make sense, because she wanted to call Samson, wanted to talk to him enough that she'd risk him sending her to voice mail. "I'll think about it."

"Do that."

"When did you get so wise?"

"It's been there all along, sis. You should listen to me more."

She grinned, happy for the sliver of humor. "Got any more wisdom for me?"

"Call Mom more."

"I'm going to." She grimaced. "I love her. I hate feeling guilty and wrong and she makes me feel guilty and wrong a lot."

"She makes me feel guilty too." Gabe lowered his voice. "But that's how she is, and it comes from a huge place of love. Ignore the guilt and try to focus on the love."

"I'll try. Be more saintlike like you."

"There you go. Also, tell Eve what a saint I am." Gabe got to his feet and dusted off his jeans. "You want to stay longer?"

The question was casual, and Rhiannon knew her brother wouldn't judge her either way. She thought of her staff, who were probably working around the clock today to help her and protect her business. This was her family, but so were they. "I'll stick to my plan and fly back tonight, after the party."

"You sure you're up for the party?"

No. But she didn't want to bail on her brother's moment of happiness. "Yup."

"Whatever you want." Gabe walked back to his ax.

"What would you have done to Peter anyway? If you'd known, at the time."

Gabe cast her a measuring look, then leaned over and picked up the ax. With a heave, he flung it. It spun in the air before it thwacked right into the trunk of a tree.

"Daaaaamn." She cocked her head. "When did you learn how to do that?"

He winked at her. "When you were off making your first million, I suppose."

Rhi found herself tensing up as they neared the Chandler mansion. She was here for her brother, and she was eager to celebrate his impending nuptials, but this town had been nosy as fuck when she hadn't gone on national television and alleged sexual harassment by a rich and famous man. What would the reaction be to her tonight?

Gabe seemed to have sensed her nervousness, because he'd kept up a running commentary on all the familiar and kind people she'd be seeing tonight. It was all *Livvy's baby is so big now* and *Jackson's opening a new restaurant*, and she appreciated the sentiment, but it would have been kind of nice to brood in silence.

". . . you know Jia, right, Rhiannon? She's actually thinking of moving to L.A. soon. Maybe you can have a talk with her tonight."

Rhiannon murmured something noncommittal when he glanced in the rearview mirror, and she tugged at her leather jacket. She'd donned her nicest jeans and a T-shirt under the moto jacket.

It was a sign of how worried her mother was for her that she hadn't said a single word criticizing her outfit choice.

Rhiannon walked into the mansion behind Gabe and her mom and almost turned around and walked back out. So. Many. People.

It wasn't all bad. She greeted Gabe's fiancée, and Eve hugged her extra tight. She embraced the Kane siblings, the grown-up children of her mother's old employer, and for a moment, felt surrounded by familiarity and understanding.

They couldn't stay with her forever, though. The rest of the party was a sea of curious faces. She met Gabe's gaze. He glanced at their mother, who was busy talking to another guest, gave Rhiannon a discreet, understanding nod, and she was off.

She snagged a bottle of wine from the open bar before sneaking out a back door. The air was cool and calm on her face, cooler than she was used to back home.

Rhiannon kicked her flats off, picked them up, and made her way away from the house. Not into the dark forest, but toward the charming little white gazebo, surrounded by flowers peeking their heads out of the ground. This estate bordered the one she'd grown up on, and she knew it like the back of her hand.

Relief ran through her when she plopped down on the wooden bench and took a swig of her wine. This was better. For her and for Gabe and Eve, who deserved to be the focus of their own engagement party. She stretched out on the bench and placed her wine on the plank floor. Then she closed her eyes. Normally, she'd be all up in her phone, but it was locked in the back of Gabe's trunk, turned off.

So she listened to the birds chirping and insects rubbing their little insect legs together and the party happening in the mansion close to her. They were all peaceful sounds, now that she wasn't required to socialize.

Wait a minute. No phone. No demands. The sounds of nature. Was this . . . a vacation?

Yes. Yes it was. She was going to claim it as one and she was going to toss it at her mother and Katrina the next time they nagged at her about taking time off. There was no greater sign of a vacation than not having a phone.

In a few hours, she'd have to plug back in. She'd see how many messages she had. She'd see if one of those messages was from Samson.

What if there's nothing?

Then . . . she'd contact him.

Peace spread through her, to the soundtrack of nature. She'd call him or text him, and she'd do it because she liked him and wanted to spend time with him, and she was so tired of shutting things down out of fear. Gabe was right. Trust was good and necessary.

"Um, hi. Sorry to bother you. Are you busy?"

"Yes. I'm on vacation," she said, but opened her eyes. A familiar-looking woman in her midtwenties stood in the opening of the gazebo. She wore a pretty, long emerald-green skirt and a black blouse. A blue-and-green hijab covered her hair, tied in elaborate folds and tucks. Rhiannon rose up on her elbows, placing the girl the second she stepped inside the gazebo and the moonlight lit her face. "Are you Noor Ahmed's sister?"

"Noor's one of my older sisters, yes."

Noor had been one of the few people in her school who had been relentlessly kind to her. Rhiannon waved at the other bench. "You can join me, then. Have a seat. Is your sister here?"

"No, she's working. My other sisters are here, though."

That's right. There were five Ahmed sisters, each more brilliant than the next. The middle one was married to a Kane, which, in the convoluted mess of relationships that made up her brother's life, made this girl *kind of* an in-law? "I'll say hi to them later."

The woman perched on the other bench and regarded Rhiannon with barely contained curiosity. "You're Rhiannon Hunter. I'm Jia. We've met a few times."

Yeah, they had, at various family events, though Jia was much younger than her, the baby of the Ahmed family. Rhiannon searched her memory. "You're one of the twins. The beauty influencer."

Jia's pink lips curved. Her makeup was flawlessly applied, her skin airbrushed levels of smooth. Lakshmi would adore her on sight. "That's one of my titles, yes."

"What are you doing out here?" Rhiannon took a sip of wine and offered the bottle to Jia, but the younger woman declined.

"I saw you come out. I wanted to thank you."

"Thank me for what?" she asked warily.

"For what you did on the show last night."

Rhiannon blinked. "There's no need to thank me for that."

"There is." Jia hesitated, glanced at the house, and then spoke in a rush. "It's not easy to speak up. There was a professor, my first year of med school, who was always making excuses to stand right next to us. He'd touch our arms, our shoulders. He would say inappropriate things, invite us to meet with him privately. I complained, other women complained, and we were told to stop being so sensitive. When he started getting a little too close to my sister, I finally told my father—he teaches at the school—and he got the guy taken off faculty."

"Good."

Jia's smile was faint. "That wasn't a universal sentiment. There were people who were so angry with me and my dad, but I'm glad I did it." She pleated her skirt between her fingers. "Not everyone has a father who can step in and help them. Not many people have a national platform, like you do." She rose to her feet in a rustle of fabric. "I know you're going to take flak for what you did and it's not going to be easy for you and no one would have blamed you for staying silent. So thank you. That's all I wanted to say. We all need to keep an eye out for each other when we have the ability to do so, I think."

She turned to leave, and Rhiannon sat up, finding her voice. "Jia."

"Yes?" She looked over her shoulder and Rhiannon was struck by how young and soft the girl appeared.

"You're moving to L.A. soon, right? That's what I heard?"

A light brightened Jia's brown eyes and she faced her. "Oh, yes. I mean, if I can get my parents to come around. I dropped out of med school, but getting them on board with my moving across the country . . ." She grimaced. "We don't have any family out there."

You made your industry better for the young men who came after you.

Jia wasn't exactly in her industry, but that didn't matter. Rhiannon made an executive decision. "Would they be more on board if they knew you had a safe place to live lined up?" Katrina would adore this woman, Rhiannon was sure of that. And in case Katrina didn't want another roommate, Rhiannon would house Jia in her own loft.

"With you?" Jia's eyes grew so big, Rhiannon feared they might pop off her cute face. "Oh my God, yes! I mean. I have to check. But yes!"

"Cool." Rhiannon fished in her pocket and then remembered she didn't have a phone. "Do you have your phone? I'll give you my number. We can connect later and figure things out."

"Yes." Jia punched Rhiannon's number in her phone. "I'll send you a text."

Rhiannon thought about the ten million texts she probably already had waiting for her response and took a drink out of her wine bottle. "Do me a favor and send me the text in a week?"

Jia nodded. "Yes. Got it. Will do. Gosh, I can't believe I came out here to thank you for taking that Peter guy down and now we'll be seeing each other in California—"

An odd choice of words. Rhiannon stopped her. "I haven't taken anyone down."

"Yeah, you did," Jia said slowly. "He quit. Didn't you hear?"

Her heart lurched. Rhiannon placed the bottle of wine on the bench with a clink. "No. I'm on vacation. I don't have a phone. What happened?"

"It broke like an hour ago."

"Gimme your phone." She made a beckoning motion and Jia stuck her hand in her pocket again.

The girl had well-hidden pockets on her skirt. Rhiannon liked her more and more.

Jia unlocked her phone, scrolled through, and handed it to her. Rhi absorbed the backlit screen like a junkie inhaling a fix. There it was, in black and white.

She didn't know what expression was on her face, but Jia drifted closer and sat next to her on the bench, placing her hand on Rhiannon's shoulder. "More people came forward after you. Peter stepped down as CEO at Swype."

Chapter Twenty-Nine

SAMSON ZIPPED up his suitcase and glanced around the otherwise empty bedroom of his borrowed high-rise apartment.

"Too bad you have to leave here," Dean remarked. He lounged in the doorway. It was odd to see him without Miley, but since they'd last had lunch, it seemed Dean really was making more of a conscious effort to not have his life be completely consumed by his child. Miley was home with Josie's mother.

"Campaign's over and so's my gig. I don't want Matchmaker to spend more money than I brought in."

"I'm glad you're staying in L.A., though. It'll be nice to see you more."

"I'm glad too." Over the last twenty-four hours, he'd made a couple of big decisions. The Cayucos home could wait. He'd found a nice place to lease, a few blocks away. It wasn't as ritzy, but it had a parking space and an in-unit washer/dryer, so what more could he really ask for? "Aunt Belle will be here in town as well for the next few months, what with

William stepping down. She's going to fight you to pamper Miley."

"Miley could always use more aunts. She going to try her hand at actively running the whole enchilada?"

"No. She's got an interim head right now. At some point she'll sell, but she wants to find the right person." Rhiannon had been the right person, but she wasn't interested.

He glanced at his phone, sitting silent on the nightstand. He would *not* check it for the tenth time in the last hour to make sure it was functioning and on. It would ring, Rhiannon calling or texting him back, or it wouldn't. He'd been trying to contact her for a full day now, since Helena's show had aired.

His heart ached for her, and he wanted nothing more than to hug her. Yes, people would be supportive, but others wouldn't. If she'd let him, he'd use his own big body to block the hate as much as he could, but no one would be able to shield her from all of it.

That *if* was a pretty big if. Whatever anger he'd felt toward her had well and truly dissolved, and he'd tried to make it clear he held no hard feelings in the messages he'd sent her, but who knew where her head was.

Dean sat on the bed. "I got a new gig lined up."

"No kidding." Samson placed the suitcase on the floor, against the wall. "What is it?"

"I'm, uh, working with Trevor."

Samson jerked around. "What?"

"It's a good organization."

"Is that why you're here? Am I your first assignment?"

Dean followed Samson out to the living room. "I like to see your smiling face, too, but sort of."

"Did you and Aunt Belle talk about this?"

"We talked, but I decided to come to you on my own. Look, I want to show you something. Can I?" He gestured to the table.

Samson gave him an annoyed look, but he sat. Dean set up the tablet he'd brought with him in front of Samson. The screen was open to a paused video. "This was from last season. Watch." He pressed play.

Samson crossed his arms over his chest. He didn't follow football much anymore, but he recognized the kid the journalist was interviewing. Al Anoa'i, a rising star who'd been drafted by the Bisons a couple years ago.

The player was sticky with sweat, his long curly hair clinging to his face. The reporter gestured to Al's arm. "I noticed you had something written there today during the game, what's that?"

"Oh, yeah." He turned his arm to face the camera. "It says LIMA. We all know about Big Joe being sick, and I wanted to show my solidarity with him and his family today."

The reporter nodded. "Big Joe, of course, a beloved former Bisons player. Why today?"

"It's the anniversary of the Charm walking off the field."

At that, Samson flinched, flummoxed. Dean squeezed his shoulder. "Keep watching."

Al continued. "Like, it was always powerful for me, as a kid, to see other Samoans in this sport that I loved, other guys who looked like me, but when Samson Lima took a stand and straight-up quit because his teammate wasn't getting the right care? I mean, that was some formative stuff. I'll remember that until I die."

The reporter spoke into his mic. "Does it worry you now, playing this game? Knowing as much as we do about head injuries?"

The twentysomething-year-old screwed up his face, the sun reflecting off his sweaty brown skin. "I mean, kind of? But I love it. And I think that's okay, you can love something and know there are problems with it. Times have changed since Samson walked off that field, and I hope the league continues to work with researchers to make our game safer so we can do what we love."

Dean hit pause. Samson looked at his friend. "Why'd you show me this?"

"To show you what you've done, and to give you an idea of what you could do. Like, don't google yourself regularly, but you might want to do it once every five years or so, enough to know that kids consider you a hero."

Samson ran his hands through his hair. "I didn't intend to be—"

"See, that's the funny thing. Sometimes you don't intend to do something, and you do it, and no one gives a fuck what you intended because you've done the thing."

There's no intent in ghosting.

"You wouldn't let them put me back in the game, because I was your brother, and I needed your help," Dean murmured. "Right?"

Samson nodded. Dean tapped the tablet. "You have more brothers out there, Samson. Whether you like it or not, you're their hero. So you can sit there and talk about how you didn't ask to be a hero, or you can simply go be the thing we all know you are."

You made your industry better for the young men who came after you, and the older men who came before you, and you did it just by living your life.

Joe didn't want anyone else to go through what his brother and nephew did.

Samson swallowed past the lump in his throat. "Not everyone likes me."

"No one's universally liked. *Beyoncé* isn't universally liked. Has that stopped her? No. Be like Beyoncé."

Samson grunted. "Being a dad has made you really bossy."

"I know. We could be teammates again, Samson. Working together for all our other teammates." While Samson digested that, Dean rose and picked up the tablet. He clapped him on the back. "Call Trevor. At least meet with him."

After Dean left, Samson wandered into his room and picked up his phone. Still no call from Rhiannon.

What the hell. Before he could think twice, he dialed Trevor.

The other man picked up on the first ring. "Samson. Hello. What a surprise."

Samson looked out the window and beat back his instinctive, immediate dislike. His personal feelings had no bearing here. "I want more information about this job offer of yours. Will you be out west anytime soon?"

Trevor paused, and when he spoke, it was cautiously, like he wasn't sure if Samson was kidding or not. "I will be, yes. In a week?"

"Sounds good. I have a condition, though. Before we even sit down to chat."

"What's that?"

"I want a public apology."

There was a beat of silence. "I'm sorry?"

Ahhh yes. He hadn't even known what he wanted until he'd said the words, and relief, glorious relief coursed through him. "What was it that you said, when I retired? What did you call me?"

"The Lima Curse. Samson, I regret—"

"If you regret it, you'll give me a public apology."

"If this is an ego thing, I absolutely understand, but we're on the same team now, Samson."

"We were on the same team then too. I walked for Dean. I would have walked for you." Samson's hand clenched tight over the phone. "This isn't for ego. Do you know where my nickname started? The Lima Charm? From my father. When he was himself, before the disease turned him into someone I didn't recognize. That was all I had of *him*. And you twisted that. That part of my legacy, you destroyed it." He took a deep breath. "I want a fucking apology."

Trevor was quiet for so long, Samson wondered if he'd hung up, but then he spoke. "You're absolutely right. I'll be on a couple of morning shows next week. I can deliver an apology right there. Is that public enough?"

"Yes." The tension leaked out of his shoulders.

"Done. We'll talk next week about the position then."

They said their goodbyes, and Samson slumped on the couch. He felt like the weight he'd carried for a decade had been lifted off him. Was that all it took? Telling someone who hurt him that they'd hurt him?

Was this . . . closure?

He didn't know how long he sat there in a relaxed haze, but he was startled when his phone pinged on his chest. He rarely turned the ringer on, it was always on vibrate.

He crunched up to look at the display, and a new kind of relief suffused him.

Rhiannon. Finally.

Hi. Thank you for texting me, I had my phone off. I'm so sorry for getting mad at you. I land at LAX in about five and a half hours. Will you come pick me up?

He didn't hesitate. His fingers flew over the screen. **It's okay. Yes, of course. See you then.**

Chapter Thirty

WHAT WOULD he say to her? What could he say?

There were about a million things that ran around his brain for the next six hours, even as he drove slowly through the packed evening LAX traffic.

He saw her sweatshirt first. It was a soft lavender, the same one she'd worn when she'd walked into a bar in central California months ago. If she hadn't been wearing that, he might have missed her. She stood on the curb with big sunglasses on, her hoodie pulled over her hair.

He didn't blame her for the impromptu disguise. He assumed, after Helena's show, those people who hadn't known the owner of Crush now would.

Samson maneuvered his car through the traffic and pulled up to the curb. Before he could get out and open the door for her, she opened it herself. "Hey," she said, her voice hoarse, and tossed her bag in the back seat.

"Hey."

She avoided his gaze as she slid in. "Thanks for picking me up."

"No problem." His fingers twitched on the steering wheel. He didn't want to spook her by grabbing her close and hugging her. But he also . . . really wanted to touch her.

Once she was buckled in, he settled for resting his hand over hers and squeezing it. "Am I taking you to your place?" He hadn't been to either of her homes yet. He knew the one she shared with Katrina was farther away, but he'd happily drive her there, let her out, and return. Whatever she wanted.

He was so gone.

She twisted her hand over so they were palm to palm. "Can we go to yours?"

"Yeah." He left his hand where it was, even if it made maneuvering through traffic one-handed a little difficult. *Sorry, other drivers. My girl's got her hand in mine.*

He glanced at her a couple of times, but she was silent, head against the window, eyes closed, her chest rising and falling like she was asleep.

It was so late the roads were relatively traffic free, and they pulled up in front of his condo in no time, which was both good and bad. Good because he wanted to get her in his home so they could talk. Bad because he didn't want to let go of her.

She stirred when he did release her and she lifted her head. He usually self-parked, but he tossed his keys to the valet this time and grabbed Rhi's bag before she could.

She kept her head bowed as they walked inside, and he used his larger body to block her from view of anyone in the lobby. Rhi kept inching closer to him in the elevator, until he finally pulled her to his side. She belonged there anyway.

She must have thought so, too, because she melted against him. He didn't let go of her even when they walked to his door and awkwardly shuffled inside. "I can order Thai for you," he said. "It's supposedly the best place in L.A., according to about three thousand reviews on—" He dropped her bag, and grabbed her, because what else was a man supposed to do when a woman he liked this much leaped on him?

She pressed her lips against his, and Samson's grip tightened on her ass. Her long legs twined around his hips and he turned them around and stumbled farther into the living room. He fell on the couch with her straddling him.

He ran his hand up her sides and yanked on the zipper of her sweatshirt. It was hard to get her undressed without separating their mouths much, but he managed to get her sweatshirt and top and bra off.

Finally, he paused. "Wait," he panted.

Her fingers were busy on the buttons of his shirt. "I don't want to wait."

"No."

Her fingers immediately halted, and she peered down at him. "What's wrong?"

"We need to talk first."

"About what?"

It was so hard to think when her breasts were in his line of vision. They were so full and lovely, the nipples perked up, waiting for his hands and mouth. "Uh."

She grabbed his ears and pulled him close. "Samson. I need this."

Well, fuck. What was he supposed to say to *that*?

He wrapped his arms around her waist and came to his feet. He carried her into his darkened bedroom, their lips fused together until he laid her on his bed. His blinds were open, and the city lights painted silver and gold across her body. He stripped off all his clothes and her jeans, then started at her breasts and kissed down her body, licking and sucking her flesh.

He wanted to consume her, but that was a bad idea. If he consumed her, there would be nothing left, and he wanted all of her. For a long, long time, no expiration date.

That was scary, the thought of indefinitely being with someone. But also . . . kind of lovely.

He pressed her thighs wide and licked her until she cried out. She tasted so good, her legs straining on either side of his head. He knew she enjoyed it, but he also didn't want to torture her.

He rose up on his knees and slipped his fingers inside her. "Fuck me," she breathed, and he nearly did exactly that before he remembered.

"No condoms," he said, regretfully, and withdrew his hand.

Her eyes flew open. "You don't have any here?"

"I'm moving soon and I don't see the point in stocking condoms if there's no one I want to have sex with. I bought that box for you."

Her lips wavered into a smile. "That's kind of sweet."

He shrugged, embarrassed. "Well, right now it means we can't have sex."

"Yeah . . ." She bit her lip. "I wish I could say condoms don't matter, but—"

"No, they matter." Rhi's trust issues wouldn't be solved in a day, and neither would his. They needed time and words before they got to a point where condoms wouldn't be an issue. And that issue couldn't be decided in the heat of the moment.

He ran his fingers back over her vulva. She was so sweet and wet. Her lashes fluttered as he played with her. "Luckily, there's about eight hundred things we can do with each other that don't require a condom." He slipped his fingers deeper, thrusting them back and forth. She moaned, and he added his thumb on her clit, rubbing the little bundle of flesh.

Rhi ran her hand up his thigh and he moved closer, until her palm grasped his cock. He closed his eyes, luxuriating in each grasping pull, and the speed of her motions dictated his own.

They played together like that for a long time, taking slow pleasure in each other's hands and bodies, but finally the need built up. He bent his head and licked her clit while he fucked her with his fingers. Her thighs tightened around his arm as she came. He gave his own body free rein and thrust against her palm, spilling on her belly.

With the last ounce of strength in his body, he leaned over the bed, grabbed his shirt, and used it to clean off her stomach. People who made penetrative intercourse the whole and sole point of sex really missed so much. This was as intimate and pleasurable as being inside her.

Samson tossed the shirt toward the bathroom. She curled into his side and he wrapped his arms around her.

"Has Annabelle offered the company to anyone else?"

Of course Rhiannon orgasmed and moved straight to business. He shook his head, a spurt of humor making him grin. "No. Are you thinking of renewing your bid?"

"Don't tell Annabelle yet, I have to talk to Katrina. But, yes, I think I'm going to counter her counter with an investment offer. It seems like she's in no rush to sell the company. She could cut me in for a slice. I can help her with her senior management issues. It could work, at a partnership level."

He laced his fingers through hers and brought their hands to his mouth to kiss. "I like the idea of a partnership."

"Yeah?" Rhiannon rolled onto her side to face him.

"Yeah."

"I guess now's the time we talk?" She gestured between them. "About us?"

"I think so." He stacked his hands under his head. "I'm serious."

"Serious about . . . me being naked and in your bed?" she asked lightly.

"No. Well, yes. But not exactly. I'm serious about you, woman. I'm looking for something serious with you. I'm not content with this just being sex for a night or a week or even a month. I want more. I want a relationship. With you," he stressed, in case she didn't quite understand him.

She wrinkled her nose. "What about your marketing campaign? Hard to be serious when you're seeing a bunch of other women."

He shook his head. "I'm not seeing anyone else. I filmed one last date for Matchmaker."

"I saw it." Her eye twitched. "She seemed nice."

"She was lovely, but she wasn't you. If we continue any campaign, it'll be the one with you and me. We still have one meetup left in the contract you made me sign, don't forget."

"William might be annoyed by that."

The relish in her statement told him she hoped he was. Samson couldn't blame her—he didn't like William much either. "William's out."

Rhi's eyes widened. "What?"

"You've missed a lot." He decided her breasts looked cold and cupped one. Her eyes fell to half-mast, but her expression remained expectant. "William and Aunt Belle decided their management styles are too dissimilar, Aunt Belle's searching for a replacement, she knew from the start that I was into you and engineered us meeting, my friend Dean told me to be more like Beyoncé, and also I agreed to hear out my former nemesis about the job at that nonprofit." He paused for a breath. "I think that's most everything you missed."

"Whoa. That's a lot." She glanced around. "I should put my shirt on."

"It really wasn't that much," he insisted and strummed her nipple. "No need for shirts."

"Sounds like a lot. What made you flip on the job?"

He told her about Al's interview, and her face softened. "I guess that's what it's all about. Making all this"—she gestured to the world at large—"better for the youths."

"That's kind of a nice way of thinking about it." He tipped his head at her. "Now you. What have you been up to since we last saw each other?"

"Well, I went on national television, told the world Peter harassed me, turned my phone off for twenty-four hours, had a real heart-to-heart with my brother about my trust issues, potentially acquired another roommate, and Peter stepped down as CEO."

He stared at her. "You turned your phone off for twenty-four hours?"

"Literally the longest I have ever turned my phone off in the history of having a phone." She blinked rapidly. "I was scared to turn it on. But when I did . . . there were so many nice messages, Samson. From so many people."

"I'm sure you'll get even more love in the days to come."

"I'll get hatred in the days to come too." Shadows darkened her eyes.

"You might." The people who hated him didn't compare to the vitriol she'd have to weather. He pulled her close so he could smush her like she liked.

"No might about it. More people for sure believe me now than they would have four years ago, but that's not saying much. There's a nice majority who are going to be livid with me." She inhaled. "But I figure, that's okay. I'm glad I said what I did. I'm not alone, and with me talking about it, neither are the others."

"I think you're brave either way, but I'm glad you feel better, having come forward. And I'm glad he stepped down."

"Me too." She wrinkled her nose. "I thought I'd feel so much satisfaction at him losing the position and power he loved. Revenge, you know? But mostly, I'm happy because it means it'll be harder for him to hurt someone else."

Samson still wanted to punch Peter. That would be the only thing that would fully satisfy him, but this was a start. "Use me for whatever you need."

"I'll try to ask for help. Old habits are hard to break, you know."

"I know."

She got quiet. "My trust issues will probably take eons to work on."

"I've been thinking about that. I told you my mom was a lawyer." Samson snuggled closer, because he could. "She used to tell me about this thing called the eggshell plaintiff rule."

"What's that?"

"I'm probably messing up the explanation, but basically, if you walk up to someone with a thin skull and hit them in the head, and they get hurt, you're responsible for the damage you caused. Even if hitting someone with a normal skull wouldn't have resulted in any damage."

"I'm not following."

"The lesson she meant for me to take away, is that you take a person as you find them." He thought of how Lulu had stubbornly stuck by his father's side. He'd been angry, sometimes with her, after the Switch. Angry that she *hadn't* been more angry at his father's fate.

Now he knew. His mother had taken life as it was. Grateful for every extra moment she got to spend with the man she loved, in sickness and in health.

"I'm patient, Rhi. I'd like it if you could give me the benefit of the doubt, not jump to conclusions without hearing me out if you're feeling nervous about me . . . but I will take you as you are, baggage and all. The flip side is, you have to take me as I am."

"Easy. You're almost perfect."

He couldn't help but laugh. "I definitely am not. I don't really know how to be with someone like this. I'm learning, and I'll probably get scared and freak out and mess up. I don't know what the future holds." He thought about one day unfolding after another with this woman. How long had it been since he'd thought about the future and not been terrified? "We can, however, communicate and be patient with one another."

"We could."

"In that case, will you answer my earlier question? Can we be serious?"

She gazed down at him. Her eyes were so pretty, endless pools of dark brown. "Yes."

"Yeah?" His smile widened.

His happiness scared Rhiannon, because God knew if she'd be able to keep him looking that happy. She'd fail. Or he would. "Though I'm not the kind of woman you probably envisioned when you wrote your Matchmaker bio," she said. "Kind and sweet and loyal."

He stroked her arm, leaving goose bumps. "You're all those things and more. Also . . ." He winced. "Uh, don't tell anyone, but Tina wrote that bio."

She huffed out a laugh, thinking of how many times she'd obsessed over those three words. "You've got to be kidding me."

"Nope. As of right this minute, the Crush bio you swiped right on is the only thing I've ever written."

Well, damn. Damn. "How about that."

"The Matchmaker quiz, though, I did take, and so did you."

Rhiannon's eyes narrowed and she recalled what he'd said, about Annabelle engineering their meeting. "Wait. Did she make us all take that questionnaire so she could see if you and I were a good match?"

"Yup."

"Diabolical." But she said it with admiration. Annabelle might not be a standard businesswoman, but when had Rhiannon ever surrounded herself with conventional people? "I might actually enjoy being her partner more than buying the business outright."

"You don't want to know our match percentage?"

"Nah. I don't believe in it." She yawned, but then opened one eye. "We scored high though, yeah?"

"Yeah, overachiever, we scored high." He rolled his eyes, but high-fived her when she sleepily offered her hand.

They lay in silence for a while. Rhiannon had a million things to do, but for the first time in a long time, she felt . . . light. Like she'd gotten closure on multiple fronts, had laid down weights she hadn't even been aware she was carrying.

He nuzzled her temple. "I'll probably love you soon."

Warmth bloomed in her chest. "I'll love you soon too. And then it's all over for you. I look out for the people I love even when they don't look out for themselves."

"Same." He pressed a number of kisses on her face, including the tip of her nose. "You said you were the only one who could protect your heart, but I'm going to protect the hell out of your heart."

Ohhhh. Well, there went said heart, turning to mush.

"I'm also going to make you take a break. Like right now."

"I'm not doing anything."

"In a few minutes you would have hopped out of bed to check your phone or email or Twitter."

"Ugh. You know, I *should* check my Twitter. See what the damage is." The dread in her voice must have been apparent to him, because it was loud and clear to her.

"I'll never tell you how to run your business, but . . . you could not do that."

"No. I have to. I should—"

"Or . . . hear me out . . . you could not."

Her smile was reluctant.

"You have marketing and lawyers, right? Let them handle it for now, and take a beat for yourself. Let's nap. We've both had a hectic time lately, clearly."

"But—"

"What did you just say, about looking out for your people when they won't look out for themselves? Seems like you should take some of your own advice sometimes. That's the fair thing to do."

She harrumphed. "Fine, damn it."

He kissed her, and after a beat, she responded. "This is going to take some getting used to," she murmured. *Delegating. It's just delegating.*

"We'll go slow. We'll talk. Trust me, we can make it work."

"I like your confidence, buddy."

"I have enough for both of us." He touched his finger to her nose. "I'm so glad I swiped right on you."

Rhiannon smiled and ran her hand over his stomach. "Me too. Now run out and get some condoms."

"There should be an app for that."

A flare of interest had her sitting up, and he shook his head. "No."

"An app that delivers condoms. And food."

"No."

"And the person who delivers it is your hookup." She gasped. "Call it PostDates."

He groaned, but again, high-fived her.

She liked him so much.

"Not now, Rhi. Make a note, but shelve the empire for a night."

Rhi. Would she ever get tired of hearing it? Probably not. "Fine. I'll take over the world tomorrow."

"Good." He yawned and hugged her tight. "I'll hold your purse."

"I never carry a purse."

"I'll hold your sweatshirt then." His smile was warm, and so was his embrace. "Or better yet, I can be your sweatshirt."

About the Author

ALISHA RAI is an author and attorney and is frequently sought as a speaker on a wide range of topics spanning publishing, media, and law. Her award-winning novels have been named Best Books of the Year by the *Washington Post*, NPR, Amazon, *Entertainment Weekly*, *Kirkus Reviews*, and *Cosmopolitan* magazine. In between deadlines, you can find Alisha traveling, tweeting, and hunting down the best place in town to get a taco. To find out more about her work or to sign up for her newsletter, visit alisharai.com.

BOOKS BY ALISHA RAI

THE RIGHT SWIPE
A NOVEL
Available in Paperback, eBook, and Digital Audio

"Alisha Rai delivers compelling emotion, fascinating characters and edgy romance in a razor-sharp, thoroughly modern voice that readers will adore. I sure did!"
—Jayne Ann Krentz

Two rival dating app creators find themselves at odds in the boardroom but in sync in the bedroom.

HATE TO WANT YOU
A FORBIDDEN HEARTS NOVEL
Available in Mass Market, eBook, and Digital Audio

"Alisha Rai blends emotional characters with passionate sensuality in some of the best examples of erotic romance available."
—Sarah MacLean for the *Washington Post*

Being together might be against all the rules...
but being apart is impossible.

WRONG TO NEED YOU
A FORBIDDEN HEARTS NOVEL
Available in Mass Market, eBook, and Digital Audio

"Rai has crafted a series as deliciously soapy as a CW drama... some of the best romance writing of the year here."
—*Entertainment Weekly*

He wasn't supposed to fall in love with his brother's widow...

HURTS TO LOVE YOU
A FORBIDDEN HEARTS NOVEL
Available in Mass Market, eBook, and Digital Audio

"True to Rai's style, family secrets and surprises add complexity to this strong story about how wealth and privilege can do as much to destroy happiness as to facilitate it."
—*Publishers Weekly*

Well-behaved women don't lust after men who love to misbehave.

HarperCollins*Publishers*
DISCOVER GREAT AUTHORS, EXCLUSIVE OFFERS, AND MORE AT HC.COM.